NIGHT
SHADOWS

Ron Ely

Simon & Schuster
New York London Toronto
Sydney Tokyo Singapore

SIMON & SCHUSTER
Rockefeller Center
1230 Avenue of the Americas
New York, New York 10020

This book is a work of fiction. Names, characters, places
and incidents are either products of the author's
imagination or are used fictitiously. Any resemblance
to actual events or locales or persons, living or dead,
is entirely coincidental.

Copyright © 1994 by Ron Ely

Designed by Deirdre C. Amthor

Manufactured in the United States of America

1 3 5 7 9 10 8 6 4 2

Library of Congress Cataloging-in-Publication Data

Ely, Ron.
Night shadows/Ron Ely.
p. cm.
1. Private investigators—California—Fiction. I. Title.
PS3555.L93N5 1994
813'.54—dc20
93–30415
CIP

ISBN 0–671–87280–X

*For Valerie, Kirsten,
Kaitland, and Cameron.*

1 🌿

No question about it, I was out of shape. My legs felt dull and springless, and I no longer cared if I was above or below the tide line. I no longer tried to avoid the sudden surf rushes.

My shoes were wet and caked with sand, yet I took a sort of perverse pride in them. They weren't designer, pump-action, psychedelic-colored cross-trainers. They were just plain, old-fashioned sneakers. An overview of the rest of me said basically the same thing. Plain vanilla. I wore sweats, baggy and cotton just like I did twenty years ago. I found it hard to imagine myself in pink and green spandex and doing the twist up, twist down in some aerobics class.

I had done five miles, but I hurt from it, and strange wheezing sounds were coming from my throat. My head was down, focused on my feet, and I seemed to have adopted "whew" as a sort of mantra my brain kept repeating over and over. Sweat leaked into my eyes, blinding me, and ran down the arms of my shirt. It flew from the tips of my fingers like the shots fired by arcade-game characters. I finally sneaked a look up to see how much more I had to run. The distant bend that marked my finish line was farther away than I expected. I knew what Lombardi had meant when he said, "Fatigue makes cowards of us all."

As I approached the last two hundred or so yards I pumped hard into a sprint and then slowed to a dog trot. A casual observer probably could not have told much difference, but to my lungs and hamstrings it was significant. Finally, I slowed it even further. I walked a leisurely walk just above the tide line toward a sun that had already lost interest. While I got my breath, and my pulse receded from my eardrums, I looked around and reminded myself that I was on one of the most picturesque beaches of the California coastline. I was still new enough to Santa Barbara to appreciate its beauty and to be slightly amazed at the way some of its denizens chose to show off money and bad taste. A good example of that was the house perched on the cliff above. I suppose you'd still call fifty rooms covered with imported blue ceramic roof tile a house. Saudi oil money, as I heard it.

The cliff face was two hundred feet high. It was just enough to insulate the estates on top from those public-beach commoners who walked the two miles from the public access to this private stretch here. I kept my eyes up, tracing the bluff until I found what I thought was the edge of my own property. It was hard to spot because my place was squeezed in up there between the big estates with only a couple of eucalyptus trees on the rim to mark it. Farther down, a good footrace away, was the next visible mansion. It had a red mission-tile roof and was built in the more traditional Spanish style. It was half the size of the Saudi's place but it was simple and elegant. To my eye it seemed grander than the blue-tiled job. Maybe I had a natural dislike for show-offs. Maybe I had to see more than what money can buy to be impressed. Or maybe I was just working very hard at being a snob. The reverse kind.

The light was going, so I resumed my trot to get off the beach before dark. There was only one way out, and I had visions of wandering through the night, fighting off the rising tide, looking for the exit. Plus I was hungry. I still had to decide whether to clean myself up and go out to eat or do a little grocery shopping. I didn't bother considering the fast-food places with the "drive-thrus." Trying to communicate through those static boxes with somebody working off a "Say It in English" book didn't appeal to me. My Spanish, and Vietnamese, and Farsi were all too rusty to make it clear that I didn't want a hamburger called a big anything. That and a view of their cooks kept me away from those places.

I drove out the card-operated gate that guarded the beach access. It struck me as a redundancy, for by the time a person got that far he had already passed through a Coco Palms entry gate and a security once-over that would do the White House proud. There were a lot of very important people living in Coco Palms, and they wanted everyone to know it.

Personally, I thought of Coco Palms as ex-ville. It seemed to me that those who lived there were all ex-somethings or other. To be sure, at every turn there was to be found an ex–captain of industry or ex–film star or ex-genius from the world of science or medicine, but then, of course, not everyone in Coco Palms was retired. Not all were old. There was the usual mix of ex-wives and ex-husbands. But there was one common denominator in Coco Palms: money. It was all around me as I turned onto Faring Lane, the main road out. As I did so, I pulled the towel up over my head and tucked it into my sweatshirt, making a sort of hood. Old habits died hard. I had spent a lot of my life with a towel draped over my head like that, letting the sweat from a workout dry.

Faring Lane was lined with palms. Bougainvillea of pink, coral, white, and purple fronted high walls and cherry bush hedges. Tropical plants of every variety flourished in the lush front gardens. As I wound my way north toward the main gate, automatic timers clocked on lights at the bases of magnolia trees and inside night-blooming jasmine bushes, as if to call my attention to the scent of the looming night. It was a heavy perfume. I put down all my windows to catch it and was reminded fondly of my convertible days. I had never known, not from my first days in Southern California, exactly what that smell in the air was. There were citrus blossoms, jasmine, honeysuckle, and any number of other fragrant beauties out there that hit you with an aroma like no French perfumery could duplicate. It unfocused me. In the deep night when those sweet smells filled the air, I would always stop and bathe in it, and do a little dreaming.

I hit the brakes hard and swerved into the bridle trail that ran alongside Faring Lane. The staggering runner toppled headlong into the space I had just vacated and rolled toward the center line. I pulled the emergency and popped the belt release as part of my move out of the car to the downed man.

The light had dimmed too much for me to see the man clearly, but I could hear the rasping demand for air long before I reached him. The thought flickered briefly that I must have sounded like that a half hour earlier. As I knelt, he groped with feebly clawing fingers at me, and spoke garbled, unrecognizable words. The claws never finished their mission. Something clattered to the pavement beside him, released from dying fingers. He never finished his thought, whatever it may have been. He simply closed his eyes, and it was over. There were worse places to die, I supposed, than on the main road of Coco Palms, the road of the rich and famous. Personally, I'd take a bed, any bed, and in my sleep, I thought, as I scooped up the squared metal object he had dropped.

I rose on unsteady and complaining legs to stand over the ex-living, ex-breathing ex-husband, father, lover, or whatever the corpse had been a few short moments before. Not for the first time did my own mortality dance into frame. Here was a guy, I thought, who went out for a short evening jog. He got all decked out in fancy running clothes, put on his pump-up running shoes, set the stopwatch on his wrist to zero, and before he could even work up a good sweat, he died.

The headlights of a car caught our strange tableau. I stood, like a jackrabbit frozen in the high beams, until the car pulled to a stop a few yards away.

"What's the matter? Is that man ill?" The careful query was delivered by a weak male voice from the leathered interior of a car that cost more than most houses in the state of Nebraska.

I knew I wouldn't like the fellow inside the car. From his voice and his style I could tell that his interest was more in getting away clean without wasting any of his own time or effort. I didn't want that to happen, so I answered, "He's dead. We better notify the police."

"We?"

"You're a witness and first on the scene. You got a phone in that heap?"

If he resented my referring to his Corniche as a heap, it didn't show. "Yes," he replied. "Who should I call?"

"911 would be a good start."

He didn't answer. I guessed he didn't like me much either.

I could hear him talking on the phone, so I turned my attention back to the unlucky ex at my feet. The light from the car caught some details I had missed before. The toup was one little item that would have been hard to catch if the guy hadn't taken such a header. The fall had dislodged the piece so that it showed a little scalp beneath it. Good toupees were hard to come by, and this one had cost a bundle. My bet was that half the people who had known this guy didn't know he'd worn one.

The watch was easy to identify. I had its twin on my wrist. It was a Citizen, good to two hundred meters. The diver's bezel, surrounded by the alarm housing and a variety of gold-colored buttons made the watch distinctive. It was not a watch for dilettantes. It usually marked a pro.

I knelt again to pick up the limp wrist. I pushed the top left button, which would activate the stopwatch if it was in that mode. A small tone should have sounded to indicate that function was active. No tone: it was not in stopwatch mode. There was no real reason why I did it. Curiosity, I guess—that and wanting to nail down my snap judgments. It was just that by the look of him, I had him figured to be the type that did everything by the book and by the watch. The running clothes, the hair, the fingernails, all spoke to me of a guy who planned things carefully and did them on schedule.

Forty, I guessed, or maybe a touch older. Thin in the way that used to be called skinny, but somehow got to be fashionable along with dope and sushi. Good skin, good tan. The guy had had it made, I thought. He lay on his back with his eyes closed, looking like something from a bad Fellini movie. The sound of the idling engine gave an eerie accompaniment. The lights, still on high beam, cast long unnatural shadows. My eyes played tricks on me. I began to imagine a stream of some dark-colored liquid leaking out of the guy.

The pool was small and mostly hidden by his head and neck, but after a moment of denial, I recognized it. This ex was leaking blood onto Faring Lane right there in the heart of dear old Coco Palms. Whatever would they say at the club the next day?

My first thought was that he had hit his head as he fell, but that became a hard sell. I replayed what I could remember of the stumble and roll I'd witnessed in my peripheral vision while I fought to keep from becoming part of the roadside landscaping. Whatever had happened to the guy had happened before he lurched out onto Faring Lane. My second thought was to drop that metal object I had picked up, back where I found it. Bad idea. There was no way I could be sure I'd get my prints clean from it.

I slowly backed myself out of the lights as the twit in the Rolls finished his 911 call. Grateful for the towel hood, I crabbed as far into the darkness as I could before the whiny voice sought me out.

"They said they'll be right here. I told them it was some sort of accident. Is that right?"

"You were perfect. Now, why don't you pull your car around the body and block the road from the other direction. Put on your flashers. I'll let the main gate know what's happening."

I waited until the Rolls started moving before I hustled to my car and took off. He was a good boy. He did just what I told him to do. His emergency flashers where working as I caught my last glimpse of him in my mirror.

I slowed at the gate and gave a casual wave toward the guard, who barely looked in my direction. They didn't care who left. They were only interested in who entered. I thought maybe I heard the siren as I was taking the 101 on-ramp but that could have been my imagination. So could the blood. So could all of it. I had one of those active imaginations, or so I kept telling myself.

I drove to a market I liked down off State Street where the shoppers were people like me. There weren't many kids running the aisles of the place and there weren't a lot of overladen shopping carts pushed by overburdened housewives clogging up the checkout counters. The older couples and single shoppers hardly gave me a glance in spite of my strangely hooded appearance. In a Safeway I'd have drawn a crowd.

Milk, eggs, coffee, minced clams and linguine was about it. There was still a lot of room in that sack and I got little more than a disgusted look back for my twenty. Maybe I didn't like that market so much anymore. I could remember when for a twenty you had to have help out with the bags.

I decided to take the beach route home and turned south on State. Santa Barbara was a pretty town. It was tight and well packaged between the mountains and the ocean. People strolled the streets and seemed at ease doing so. I knew some places where that was a foreign concept, especially after dark. That brought survival to mind, which opened up a bag of lots of other things like why some do and why some don't, and what's the use of being the one who does when you lose the ones who don't. It was a big bag, and a dark one. My maudlin side was knocking.

Ocean Avenue took me on a winding route into the high-rent district. At some point Ocean became Coral Ridge Road. As far as I could tell, it was the same street, but who knows. Maybe it was a county thing. It was clear, though, that as soon as it became Coral Ridge Road the real estate got richer. It led right into what most thought of as the back entrance to Coco Palms.

I tossed aside the towel from my head and slowed as the guard stepped out of the kiosk. He shone a light on the small blue decal in the upper left part of my windshield.

"Sorry to stop you, sir, but we've had an incident in the Palms tonight. Nothing to worry about, but there was a death over on Faring Lane about an hour ago."

An incident, huh? So that's what they called it these days, I thought. I looked at the county sheriff's car parked to the side. "Someone hit by a car?" I asked innocently.

"No sir," he answered, and became conspiratorial. "We can't say for sure just now, but it looks like it might be a homicide."

Until then I had never connected those security guards with the real cops. He was one. He was either moonlighting or retired, but he was one. I should have spotted that before. Just another sign I was slipping.

He produced a clipboard and said, "And your name, sir?"

"Jake Sands," I answered. "I live right up the road here."

"Yes sir, Mr. Sands, I saw the Coco Palms decal, but tonight we're taking some extra precautions. 713 Coral Ridge Road?" He kept his eyebrows raised at me until I nodded. "Call the patrol if you see anything odd or suspicious, and we'll be right over, sir."

"Yes, I'll do that. And you be careful."

He gave a tight nod as he opened the gate for me and said, "I'll be fine, sir."

"*Semper fi,*" I almost said, fairly sure he was a fellow ex-marine, but waved a sort of left-handed salute instead, which he answered with the real thing. The sheriffs let me pass without comment.

Half a mile from the entrance I turned into a gated driveway that opened to the touch of a button on the device stuck to my sun visor. The garage door opened the same way. I punched in the right numbers, for a change, and the door into the house itself opened without setting off a wail usually reserved for nuclear alerts. Hell of a way to live, I thought, having to pass through two gates and a high-tech security system just to fix dinner for myself and eat it alone.

• • •

I took a mug of thick black coffee outside. The air was cooling to a just-right temperature where it felt good and smelled good. I settled onto a too soft chaise with the clumsiness I'd come to expect from myself when dealing with such extremes of comfort. I was better with rocks and tree stumps.

I had left some music on inside. I could have hit a switch and heard it from speakers attached to the exterior of the house, or hidden behind bushes, or even from beneath the surface of the pool. I didn't, because music had always been a sort of inside thing for me. I couldn't get comfortable with a piano riff coming at me from a bougainvillea. It sounded faintly and drew most of my ear to it. It was music I chose when I was alone. It was old-fashioned and fit well with the jasmine and orange blossoms. It was Nat King Cole. A long time ago I had stopped trying to follow the trends of things. My suit jackets all had a medium-sized lapel and twin vents in the back. My pants legs were straight and roomy. My shirt collars were high with medium to long tabs. My ties, those I had, did not change, nor did my shoes. I had penny loafers, plain loafers, and tassel loafers. I liked them, and that is what I wore. I liked Nat King Cole, and that is what I listened to. That and Gleason, Bobby Hackett, some Sinatra, and a few of the New Age musicians that played with Old Age soul.

I tried not to dwell on the dead man, but a situation like that has an impact. It's not the sort of event that crops up on a daily basis. Who he was or what he was I did not know, but one thing was sure. He was taken down by a long-range hit. A scoped gun, probably, of small bore. My bet was a .22 long, high velocity. It was most likely a mercury pill, that little deadly drop of mercury encased in lead that is the most effective of all the dumdums. It explodes in the soft tissue and stays right inside. There was no exit wound on my man. There was no violent lift forward. He stumbled into a forward collapse. It fit.

Then came the questions. Who hit him? What was he doing out there? Was he on an evening run when some nut took him out? Not hardly. That was a high-quality takedown. My guess was that it all depended on who the poor sap was. Not my problem. But the watch bothered me. He struck me as the kind of guy to tap the stopwatch function the minute he hit the street, but he hadn't. And why that watch? Was he a sport diver? Too many questions. Not my problem.

I sipped the coffee and contemplated the sky. Stars. Lots of stars. And to think that all those poor souls just ninety miles away couldn't see a one of them. They could sit all night in the center of Los Angeles and never see a glimmer. Too much light reflected back from the atmosphere. Too much smog. Too damned many people. What a relief not to be there, even though it had had its moments.

The phone rang at my elbow, and I thought about not answering it. It managed two more bird imitations before I finally picked it up. I didn't say anything. I listened.

"So what's happening over there? Know anything about it?"

"None of your business," I answered.

"You do it?"

"None of your business," I answered.

"You better run, pal, they may start looking under rocks."

"What have you heard?" I asked.

"Same as you. Just what the robot on the eleven o'clock news reads us."

"I haven't seen the news. What'd you hear?"

His tone changed. He hesitated just a beat, but when he spoke again he was all business. He was one guy who could give a straight report.

"A very important person, name withheld, was shot to death in the Coco Palms section of Santa Barbara. He was found on Faring Lane moments after his death. They say there is a possibility it was an accidental shooting. That's about it."

"It was no accident," I said.

"Go on," he urged. "This should be good."

He was older and gruffer than I. He was richer and more erudite. He was probably smarter in some ways, and in his day, maybe even tougher. But I could take him in poker and chess, and I knew how to hook his curiosity. I could have played him for a long time if I'd wanted.

"I was there," I said. "I found him."

"The robot said a car dealer named MacGribb found him."

"He came along. I left him to stand guard while I went for the cavalry." I took a sip of my cold coffee and waited while the throat at the other end of the line cleared.

"You're not in any trouble with this thing, are you?" He gave it a hard delivery. He gave most things a hard delivery. It was a good disguise.

"Not yet."

"You up to some chess?" he asked with the same hard edge.

"Sure. When?"

"Say about ten, ten-thirty tomorrow night. I've got something to show you."

"I'll be there," I said. "Oh, by the way, Jason, any on-the-scene coverage of the incident?"

"Just a still of the car dealer."

"MacGribb? How'd he read?"

"He's what he is, the son of a rich man, and not much else. Weak-chinned and arrogant. The type that gets caught embezzling and turns state's evidence on his best friend. You know Beverly Hills—the streets there are filled with them," he said with the monotone delivery that parodied the type he was describing.

"I had a feeling I wouldn't like him. See you tomorrow."

I felt better. I was less inclined to think of L.A. and all that might lead to. Jason Meddler's call had put aside what might have been a nudge at the past with a loose-cannon memory.

I reached down for the object I had picked up from beside the dead man. It was cold and smooth and spoke to me in a voice I knew from long ago.

Earlier when I had returned home I had looked closely at the object. It was nothing more than an old-fashioned Zippo cigarette lighter, which in other days had been as common to a G.I. as dog tags. However, this particular Zippo lighter had caught my attention. For one thing, it was not the usual one that most G.I.s used. This lighter had been waterproofed. I hadn't noticed right away because most of it was worn off, but as I looked more closely I'd seen where the rubber seals had been glued. I had screwed out the flint plug, and sure enough, there was a tiny rubber washer. The waterproofing was a poorly done job in comparison to some I had seen. Probably just enough to keep the wick and flint dry, but if it had worked, what difference did it make?

The surface of the lighter was smooth from wear, the emblem that had been affixed to it long gone. There remained only a blemished spot with a small residue of solder. A magnifier had helped me read the letters imprinted or etched into the metal. "Subic Bay," was all it had said.

It didn't go with the guy I'd seen on the pavement. It was more likely a last remnant of a father or uncle or maybe even an older brother who had been stationed at one time in the Philippines. I had spent a short time at Subic myself. I could still smell the river that separated the base from one of the wildest towns in the world, Olongapo. I had to quickly suppress the images of the hookers and their male counterparts, the Benny boys, who had waited across the bridge for the servicemen with full pockets and empty heads. I fought to keep a tight control on those little peeks into the past. It was too easy these days for me to get sidetracked with old memories.

I leaned back into the soft extravagance of the custom-designed cushion as the air grew cooler around me. That scent, heavy and rich, closed in on me. That scent which I could never quite identify, but knew only as the sweet smell of paradise.

2

My pants were too snug at the waist, and I was beginning to accept that the laundry wasn't shrinking my shirts, so I didn't eat the potatoes. I waited while Peggy Cooley poured coffee for the other early risers, hoping that my willpower could hold out until she picked up the plate. She was slow this morning.

I knew every coffeepot in the area that was hot by six-thirty. There weren't that many places open at that hour in this town. Santa Barbara wasn't exactly a workingman's burg. It was more a banker's town, where stores opened at ten, and places opened for brunch. I hated brunch. I wasn't even sure I liked Santa Barbara anymore.

Like Coco Palms, Montecito was an unincorporated area of the city. Unlike Coco Palms, it was ungated and had shops and restaurants. The Montecito Coffee Mill was well positioned at a crossroads of Montecito's two main streets. It had a local reputation for serving good food, which was justified, but it also had a reputation for characters. I guess that's why I liked it, that and Peggy Cooley, who just might have been the biggest character of all.

I watched the other customers react to Peggy's banter. Even

those who did not smile easily succumbed to her misplaced Texas twang. I say misplaced because it didn't quite fit the chichi pretentiousness of Montecito. What it did was strip people down to the basics, settle a lot of phonies back on earth. I guessed, if truth be known, I was in a mood not to like Montecito or Santa Barbara or Coco Palms.

She punched an old, retired L.A. real estate lawyer in the shoulder with one hand and held the coffeepot high and wide in the other. The rasp of her voice found every ear in the place, which is just what she intended.

"Why Lenny, you old reprobate. You rub your paw across my bib one more time and my pa will shotgun you right to the altar." She laughed with a loud cackle. "I tell you what, Lenny, I marry you and I won't eat another red bean the rest of my life."

The old man reddened. She had taken him down good but at the same time had left him something to walk out on. I supposed that was called diplomacy. I never was much of a diplomat myself. If I took them down, I kicked them.

The coffeepot moved in my direction. I pushed my empty cup toward it. She pushed the cup back to me and leaned in to pour. When Peggy leaned a man paid attention, unless he'd lost some key equipment along the way.

"My bark is worse than my bite," she said in a voice much softer than she'd used before. "Course, my bite's not all that bad, you know?"

She finished her pouring and stood up. I just looked. I knew when to keep my mouth shut. She grinned impishly at me and shook back some hair.

"You look but you don't talk, is that it?" She teased me with everything she had, which was considerable. I nodded and bit the inside of my lip. She grinned with all the confidence of one who had been there. "I bet you got some story."

I leaned back as she reached for my empty plate. Damn all, I had eaten the potatoes. She pulled the plate and herself away slightly and said, "I'd like to hear it sometime."

All I could do was nod. She looked at me as if for the first time, and her smile was gone before she turned back to the counter. I watched the short skirt ride up the backs of her thighs, just like all the other drooling oglers did. Old habits were hard to break. I had to say this for her, though, she had damn fine legs, tan and lean. I was glad they were tan. I was tired of tan. In fact, I hated tan, I told myself, along with Montecito and Santa Barbara.

I devoted the rest of my cup of coffee to the crossword puzzle. The two were finished together. I flipped the paper over and glanced once more at the front-page story. Big headlines shouted, "COCO PALMS MURDER." The only new information in it was the dead guy's name and a brief bio. It rang a bell. The name was Wendell Leeds. He was somehow related to the family who owned and operated the Leeds Leather Palace stores; a chain that had started in the heart of Beverly Hills. It rang a bell because I'd once bought a suede coat from the bastards. The lining had come apart and the shoulder seam split the second time I'd worn it. Leeds Leather Palace was sorry but not responsible. The shooting was no longer a mystery to me. It was clear he was killed by a customer.

Something caught my eye as I started to turn to the inside pages for the continuation of the story. At the bottom left-hand corner of the front page was a story about a homeless man burned to death in an abandoned house. They had no way of identifying him. He was another of those anonymous vagrants who had become the focus of so much recent attention. The house had burned completely to the ground. It was one of those abandoned shacks that stood on land worth millions, which the city fathers refused to allow to be developed. I had no thoughts one way or the other on that. However, the sign the homeless fellow had left as his last statement to the world, clearly visible in the newspaper photograph, did get my opinions moving. On the lawn in front of the shack, hammered into the weeds, was a piece of plywood with crude lettering. It read, "Care for the Homeless."

I had seen the homeless. They were not all helpless little old men and women. Neither were they all simply poor creature families down on their luck. There were a lot of able bodies in there. More than a few. To my eye, I would say the preponderance of the homeless were people able to function in society and by society's rules, but chose not to. Maybe this fellow had been one of those. One of those protesters who demanded the right to sleep on the steps of city hall. One who paid no taxes, contributed no service, offered no investment of self in the community. One who urinated in the streets, one who demanded change from passersby with an air of thinly disguised intimidation, one who cluttered and dirtied the parks and beaches. In short, one of the reasons people felt less safe walking their own streets these days. Yes, maybe this fellow had been one of those.

Or maybe I was just in one of those moods. Maybe he was a good soul on his way to a better life who just happened to be in the wrong place at the wrong time. In reading the story, I saw there was some speculation that the fellow had committed suicide by pouring gasoline over himself and lighting it. It was unclear to the officials whether or not this had been an accident. It may have been his last protest. It was a bad way to go, whatever it was—suicide, accident, or futile protest.

"More?" Peggy leaned on one hip with the coffeepot lazily held to the side. She was showing me more Peggy than coffee. I looked. I looked hard, and I won that showdown. Something gave inside her.

"I've had about all I can handle at my age," I said, and got to my feet. I was a lot bigger than she was. "But thanks anyway."

"Y'all come back now," she said with a flippy walk away. I hadn't noticed until then that she had not had much of an accent talking to me. Well, well, Peggy Cooley, all things were not what they seemed. More of life's little deceptions. I knew of an ex-hooker, at least one, who had married money and now roosted at the top of local society. And here was a waitress from Texas who maybe turned her accent on and off.

They were not the same, and yet something inside tried to say they were.

So what? Take it easy, Sands, it is not a perfect world. Or as the New Age yuppies would say, chill out. I started my car and rubbed my eyes. I hated deception. It was theft to me. I pulled onto Mountain Road with a soft look back at the windows of the coffeeshop. I wouldn't chill out, that was for sure. I only responded to the idiom of my own generation.

• • •

The day idled along without much happening to catch my attention. My phone rang. Once. I let the machine answer it and listened in. It was Bob Claiborne wanting to see me for lunch the next day, saying he had something personal to discuss. My curiosity was too dead to wonder if he meant personal to me or personal to him. I didn't much care either way. I exercised the shoulder as much as it could take with light weights. It felt good, so I decided to increase my routine. I shadowboxed the mirror until my sweat made the Spanish tile floor a danger zone. I quit with a draw.

I settled into the hundred-degree water of the spa attached to the pool, faced away from the sun, and closed my eyes. In the past I had used the ocean to heal, but it was a lot easier to loll in heated water churned by a machine. No rocks, or sand sharks, or riptides to disturb one's thoughts.

My mind jumped about. I thought briefly of the dead man. Nothing in the paper about another person having found Leeds. That could mean the police were holding that information because they considered me a suspect, or the car dealer had not mentioned me. It wasn't my problem.

I had a little sorting out to do with other things. I had a whole life to contemplate, or what was left of the rest of it anyway. Mostly, I thought about Trinia . . . Trinia and Josh. Some of it didn't hurt anymore. It was bearable. There were even times when it was like something that had happened to someone else. I didn't let myself dwell too much on the loss. I didn't let myself think very often of how old Josh would be now, or of the baby who never had a chance to see this world, or the wife, mother, daughter, friend who made the world a better place.

It grabbed me, of course, when I did wander into it. Almost four very long years had passed, but I could still smell the wet, charred remains of our house, and I was still chilled by flash moments of what I'd learned about the way they had died in that fire. It was guilt. I knew that. They had died because of me and what I did . . . because a man named Clyde Walls had thumbed his nose at the courts and the law and the people he had stolen millions from . . . because I had tracked him and found him and brought his hidden assets back into the system for the people he owed. Trinia and Josh had died as a part of his revenge. The years we had together seemed short compared to what we might have had.

It was those thoughts that got to me. I sometimes tried to counter them with thoughts of my own revenge, executed deep in a jungle in Paraguay. It had taken me time to figure out who had done it, and more time still to track him down again. His bodyguards had cost me a separated shoulder and some fractured ribs, but in the end I had gotten to Clyde Walls and done what I had to do. It wouldn't bring Trinia and Josh back, but for the first time since they had died I could sleep without dreaming of fire.

I opened my eyes to shed the remains of it from my mind. It was no longer painful, but it wasn't healthy. I could get maudlin real fast. Not good for a big tough guy like me. Somebody might see me feeling something. Not good.

It was so quiet I could hear the waves breaking down below. I faced toward the sun and looked out on the view. The ocean and the Channel Islands peeked back at me. Funny that I would wind up here, of all places. I wasn't the Santa Barbara type, whatever that was. I was more for the big city. I liked it where a guy could get lost in the crowds. At least, I had liked it. Now, I wasn't so sure.

The ironic part of it was, I had bought this lot for Trinia, who had a thing about Santa Barbara. It was supposed to be a surprise and part of my promise to her that I would quit the recovery business. She never got to see it. She never got to plan a house for it or dream any dreams about it. It was just as well I didn't have those memories stacked on here.

I had to smile when I looked around at the house. It was designed by an architect named Albert who owed me one. It was built on the insurance money from the other house. I never saw the plans and I had never seen the house until one month ago when I moved in. Albert the architect still owed me one as far as I was concerned. He built a house for me like he would have built for some swinger in the Hollywood Hills, which is exactly what he was. And exactly what I wasn't.

Actually, Trinia would have probably liked it. It was a bachelor pad, but it had all the amenities that women liked. She would have liked the shape of it, with its big circular sunken living room and high ceilings. She would have liked all the glass and the gourmet kitchen. She would have liked the size of the master bedroom with its sunset view of the ocean. It was possible that down deep inside, I might grow to like it. I was just embarrassed by it.

I toweled off. It was really like living in someone else's house. Even the towel I was using had been picked out and bought by the decorator, a fellow named Lonnie, who was a very special friend of Albert the architect. That was another miss, high and outside. I didn't worry about what it had cost me as much as how it had nothing to do with me. I was a sort of guest to my own house and its furnishings. The bottom line was, I didn't belong in Coco Palms, and the house knew it.

• • •

I drove south along the coast on a deserted stretch of the Pacific Coast Highway just north of Malibu and Zuma. I was an hour from Santa Barbara, looking for a turnoff that I'd tended to miss on a few occasions when my mind wandered.

That was because it was unmarked and looked like a private driveway leading to the ocean. It ended abruptly before the porticoed entry of a classic Mediterranean building with arches and columns and all the other stuff a high-class joint had to have. I pulled up before the double-doored entrance with a blue neon sign in script that read "Meddler's." I looked at my watch. I was on time.

I liked entering this place. It was like stepping into another world, or at least another time. I'd put it at about 1945. It was like the supper clubs they had in those days. It had a roving piano and a torch singer. It had a long bar in the tradition of Raffles in Singapore. That was something I knew about. Most of all, it had people that made it work. There was a fellow behind the bar who was supposedly descended from old Russian nobility, known simply as the Count. He had a never-ending string of stories. If you listened closely, you'd notice his accent changing. I didn't know if he was Russian or Australian. Brooklyn was also a possibility. I gave him a nod as I passed and said, "Count."

He snapped to with a Prussian salute and said, "Goot efening, Chake," in something akin to a German accent. I saluted back and headed toward the music and the main room.

The piano player was a guy named Eddie. He was an ex-fighter. Not bad. I'd gone a few rounds with him down at Main Street in the old days. He had an ex-fighter's face and eyes. His hands were a little scarred but delicate. He played my kind of music.

The singer, Lorna, had a Veronica Lake hairdo and an ice maiden reputation. Fact was, she was a hard-luck lady who went for the gigolo type and always wound up swearing, "Never again!" She showed up in the spotlight now and then and added spice to the evening. She sang my kind of music.

The man who really ran Meddler's, greeted people at the door, in any one of more than five languages he spoke, and was generally thought to be Meddler was an enormous man in both height and girth who bore an amazing resemblance to the late Orson Welles. His name was Sebastian Kule. I'd once heard it said of him that he had "a greeter's smile, but a bouncer's eyes." I had always thought that summed him up pretty well. He took my hand as one would an old friend seldom seen.

"Too long, Jake, too long. You know we worry if we don't see you on a weekly basis." His voice was deep and warm. He had moved his hand to my elbow and was guiding me into the main room.

"I've found better food at a dive in Lompoc," I said for no real reason.

Sebastian laughed exactly as loud and as long as I knew he would. It was not phony, it was just that I knew Sebastian.

"I'll pass that along to Jason," he said. "He's waiting for you upstairs." With each hand he indicated a choice: the elevator at the other end of the bar, or the flight of stairs at the back of the main dining room, both of which led to the upper level. The elevator, however, was primarily used by patrons with an interest in the card games available in the upper front clubroom, and of course, by Jason Meddler himself. Sebastian always offered the choice. I always took the stairs. It was another ritual.

He waited, I suppose afraid I would lose my way, until I had managed to ascend the stairs. I saluted from the top before Sebastian gave a jovial shake of his huge head and pushed the button that popped the door open with a little buzz.

Jason was on the phone and motioned for me to go on back through the open door to his private quarters. The dining room was set up for dinner for the two of us and the chess table stood beckoning from the window that looked out to a well-lighted beach. Jason knew how to live. I poured coffee from the carafe on the side table. It was for me, as the cigars were for him. I heard his chair creaking toward me, so I went to greet him.

His handshake was firmer than any man's I'd ever known. Most people probably assumed it came from using the wheelchair. I knew different. I knew Jason Meddler before the wheel chair, long before. He always had hands that could strangle an elephant. He always shook hands, too. It was custom with him even if you had seen him that very morning, he shook your hand. There was something to it. It gave you a chance to look at a person and make a tactile contact.

"Hungry?" he asked, like a mother to a son returning home from college.

"I ate in Lompoc," I replied, hoping Sebastian would keep his word.

"Too late for you, huh, Jake? And I'll bet wherever you ate, you ate alone. Right? You know you're turning into a regular old maid? Early to bed and early to rise, is that it?"

I shrugged. We had been through this before, in one way or another, many times since I had returned.

"Now, you know I'm not talking about dinner, Jake, you know that. I am talking about you though. What I say is true. You've developed this tendency to hole up. You know that? You get into streaks where you don't want to see anybody, and I'm saying that's not healthy. You've got to snap out of it before it becomes what you are."

I shrugged again, but maybe it was too small a shrug for him to see.

"And this thing you have about not letting anyone do anything for you. You had that decorator send my check back to me. Why? Do you think I could ever get a favor up on you? I owe you my life, so tell me how can I ever get even on that score, huh? Don't you see the craziness here?"

"Jason, calm down. Look, if I ever needed anything, money or anything, I'd call you, okay? But I don't. I've got more than I need. It's just easier if I pay the folks that do things for me, that's all. It makes it easier to tell them to go someplace and die if I've been the one to pay the bill. That's all there is to it. And as for the other thing, you don't owe me squat. We're even, if you're keeping score. I'm not. And I did find a better place to eat in Lompoc."

He put his head back in a silent laugh. He looked at me long and steady for a moment. "How is it that I'm the only one who knows how long-winded you really are? Most people who know you call you the Sphinx, or silent Sam or something."

"You're just lucky, I guess," I said. "Chess?"

"Damn right, and you better be on your game. I've been studying the middle game. That's where you get me, and that's where you'll lose. I warn you."

"You sound a lot like Saddam Hussein proclaiming 'the mother of all wars.'"

"We'll see," he said, taking a cigar with him as he wheeled himself to the chess table.

It was a perfect time and a perfect place. There was no one in the world I liked better than Jason Meddler or trusted as much. In schoolyard terms, he was my best friend. In a distant past he had put his life on the line for me, and I had done the same for him. He was the best company I could have. He was family to me and would always be so.

Jason began to mutter about an imbecile named Lasker. I assumed he was referring to his maven on the middle game, because he was losing that aspect of our contest in a more brutal manner than usual. I tried not to smile when he toppled his king in the universal representation of defeat.

"A revenge?" he asked, knowing without asking that we would play another game.

"Your choice," I replied.

"Black," he said without hesitation. "I'll defend. This time you will suffer."

"You forgot to call me the evil Satan from the West," I said with an unrepressed sense of glee. I was one of those guys that liked to rub it in.

He played better, but not better enough. I quenched his appetite for war just as Stormin' Norman had done to Saddam. I liked the comparison. He had to suffer the humiliation of hearing me say the word: "Checkmate."

I teased him. "You know, Jason, I think you're really onto

something. That middle game was, well, very unusual. I especially liked the sacrifice of your knights. What's this fellow's
name again? Lasker, is it?"

"You're a lousy winner, you know that?" he answered back.
He clipped a fresh cigar for lighting, with a look up at me to
let me know he was giving me all rights to my victory.

I waited while he puffed the cigar into a small replica of in-
dustrial America gone bad. The smoke, of course, took a direct
path to me. I think he knew that, and I think he took some perverse pleasure in it at that moment. I tried not to cough.

"You said you had something to show me," I said after I
found a tiny space of fresh air to breathe.

"Did I? Oh, right. It's a file Tim Brandt left for you. You remember Tim, don't you?" He said it in such an offhand way I
became instantly alert.

"Sure. Good lawyer."

"Yeah, well, if there is such a thing, but anyway, he wanted
you to look over the file and maybe get together with him this
week." His eyes were set on me through the heavy plume of
cigar smoke.

I played along. "He want my advice on something?"

"Well, that yes, but I think he might have something more
in mind."

I refused to do it for him. I still played. "What's that?"

He patted the end of the cigar into the ashtray. A perfect
circle of ash was left deposited dead center. Jason was not a
sloppy man.

He said, "I think he'd like you to do a recovery for him. It
seems simple enough, jewels and bonds and that sort of thing,
stashed out of country."

"I don't do that anymore," I answered simply.

"Yes, I know, I told him, but this really does seem like a
snap. I read the file, and this guy should be easy to find and no
threat. He's no tough guy."

"That's what they said about Clyde Walls," I answered, and
let it hang.

He was quiet for a while. He put another perfect circle next to the first one.

"Jake, you're not even fifty years old yet," he said finally.

I answered. "I'm closer to fifty than I am to forty."

"You haven't worked in three or four years," he said. "They'll stop asking if you don't get back in soon."

"I don't want back in. I'm out, for good." I let that sit for a second or two. "I've had enough adventure, and I don't need the money. And Jason, don't worry about me. I'm fine. I'm over the hard part."

"Really?" he asked with a kind of concern that can't be faked.

"Really," I said, hoping to put it all to rest.

"So what now, pal? You got any plans?"

"Nope, and I don't want any. Where I live there are a lot of people that don't do a damned thing. I'm going to learn how they do that," I said.

"Santa Barbara," he muttered around his cigar. "Of all the damned places. Why Santa Barbara?" I shrugged my response. He continued, "How's the house? You getting used to it yet?"

"Not yet. Probably not ever. It's sort of like having a pet that hates you."

He laughed. I laughed too. I was getting used to looking at myself as a humorous anecdote.

"I'm not too surprised. Albert and Lonnie loose to do their own thing? . . . Talked to Vera since you've been back?"

"Nope, not yet," I replied. "She okay?"

"She's Vera. Sure she's okay. She'll be okay until she croaks," he said. He examined the neat residue of ash in the ashtray. "I miss those days sometimes, don't you? Those long Sundays at Vera and Henry's?"

"I suppose," I said, trying not to add any fuel to the fire of his memory.

"Until the day he died, Henry felt regrets about forming the Orion unit. He never thought it was a success, but like I tried to tell him, he was looking at the men we lost, not what we managed to do," he said, determined to dredge it up. "When you think about it, we did one hell of a lot in the two years and change we were in operation. We took out some of the big players in the terrorism game, that's for sure."

"We paid a big price," I reminded him.

"Yeah," he said with that ironic twisted smile of his. "I guess it was too much for Henry. I'll always think he finally pulled the plug on Orion to save your tail, amigo, and maybe a little guilt over what happened to me."

"You're probably right," I replied as tersely as possible. I was afraid to look back. It was a vulnerable area for me.

"You know something, I can still taste that red wine stew that Vera and Henry used to fix so often, with the oregano and basil. I haven't thought of that in years." He squinted into the smoke of his cigar. The fun of the memory faded fast from his face. "I guess some things are gone forever, aren't they?"

"Some things," I agreed. "The past is a lousy place to live, Jason."

"Yeah," was all he said in response. Then: "Stay and play one more," offered without enthusiasm. He was suddenly tired.

I got to my feet and put out my hand. "Not tonight, Jason. I'll see you in a couple of days."

We shook hands, and he saw me to the door.

"I'm here," he said.

"I know."

On the way out I stopped and listened to Eddie and Lorna do "Tangerine." I sat at the edge of the bar over a cup of coffee the Count pushed silently toward me. It was more ritual, and it felt good. I said goodnight before they did a reprise of other songs they knew I liked, and before I began to notice that I was alone.

3 🌿

I parked my car in front of the Lighthouse on Chapala and sat for a moment listening to the end of a Klemmer record that brought back some good memories. Memories of a big Roman tub in front of a window that looked out on a 180-degree city view. City lights, and scented candles, soft touches from wet, tender fingers, and her John Klemmer music. Funny how the spirit relives what the senses recall. Cut grass, for instance, often brought back spring training to me. The taste of spearmint reminded me of summer tea with fresh mint sprigs served on porch swings Another smell, diesel, made me think of early-morning liftoffs from places like Quang Tri or Da Nang. Klemmer, and solo horns, and sweet, sad songs brought back Trinia.

I switched off as some tone-deaf juvenile started to do his stuff on a synthesizer. It was leading to what music would be in the future, I supposed, but I would hold out for the old, pure, imperfect sounds of the real instruments as long as I could.

I unfolded from the car, an older Porsche 928, which had been part of my fee for a recovery some years back. It was oak green with deep yellow pin-striping—I still considered it the best design ever put to an automobile. Its big V-8 was a match for anything on the road, and no other car handled as well in the curves. It still got the look-over from people who had a discerning eye.

I spotted Bob Clairborne in the back and waved off the hostess. He had a cup of coffee waiting at the place across the booth from him. I had to smile at that.

He explained it by saying, "I saw your car pull up."

I had known Bob Claiborne in L.A. We were neighbors on Mulholland Drive and had met one night when he turned into my driveway followed by a couple of tough numbers intent on robbing him or killing him or both. It was simple enough for me to take the two down, but to Bob Claiborne it seemed like far more than it was. He had never forgotten it and probably was still having flashbacks on it. The incident had soured him on Los Angeles and in looking around he was smart enough to see the future for his kind of business in Santa Barbara. He was a real estate man who specialized in high-priced properties. Occasionally he touched deals that weren't beyond the common man, but rareley, and only for special situations. For instance, he had found my Santa Barbara property for me through an estate sale. In real estate terms, he had helped me steal it. Now that I had built a house on it, I suspected he had visions of one day selling it and turning a profit on the deal. I had become a cynic.

"How goes it?" he asked. "You all settled in yet?"

"You might say that." I was noncommittal. "How's your tennis?"

He loved tennis. He loved to play it, watch it, talk about it. I had seen him play, and the only thing was, to my eye he wasn't very good.

"Great, just great. My backhand has finally come around. I think I found the answer. I wasn't turning my hips around enough."

"Yeah," I said after a sip of tepid coffee, "it's usually the hips. Most moves work off the hips."

"You don't play tennis, do you?" He didn't wait for an answer. I was glad because I would have probably made a wise-ass comment that pricked his tennis ego. "Shame, because it really is a great sport. Golf?"

"Do I play?" I asked in return. He nodded. I shook my head. "It seems like every so-called sport I've touched has had something to do with taking out the other guy. I can't quite visualize myself jumping a net and congratulating some fellow for ruining my day."

"No one jumps the net anymore," he said with a smile, as if that was what I was talking about.

"That's too bad," I said, meaning it.

It read like a reversal to him, and it came too fast for him to deal with. He was quick to jump out of the way of things he either did not understand or was afraid to confront. He was not a man who liked controversy.

"You hungry?" he asked as he waved to the waiter who was lounging at the bar talking to the bartender. The waiter saw the summons but continued his conversation. Bob shrugged as if to say, what can you do? I almost told him but decided to pass. It didn't seem worth it.

"Not too," I finally replied to Bob's question.

"Fish is good here. They have sand dabs today. I love sand dabs."

I sipped my coffee. Bob put his hand up to wave again. He held it at half-mast, waiting for the waiter to deign to turn in his direction so he could repeat his summons. The waiter was practicing the fine art of customer avoidance.

"I know you're not a lunch person, Jake, but I wanted to touch base with you, see if you're moved in okay, and just in general offer help in anything you might need." He waved and pulled his head in a motion that a Martian would have understood to mean, come here. "Lunch is the only time of the day when I can get away and deal with things other than real estate."

Bob's waving and head bobbing was successful. The waiter

made his disinterested approach. "You ready to order?" He
said it from a distance of about ten feet. I looked him over
pretty good. Fingernails and hair hit me the wrong way, especially for a waiter. Attitude too was a giant zero. This guy did
not score very high on my chart.

"Yes, I think so," Bob said brightly, trying to win the ap-
proval of the slob with the order pad. "You want to try the
sand dabs, Jake?"

"Just coffee for me, Bob. Thanks."

The slob looked at me as if I'd shoved his grandmother. Bob
knew me better than to press the point, although it was clear
he considered it.

"Right," Bob said. "Okay, then I'll have the sand dabs and
another glass of sangria." He couldn't resist asking, "You're
sure?"

"I'm sure." I couldn't imagine eating anything delivered to
me on a plate handled by the slob.

"Right," Bob said again. Then, to the waiter: "I guess that
does it."

The waiter made an ungracious exit. I had no idea what we
had done to make him angry, other than interrupt his conversation with the bartender. I took another look and understood
it a little better. The bartender was a girl. Not a bad-looking
one at that.

"So," Bob said, clapping his hands together and reposition-
ing himself in the booth. "This is great. No one seemed to
know where you were for a couple of years there. After they
started on your house, I'd go by whenever I was in Coco
Palms to see if you'd been around. No one had ever seen you."

"I was out of the country quite a bit," I said, as if I were
telling him something, without really telling him anything.

"Yes, I can understand how you would be, in your business,"
he said. He found himself suddenly at a mental crossroads he
had not expected to reach for some time. He stalled out.

"You've got some sort of problem?" I decided to help him
through his vapor lock.

He breathed deeply to get himself started. "I had a call yesterday morning. About you." He stopped while the waiter slid his sangria in front of him. I drained the remainder of my cooled-down coffee, which prompted Bob to ask, "Could you bring more coffee, please?"

The waiter gave his back to my host in reply. Bob pretended not to notice and toasted me with his fresh glass of sangria. "To waiters the world over," he said sardonically.

"Let me cut to the chase here," I said. I had a habit of getting to the point. Another old one that was hard to break. "You wanted to meet today because somebody's trying to get a line on me, and you don't know what to do about it, right?"

"I suppose so, yes, something like that. You're the only person I know who does the sort of thing you do. I mean, I don't know how secret you need to keep your life, you know?"

"Hear this. The sort of thing I did do, I don't do anymore." I laid it out flat and simple, giving it a moment to take hold. "Now who's asking and why?"

"The Coco Palms security people," he said, trying to keep his voice down. "Since I'm your realtor of record, they naturally called me for what I knew of your background. I told them I didn't know much about you. I don't really, when it comes down to it."

The waiter was back with Bob's sand dabs. They did look good, even with the waiter's unappetizing thumb sharing the plate. I wondered if he moonlighted as a mechanic: the creases of his thumb were black with some foreign substance. Bob nodded in puppy dog appreciation. "Coffee?" he persisted with a nod once again at my empty cup. It was more of a plea than a demand this time.

The waiter ignored him again. Nothing overt, yet nothing too subtle either. I was getting tired of this guy.

"And why?" I prodded.

"I don't know. I really don't know." He fumbled with it while he looked for some good explanation. "Coco Palms is very security-conscious, I do know that. You're a new resident, and my guess is, they were simply trying to complete their file on you. Something like that, maybe."

A busboy passed with a load of dirty dishes. I leaned out from the booth to get his attention and said, "*Más café, por favor.*"

He nodded and replied, "*Sí, señor.*"

Bob pushed at the sand dabs and I watched him. Neither of us said anything. It was slightly uncomfortable. The busboy was back in a moment with a pot of coffee and poured my cup full. "*Gracias,*" I said, and he replied, "*De nada.*" I tasted the coffee and for the first time detected the slight flavor of cinnamon. It was very good coffee served hot.

"There's something else?" I asked from instinct.

He tried a brave grin. It failed in the eyes.

"No, no, nothing. That's all," he said, saying too much. "What do you think of Coco Palms now that you're living there?" He put on a more realistic smile finally.

"Not much," I managed to say without sneering.

"Yes, I know what you must think. It's not exactly from an Andy Hardy movie, is it?"

"It's about as real," I sneered.

"What did you think of that murder?" He raised it as if it were a new issue, but it was clear to me that the murder was the linchpin of this little meeting. "Do you know I had just gotten an exclusive on Leeds's house, not more than two weeks before he was killed? I had already showed the house once, and we were going to have an open house this coming weekend. Now God only knows what will happen with it. I suppose it will have to go to probate and such. He was on the outs with the rest of his family, so I would doubt that they'll be up here." A beeping sound came from his inside coat pocket. He reached in and pulled out a small foldup cellular phone. "He wasn't married, so there's no one to give me any instructions in the thing. Excuse me," he said before turning his attention to his phone.

I had an empty cup before me again. I tried to look around and not listen. It was clear that he had forgotten some appointment, or was late, or both. He gave an E.T.A. of fifteen minutes and folded up that little wonder of modern electronics.

"Jake, I'm sorry," he said with a frantic wave at the slob. "I forgot completely about a showing this afternoon. I have a family up from Los Angeles waiting in my office now. I have to run." He made a writing gesture in the direction of the bar, and the bartender passed the word to her admirer.

"Don't worry about this," I said, not letting him see how easily I read into his lie. It was clear to me now the call had been preset. "I'll take care of it."

"No, no," he protested. "I'll do it."

The insolent waiter sauntered over and placed what looked to be a passport folder on the table. Before Bob could pick it up the slob had walked away again. Bob shook his head in frustration and looked at the bill. He took some money from his wallet and placed it inside the folder.

"Thanks for the coffee," I said as he got to his feet. "I'll see you soon."

"Thank you for meeting me, Jake. Good luck in the new house," he said in an uncertain effort to depart.

"I can use it," I answered. He seemed unsure what to say next. "Relax, Bob. I don't know any more about the dead guy than you do. Okay?"

"Oh, no, Jake, I didn't think anything. It's just that they called with all those questions, and I owe you. I mean, I'll never be able to repay you for what you did for me that night."

I shrugged it away.

His voice moved up slightly. "Those guys would have killed me. Sometimes I can remember it like it just happened. Thank God you were there and thank God you had a gun, or I'd be dead. That's a fact. I'd be dead."

I had not used a gun that night, but there was no sense in trying to rewrite his memory of it. I simply nodded and let him spill it out. He shook it all off with something akin to a shiver.

"Well, on this other thing, this inquiry about you, I wanted you to know, is all." He fumbled it again.

"I know, Bob, thanks."

"If there's ever anything I can do. I mean it, Jake, anything."

I nodded. Finally, he merely gave a small wave and hurried away. I sat alone at the table with an empty cup and the folder holding the bill and the money. Since there was nothing in the cup, I picked up the folder.

Bob had left a very nice tip indeed. By my quick calculation it was about fifty percent. I got to my feet and walked to the bar with the folder in hand. I sidled in next to the waiter and looked into the eyes of the bartender. Up close she was not much.

"Little lady," I said, hoping she hated being called little lady, "tell your feeble-minded boyfriend here that he needs to wash his long greasy hair, clean his fingernails, press his clothes, and bathe at least once a month. You might also tell him that the peace symbol he's wearing for an earring is becoming an irritant, so he shouldn't tempt me."

I left enough money to cover the exact amount of the bill and put the rest of Bob's money, a ten, in my pocket. I did it openly and obviously so the slob could get the full meaning of it.

On the way out I passed the busboy and slipped the ten into his hand.

"*Gracias*," he said.

"*Por nada*," I replied.

I took the long way home, mulling over what I had learned from Claiborne. It depressed me, in an odd sort of way. I decided for the rest of the day to fall into one of those deep holes Jason had accused me of inhabiting. Once home, I closed the gates behind me, turned off the phones, exercised until I was tired, and then watched television in a mindless stupor until sleep became the best alternative.

• • •

I made my own breakfast the next morning. I scrambled up some eggs with diced potatoes, diced ham, and some sautéed onions and jalapeños. I grated Monterey and cheddar cheeses over it. I was breaking a lot of my current dietary rules, but I used the old "to hell with it" rationalization and ate it anyway.

When I finished I took a carafe of freshly brewed double-roasted Guatemalan coffee outdoors, poolside. The sun was just coming up, so I watched it. I didn't think much. I let my senses take the moment. Life felt good just then. I loved the morning when the day had not been decided quite yet. I wondered how people could be night people and miss this. How did they ever get their souls clean? Not my problem.

I did have one recurring thought I could not quite control. It was a flickering memory of Wendell Leeds as he stumbled awkwardly into the center of Faring Lane. I did not dwell upon it, but somewhere working in the back of my mind was an inconsistency picked up by my eye but not yet recognized by my brain. I did not like it when that happened. I didn't like it especially because it was not my problem.

The six-cup carafe was empty. I began to look ahead to my day and what, if anything, I must do about it. I picked up the cordless phone and activated the clever little device on it that connected the answering machine to an intercom line. I played back the messages that had accumulated while the phone was off.

Jason had called four times. His impatience was quite evident in his last message. There were two hang-ups and one call from a Captain Jessup with the Coco Palms patrol. Would I please call him at my convenience, etc. I played that message back several times, trying to get the measure of the man through his voice tones. I wondered if Captain Jessup was on duty at this hour. I pushed the auto dial function and the three-digit patrol number.

"Coco Palms patrol. How may I help you?"

"This is Jake Sands. I'm returning a call to Captain Jessup."

"One moment please, sir."

Efficient, courteous, soft-spoken, all the things one might
want from a self-contained security patrol service. Why was I
reading "too good to be true"?

"Sir, are you calling from your 287-1000 number?"

"Yes, I am," I replied, impressed again by the efficiency.

"If you will stand by, sir, Captain Jessup will get right back
to you." The voice at the other end said it as if there was no
alternative but to comply.

I did. I said, "Fine," and hung up.

Captain Jessup called five minutes later. I was inside rinsing
off my breakfast dishes. I took it on the wall phone.

"Captain Jessup?" I said.

"Why yes, Mr. Sands, it is. Thank you for returning my call,
sir. I see you're an early riser."

"I am," I replied.

"Yes, well, so am I. This is nothing important, sir," he began, which of course meant that it very well might be, "but I
do have to run a couple things by you, as we are doing with
some of the other residents in regards to this homicide we had
a few nights back."

"Shoot."

"Sir?"

"I said, shoot. Begin. Fire your first question."

"Oh, yes sir, I see. Well, sir, you drive a Porsche 928, do you
not, sir?"

"I drive a 928."

"Were you out on the night of the incident, sir? Do you remember the night I'm referring to?"

"I do, and I was."

"Do you remember any of the details of the evening?"

"I think what you want can be verified by your Coral Ridge
gate guard. I came in that gate evidently after the incident had
occurred. He told me about it."

"Oh, I see. Well, then, I have no further questions for you,
Mr. Sands. Thank you for your cooperation. It was reported
there was another person on the scene that night, allegedly
driving a 928. We haven't been able to locate that person yet. I

was hoping you might be able to help in some way."

"I understand. Goodbye, Captain Jessup."

"Goodbye, sir."

I wondered if he was as curious about me as I was about him. This was no rent-a-cop patrol. These guys were pros. I figured them all to be cops and probably ex-military. It seemed that Jessup was making moves that were more police than security, and it made me wonder just how far he was willing to reach beyond his sanctions. Ex-ville was beginning to have some layers to it. Coco Palms did not strike me as a place that needed that kind of heavy protection. Maybe I was wrong. At any rate, something did not fit.

I don't know why, but I was reminded of the old studio days in Hollywood. Legend had it that the studios had such powerful security forces that they could fix all kinds of crimes for their V.I.P.s, up to and including murder. That was in the old days, of course, but they did it then by hiring cops and ex-cops. I tended to like cops. I knew a lot of them—I had to in the work I used to do—and a lot of them were good men. But I knew some bad ones, too. There was nothing worse, to me, than a bad cop. The question that seeped into my gray matter was whether Captain Jessup and his crew were good cops or bad.

I did my dishes, made my bed, and had a light workout. I felt a little dulled from all the television I had watched. Dulled and somewhat amazed at the utter failure of that medium to aspire to its potential. I stayed under the hot shower for a little longer than usual. Those television cobwebs were hard to clear.

I answered the phone on its third ring. I was still wet from the shower, but I couldn't stand the ringing. As soon as I got it to my ear I heard Jason's voice.

"You don't return calls anymore? I've left a dozen messages there for you."

"Four," I corrected.

Jason snorted into the phone. He took another moment to light a cigar. I could hear the puffing sound. I was glad I was here and he was there. I hated smoke.

"You fall in a hole someplace or what?" he finally said when his cigar was pulling smoothly.

"If that's my only choice, I'll have to pick 'or what.' " I dried myself with a beach-sized towel while I held the phone against my shoulder. He waited me out. I tried to find a way to defuse his curiosity. "I was clearing my head. Doing myself a little favor."

"I see," he answered. "A favor."

"Yeah, a favor," I replied, and tossed the towel.

"Well, I'm happy to hear that you're in the favor-granting mood, because I'm asking one."

"I'll bet," I said, not taking him seriously. "And what do you call a favor?"

"That you meet somebody, and listen to her, and help her if you can. That's what I call a favor."

"This somebody I know?"

"Nope," he answered. "This is somebody I know."

"I thought I knew everybody you knew."

"Not quite. How about it?"

"Okay. Where?"

"Actually it's pretty much in your neck of the woods. You know Summerland?" He paused for my sound of acknowledgment. "Can you meet her out there today sometime?"

"Okay, have her meet me at the White Gull. I'm always looking for an excuse to go there."

"Food is better here," he snorted.

"Yeah, but they don't allow smoking," I said. "Tell her eight o'clock. What's her name?"

"Katherine Burley. Mrs." I knew he was smiling at that.

"Just tell her to ask for Jake Sands. Mr."

I hung up quick. I didn't want to hear his topper.

Jason Meddler did not ask for favors. Sometimes he would tell you he was asking a favor when he was really trying to do something for you. I had seen him do that with others. Ordinarily, we didn't play that game, so I had to assume this was, simply put, an old-fashioned favor. I began to get curious.

4

The White Gull was the ground-floor restaurant in an old, four-story Summerland hotel. The hotel had been renovated back to the charming level. The restaurant was a classic. It had very high ceilings with natural exposed beams. The walls were bricked up to about eight feet, with plaster the rest of the way. There were slow-turning ceiling fans that reminded me of an old Gable movie.

The chef was an ad man turned restaurateur. His wife tended the front door. Together they had turned the place into a gourmet's find. Their name was, of all things, Parsley. Bernice and Todd Parsley. They had had a partner a few years back who stole from them. They sued and won big. He came up with empty pockets, and an escape route. Their lawyer found me, and I found their partner and the cache into which he had emptied his pockets. Now they not only owned the restaurant, they owned the hotel as well.

The place was always packed and this night was no exception. That was never a problem for me. If I had wanted, they would have emptied the place. Gratitude is expressed better by some than by others. Bernice and Todd did it very well.

She grabbed me and gave me what to her was a hug. Actually, there was a lot of empty space between us except maybe around the neck and shoulders. She pushed back and at arm's length said, "We were worried."

I pushed my chin at her in response. "So you see, it was for nothing."

"I heard you retired. Is that true? You're not doing that same work anymore?"

"Not for a while now," I replied. "How's Todd?"

"I'll let you see for yourself," she said, and led me to the kitchen.

Todd and I greeted each other with an exchange similar to the one I had had with Bernice. It all dwindled down pretty fast. I muttered something about letting them get back to their work. They went through the motions of protesting, but I helped them along by waving and backing my way out of the kitchen.

I said, "Bernie, I'm meeting someone here tonight. Her name is Katherine Burley. We could use some privacy."

Bernice nodded efficiently. "Done," she said. She led me through an alcove to a private dining room. It would have been tight for a party of twenty, but for two it was roomy. A waiter appeared with a cup of coffee before she cleared the door. I knew there would be no menus. There never were. The choices would be theirs.

Katherine Burley was a knockout. The kind of blonde you can't get out of a bottle. The kind of figure you can't get from a workout tape. Either you were born with those things, or forget it. There used to be an artist named Vargas who painted ladies in small nothings. They were famous enough to become a generic term. Vargas girls. You couldn't go into a garage or machine shop without seeing two or three tacked up on the walls. They were lush, soft and curved. They were long and graceful. They were like Katherine Burley.

Her hand was a butterfly kiss. Her eyes played straight and true, and probably photographed blue, but they were green. Her mouth made a Loretta Young smile, which somehow read

brave and a little sad. I suddenly had the feeling that maybe
this was one of Jason Meddler's upside-down favors. It didn't
make me mad at all.

"Thank you for meeting me, Mr. Sands. I know it's a great
imposition." She had a good voice. I listened for an accent or
a diction malfunction. There was none. So far, perfect.

"No imposition," I said, holding a chair for her. "I had to
eat anyway, and this is the best place I know."

"So I've heard," she agreed. "We've intended to eat here several times. We're originally from San Francisco, where there
are supposedly the finest restaurants on the west coast. We've
heard this place matches anything we have up there. It's hard
to get a table." The last she said with an eye on the private
room, and a question left unasked.

I left it unanswered. "You say we. I assume that's Mr. Burley you're including there?"

"Greg, yes." Her eyes lowered away from me. Not coy. Not
theatrical. It was a sort of withdrawal.

The waiter entered with an appetizer, a Nova Scotia salmon
in yellow tart sauce with golden Iranian caviar mounded in the
center, and an open bottle of fumé blanc. She accepted a glass.
I let him top off my coffee.

"You live here in Summerland. Is that right?"

"Yes. On Palmetto Lane. Do you know it?"

That was like asking any woman in Beverly Hills if she
knew Rodeo Drive. Palmetto Lane was strictly high-rent. It
was a short road that ran along the beach just to the L.A. side
of Montecito. The properties there were estate-sized, with
large homes, ocean views, and high walls for privacy. There
were few enough to make it a very exclusive part of the coastline. It was often referred to as Fame Lane, for so many movie
stars had at one time or another resided there.

"Well enough to know that if you're living there, you're not
on food stamps," I answered.

She smiled. "Yes, I suppose it does have its own reputation.
Had we known when we moved in, we might have chosen

otherwise, but then the house is so perfect for us. We look out at the ocean in all directions practically. We would have taken this house wherever it was located. It just happened to be on Palmetto Lane."

"How long have you lived here?"

"About a year."

I tried to get some feeling for her mood. I tried not to press. I kept soft subjects afloat as we worked our way through foods delivered in small portions on good china plates. The wines changed, but the coffee stayed the same. I was happy. I still could not detect what she was.

It wasn't until we had dessert in front of us that she got to it. She tasted the torte in raspberry sauce, liked it, and pushed it to the side. I did the same. It was time to talk.

"Jason Meddler seemed to think that you would be able to give me the best advice of anyone he knew," she said in preamble.

I cut in there. "Is that what you want from me? Advice?"

She looked rattled. "Yes, I guess so. I am very disturbed by this. I need some direction. I can't just do nothing."

"About what?" I prompted.

"I thought you knew." I shook my head. She cleared her throat. "My husband, Greg, is gone, disappeared."

"You say disappeared? Does that mean without any prior indication that he intended to leave? Without clothes, without cleaning out a bank account, without a note? Does that mean he just dropped out of sight?" I asked all this in a monotone, as simply as I could.

"Yes," she nodded to all of it. "That's it exactly. Monday morning he left in his car and never returned. I called the police, who wouldn't do a thing until he'd been missing forty-eight hours or some absurd amount of time like that. When they finally accepted a missing persons report it was already too late for anyone they talked to to remember anything. Or so they said."

"And the car?" I asked.

"I'm sorry?"

"Did they find the car?"

"The car? No, not yet," she answered as if bewildered by the question.

"Did you get the feeling that he might be meeting somebody that day?"

She took a moment with her eyes away from me. She was weighing something on the mental scales. She looked at me before she spoke. "Mr. Sands, to tell you the truth, Greg and I were not on the best of terms. He did a lot of things I had no knowledge of. He knew people I did not know. He had interests I did not share. We were living in the same house, but our marriage was nearing an end."

I could detect no remorse. There was also an absence of bitterness. I tapped my spoon on the table in what would have been perceived as an unconscious mannerism. I wanted to see if it annoyed her in any way. I was curious about her nerves. She showed nothing outwardly, certainly no annoyance.

"Do you think he's dead?" I dropped on her without warning.

She looked at me as if I had blasphemed. She looked, but she did not answer. I got the impression that until that very moment, the possibility had never been raised. People are very polite about death and murder. They leave such things to others to bring up. Others such as me.

"I take it you want to know," I persisted, "one way or the other?"

"Yes," she said from behind a fog. "I suppose he could be, couldn't he?"

"Is there any reason why he wouldn't tell you if he wanted to go away somewhere?" I watched her eyes.

"No," she said. The fog lifted. "It wouldn't make a difference."

"Is it possible that he could have stashed away some funds, like say in a bank in Switzerland or the Grand Caymans?"

Again she answered, "No."

She focused in on me with those green eyes and drew my

full attention to her. She said, "He is not that kind of man, Mr. Sands. We have a compatibility problem, but he is a man of high morals and very good character. Otherwise, I would never have married him."

I believed her. I took a pad and pen from my coat pocket. I wrote my address and phone number on the top sheet and tore it off before pushing the pad and pen to her.

"That's so you can reach me if you need to. Now you give me yours, and I also want the make, model, and year of your husband's car. And if you can remember, write down the name of the police officer you have contact with on this matter."

I watched her write in a classic calligraphic hand. It made me ashamed of the scribbling I had passed to her. She was still perfect. When she finished she passed the pad and pen back to me. She said nothing. Her eyes did not waver.

"And the car?" I asked when I noted that she had not included that information.

"I'm sorry," she answered, "but I'm so stupid about cars. I don't know what he drove. He changed often, and they all look alike to me anyway."

As odd as that may have sounded, I understood it. I had trouble distinguishing one from another myself. A few years ago I could identify make, model, and year of anything on the streets. It was like a lot of things I could do years ago. I made that thought stop there.

I said, "Maybe you can find a registration among his things. It would be helpful. When you get home, I want you to think of everything you've heard your husband say about those things he does apart from you. I want any names you can remember, and activities, and events with or without dates. Any person you may have seen him with, and his habits. I especially want a list of his most firmly entrenched habits. I want anything he may be excessive about, drinking, smoking, and so on. I want a list of his friends, his enemies. I want you to write as thorough a description of him as you can. Include every detail, no matter how strange or insignificant it may seem to you. And a picture too, as recent as you've got. Give me that, I'll do the rest."

She hesitated over something. I thought I knew what it was, but I let her get it started. "Mr. Sands, I really appreciate your helping me like this. I want to do this right. I don't know how to approach this except to just say it. I would like to have some idea of your fee, if that's not a rude thing to bring up at this time."

"Jason Meddler has taken care of it." Again I watched her eyes.

"Oh, no," she said. "I can't let him do that. I went to him because I thought he might know something about Greg. Greg spent a lot of evenings there."

"Greg gambled, I take it?"

She nodded.

"Well, let's not worry about it. Let's just get the answers, okay. You do your part with the information, and I'll do mine." I pushed my chair back. I knew better than to ask for a check, so I dropped two fifties by my plate.

I helped her back with her chair and stood aside as she got to her feet. She did a funny turn and for a moment stood facing me. She seemed surprised by my size. For a crazy moment I thought she was going to run her hands up my shoulders to the top of my head. Her green eyes opened wide, and I fell in. I suddenly wished my nose were straighter and the scars across its bridge and along my eyebrows that separated me from the church deacons and clubhouse gentlemen weren't there. I could have explained them all away as evidence of a life spent doing dangerous things in the company of dangerous people, but I didn't want to be that then, there, with her. I wanted to be smooth, and charming, and Cary Grant. I wished I were richer, and stronger, and braver, and a lot of things I wasn't, but most of all I wished I were younger.

She let me swim around before she turned the green pools away. I had drowned and didn't know it. I have no idea what gibberish I must have spouted to Bernice as we left. I said something, and Bernice responded and leaned up to give me one of her spinster hugs. My feet worked well enough to follow Katherine Burley to her car, and my hand worked well enough to open the door for her. It was my mind that was numbed.

It was only after she was inside and the engine had started that life returned to my brain. I bent down as she lowered the window.

"One question," I said. She nodded and waited expectantly. "Did Jason Meddler know that you and your husband were not exactly, you know, the perfect couple?"

She thought about it but nodded as she did. "I think so," she said. "I confided that much in him."

"I see," I said. "Drive safely."

She gave me a little finger wave, and then as an afterthought blew me a kiss. I watched the lights of her BMW vanish toward the foothills of Summerland.

"I see," I muttered again, and muttered it several times more before reaching the cloistered confines of Coco Palms. I set off the alarm by punching in the wrong code and had to suffer the indignity of confessing that to the Palms patrolman who answered the alarm.

I brewed some strong Turkish blend and wandered outside with it. The sea pounded below. The paradise scent covered me like a memory. I picked up the phone.

He answered on the first ring.

"I thought we didn't play games with each other," I said.

"I've been expecting you to call. She's quite a woman, isn't she?"

My voice had an edge to it. "I don't need a dating service, Jason. I thought we'd been through all that."

"I knew you'd read it that way, but you're wrong. I'd have asked you for this help no matter what she was like. Fact is, they're both damn fine young people. I don't like to see either one of them stuck out in limbo like this. She needs some answers and he may need some help. Who knows, he may have conked his head and be wandering around with amnesia or some damned thing. The point is, the police are useless as tits on a boar hog on this thing. I couldn't think of any way to help them other than you." He paused. I heard the sound of ice in a glass and could imagine him pouring a fresh Glenlivet to chase the cigar.

"He owe you money?" I asked cold.

"Yes." He answered without hesitation. "Not much. Not enough to make him run. He could cover it without making a wrinkle."

"I see," I said for the fortieth time that evening.

"If you've got a problem with this, we'll forget I asked the favor," he said in a husky, tired voice.

"No, no problem," I said in a more subdued fashion. "But I don't do this kind of thing, so don't ask again. Got it?"

"I got it." He let dead time pass. "You like her?"

"What's to like? I don't know her." I started to say something about her eyes, and how deep and clear and green they were, but there didn't seem to be a way to do it. "Goodnight," I said after another silence.

"Sweet dreams," he answered. I listened, but he didn't laugh.

5 🌿

I sat over an empty coffee cup at a window table in a State Street café. It had been empty a long time. I waved off the reluctant offer of a refill from the waitress who preferred to motion rather than move. I could hardly blame her, considering the bulk she would have to move. The coffee was so bad I wanted no more of it, yet there was Big Bertha hoarding it like it was gold. Maybe she was just afraid she would have to pick up the congealed remnants of my breakfast which I had pushed to the other side of the table. Maybe she resented having only one customer and was punishing me for being it. It had occurred to me that she might be the reason for all the empty tables. Perhaps it had not yet occurred to her.

I glanced at the pad in front of me, with the addresses of all the auto service houses in the Summerland area. I wasn't looking forward to the job, but it was one way of checking out Greg Burley's car. Given his affluence, I had made a listing of the more exclusive automobiles and their service outlets. I was hoping that at one of them I might discover the make, model, and year of the vehicle along with some additional information on Burley himself. It was a long shot, but I needed a starting point. Beside the pad was the paper upon which Katherine Bur-

ley had written the night before. The careful, neat script was as
easy to look at as she had been. I let myself think about her for
a moment, as a little reward for the drudgery I was facing.

It was getting close to the hour when the places I wanted to
check out would be opening. I dropped some bills on the table
and left the State Street house of fun, with some inner grumbling about bad coffee and bad service. I had already checked
this place off my list of early-morning cafés by the time I
pulled away from the curb. It was no wonder to me so many
of them failed. The employees had not caught on to the fact
that they were partners in the game. In a sense, where service
is involved, everyone is self-employed. A month or two down
the road, Big Bertha would be looking for another job, blam-
ing management for the failure of the café. I wondered how
many joints she would kill before she caught on.

The speed limit was fifty-five on 101. I was in the left lane
going ten over that and passing the traffic on my right without
blowing off any doors. My rearview mirror filled up with one
of those quick little Japanese jobs. It squirmed and moved up
and back on me in a real show of impatience. I would have
moved willingly had I not been over the speed limit already
and passing everything right of me. He stood it as long as he
could, before he found a tiny slot where he could risk his life
and the lives of those in the minivan one lane over. The fellow
in the Toyota swerved close enough to the van to make that
driver flinch onto the shoulder. Both of them almost lost it.
The Toyota then made another, equally stupid move back to
my lane in front of me. Before running his needle up to eighty
he took time to flip me what is commonly known as the
"bird." As long as I had been driving, I still could not figure
that mentality.

I started my search at some of the places on the fringe of
Montecito and Santa Barbara and worked out to Summerland. I wasn't having much luck. It did, however, give me
time to think about this guy Burley and try to get some of
my ideas and questions about him in order. I tried to assem-

ble what I thought I knew about him. He was from San Francisco, married to a beauty, wealthy, probably conservative, gambled, and moved from the big city to a small, confined community. That gave me pause. The disappearance of a guy like that didn't sound too good to me. Maybe it was just that I couldn't imagine any red-blooded fellow bailing out on Katherine Burley.

It was late morning when I made my way through my list to the D and J British Motor Car Service. It was not like most independent garages. It was very neat and well appointed. There was even a waiting room with some amenities. I figured a hundred-dollar bill might cover an oil change at D and J's.

A fellow with the name "Jon" stitched on his shirt looked at me with the raised eyebrows of one willing to field a question. I threw him one. An easy one.

"Are you Jon?"

He brightened. I'd found a guy who didn't read his own shirt. "Why yes, how may I help you?" The British accent did not surprise me. The garage was loaded with high-priced wheels from the Anglo homeland.

"My name is Sands. I was sent over by Mrs. Burley to look at Mr. Burley's car." I figured people looked harder for something if it was supposed to be there. Then when it turned out not to be, they tended to talk a little more freely about it out of some undefined guilt. It was the same approach I had used at all the other places that morning. I primed the pump by adding, "Greg Burley."

"Oh yes, of course," he said. "Are you here to pick up Mr. Burley's car?"

My surprise must have showed. I tried to cover it by asking, "You mean you know the car without checking your records?"

"Certainly, sir," Jon answered. "Mr. Burley is a very good, and regular client."

Client? I'd never heard a garage mechanic refer to customers as clients before. I figured "sucker" was the only other term they had for them.

"Is there one particular mechanic who usually takes care of Mr. Burley's car?"

"That would be me, sir. I always accept the car and write up the work order."

"Could you show me the car, please?" I looked around, wondering which of the fine, expensive automobiles was Greg Burley's. The garage seemed to be filled with Rolls-Royces and Bentleys.

Jon was very helpful. He wiped his hands and led me to the parking area outside. "I'll fetch the keys?" he offered in a sprightly way as he pointed to a deep bronze vehicle. I loved the word "fetch." I never used it, is all.

The Range Rover was in perfect condition. I could see the interior was gray leather, with all the bells and whistles I guessed you could put on one of these little babies. Disc player, car phone—you name it, it had it. I had the immediate feeling that Jon had made a mistake. A Range Rover was an off-road-type vehicle. It was four-wheel drive with a high undercarriage designed for rough terrain. Granted it cost as much as a midrange Mercedes, and had a luxurious interior, but it did not quite fit the image I had formed of Greg Burley.

Jon returned and opened the car. He stood to the side like a patient sentry. I had expected him to. This was that kind of place. Unlike most cars', the foot wells, front and rear, were uncluttered. There was not a scrap of anything on the floors or seats of this pristine vehicle. I was impressed.

"Did you clean the car after you worked on it?"

"No sir, we merely changed the oil and filter. Mr. Burley keeps a fine car."

That was an understatement. Mr. Burley did indeed keep a very fine car. It was too clean for my purposes, whatever they were. It seemed to me that I had spent half my life looking for things, without knowing what things I was looking for, and not finding them.

"Oh, it was just a regular service, huh?"

"Well, actually," the elegant mechanic corrected, "it was

slightly early for a regular service. We recommend three-thou-
sand-mile intervals. He had slightly over two."

"Say, Jon," I said, as if I had known this fellow for more
than six minutes. "I was wondering if you could tell me a little about the morning that Mr. Burley dropped off his car.
Were you busy? Did he have to wait? Was he anxious? Did he
talk to any of the other customers? Where did he go when he
left here? That sort of thing."

"What was your name again, sir?" He asked it in a polite
way. This was a fellow I would want working for me, if I had
anyone working for me.

"Sands," I said. "My first name is Jake."

"Mr. Sands, please forgive my candor, but you seem to be
asking for rather personal information." He smiled behind his
statement.

It was time to level with him. I had found the car, so I
figured anything else was gravy.

"Nobody's seen Mr. Burley lately. He's been missing since
about the time he dropped the car off with you." I said it that
way on purpose.

He looked properly shocked. "Good heavens. Are you with
the police?"

"No," I said, and shook my head in emphasis. "I am simply
here as a friend of the Burleys."

"I see," Jon said, nodding in the information. "I do hope
nothing has happened to the poor man."

"Yes, so do we. Now, about that day?"

He collected himself. "It was an average day, and there was
nothing extraordinary about anything Mr. Burley did. It was
the afternoon, incidentally, not the morning, but he spoke to
none of the other customers to my notice nor did he leave in
another vehicle. Well, perhaps he did. I can't say positively. He
might have walked toward Channel, which is our main street
just two blocks from here. I can't say."

I watched him for any signs of fabrication. It seemed forth-
right enough. One item caught my attention.

"You say it was in the afternoon when he dropped the car off?"

"Yes sir, it was well into the afternoon. I would say close to three o'clock."

I nodded. My attention was back on the car. I had worked my way to the rear, where there was a large cargo area behind the seats. I could see some faint impressions on the carpeting. I opened the large rear door and leaned in. Most of it had been brushed away, but what was left appeared to be traces of rust. There were depressions where it seemed that something heavy and rusty had been dragged out. The meticulous Mr. Burley had, no doubt, intended to vacuum up the rest at a later time.

I walked around the car again. If it had been for sale, and it had been my type of car, I would have bought it in a second. On a whim I reached in and checked the car phone. It responded with a dial tone as soon as I pushed the power button. I saw Jon's eyebrows raise slightly as if he had just remembered something. I gave it a second, but nothing came out of him.

He locked the car and led me back into and through the garage. I was at the door and had already thanked him when I asked, "So you heard him talking on his car phone? Did you get any idea who he was talking to?"

Jaws do drop. His did. He was not good enough to catch himself. I could see that he wondered how I knew. I nudged him.

"Let me put that a little differently, Jon. Just how much of it did you hear, and did you hear a name mentioned?"

He said, "His window was down, and he was making no effort to speak privately. I don't repeat conversations I overhear, Mr. Sands, even in these circumstances. However, I will say the conversation appeared to be with his wife."

"His wife? He called her by name?" I asked.

"Possibly. I don't recollect. I did have the distinct impression he was speaking with a woman. He was agitated, now that I recall."

I took it all in and let it settle. I rummaged for any nagging questions that might have surfaced. I seemed to have everything I could use from Jon at the moment.

Jon had a question of his own. "Will the car be picked up, or should we deliver it?" He took a short moment to consult his memory. "Palmetto Lane, isn't it?"

"Yes, I'll tell Mrs. Burley to call." I liked a place that delivered. I wondered if I could afford it. "Do you work on Porsches?" I asked with a nod at my machine.

"Strictly British motorcars, sir," he responded with a swell smile. I was grateful he had not tilted back his head to look down his nose.

"Pity," I said.

"Indeed," he said as he tilted back his head.

• • •

She was more everything than I remembered. More tall, more curvy, more graceful, more beautiful, more everything. I had to resist the urge to touch her to see if she was real. The feeling had started when I called her to tell her about the Range Rover. The sound of her voice had cast me into a world without any hard edges.

She had tea and I had coffee in a roundish room of windows facing out to the ocean and the Channel Islands. I tried to concentrate on the yellow legal pad, but my eye kept lifting to see if she was still there, and to see if she had suddenly turned ugly.

I read it all, what there was of it. It could hardly be called an in-depth piece of work. It was surprisingly impersonal. Even allowing for their estrangement, it did make me wonder. The pictures she had assembled of Greg Burley would require more study. I did notice that she was in none of them. When I finally put it all aside, she said, "Is that what you wanted?"

"You did a very good job. I think maybe there is a lot to work from here." I leaned back on my lie and let myself have a good look at the view outside the window.

"Awful, isn't it?" she said.

"Awful?" I didn't get it.

"Those drilling platforms."

Then I focused on them, and she was right. "Awful" might not have been the best word for the sight they presented. It needed a word more awful than "awful." Somehow, this area of the most beautiful coast in the western United States has lost in the battle between the big oil companies and the local interests. Just off the beaches of Summerland and Santa Barbara are the most unadulteratedly grotesque structures conceived by man. They could not be more horrible to the eye and the spirit had they been planned only for that purpose. The oil-drilling platforms sit in the center of the channel between the beaches and the islands as a testimony of some men's callous greed and the helplessness of the majority who oppose them. The politicians who allowed it to happen should be hanged, publicly and slowly. I would be happy to set the noose.

"Yes, it is. It is awful." I tried to defocus my view of them again. It was not possible.

"Greg doesn't feel that way. He likes them because he says they make for some good diving," she said with the slightest hint of nostalgia. "Why, I don't know."

I referred to her notes on the yellow pad once again. "Yes," I said, "I see that you mentioned diving as a hobby. Then you added that it was more than a hobby. What does that mean?"

"Well, I guess I should have said avocation. It would be a vocation if he could get well paid for it. What I meant was that Greg is an avid diver. And I do mean avid."

"Scuba?"

"Does that mean with the tanks and masks and some kind of rubber suit and all?"

I said, "That means self-contained underwater breathing apparatus. Yes, tanks, masks, neoprene suits, and all."

She smiled. "Then yes, it is. He is. That's what he does."

"You don't dive, I take it?"

She shook her head.

I took a deep breath and jumped in. "Now, you mentioned that you and your husband were to some degree living separate lives? Did I understand that right?"

First she nodded, then she added, "Yes, that says it quite well, frankly. It's not a bitter thing, or angry in any way, it's just the way we want it. I suppose I should be completely honest with you on this, so you know. It's a condition of separate bedrooms and separate phones. That's how separate it is, Mr. Sands."

"I understand," I said, not knowing how to respond.

She laughed. "It is not a tragedy if that's what you're thinking. We're both happy, and we love each other."

I started to say "I understand" again but the fact was, I did not. I said, "You know people in common, but you also each have friends the other doesn't know, is that it?"

"That's right," she said. She smiled.

I tried a smile myself. It felt as if my lips were pasted to my teeth. It only made it to about the point where I looked slightly foolish or loony or both.

I got to my feet, thanking her for the coffee as I rose, and muttering something about all the fine work she had done in assembling the notes for me on the legal pad. She rose with me, more agile, more graceful, more everything. She touched my arm.

"Mr. Sands, I can't tell you how grateful I am. It's simply remarkable that you found Greg's car the way you did, and so quickly."

I tried to mumble it away without saying, "Aw shucks."

She said, "Last night, I tried to discuss your fee with you. Can we talk about it now?"

Was it only last night? I answered her: "There's no fee. Look, Mrs. Burley, I'm not in business. And looking for husbands is not what I did when I was. I don't work at all now. So, what I'm doing here, don't take too seriously. I'm just nosing around a bit, asking a few questions here and there that maybe nobody else is asking, and looking for some sign of Greg. I might be a little better at this sort of thing than the average guy, but not much. And like I said, don't put much weight to it. I may not deliver. So, there is no fee. Forget it."

"But why are you doing it?"

"Because Jason Meddler called me and asked me to. And because Jason Meddler thinks that I ought to be busy doing something instead of sitting around my house doing nothing. That's it in a nutshell."

She finally moved her hand but grabbed me hard with her eyes. She said, "He told me a little about you. He paints a far different picture of you than you do of yourself."

"Yeah," I said, "I can imagine. Don't believe it. Any of it. He likes to make up stories and create people that don't exist."

"How do you know what he told me?" she teased.

"Like I said, I can imagine."

She studied me. "He told me you were the only person in the world he trusted completely. I thought that was quite a statement."

I studied back. "Was he slurring his words? He drinks, you know."

We just stood there.

"He said you had lost your wife?" she asked.

I nodded. I seemed to nod a lot with her. "Yes, that's true. And son. But Mrs. Burley, I'm not in mourning. That all happened a few years ago. It's not a pleasant memory, but it doesn't chew my insides."

She looked slightly surprised. "I thought it was more recent. Jason said you had just put it behind you or something in that vein."

"Well, yes, something in that vein. There were some things which needed to be done. But I'm okay. I don't need special care."

"I think I understand," she said, leading me through the kitchen toward the front door.

I stopped by the telephone as my eye caught a phone list

posted on the wall next to it. The list contained eight numbers, printed in a very neat and precise hand. I could see they
were the usual choices of important, yet seldom called, numbers most people might list. There was also a pad of paper
hanging next to the list, with a short notation on it. It read,
"Reset appointment for cleaning. Ask for Sharon. 770-4439."

Katherine Burley turned to see what had captured my interest. "That's the list of the doctor, dentist, cable TV company,
and such," she explained.

"And this?" I said, indicating the notation.

She took a step closer to read it. "It's some reminder Greg
wrote for himself."

The handwriting matched the printing on the phone list. It
told me a couple of things. Greg Burley was a very precise and
organized man, and he did things for himself. I compared the
number on the note with the list and found a match with the
dentist named Dunn.

"Do you mind?" I asked as I lifted the phone. She shook her
head in a slightly bewildered fashion while I dialed the number. The dentist's receptionist answered and after checking her
calendar informed me that Greg Burley had canceled his teeth
cleaning the month before and had not rescheduled as yet. The
hygienist's name was Sharon.

"Nothing," I said as I replaced the phone.

She shrugged it off and led me to the front door. I let her
open it for me while I mentally phrased a question I had been
holding for the entire meeting. I looked for a way to time it so
it would not bring undue notice. She gave me the opportunity
when she stepped outside behind me.

"I never did get the exact time of day when you saw Greg
last. Is that here somewhere?" I looked down at the yellow pad
as if trying to locate what I knew was not there.

"I don't know the exact time. It was fairly early in the morning when he left. I would say probably around nine or so."

"I see" slipped out of me again. "And you never saw or
heard from him again after that?"

"No."

"Not even a phone call? Nothing?"

"No."

"I noticed that he has a phone in his car. Did you ever try to reach him on it?" I was at the door of my own car by that time and was able to mask my interest with the actions of opening the door and tossing the yellow pad inside. I listened closely though.

"No." Again.

She bent down to face me through the open window. I did not want to start the car. I wanted to stay there gazing at her beautiful face framed by the distant islands of a sun-dazzled ocean. Some moments are just right.

"What do you look for now?" she asked.

"A perspective." I shrugged, trying to leave it there.

"How does that apply?"

"Perspective? Doesn't life really come down to a matter of perspective? Whether something is good or bad, and I don't mean good or evil, often depends on which side of it you're on. If you bet the red in roulette and the black comes up, it's bad. But then how about the guy that bet the black? Sometimes it pays to take half a beat and think about the guy on the other side. I can do that. I just haven't learned to root for him yet."

She smiled. That was my reward for the day.

I started the car. She stood and backed away. I leaned out and asked, "Does Greg have a girlfriend?"

She shook her head, not at my question but at me. She said, "I don't know much about what Greg has or hasn't got. Not for the last year anyway."

I had another question. She stood braced for it. I put the car in motion and watched her watch me, still braced and ready to answer the question which had been locked and loaded but never fired.

She was still perfect.

• • •

I had presented myself as a friend of the family, and in as circumspect a way as I knew how, to the sheriff's department investigator assigned to the Burley disappearance. He was polite and seemed to share openly with me what sparse detail and information they had. I was in the process of leaving when a beefy wall of a man entered. I was taller, but he was broader of shoulder and hip.

"You Sands?" he asked without preamble and with his hand out.

"Jake Sands," I replied, taking the side of beef to shake.

"I'm Tex Flanagan, special investigator for the department here. Pleased to meet you. You all done with Deputy Morris?" He looked at the deputy for affirmation. The deputy nodded.

"How about joining me for a doughnut? They fresh-bake 'em at a little place I know. My treat." He had one hand sweeping me out the door he was holding open with the other. I waved my thanks to the deputy, who seemed to take our departure in stride.

I followed Tex Flanagan to a bakery in a Goleta shopping mall. He bought the doughnuts and brought them to a table outside. We had a great view of the big parking lot.

"You're a big bastard," he said. "I thought I was big, but you got me lookin' up a little."

"No thanks," I said to his offer of a doughnut. "What is a special investigator?"

"You sure? They're real good," he said, a look of disappointment at my refusal. "Well, what I am is a sort of a freewheelin' linebacker, you see? I sort of move into a slot and take a peek when it looks like a play might be breakin' out there."

"I get the picture," I said. "And you think the ball might be moving through the Greg Burley slot?"

"What I think is this. When I see a big old guard pull out and start around the end, I want to get my tail movin' the same way, 'cause sure as hell has heat, some quick little tailback'll be scootin' in right behind him. Now, if I don't move

pretty sudden like, then all I got to look at is that tailback's
ass and elbows. I never have much liked that view." He took
half of one of the big glazed doughnuts in one bite.

"You know a bit more than my name, I take it?"

"There's a fella I've heard about that's what you might call
a big-league bounty hunter. He does 'recoveries,' but most
folks can't make the distinction between recovery work and
what they'd call bounty hunting. 'Cept maybe recovery work
pays better. I heard tell this fella's pay is about half of what he
recovers. That could add up to some pretty big bucks there,
podner." He chewed happily and let some smugness creep into
his face.

I kept my eyes on him, letting him take his time with it.

He enjoyed showing off what he knew almost as much as he
enjoyed the doughnuts. "Some people down in L.A. that know
about this fella say that most of the time he works for lawyers
or the courts looking for folks that try to hide away what they
owe in court awards or settlements. They go outside the law,
and he goes right out there with 'em. Ain't a fella to mess
with, way I hear it."

"Sounds very interesting."

"Interesting ain't the half of it," he said, relishing his moment. "Ever hear of the Orion unit? Antiterrorist group? Secret as hell? Answered only to the N.S.C. or the President?"
He squinted his eyes hard at me, trying to read something
from my face. "He was part of that outfit before he got into
doin' recoveries. Well sir, that makes this fella a lot more than
just interestin' to me."

"And your point?" I prompted.

"You remember the junk bond fella, Tyler? The savings and
loan operation? Victory Savings and Loan, was it?"

"I remember," I said, reaching back a few years for it. "It
cost the taxpayers a bundle."

He grinned around the other half of the doughnut. His eyes
were the kind that could go mean or merry. They were merry
at the moment. I never wanted to see them mean.

He said, "Of course, you only read about it in the paper?"

"Like everybody else," I said.

"Well, podner, not exactly everybody else. See, this same fella I was talkin' about took this Tyler down and brought back a big share of the loot he'd stashed. It helped a lot of old folks who'd have lost their life savings otherwise. I was close to folks that was part of the Texas group that trusted that snake Tyler, and when he was brought back, and them folks seen some of the money they'd give up for lost returned, well, I always figured I'd like to shake the hand of the fella that made that happen. You see, I figure I've done that now."

I shrugged into his intense but friendly gaze. There was something there I didn't believe, but I decided to roll with it. I said, "I was well paid."

"Whatever it was, you wasn't paid enough," he stated emphatically. "So, you can see that I'm inclined to line up on your side of the ball. I do need to know which side that is though."

"I'm nothing more than what I presented myself to be," I said as simply as I knew how. He studied that for a moment, as if he needed to measure it for truth.

"The story is that you'd hung em up. Quit."

"True."

"You sayin' you're not doin' some lawyer's chasing on this one?"

"I'm in this as a friend of the family," I replied.

"And Coco Palms?" His eyebrows made cartoonish lines well above his eyes.

Mine must have done the same. He grinned again. "Huh?" he added as I hesitated.

"I don't get your question, Tex. What does Coco Palms have to do with anything?"

He brushed away the crumbs left from the ravaged doughnuts and said, "Maybe nothin', maybe a lot. You tell me."

"Nope," I replied, "you tell me."

"You've moved in there, right?" He didn't wait for an answer. "I was just wonderin' why."

"None of your business, Tex," I said, pushing him to commit one way or the other.

He didn't lose his grin. I was glad about that.

"You meet Charlie Jessup yet?" he asked.

"The captain of the Coco Palms patrol? No, but I've talked to him. He from the department?"

The grin changed to a little bit ugly. He answered, "Not from this sheriff's department, no. He's got police background, military and civil though."

"He got a story I should know?"

He considered it but shook his head. "Probably not," he said.

"So, what is this all about here, Tex? You just wanted to tell me that you've run a check on me and that you know a few things about me? Is that it? Or is there more?" I tried to say it in a pleasant manner. My delivery must have failed.

"Don't get on your high horse there, podner. I told you I'm on your team."

We let that wander the air between us looking for a place to settle. I let it fall on me. "Okay," I said, "good. If I need a friend, or some information, I can call you, right?"

He did not hesitate. "Right," he said. He was serious. I had been facetious.

That floated for a minute too, until I pulled it in with a nod of acceptance.

"Then maybe I'll keep you up-to-date on what I find out on Burley. If you'd like?" I tested him.

"That's up to you, Jake. I'm offerin', not askin'."

I rose from the table. He stayed seated but thrust up his big paw.

"You're a piece of work, Tex," I said, shaking his hand. "I hope you're on the level, because I think I'd hate to have you against me."

"Oh, you would, Jake. You got that right." He grinned his grin again. I was beginning to like it.

I was a few feet closer to my car when I turned and said back to him, "You might check out Greg Burley's car phone

for the calls he made on the fourteenth. You might pay particular attention to one made or received around three in the afternoon. I'd like to know who was on the other end of that
one myself."

"You could find that out easy enough yourself just by checking with his cellular company," he said with that studying
squint back in his eyes. "Course they might ask Mrs. Burley's
permission to give the information out to you, but that's not a
problem, is it? I mean, you're not trying to protect her from
the truth already, are you?"

I kept my face closed to his scrutiny. I did not want him to
see how close to the mark he had hit.

"Why you tossin' me this little bone here now, podner?" He
asked.

I didn't answer. I threw him another little bone.

"His car is at the D and J British Motor Car Service in Summerland," I said.

His expression did not change. There was no indication that
he had heard me.

Instead he said, "You watch yourself with Charlie Jessup."

6

I awoke in the early hours of the morning in my circular sunken living room. My own notes lay scattered about with the yellow pages from the legal pad and the pictures of Greg Burley. My ears opened first from force of habit, followed slowly by my eyes. My body stayed completely still until my mind had reached full wakefulness.

I remained motionless while something replayed in that soft gray area of subconsciousness. A sound? Sensed movement? Something had awakened me. I listened alertly while my eyes brought basic pertinent data to me. Lights on in kitchen and living room, as well as outside. Doors open to the back lanais. Heavy surf sounds. Some wind. Maybe a door blew or a cushion toppled. According to my watch it was three a.m.

I rolled from my spot on the floor and got quickly to my feet. In a few moments I had more or less checked the house to my satisfaction. I am not the jumpy type, so I felt a certain absurdity in what I was doing. However, better absurd than interred, I thought, giving myself the lift derived from silly word play.

I finished the night in my big, too soft, too satiny bed. Dawn sneaked in on me. It slipped by, pulling with it a bright, hot sun. I hated to wake up with the sun in my eyes. It made me feel I had missed half the day.

I was half finished with the paper when the phone rang. I ignored it. Whoever it was did not wait for the machine to answer. In the next two hours I showered, shaved, and renegotiated my lease on the day. I made myself a late breakfast of country ham, eggs, biscuits, and red-eye gravy, which is made with coffee. I suppose I was influenced by my meeting with Tex Flanagan, because I even made cowboy coffee. That's done by adding egg shells and salt to your grounds and boiling it all together. I strained it into a thermos carafe and sat in the sun with the last of it. I was awake and ready when my phone chirped at me again.

I could almost feel her lips against my ear when she said my name. I must not have said anything back, because she said, "Jake? Are you there?"

"Yes," I answered. I liked the way she said my name. It sounded intimate. I wondered if unnoticed by me we had passed to some new plateau where we would speak in the familiar tones of friends or lovers.

"I have found some scraps of paper with names and numbers on them. Some could be very old. I have no way of knowing. I found them in desk drawers, in his briefcase, coat pockets, even some in a kitchen drawer. Should I save them for you?" Her voice had a throaty sound. It was a sound I liked.

"Yes," I said, "save them, but look through them and see if you can identify the scraps they're written on. Napkins with café names, that sort of thing."

"Right now?" she asked.

"Look for Greg's handwriting and names that clearly indicate man or woman. Also, separate any that might have been written in haste or by another hand, and look for those written on the same type of paper—like a hotel pad, for instance."

"Would it be better if I brought them to you? I'm coming over to your side of Santa Barbara anyway." She made it sound silly not to do it that way.

"Sure," I said as casually as possible. "What time?"

"I should be there in an hour if that's okay."

"You know the way?"

She laughed. "Everyone knows the way to Coco Palms."

I opened my own front gate and left her name for entry with the patrol. I thought I could detect a strangeness from the patrolman who answered. It was nothing overt. It was more of a feeling. Maybe I was in the early stages of paranoia. Maybe they frowned here upon unescorted women visiting single men in the middle of the day. I was growing to hate Coco Palms.

I was in the pool having a good workout, when my phone got very busy. Jason called to see how I was doing and if I needed anything. I agreed to come for chess that night. Then Tex Flanagan called.

"Well, well, you taught us a thing or two," he said in opening. "I put the boys through it for getting outplayed on that Range Rover. They don't take a tease worth a damn. Not too many left that do. You ever notice that?"

I felt like smiling. He did that to me. "I've noticed. Did you check out the car phone?"

"Yep. I'll tell you about it if you'll tell me what it means," he bargained.

"I will if I know," I accepted.

"Well, he had a quiet morning on that car phone, compared to what he usually did. He's got a big bill coming. Did you know that he's charged for every call he receives as well as the ones he makes? Why, hell, if somebody gets it in his head to call him from Atlanta, he's got to pay the charges from Atlanta. Somehow that just don't seem quite fair to me." He paused to see if my impatience was showing. I knew he was playing with me and I was determined not to rise to the bait. He waited until he knew I wasn't playing. He laughed.

"Okay," he said, "you're a cool one. You want all of 'em?"

"What was the three o'clock? Incoming or outgoing?" I asked.

"Outgoing," he answered. "To another car phone. Now

who would pay for that one, I wonder? You suppose they both have to pay? And it was a long-distancer, too. Area code just south of San Francisco. That phone company gets 'em comin' and goin', don't it?"

"You got a name with it?" I asked, with both feet on my impatience.

"Nope, and that car phone ain't in service. Probably don't want to be charged for the call." His voice had become a little muffled. He was chewing on something. I pitied it, whatever it was.

"The man at the garage thought Burley might have been talking to his wife." I found the word hard to get out. "Maybe she has a phone in her car."

"Could be, but the cellular bill goes to a San Francisco corp. Frisco address and all that sort of B.S. We'll get a local though, if there is one." Now he spoke through a whole mouthful of food.

"What about the other calls?"

"A couple of incoming from local pay phones. Now that raises another interesting billing problem, wouldn't you say? And then there was an outgoing to a local real estate lady named Chandler."

"Selling or buying?" I asked it simply out of curiosity.

"Didn't ask and don't care. One other outgoing was to a coffee shop in Montecito. Must have been callin' for a customer, because no one there connected to it." He gulped some sort of liquid down after the food.

"Which coffee shop?" I had a feeling about it.

"Coffee Mill," he said, and took a fresh bite. "Know it?"

"I do," I answered. "Well, you get back to your snack and I'll carry on. You don't happen to have that cellular number he called handy, do you?"

"667-7766. I had a feelin' you might ask." He spoke through food again. "See ya."

"*Bon appétit,*" I said.

Five minutes and a few laps later I answered a dial tone. A

wrong number would have waited for a voice. Three rings and a hang-up when the receiver lifted said other things to me. Either someone was verifying I was home, or someone changed his mind about talking to me. Then again, maybe it was a she who admired me from afar and had lost her tongue to shyness. Big Bertha perhaps? I had a tendency to chase unjustified suspicion with silliness.

I slipped back into the water to complete my workout. I was determined to ignore the phone and get the swim done. I swam earnestly, working the shoulder hard through the down pulls. I broke the crawl with underwater lengths to check the ribs. I was feeling good. My mind freed, my body loosened, and I entered that other world of cerebrally administered euphoria.

I dug down hard for the last length. One breath, six strokes, and I was holding to the brick coping at the shallow end, gasping in the scented air of paradise. I dropped beneath the surface and came up with my head tilted, letting the water take my hair back off my face. My head was still up as I shook away the water and opened my eyes. I looked up the damnedest pair of legs I'd ever seen. All the way up to hips wrapped in a short, pleated tennis skirt.

I wiped at the liquid blur. My eyes stung from the chlorine and the bounce from the sun. I had to squint, but I had to look. She stood quite still and let me.

She said, "You're a terrific swimmer. Did you ever compete?"

"Yeah," I answered, "but not the way you mean. How'd you get in?"

"I found a side gate. I got no answer at the front door."

"I'm sorry," I said with a quick glance at my watch. "I lost track of the time."

"I could tell. I've been here watching for a while," she said.

Katherine Burley took her great legs away from me and wandered off to look out at the ocean. "Nice view," she said back over her shoulder. I almost bit on the obvious but kept my mouth shut. I think she knew she presented a nice view too, without my saying it. I felt proud of myself.

Instead I said, "If you'll give me a minute, Mrs. Burley, I'll be right with you. You want to wait inside or out?"

"Out," she answered without looking at me. "And I like to be called Kate. You might try it sometime."

I excused myself and went inside to dress. I slipped on a pair of white sailcloth pants and a batik shirt from the islands. I felt like dressing for paradise. I didn't have a pair of white, low-cut Bally loafers, so I settled for a pair of fairly white sneakers. I hurried back to her with hair still wet but slicked back.

She rewarded me for my efforts. "You look nice," she said. "I knew you weren't the type to use a blow dryer."

There was a giggle in her voice, and I was not quite sure if it was at me or with me.

"I'm afraid I'd electrocute myself," I said.

She took her eyes off me as she made a quick sweep around the place and said, "I don't think that's it." She took some steps toward the house. "This is not quite the kind of place I had imagined you having. I pictured something a bit more, how shall I put it, sedate? Yes, sedate. This, Jake, is not at all sedate."

I looked around with her. It was still a stranger to me, too. "Nope," I agreed, "it's not sedate. Now what can I get you? Food? Drink?"

"Nothing," she said. "I'm on my way to a tennis lesson. I don't want to slosh."

"Let's go inside and I'll look at what you've brought," I said, leading her into the living room through the lanai doors.

"Oh my," she exclaimed. "Jake, this is getting to be less sedate by the minute."

I extended my hand for the envelope she carried. "Take a look around if you want while I see what you've brought me."

"I think I will, thank you," she replied. That giggle was still there.

I dumped the envelope onto the glass and brass that the dec-

orator called a coffee table, and sorted out the scraps of paper.
I took a pad and pen and listed all the notes that bore only
numbers before I listed those that contained names or initials
as well as numbers. As I wrote them down, one jumped out at
me. The block letters, "TONI," didn't mean anything but the
number with it did. It was 667-7766, with a small "c" in front
of it. In my book that had to mean cellular or car. Just to be
sure, I grabbed my notebook where I had written the number
Tex had given me. It was a match.

Katherine Burley glided back into the living room. For the
first time I realized that it was not the sweet smell of paradise
I had breathed in at the pool but Katherine Burley.

"What is that?" I asked without thinking.

She hesitated only a moment before she answered. She either
read my mind or the flare of my nostrils, because she said,
"It's called 'Night Flowers.' It's a combination of scents,
mostly jasmine and honeysuckle. Nice, don't you think?"

"Yes, it is." I tried to hide from her just how very nice I
thought it was, and she was. "You know somebody named
Toni?" I asked.

"No, should I?"

"Your husband does. I'd guess it's a female. It's spelled with
an 'i'."

"It's probably not what you think it is." She gave a quick
look at her watch. "I'm late. I'm always late to my lesson. If
there's anything, you'll let me know, okay? And Jake, I love
your house. It says a lot about you."

"It lies," I responded with a feeling somewhere back in my
brain that I was caught in a momentum I did not understand.
I pulled one of the too tall, too heavy front doors open and
had to brace myself to keep it from slamming me into the
wall. That was the thing about momentum.

"Bye," she said.

"Kate," I said.

She turned from her car and waited with her head cocked in
my direction.

"Nothing," I said. "I was just trying it out."

She did not smile as I thought she would. I did not know how to read the look on her face. It was sad and sweet and a lot of things that don't come with words attached to them. She sat for a minute behind the wheel of that 9 series BMW and let me see the look again, before she turned the key.

She didn't wave, and I didn't watch. I was inside as she drove away.

● ● ●

Jason checkmated me in the second game with such glee I actually felt good about losing. He leaned back, and clapped his hands, and laughed out loud.

"I've got your number now, old boy," he said. "Do you feel the gentle change of tide here?"

He wheeled back, in that swift, sure way that always impressed me, to his Glenlivet. He toasted me with glass raised high above his head. "The king is dead, long live the king."

"I never did understand that one," I replied in a grumpy way, to make his victory more enjoyable for him.

"Oh, I love a sore loser," he said. "It makes it all the sweeter."

"Again?" I offered with a backhand motion toward the board. I knew he would refuse, which he did with an impish shake of his head.

"Not on this night, my friend. I am going to take this little victory into my dreams, unclouded and pure." He clipped the end of a fresh cigar. "Have you called Vera yet?"

"Vera?" I asked, caught unprepared for his quick shift in gears.

"Yes, Vera. Your dear and old friend Vera."

"No," I answered guiltily, "I haven't. And yes, I know I should, and yes, I will, and I want to. I just haven't, so stow it. Okay?"

He grinned around his cigar. He loved to stir things. "How would you like to sit for a moment and talk about Katherine Burley?"

He always tried to surprise me. I suppose it was a game we

played, had played, both ways, for a number of years. We had both become masters of noncommittal response. It was possible that such nonresponses were now more readable than raised eyebrows and gaping mouths. That seemed to be the case, for he raised his own eyebrows and grinned.

"Well," he said, "I've touched a nerve."

"You fantasize, Jason."

"That I won't deny," he admitted. "How about you? You been doing a little fantasizing lately?"

I tried to slough it away with a tilt of my head. I poured another cup of a nice, nutty-flavored brew he had discovered for me, to bridge the silence.

I said, "Do they fit? I mean together? Would you have put them together as a couple?"

"Katherine and Greg Burley? Never saw them together. Never saw her at all until he came up missing. But no, he's too much of a boy for her, to my eye. He's the same size and almost as pretty. She's not the type, I don't think, for that twinning you see so much of today. God, that's just another thing I hate about this screwed-up society of ours, Jake. You can't tell the girls from the boys sometimes. The women are tough, and the men are clever, soft slimes who think life is inside deals and angles that can give them an edge over the hardworking slobs of this world." He tossed off the last of his drink with an angry flick of his head.

"You're talking about Greg Burley?"

"No, not at all. I was just ranting against the times. No, I suppose he's a good fellow. And so is she. She's modern but not butchy like a lot of them, don't you think? He alive, Jake?"

"I don't know," I said. "So far I can't find any reason for him to have split. You ever hear him mention a girl named Toni?"

"Girl?"

"Yeah, with an 'i.' Could be a little fling here that maybe took them off to an island someplace. Who knows?"

He shook his head. "No. And as for the fling, I would say no."

"Reasons?"

"None, just a feeling." He mulled it a moment more. The scotch and his victory had gotten to him. He was just short of slurring. "Who knows, maybe he's a fag. In this day and age I wouldn't be surprised. It's this society, Jake. It's confusing the hell out of people. They think being gay is a normal option anyone can take. They think it's just another thing to try. God in heaven, how did we get so screwed up? You look at that damn television, and see the wisdom of our time expressed in condom ads. Can you imagine that? They're telling the young people to bang away, but just use condoms. When did sex become just another recreation without regard for procreation? Where the hell is the moral factor anymore? Where the hell is monogamy and love and family? Where the hell does that fit in this screwed-up world we've let get away from us?"

"Maybe it's just us, Jason. Maybe, the parade got away from us." I offered it without much conviction. I looked on as he fed more Glenlivet to his anger.

"Bullshit," he said, wiping a small spill of scotch from his chin. "We let our appetites get away from us. We're becoming a people that's overfed, overdoped, and oversexed. Do you believe the gross stupidity of people to sniff that white powder or smoke it from a pipe without really knowing the consequences? The harmless experimentation with grass in the sixties and seventies became a runaway train. That time and the voices of that time mowed down the decency that existed in our society, and labeled any effort to maintain discipline against it hypocrisy."

"How does any of this relate to Greg Burley?" I asked when he paused again to sip his Glenlivet.

"Don't ask me. I don't know how any of it relates to any damned thing anymore. Aren't you sick of it, Jake? Aren't you sick of every movie having an obligatory scene where you are exposed to some director's fantasy of how he thinks two people mate. I mean, here is some actor showing you his ass and some actress faking an orgasm. Why? Have they all lost their imaginations? Do they think they're showing us something different? I tell you, Jake, I used to admire actresses and actors too, I guess, but not anymore. I think of them as whores. They're the same as the performers in those sex shows that used to be put on in the back alleys of places like Juarez and Tijuana."

"That may be taking it a step too far, Jase," I offered in an attempt to lighten him up a bit.

"That's not even the half of it. Decent people don't have a chance anymore. Where's their forum? And by decent I mean the average Joe with the average kind of instincts, desires, appetites and all the rest that come with being a human being, who exercises some control over it all from a moral basis. That's what the hell I'm talking about, and you think the same damned way about it. So don't go calming me down on it."

I let him spew it out. It was as if a pressure valve had opened. It came out and he sputtered to a stop. He poured a short shot of scotch and held it up in ironic toast.

"To the inmates who now control the asylum," he said.

"Not quite yet," I countered. "Decency has a way of rising up and kicking ass."

He shook his head. "Not many of us ass kickers left, Jake." He smiled a wry inward smile, before setting his face into a serious mask.

"How much does he owe you?" I asked.

Without much of a moment for thought he answered, "Thirty-three thousand dollars. If he is dead it's not a debt which transfers to his wife. Does that answer your next question?"

"Yep," I said.

"You think he is?" he asked.

I shrugged. "That's not my problem."

Again that wry smile peeked over the rim of his Waterford double old-fashioned. "No? If he's dead then maybe somebody helped him die. That brings up a list of suspects. At the top of the list would be the wife, wouldn't you say? I wonder if you would still think it was not your problem then. Just wondering." He held up his hands in a show of innocent speculation.

I got up in a heavy, slow way. I set my cup back on the side table and went to the door. He wheeled along behind me all the way, the little smile firmly in place. I stopped with the door open, extended my hand, and said, "Glad you finally won one. It was beginning to get monotonous."

"It was a pleasure," he gloated, with a little extra pressure on my hand. "I hope you'll continue to be such a gracious loser."

"Like I said, you fantasize."

• • •

Much of what you learn about fighting, you learn from the guy facing you trying to knock your brains out. That is, if you survive the fight. I had learned most of what I knew about perimeter-invasion detection from the people I had invaded. I had learned the use of simple devices, for instance, to alert me to the presence of an intruder, either past or present. I had put a couple of such devices in place before I went to Meddler's.

It was only half a toothpick. I had left it tight up against the jamb leaning against the door. It would have been hard to see unless someone knew where to look. It was still leaning just as I had left it. It's tricky depending on such things though, because a stray draft can topple a toothpick. It serves to alert you, but it doesn't stand alone as proof of entry. Also, there is the other side—a clever intruder might spot it and replace it. It is not foolproof. However, I tend to believe the toothpick.

The alarm system showed nothing amiss. I punched in the code and entered. Everything appeared to be in order as I checked the house. I opened the doors to the lanai from simple force of habit. It seemed that all my life I had been opening doors to let fresh air in and stale air out after even the shortest of absences. I stood for a moment and listened to the surf.

I did not feel ready to sleep. Something was stirring in my mind. Something I could not hold on to long enough to identify. I put on some Nat King Cole and made myself half a pot of decaffeinated Irish Cream. I settled down in the living room with the yellow pad, pictures, notes, and paper.

I fiddled around with the scraps as one might with a jigsaw puzzle, looking for I knew not what. I knew it when I found it though. It had been there all along, but I was too dense to see it. Two of the scraps fit together. Both papers had initials on them. One was the TONI paper. The other also had large block letters, W E N, and a number. They both had been written on the same piece of paper. It had been torn in half, and when I placed the pieces together they made a perfect fit. The W E N notation had been on the top half.

I played with those initials for a while. William, Willy, Winston, and Edward, Eddie, Ellis, Eliot, and Nunn, Nader, Nelson. Nothing clicked, except Willie Nelson. When that lodged in my brain I knew I was through. It was hard enough to think without having the image of some nasal-toned country singer popping up in the way. I would run it by Katherine Burley. Maybe she could fill out the initials.

On a whim I dialed the numbers on both pieces. No answer. I can't say why I expected there would be no answer, but I did. I was getting a feeling about this thing that was taking up residence in the base of my neck. There was no explaining it in a rational way.

I leaned back and sipped the very good decaf and read the empty profile Katherine Burley had written on her husband. It possibly revealed more about her than it did about him. That was one of the purposes of it, the hidden purposes, about which I now felt a twinge of guilt. What she had written was about as personal as a *New York Times* obit. "Sterile" was the word that came to mind.

The sound of the surf, old-fashioned music sung by an old-fashioned voice, and a warm mug of coffee pulled me into a lazy sort of contentment. I put my head back against the cushions of the sofa. A small breeze danced over my eyelids and the heavy night scents of jasmine and honeysuckle filtered into my brain.

7 🔥

For the next couple of days I used the phone a bit, exercised a lot, and did not accomplish very much. I was floundering. I found myself wishing Greg Burley would suddenly reappear with a story of a sordid little escapade in Baja with one very naughty lady named Toni something or other.

Various scenarios played through my evening runs. They chased me into my dreams at night. They took the place of my usual discontentments with the condition of the world. I had an unease which I could not explain. Yet with it I felt no need to hurry. Whatever it was, I knew I was already too late.

After two bright, clear mornings, I awoke early to a foggy one. The locals liked to refer to it as a heavy marine layer, or morning haze. Some called it the June gloom. Anyway, it was foggy and I did not feel like sitting in my own kitchen or making my own coffee on such a morning. I drove to Montecito and the Coffee Mill.

It has always amazed me the way accidents happen. A guy takes a wrong turn, and bingo, a truck hits him, and he winds up in the city morgue. One minute either way, or he doesn't miss his street, or he doesn't drive to work that day, and he's home with his family watching TV and snoring through the evening news. Why one guy lives and one guy dies in a plane crash into an Iowa cornfield is one of the great mysteries. That little edge that fate brings to life is what gives us both hope and fear.

In my life it was sometimes that element which broke the inertia. I guess I could have gone a dozen places that morning, but I chose the Coffee Mill. I'm sure Big Bertha was on duty ready to ration out her muddy brew, but without any prior thought I went directly to the Coffee Mill. I wondered about it later, but at the time it was unremarkable.

Peggy Cooley was in her usual good spirits, laying out equal measures of food and folksy homily. She gave me a good minute of attention when I entered. All of it was from across the room while she listened to the end of what must have been a long-winded story and I seated myself next to a window. As soon as she could make a graceful departure from the local raconteur, she brought the coffeepot.

"You've been missed," she said as she leaned over to pour the coffee. She made sure I could see what the loose-topped blouse displayed. "You need a menu, or do you know what you want?"

There was plenty of sexual innuendo there, and it made me wonder. Was it so ingrained in her at this point that it was automatic, or was it boredom? I gave a simple answer: "Eggs over easy, ham, wheat toast, no potatoes."

She was not going to let me off easy. "You sure that's all you want?"

I felt slightly absurd. "No, I've changed my mind. I'll have the potatoes."

She grinned as she pulled her ample bosom up from my view. "I like you," she said. "You have a way about you, don't you."

It wasn't presented as a question, so I didn't bother trying to answer. I withstood her gaze like a man standing against a gale, until she released me from it to place my order with the cook.

I sipped the hot coffee. It was a form of refuge, like cigarettes and worry beads. I let the little coffee shop become a vague backdrop to my thoughts, and drifted mentally through smoky fragments of reflection. There was something in there pulling at me, tugging at my sense of logic. I played with all the surface things, not wanting to miss the obvious.

I went deeper and deeper, placing the pages of the yellow legal pad before my window of memory and comparing what was written there against any other information or speculation. I reconstructed Greg Burley for what was probably the hundredth time and in the hundredth different configuration. I was looking for the illusive perspective that would make the picture change enough to mean something.

I pondered it through my breakfast and two coffee refills. I got lost in it to such a degree that I was unaware of what was going on around me. My face was turned to the window, but I could as easily have been looking at a blank wall. Only one thing penetrated. It was the sight of a man stopped at the corner talking with great animation into his car phone. The inner tug again, pulling hard.

"No crossword this morning?" Peggy asked at my shoulder.

"I didn't get a paper," I answered in rather lame fashion.

"Try this one," she replied, and dropped a paper in front of me which she had just cleared from a table. "It's a *Chronicle,* but the crossword's probably same as the *Times.* Beats me why so many people here buy a San Francisco paper, but they do. More coffee?"

I nodded and mumbled some sort of thanks for the paper. She took a long grin at me before moving on. I thought about her a little bit while I absently opened the *San Francisco Chronicle* to the front page and just as absently glanced over it. I had turned to the second page without anything registering before I comprehended what I was seeing. It was a picture of a car being crane-lifted up a cliffside. Its rear end was to the camera, and the license plate was clearly visible: "TONI."

"T-O-N-I," my brain spelled out, as if I were seeing it on a small scrap of paper. My instincts took on a familiar buzz. It was a moment like a fisherman must have when he thinks he's hooked a fish but doesn't know how to land it.

I quickly scanned the story, looking for the part where it said that two bodies were recovered, a male and a female. It did not read that way. The story did say there was a female body identified as Toni Spence, but there was nothing about another body. I searched the story over twice to no avail. It said simply that the car had been at the bottom of the deep ravine for probably ten days to two weeks, judging from the condition of the body. It appeared to be an accident, possibly alcohol-related.

I sat staring at the picture as if I could glean some extra information from it. This did not fit with my scenario. They must have missed something. Possibly his body had flown into the brush some distance from the car and they had not discovered it. Yet even as I reached for such possibilities, another part of my mind was saying no. This was a different Toni. He had not been with her. Greg Burley had not run off with this Toni Spence. Greg Burley was still missing, and I was grasping at straws.

Peggy sashayed by with a quick glance down at the paper. She hesitated a moment before coming back to look over my shoulder. She made a funny tongue sound as she shook her head.

"Yeah, Barney showed me that. Awful, isn't it? Nice lady. Did you know her?" She asked it as if I should have.

"No," I answered. The buzz returned. "Did you?"

"Sort of. She came in here a lot. Used to sit at that back window if she had a choice. Very showy type, if you know what I mean."

"I'm not sure," I said, using a very subtle and slow pull on the information rope.

"Lots of pizzazz. Dressed to the nines, even at ten o'clock in the morning. Makeup, jewels, the whole nine yards." She cocked her hip and her head in that unique way of hers and added, "Barney, Lenny, Big John, all the old leches were always drooling over her."

"This Barney knew her, did he?"

"Barney? No, I don't think so. That's his paper you're reading. He's from up there and can't seem to break the tie." She started away.

"How did he know this was about her? How did he know her name? There's no picture." I had to turn to catch her with it.

"Everyone knew her name," Peggy said with arched eyebrows. "She had it on her car, and two or three times there were calls for her here. All the regulars heard her name then."

"Phone for Toni Spence? Just called out like that?"

"Sure, why not?" she said as if offended by my characterization of the action.

She started away again, and I got to my feet to stop her.

"Can you remember the last time you saw her in here? When it was?"

Peggy's eyes took on a sharper glint. She looked at me with a different quality than before.

"A couple of weeks ago," she answered, and added, "Why?"

"And did she get a phone call that day?" I pressed.

She shook her head. "Not that day, but one of the days after that she did. Some guy called and made sure I looked everywhere. He was pretty upset that he couldn't find her."

"A day or so after the last time she came in?"

She simply nodded, but her eyes were dancing all over me. "Now that empties the well. You want to know anything else from me, make it about something I know. I know a lot. I was a history major at U.T. Make it about Texas. I know everything there is to know about Texas." The eyes still did the old soft shoe. "What I don't know much about is you," she said, "do I? Are you some sort of cop?"

"Lord, no," I answered, turning back to the table to drop some bills next to my plate.

"Then why the questions, chum? They're cop questions, if I'm any judge."

Without waiting for an answer, she turned away from me with absolute dismissal, her Texas twang taking on the room. By the time I reached the door she was in full stride.

"Now, I'm as friendly as the next girl, but there's a time and place. I said to the old fool, 'You can peek, but you cain't pet. You grope me again and I'll rotate your liver.' "

There was a mystery there, to be sure, but I had my hands full at the moment.

* * *

When the cellular number checked out to be the one in Toni Spence's car, Tex Flanagan grudgingly sought the facts on the accident for me. He had the authorities in Monterey fax a copy of the accident report down to him, and he read it to me over the phone.

"Car must've been at speed when it went over the edge, because it flew the slope completely. It landed almost in the flat ravine below."

"No skid marks, you said?"

"It only states that none were noted."

"They think she was drunk?"

"Either that or asleep. They'll do an autopsy when they get the time. What they really think is drugs. That's what you always have to consider when some idiot takes a flyer like this."

"Or suicide?" I don't know why I said it.

"Or suicide," he confirmed. "Suicide's a possibility, but there would have to be a hell of a lot of prior indicators before it would be listed as one."

"There was no luggage listed in the contents of the car?"

"Nothing. The car was clean. Nothing in it at all except her handbag. Hell, if that was my car, it'd take them a year just to sort through all the crap I've got in there."

"And no sign of Greg Burley with all this, huh?" It was one of those thoughts you sometimes asked aloud.

"Why should there be?" he asked, meaning it as a real question.

"Because there's a connection."

"Yeah, they knew each other. Or is there something I don't know." His voice had become serious.

"No, but I have a feeling about it."

He gave a little humming sound. "Well, Jake, I've been a cop long enough to know that there's something to those feelings about things, but all that shows here is that they talked on the phone. That don't seem like much to me."

"That and the fact that he's gone and she's dead. It doesn't feel right."

"Well, podner, the ball's in the air. You catch it and run. If there's something there let me know, okay? I'll be right happy to kick the extra point."

I put down the phone and mulled it over for a few moments before forcing myself into motion. I donned sweats and started a halfhearted workout. My mind wouldn't unload. There was a vague form, a sort of mental shadow, that muddled my thinking. I worked through it and finally managed to get mind and body together in the workout.

My body was getting back into some semblance of condition. It was a tough road back, but I could at least begin to see some signs of progress, especially in my endurance. My shoulder was working in full rotation finally without the pain grabbing halfway through. The ribs were not complaining. Life on that end was good.

I took twenty minutes of steam, showered, and dressed before eating a light lunch of gazpacho and cold chicken. I brewed a blended cocoa coffee and poured it over shaved ice to take outside with me. I settled back onto the chaise, beneath the shade of an umbrella, and sipped at the iced coffee. My mind had cleared somewhat, allowing me to begin a sorting process.

Something caught my eye. A movement from the far edge of the garage wing of the house put my senses on alert. I quelled the impulse to rise immediately and instead pretended a state of languor. The front gates were closed, there was no question about that. This was neither the gardener's day nor the poolman's, so I could reach only one conclusion. I had a midday prowler.

I made a lazy roll to my feet and stretched, as if all I had on

my mind was where to take my nap. The movement I had noticed earlier was stilled now, but I could detect an unusual
outline in the hedges by the house. I lazed my way inside and
made a quick shift to the kitchen window where I could get a
good view of the end of the house. I saw the movement again.
A spot of sun shot the shadows and hit the man squarely as he
moved away from the back garden entry.

Two minutes later my front doorbell rang. In that time, I
had prepared myself for almost anything.

I opened the door to a man in his mid-thirties with the kind
of size and shape pro football scouts dream about when
they're looking for middle linebackers. This guy met me on a
level eyeline. His hair was close-cropped, like a boot fresh to
camp. His eyes were hard and steady, and about the color of
fine finished walnut. He would have made a great poster boy
for World Championship Wrestling.

"Mr. Sands," he said in a voice a little too thin for such an
imposing physical presence, "I'm Captain Jessup."

"Captain's your first name?"

He hesitated. That was all I needed to see. He said, "My
first name is Charles."

"Well, Charles, what's on your mind?"

"I've come to have a word with you about the man who was
killed on Faring Lane Monday of last week. If you remember, I
spoke to you in regards to your car?" He clipped his words as
if English were a second language to him.

I squinted a bit and said, "I remember, but now we're going
to have a little talk about *your* car." I nodded my head in the
direction of the Wagoneer four-by-four parked in my circular
drive. "What's it doing in my driveway? And how did you
open my gates?"

No reaction showed, though I'm sure he was trying to con-
vey innocence. "Would you rather I park on the street?" he
answered with his own question.

I took that moment to try to decide if I could find anything
about the man that I might like. I came up empty. I had the

feeling he was doing the same about me, with the same result.

I said, "You're not going to win if you try to make this some kind of game. Answer my question."

He took his time. "With a remote opener. Just as you do."

I had to laugh at that. "Well, it strikes me that there is a bit of difference here. It's my gate. You have one of my gate openers?"

"Not one of yours, sir, no. We were given the transmission code when your gates were installed. We logged it into one of our master units. It is customary here for the patrol to have access to the properties. I assure you I was doing nothing outside our charter, sir." He spoke with a heavy tone of condescension.

"I see," I replied while I thought it over. "Well, you better delog my transmission code. This is the last time you are ever to enter my property uninvited. Is that clear?"

"It is, but if I might advise you on that, it is in your best interest that we have the capability. In the event of fire or break-ins, it can make the difference between life and death." It was a well-rehearsed line.

"I think not," was all I said.

He nodded in tacit acceptance. We each awaited the next move. I figured it was his.

"If you have a moment, I would like to discuss the Leeds case." He continued to look at me like I was lunch.

I decided to give him his lead and see where it took us. I stepped back and said, "Come in." I had the uneasy feeling he knew the inside of my house better than I did.

We settled in the living room and stared at each other for a second or two. He was less comfortable than I, because I had already made up my mind that he was someone I did not want to tangle with. He was still trying to decide about me.

"You know the man who discovered Mr. Leeds, or was credited with it, owns several car dealerships?" he began. "He gave a very good description of your car, Mr. Sands. That's why I'm here, to ask you again if you saw anything that night."

"MacGregor, is it? No, MacGribb. Isn't that the fellow you're talking about? The one who found the body?" I asked with all the innocence of a thief. I waited for his nod. "I'd be interested to know just how he described my car. What did he say about it? Did he mention the color?"

"He did," Jessup responded. "He gave the color, make, model, and year. Hit it right on the nose."

"Did he now? That's truly amazing if he did, because I've never met anyone yet that could tell you what color my car is in the dark. What's even more amazing is that he could tell you the year. For ten years that model looked the same on the outside. The only way I could ever tell a year was by looking inside on the door post. Did he do that?"

The funny thing was, I knew the little twerp, MacGribb, had not told them a thing. Possibly, he could have noted the make of car, but even that would have been difficult in that light, and with what was happening. Yet they knew I was there. Jessup knew it for certain. He was not being truthful about his source. That made me wonder.

"I can only tell you what was in the report. It would be helpful if you did tell us all you know about that night, Mr. Sands, and then we can put it to rest." He did not persuade me.

"It seems to me that someone has given you some bad information." I wanted to keep the ball in his court as long as I could.

Again he took his time. He looked around the room, letting me see his immediate assessments. I decided to give him a peek at my assessment of him. I scowled.

"I assumed you would be more helpful," he said. "We don't like to let these things get to a critical stage."

"I'd say it sort of started out there with Leeds, wouldn't you? Death has always struck me as critical."

"I'm talking about your involvement. I'm sure you'd rather keep things on an unofficial basis." He was patronizing me again.

"You got that wrong," I replied. "I like official. What I don't like is overblown unofficial meddlers stirring the waters. I would guess the local gendarmes might feel the same way."

We stared at each other.

"You don't mince words," he said finally.

"I was hoping that wasn't too subtle for you."

He got to his feet and said, "No, it came through loud and clear." The rough edges were beginning to seep through his carefully controlled demeanor. "We don't seem to be hitting it off too well, do we?"

"Let's just put it down to an employee overstepping his bounds," I replied.

For the briefest of moments I thought he was going to get physical. It was in his eyes, to be sure, but his control kicked in. He was a dangerous man. It was possible I had under-assessed him in that department.

"I'm not your employee," he snapped.

"No? That's odd. I thought you worked for the Coco Palms Homeowners' Association, which I was obliged to become a part of when I bought property here."

"Me and my men answer only to the board of directors," he said with open insolence. "And so do you, you'll find out soon enough."

He turned away from me and headed for the front door. I followed him outside, allowing myself some assimilation time for the little teaser he had dropped on my plate.

I tried a teaser of my own. "Tex Flanagan calls you Charlie. You don't look like a Charlie to me."

That stopped him. He turned from his door, halfway in the car, with his stare firmly in place. "You think by mentioning Flanagan you're sending some kind of message?" He sneered at me and slid under the steering wheel. He put a huge arm out the window in my direction. "You remember, it was you that turned things bad between us. I came here in good faith, trying to do my job. You remember that."

"You came here like a burglar sneaking around the back. You come here like that again, and you'll have more trouble than you can imagine." I took steps toward the car. "That's the only message I'm sending you, Charlie."

We stared at each other again, before he started the Wagoneer and slowly departed my driveway. It took a while for the adrenaline to drain from my system, a sensation I had learned to hate. It always left me with a slight tremble and a feeling of disgust.

I fixed more iced coffee as I replayed our brief exchange. There was something he had said that nagged at me. He had imputed unusual power to the homeowners' association. That was interesting to me, though I could not say why. I vaguely remembered a recent notice of a general membership meeting sometime soon. I went through the recent stacks of mail until I found it. I would be there. I wanted to get a good look at that board of directors.

8 🌿

The parking lot of the Coco Palms Country Club was like a new-car dealership. It was amazing to see so many clean cars in one place that weren't for sale. I did a quick calculation with all the Rolls, Mercedeses, and such, and totaled it up at around three million dollars in parking lot inventory.

I entered the clubhouse with that faintly bewildered look people get when they step from bright sunlight into a darkened interior. I groped forward, sure that just ahead were two or three steps down, which were designed to cripple and embarrass. I had visions of myself catapulting into some elegant dining room where I would go sprawling into a carving trolley or pastry cart.

I found light again just beyond the entry and with it a large open dining room. The maître d' approached with the smile of a great aunt. "Yes sir," he said. "Are you meeting someone?"

I nodded and mumbled, "Mrs. Burley. I may be a bit early."

"Indeed," he confirmed as he consulted his seating chart. "I don't believe she has come in from the tennis pavilion. If you'd care to join her there, you may use that door off the terrace."

I seemed to have no choice, so I used the door off the terrace. The tennis courts were a short, pleasant walk from the main clubhouse. I used the walk to straighten my clothes and finger-comb my hair. I was like a schoolkid on a date.

She was easy to spot. I stood on the pavilion and watched her hit balls back to the pro. She had good timing and better-than-average power. She hit a two-handed backhand, reminding me of Chris Evert. It was obvious she could play. I wondered why she was taking lessons.

When she saw me she waved, hit two more volleys, and then exited the court with a graceful goodbye to her pro. Still perfect. She zippered up an expensive-looking warmup outfit of hot pinks and greens. I could remember when people didn't think those colors went together, but of course, all the attitudes of those times have been reversed. With a quick flip the headband came off. She shook her head and fluffed her hair with her hands as she approached me.

"Give me one second and I'll be right with you, Jake," she said with a graceful lope toward the ladies' locker room.

It was more than a second, but it was worth it. When she returned she was clad in a casual dress which had designer written all over it. What a waste, I thought, because she would look good in anything.

"I'm starved. I hope you are too. I hate to make a pig of myself in front of someone who's only having a salad or a half order of something. You won't do that to me, will you?" she said as she closed the distance between us.

I was in the process of stumbling with my answer when she took my arm, in the manner of one well acquainted with it, and turned me toward the clubhouse. Jasmine and honeysuckle surrounded me, and I walked on rubber legs beside her.

Below us men were walking with heads down toward balls nestled in sand traps and behind trees. They did not seem happy. They did not care about the ocean view, or the mountains, or the beauty of the day. They were plodding, grumbling, and occasionally cursing the fates that conspired against them.

She saw me see them or took for granted that I did. She said, "On the first tee those same men are laughing, joking, making bets, and commenting on the glories of the day. Now look at them."

I laughed, more at the fact that she had captured my thoughts exactly than at what she had said. "How do you know that?" I asked.

"My father," she answered. "He was an avid golfer. I used to go out with him and ride in the cart. He would always tell me to watch the personality changes in the men he played with. He was good at calling it. But even he was a little grim sometimes by the eighth hole."

"Does he still play?"

She ignored my question. Instead she said, "You never answered. Are you hungry?"

I shrugged. "I'll try to hold up my end."

She greeted the maître d' with the sort of nonchalance I envied, but never sought to emulate. It was that casual acceptance of positions that made it natural for her to say "David," and for him to say "Mrs. Burley." I had never been completely comfortable with that kind of attitude, and I hoped I would never be.

We ordered a lot of food and ate most of it before we got beyond the small talk. I did not push it. This lunch had been her idea, so I let her lead.

After a short silence she said, "Are you discouraged about finding him?"

I shrugged. "Like I said, it's not going very well. You might be better off hiring a private detective at this point."

She gave that no time for consideration. "No," she said. "I'm sure a detective could do no more than you are doing. I really do appreciate your efforts, Jake. I want you to know that." She paused for that to settle in on me before she reached into her large bag and pulled out an envelope. "I found these. They're just more pictures Greg had, but I thought I'd bring them anyway. They seem to have been taken on one of his diving trips. I don't recognize any of the other faces, but then I didn't know any of his diving friends. They never came to the house. They called, but they never visited. It was like a separate life for Greg."

I glanced at the few pictures she handed over. They were unremarkable in both composition and content. I could identify Greg, barely, as most of the pictures were taken into the sun with a glaring backlight. In most of them Greg and his fellow posers were clad in wet suits, either just out of the water or just about to go in. There was one picture, however, that caught me immediately. Greg was standing with his net bag held high, displayed for the camera. A man with a baseball cap pulled low over his eyes was beside him, his arm around Greg's shoulders. The picture had been taken in a marina parking lot, again with the sun at their backs. What caught my eye was the car behind them. It was an XJ Jag with a license plate clearly reading, "TONI," just as I had seen in the paper.

Something about seeing a picture of that car again jogged my feeble mind. All at once I knew what had been bothering me ever since I'd read about the accident in the *San Francisco Chronicle*.

"Would you excuse me," I said. "I need to use a telephone."

She seemed surprised by my abruptness, but pointed me in the right direction. I hurried as if there were something immediate about it. There was not, because what had happened had already happened, but I was anxious to know.

"Tex," I said when Flanagan finally came to the phone, "I wonder if they could detect whether Toni Spence's car had the cruise control in an on position or not. Was there anything in the report that indicated that?"

"No," he said with a long, thoughtful pull on the word. "What are you getting at?"

"I'll tell you when you get that information. One other thing. Were the windows of the car up or down?"

"They don't put that kinda crap in accident reports, Jake. If you don't tell me what this is all about, I'm gonna look a damn fool asking for this stuff. You wouldn't want that, would you?"

"Better you than me," I answered. "Call me as soon as you find out. Oh, by the way, I got to know your pal Charlie Jessup a little better. I'd like a word or two with you about him."

"I can give you that now," he said, suddenly more interested than before.

"Later," I stalled, "when you've talked to the folks in Monterey. They may have to check the vacuum connections to determine if the cruise control was on, but they should be able to tell. I think it might be important, Tex."

"I'm guessin' you're thinking maybe the little lady did herself in on purpose, am I right?" He waited into a short silence. "They're not gonna like this up there, you know. They're gonna think I'm horning in trying to tell them they didn't make a complete report, you know." Again a pause. "Okay, I'll see what I can get. I'll call you."

He hung up. I sat for a moment before I replaced the receiver. I was not too content. The nagging little itch in my mind had returned, and I couldn't scratch it. I tried to let it settle before I returned to the table.

"I'm surprised you haven't joined the club here, it's so convenient to your home," she said as I returned to my place across the table from her.

"Is that what you've been thinking about while I was away?" I asked, hoping it sounded playful, the way I meant it.

"No, actually I was thinking about myself, if you must know," she answered. "I was thinking about myself sitting here enjoying lunch with you in the surroundings of a beautiful club when Greg might be . . . who knows where."

"I was wondering why you were a member here when Birnham Woods, Valley, and La Mirage are all closer." I sought a subtle change of subject.

"It's not as far as all that. Besides, now that I've had a chance to compare, I would have to say that Coco Palms is the best club for my purposes. La Mirage has the most snobs though." She laughed a little, and I could see it was partially at herself.

"Kate?"

She answered me with eyes only. Eyes that were green and alive with good humor. If I were an artist I would beg to paint such eyes.

"Kate, I asked you before if you knew a person named Toni. Her last name was Spence, by the way." I looked but there was no reaction, so I continued. "Well, she's dead. She had a car wreck up near Monterey. She was somehow involved with Greg. This is her car here." I showed her the snapshot of Greg and his friend in front of the car. "Are you sure you never saw her or maybe even her car?"

She looked at the photo closely before replying. She was very serious when she did.

"I had never heard her name before you mentioned it. As for the car, I don't know. It could be that I have seen it. It's a very sporty car, right? Bright red?"

"It's a sport coupe. An XJS12 Jaguar, to be exact, and until this photo I didn't know what color it was, but in this it does appear to be red, yes." My eyes never left hers as I spoke.

"I think I've seen that car somewhere, but I can't remember exactly. Do you think it's important?"

I answered frankly. "Yes, I do. I don't know how just yet, but I have to believe there is some connection between that girl and the fact that Greg is missing. I'm working on that assumption for now, so we'll see soon enough if I'm right."

"You have no children?" she asked from deep in left field.

"No," I said, adjusting as quickly as my slow mind would allow. "Not living. I had a son, but no, I have no children now."

She reached across and touched my hand with her fingertips. She said, "That's too bad. You would make a wonderful father. I learned everything from my father. He taught me to ride, to swim, even how to shoot. I learned everything important about life from him. You have his qualities, Jake, of gentleness and strength. He could always make me feel as if everything would be just fine if he was there. I feel that way about you, Jake. I know you will do what has to be done, and I trust that."

The place on my hand where her fingers had rested seemed to burn when she pulled them away. I was frozen in mute contemplation while she readied herself to leave. She signed the check with an almost comical discretion. I made no feeble effort to pay, knowing cash is not accepted at such clubs. I simply tried to deal with the little roar inside my brain.

She rose too quickly for me to tend to her chair. I stumbled along after her as she regally swept past "David" and the other underlings who staffed the place. I was not shocked to see David bow as she passed, for he too knew his part and played it well. After all, that was what it was. People playing at roles with a part of themselves that had very little to do with what they really were. At least, that was the way I hoped it was.

After she drove away I stood at the edge of the parking area and looked out at the shimmer of ocean with the Channel Islands in the distance. Those golfers should look up once in a while. It was a hell of a view.

• • •

It was dark when I returned from my run. I was grateful for the automatic sensors that turned on my exterior lights: I was able to get into my house without killing myself, and just in time to answer a ringing telephone. It was Tex Flanagan.

"The cruise control was engaged," he said without preamble. "So what? Most people that have it use it on the highway, don't they?"

"I would imagine," I replied. "How about the windows?"

"One window was down. So?"

"Which one?"

"The driver's side," he answered impatiently. "Now tell me what this is all about. What's in your craw?"

It was as I had figured, as I had known. It was amazing

what those little itches told you if you only listened.

"I'd lay odds that Toni Spence was already dead when she went over, or at least unconscious. It's my bet that what happened to Toni Spence is murder."

He asked quietly, "Would you mind laying that out for me, please?"

"Just this," I said, trying to simplify it. "Cruise control engaged means she was going at speed, and on a highway, that's over fifty-five. I don't know many people who drive at that speed with their windows down. Not women at any rate, and not the driver's-side window. Another window, maybe, but the window next to you blows your hair and puts a roar in your ears that makes it too uncomfortable. It's unlikely that a woman would be driving on the highway with her driver's-side window down."

"But it was down," Tex said, not quite getting it yet.

"Which should say something else to you. It was down for a reason. It was down so someone could reach in and put her in motion from the outside." I waited while that image scored with him. "Somebody set the cruise control and sent her on her way right over the edge of the cliff."

"No, no, that doesn't work," he argued. "The cruise control only works over thirty or thirty-five miles an hour. You can't set it from a standstill. No, it doesn't work out, you're runnin' at the wrong end zone, podner."

"You ever use your cruise control?"

"All the time."

"Do you ever have to hit your brake because some slower traffic gets in your way and the cruise control disengages automatically?"

"Yep, that's how she works. What's your point?"

"So what do you do when you've got clear sailing again? Do you turn your cruise control back on and then set it the way you did the first time, or do you simply push the reset button?"

"I push reset," he answered, beginning to catch on.

"What if someone drove her car at speed, setting the cruise control at, say, sixty-five, and then brought the car to a stop with the engine idling? Then they moved her behind the wheel and from outside reached in and simply pushed reset, and away the car sped, automatically pushing its way back up to sixty-five. Get it?"

"Yeah, I get it," Flanagan said, and was quiet for a moment. "So?"

"Tell them in Monterey and have them look for any signs that might indicate she was either unconscious or dead when the car hit. It's my bet that the autopsy will show an inordinate amount of alcohol or drug overdose or something chemical. I doubt that there'll be a physical mark, but have them check it."

"Let's say it's the way you've got it figured. What's your move?"

"My move?" I asked, not getting his drift this time.

"Yeah, you're a friend of the family, aren't you? Isn't that what you said you were when you came into this thing? If you've got this figured right, then look who comes up as a pretty good suspect."

"You mean Greg Burley? I wouldn't go that far. I'm just trying to locate the man, that's all. I'm not thinking beyond that. I'm just taking it one step at a time. That autopsy could be important." Experience was yelling loudly at me not to say too much.

"Look, I can't keep bugging them about this thing without some solid reason, and your theory is cute, but it's not good enough." Tex spoke as if he were closing the issue.

I said, "I don't suppose you're planning to go up there yourself, are you?"

"Podner, you are one pushy cowboy, you know that? What is it you're looking for?"

I thought it over. "I told you. This is pretty simple stuff here, Tex. I'd like to know what really happened to that lady."

Tex sighed, in that way designed to tell me he'd had enough.

"This thing is being handled by a sheriff's substation in Monterey. They see it as an accident, pure and simple, and they don't want to see it any other way. I pretty much agree with them."

"No, Tex, it was no accident." I was beginning to feel some frustration. I decided to test this good old boy from Texas. "I want to get a look at things up there. Think you could set it up for me with the deputy in Monterey?"

There was a long silence. "What things?"

"The car, the body, the location where it happened. Things."

"Nope, I don't think I can do that, pard. You'd be too far away to keep an eye on. I don't know you that well."

"You got a point there, Tex. That might be good for me to keep in mind too."

"Fine," Tex said. "Now what was this about Charlie Jessup?"

"He's tweaked my curiosity. I'd like what you can give me on him." I threw it out as flat as I could.

Tex's voice grew very calm and serious in tone. "I told you to watch out for him, and I'm doubling up on that. He ain't a guy to fool with, Jake. I like you, and I'd sure hate to see you get a tit in a wringer with that one. I'll just give you one little piece of background. He's a product of the military police, if that gives you anything, but after the service he became a top collar ace with the Chicago police force. Went to plain clothes in record time. Lots of beefs on his record about brutality. Lots. Even got noticed on deaths-while-apprehending. Not a cop in Chicago history ever had so many pursuit deaths. God only knows how many were not reported. Anyhow, he was brought up on charges by his precinct captain. That captain is suddenly dead, and next thing I know, Charlie Jessup is head of the Coco Palms patrol. His protection is very deep. Very."

"How do you know this, Tex?" I had to ask.

"Well, let's just say I knew his precinct captain," he said.

"Anything else?"

"He's a very bad man with the ladies. If you have any you

particularly care about, I would keep them miles away from
him. He doesn't take no for an answer, if you get my meaning.
That was also part of the charges against him."

"I think I get the picture."

"There's been a lotta fellas thought they could handle themselves with Charlie Jessup. So far as I know, they was all
wrong. Adios, podner."

I put the phone down and thought about what I had learned.
Flanagan had gone a long way to warn me off of Charlie Jessup. It made me wonder about a lot of things. I wondered just
what deep protection meant. I also wondered how it would go
if Flanagan and Jessup finally came to it. I'd be hard-pressed
to lay a bet on that one.

• • •

Highway 101 North above Santa Barbara is a drive that I'd
always enjoyed. I hit the on-ramp while it was still dark, and
was just passing Gaviota when the first light broke into the
sky. There was no stretch of highway like it, to my way of
thinking. It had the Pacific on one side, mountains on the
other, and plenty of open ranges to get your fancy going. It
moved inland from the ocean a bit, giving some variety to the
countryside, which was still verdant and rolling. It was like
that, more or less, all the way to San Francisco if you stayed
on 101. The alternate took you back to the coast, and Big Sur.

The morning was not very far along when I stopped at a
place that beckoned to me mightily when I was on the road
near San Luis Obispo. The Madonna Inn was a fix I had to
have every couple of years or so. I ordered an omelet and coffee, and took my pilgrimage to the men's room. The inn was a
tourist's delight; it was graced with design and detail that
were meant to be enjoyed. No expense had been spared in presenting unique and artistic features at every turn. The banister
on the staircase was hand-carved hardwood, done by an arti-
san from Italy. There was ironwork, plasterwork, and tile-
work, all equally as impressive. It was for this I had stopped at
the Madonna Inn, so I took my time.

Funny how things play on the mind, how thoughts pop up unbidden. By the time I returned to my table I was thinking of this woman, Toni Spence. The omelet had been delivered in my absence and was diving toward room temperature fast. The coffee was at that terrible stage called tepid. I ate the potatoes and fiddled around with my thoughts on Toni Spence.

There were two possibilities, the way I saw it: suicide or murder. The first did not hold, and the latter was an open door. With murder came all the questions of who, why, how, on and on. And Toni Spence? Who was she? Other than Greg Burley's girlfriend, that is. That was another big problem I was having, imagining any lady who could pull a man's eyes off Katherine Burley. This Toni Spence must have been some doll.

I tried to remember what Peggy Cooley had said about her. "Pizzazz" and "showy" were the words she used, at least the words I remembered. No doubt a looker of the highest order. I sipped at my cold coffee and pushed the yellow pile congealing on my plate with my fork. It felt like something that should carry a forty-thousand-mile warrantee with road hazard protection. At least the potatoes had been good.

Back on the road again, I set my cruise control at sixty-two and let my mind roam. What had started to gnaw at me at the Madonna Inn was, what did this Toni Spence have that was so all-fired great? And was that what had gotten her killed? I drifted so deep into my speculations I almost missed the turnoff to the coastal route.

I could feel the cooler air coming through the vents as I neared Morro Bay. I lowered my window to breathe it in, thinking how unlikely it would have been for a woman to do the same thing. It was possible, though, that she had taken just a breath of fresh air and, at that moment, lost control and gone over the edge of the cliff. It could have happened that way, I thought, but my instincts said it hadn't.

I made better than average time all the way to Big Sur, which was always worth a food stop. It was amazing how good a plain sandwich was in Big Sur. It was a rustic and simple place with a mix of native people who fit the land and transplants from the big cities who did not. The land itself was of the spectacular variety, offering high trees in woods that competed with the sea for attention.

I stopped at Ventana's, where I could view the ocean and collect my thoughts, but I made it quick. The more I thought about that supposed accident, the more I wanted to get to the scene myself. I was also getting anxious to see the results of the autopsy.

The serpentine coastal road was no problem for my car: it had been designed for roads like this. It made me think of the Jaguar. Certainly the XJS12 Jag was a good road car. It could hold a corner with the best of them. Not a likely candidate for an accidental plunge over the side.

I got to the Monterey County sheriff's substation just before their lunch hour. It was going to be tricky, but I had always found the best time to be a little tricky was when a man was hungry.

"I'm Jake Sands from Santa Barbara County. Up here for the autopsy on Toni Spence," I said to the calm, receptive face of the female deputy behind the desk. "Could you please put me in touch with the investigator handling the matter?"

"One moment please, Mr. Sands," she said with an efficient tap-tap on the keyboard in front of her. "Spence?" I nodded. She flicked a switch and said into a phone, "Bill, there's a Mr. Sands here from Santa Barbara to see you." There was a pause before she answered, "Spence. Toni Spence. 11642."

A moment later I was met at the door by a tall, hatchet-faced man who was probably thirty-five and looked sixty. He extended his hand and said, "Bill Arness, Sands. Come back to my office here and have a seat."

I followed him through a maze of small glass-sectioned offices to one slightly larger and more private. I sat.

"I know you've talked about this with Tex Flanagan in our Santa Barbara office, but I thought one of us ought to come on up and get with this thing on a firsthand basis." I talked quickly and authoritatively, hoping he would not ask me for identification. "We've been trying to locate Miss Spence for some time. It was a surprise to learn of the accident. It *was* an accident, wasn't it? I mean, you still see it that way?"

Bill Arness was not a man to be rushed. He leaned back and gave me a careful look. "You're a ways ahead of me, Mr. Sands. I better get the file you're talking about so I can get up to speed on this. This the Spence woman, right? Just a second."

He left me for what seemed to me to be too many seconds and returned with an open manila folder. I was happy to see that he could read without moving his lips. His eyes remained on the file while he said, "Hmmm, yeah, seems pretty clear it's an accident. You have some reason to think it was something else?"

"No," I answered with wide-eyed innocence. "I'm just wrapping things up. Mind if I look at that file?"

He gave me a show of a shrug and passed it over. I read what was there as quickly as possible, unsure of my footing with Arness. He displayed little moments of hesitation that bothered me. The only new information I was able to glean from the file was the exact location of the accident. It was on the road to Big Sur, about five miles out.

"How about the autopsy?" I asked, handing the file back.

"Probably doing it as we speak, Mr. Sands, over in Salinas. We're headquartered there, you know. Anything in particular you're looking for?"

I tried to sound offhand. "The usual, I guess—blood alcohol, any unusual drugs or chemicals, any marks on the head that might've come before the crash, that sort of thing."

He was dialing as I spoke. To me he said, "This thing would've been different if the highway patrol had handled it, the way I wanted. It was our boys that got there first, so somehow it became our baby. Just a lot of work over nothing, you know what I mean? I even tried to pass it to the Big Sur substation, but we were closest to it, so they passed it right back." I waited while he worked his way through the layers of underlings to the person he sought. "Oh, yeah, Jay, how you doing? I was wondering how you're coming on the Spence autopsy?" He raised his eyebrows with a short accompanying nod to let me know he was hearing a report. "Alcohol, or drug level? And marks on the face or head that didn't figure for the crash, that sort of thing?" Again he listened intently. He sobered considerably before he thanked Jay and faced me.

"Not sure about the marks around the head," he said, making a tent with his fingers on the desk in front of him. "Alcohol level was way up there, and there was some sign of drugs, but I'll let you see for yourself. He's faxing it to me now."

He excused himself and returned moments later with the faxed autopsy report. I read it while he watched me. I raised my eyes to his. "Well," he said, "not much question about it now, is there?"

"I shouldn't think so," I replied. It took a great deal of effort to keep any reaction from my face. I looked back down at the report in my hands. I took a long mental pull at it, memorizing two key passages.

He seemed oblivious to my focus of attention. He droned, "I just wonder how the hell she got that far. Had to've been drinking while she was driving, I'd think. Scares me to death to think how many there are like her out there. We're cracking down on drunk drivers up here though, I can tell you."

"Same with us. Thanks for your time," I said, and stood, dropping the report on his desk. "I guess I can close my file on this one. I suppose the car is in Salinas too?"

"Her car? Nope, it's here. No reason to haul it all the way to Salinas. It'll go to junk if no one comes to claim it."

"Have you contacted her family?" My innocent delivery of questions was beginning to wear thin. I hoped he had not noticed.

"We notified some corporation up in Frisco, but so far no one has contacted us about her. Most likely it's one of those private corporations people set up for income tax purposes. Could be there aren't any relatives close enough to count.

You'd be surprised how many people are out there all by themselves. Seems kinda sad to me. We were talking about that very thing just last night."

"So the car's sitting at some garage someplace? Here in town, is it?"

"You want to see it?" He asked as if the thought was extremely odd.

I shrugged. "Yeah, why not? I've come this far."

He wrote down the address for me and walked me to the front. He put his hand out and said, "Just show 'em your badge, and they'll let you right in."

"Uh, oh," I said as if it were an afterthought, "no badge. I always forget ID when I travel. Do you do the same thing, leave your badge and gun home?"

He nodded in understanding. "No problem, I'll call over. Have a good trip back."

He was as good as his word. I was passed into the car lot without a hitch. The Jag was in a corner by itself, which made it easy to spot and easy to look at. I could see it was beyond repair, but some sections of it seemed almost untouched. I made a cursory pass at it before seeking a bit more detail. It did something to me to see such a beautiful machine ruined like that.

The rear lid was down but had been sprung, supposedly on impact. I pushed it up. The slender hydraulic rods were still in place and functional enough to hold it raised. I leaned in and examined the trunk area. There was nothing there, just as the report had said. No baggage. Only a purse with the most basic items in it. I had just reached to close the lid when my brain registered what my eye was seeing. There were two parallel indentations in the trunk's carpet. They were approximately two feet long and about that far apart. They were marked with rust stains. I had seem similar ones before in the rear section of Greg Burley's Range Rover. I was getting curious about that cargo. Even more than what it was, I was wondering where it was. I couldn't help but wonder if maybe it was back in Greg

Burley's possession. Had he transported it first or had she?

After leaving the crumpled Jaguar, I took Highway 1 toward Big Sur. At about the five-mile mark I found the location of the accident. There was little evidence of it left, if there had been any to begin. The car had simply catapulted into space from a well-banked, well-shouldered road. The odd thing about it, which made me feel somewhat foolish, was the fact that the car had been traveling south. I had automatically assumed she had been going north away from Santa Barbara. It now seemed that wherever she had been going, she had been and was on her way back.

With that to chew on, I drove on in to Big Sur and gave myself a break. I took a corner room at the Rocky Point Inn. After a shower and shave I sat on my terrace overlooking a spectacular view of the coastline to await the dinner hour and think.

I was feeling numbed by what rumbled in my brain. South, she was going south. But from where? Carmel? Monterey? Santa Cruz, or maybe even San Francisco? The big question was why she had been there. What had she done there? Had she delivered something that left rusty tracks?

The sun drifted lower, softening its light. I had to stop myself from staring straight into it. It tantalized me like a tide pool at the base of a cliff. At the same time, my mind mulled over the new complications raised by the autopsy report. Unexplained bruises on the nostrils and beneath the chin on the neck. It fit too well with a very ugly scenario. It was easy to visualize the arm holding Toni Spence still, pressing down against the trachea, and up against the chin. I could imagine the panic she must have felt when the fingers closed her nostrils, forcing her to breathe through her mouth. The gagging, suffocating feeling that must have come when the bottle was held to her mouth and the harsh liquid filled her only source of air. Vodka, rye, or was it a good scotch whiskey that they forced into her? Or was it one man alone who did it?

How frail and weak she must have felt in those last moments, choking and struggling for air, coughing back up the burning liquor that seared her lungs. I knew the life had gone out of her long before she went over the edge of that cliff. The terror seemed real to me, as it always did when I let myself think of the horrible things some humans are capable of doing to others. For the first time I felt a sort of pity for this woman who had been vain, and happy, and showy, and full of pizzazz. I knew so much more about her now that I had seen the autopsy report. I knew that I had made a foolish assumption. I had assumed she was a young, frivolous playmate for Greg Burley. Now I did not know what to think. I could see the first line of that report as clearly as if it were before me still: ". . . the body of an adult female of approximately fifty years of age . . ." *Fifty.* It stood out like a beacon reminding me that all things were not what they seemed.

I watched the sun turn orange and then disappear. The breeze from the ocean picked up and stirred to life the things around me. I remained as I was, feeling more than seeing the light leak away, missing the comfort of having someone to share moments with, good and bad. I thought a lot about Toni Spence. I was sad about her in an undefined way. Fifty years old, with the last moments of her life lived in terror and pain. I wondered if there was someone who would miss her. A child somewhere, a parent, a lover? Was there someone she thought of in those last moments and, maybe, cried out for?

I shook my head as if I could clear away the images forming there. In the long run it didn't make much difference if there had been someone in her life or not, someone who had shared her ups and downs. She was alone at the end, but then, aren't we all?

9 🌿

There were messages and mail for me to deal with when I got home, which helped pull me back into a more normal frame of mind. There was some value to the mundane after all. I pushed the playback on my answering machine and listened while I sorted through the mail.

"Jake? . . . Tim Brandt here. Jason gave me your number and said I should talk directly with you. I was wondering if we could get together and have lunch or dinner, whichever, and I could give you some deatils on this case. . . . I believe Jason mentioned it to you. It would be a snap for you, and my client would be willing to make a very healthy up-front payment. . . . Anyway, give me a call either at the office or here at home. Just in case you don't have that home number, it's 668-7171. Talk to you soon."

I jotted down the number while two dial tones played through. I pushed aside most of the mail, after a quick look at the return in the upper left-hand corner. If it didn't grab my immediate interest or jog my memory, it was destined to join a growing pile of other unopened missives.

A voice I did not recognize brought my ear to the machine. "Mr. Sands, my name is Garvey . . . Samuel Garvey, and I'm a neighbor of yours, so to speak. You may be familiar with my name from the mailings I've sent out recently. . . . As you probably know, I'm opposed to many of the current actions of the board and I'm trying to make the membership aware of what's happening here. . . . So, if you have any questions, please give me a call . . . 934-8000. Also, I strongly recommend you attend the meeting tonight if that's possible for you. Thank you, Mr. Sands. Goodbye."

I wrote down the name and number. The name rang a bell. I had just tossed aside a letter with it on the return address. I retrieved the letter and opened it while another dial tone signaled another hang-up. I switched off the machine after the four beeps sounded and devoted my attention to the letter from Samuel Garvey.

It was a rebuttal letter for the most part which called the last communication from the board a pack of lies. I found it interesting enough to seek out the board's letter. In so doing I discovered that I had several such letters in the pile of unopened mail. I set them all aside, the ones from Samuel Garvey and the ones from the board of directors of the Coco Palms Homeowners' Association, and a few others, some of which bore the return "Concerned Residents" and others I simply guessed might be of the same ilk. I made coffee, placed all the letters in chronological order, and settled down to read.

After the better part of an hour and a pot of coffee, I felt I knew a great deal about the war being waged against the board of directors, who were stonewalling the efforts of the membership to get more information on the board's actions. There were substantial charges of personal agendas being fulfilled by the directors. One thing that caught my attention was the issue of the patrol's abuse of authority. I had to wonder if Samuel Garvey knew what it would take to bring a definitive action against an entrenched board. Most homeowners' associations were corporations, and any stockholder could tell them how hard it was to dislodge the corporate thieves.

I decided then to attend the meeting. I needed a clearer picture of Coco Palms. I especially needed to hear more on the protests about the security patrol. There was definitely trouble in paradise.

I spent the remainder of the day exercising and trying to clear my mind so I could get a fresh perspective on Greg Burley. I was completely lost there. It was becoming something I wanted no part of. I came close to calling Kate Burley and dropping the whole thing, but I didn't. I could imagine how her voice would sound when she answered the phone, and knew that I was captive to it.

I was preparing to poach a chicken breast in Dijon sauce for dinner when the phone rang. I answered it to a very disturbed Tex Flanagan.

"You stepped over the line, cowboy," he fumed. "You've made yourself a pot of trouble now. You know the penalty for impersonating a police officer?"

"And how is Deputy Arness today?" I answered, acknowledging that part of his information was correct.

"Cute ain't gonna cut this one." He was angrier than I had thought.

"Did you call him, or did he call you?" I asked out of nowhere.

"That makes a difference, does it? Well, cowboy, you've pulled your last word outta me. Don't think you can wave your fanny in the face of the law and not get it bit. I'm gonna want you in here to face charges. You can come in the morning or I can come get you. It's your call."

"You got it wrong, Tex. I didn't impersonate anyone. I maybe left the door open for that assumption, but I never claimed it. Do you have a few minutes?"

"I ain't taking your bull. That deputy up there called me and told me all about your visit. You didn't really think you could get away with that, did you?"

"So he called you? I thought so. Now, do you have a minute?"

"Yeah, he called me. To see if we wanted copies of the autopsy report sent down for our files. A real accommodating fella. Thought you were a real fine representative for the Santa Barbara sheriff's department."

"I've got something I want you to hear," I said while I affixed an attachment to the mouthpiece of the phone. "I have the entire interview on tape from a pocket recorder. I had it on while I was in the sheriff's office. It picked up everything, loud and clear. So you listen, and you decide."

I played the tape for him all the way through. He listened to the exchanges between Deputy Bill Arness and myself without saying a word. When it was over I said, "Well?"

He grunted, not giving up his anger easily. "You play too close to the sidelines and sure enough you're gonna step out of bounds, cowboy. I figure you leaned mighty heavy on my good nature this time. Don't do it again."

"Now let me tell you something, Tex," I said with an edge to my voice. "I'm not of a mind to take any more browbeating. You better worry a little less about your good nature and more about some of the questions I've put on your plate. That was a murder up there. Look away if you want, but it's not going to disappear."

"You're a nervy bastard, Sands, I'll say that for you," he responded.

"I'm a lot of things, Tex, and like you said before, you don't really know me. Now, if you've got nothing more to say, I'll have my dinner. You'll appreciate that, I'm sure."

He let me hear a grudging chuckle. "Podner, never let it be said I'd stand between a man and his dinner. Okay, forget I called. I just wish I was as smart about covering my tail as you are about yours. One little question. Do you carry that little recorder all the time?"

I kept my answer ambiguous. "I've got a poor memory."

"Oh, I'd bet the ranch against that." He chuckled again. "Okay, podner, be talkin' to you."

I put the receiver down, surprised by the residue of adrenaline I felt in my system. I had been unaware that my reaction was that strong. I took careful note of it. I had learned to listen to what my instincts told me.

· · ·

I had never belonged to a homeowners' association before, therefore had never attended a homeowners' association meeting before. Even if I had, I doubt that anything could have prepared me for the Coco Palms Homeowners' Association meeting. The parking lot of the small local elementary school was filled with the same assortment of vehicles that was so evident at the Coco Palms Country Club. Possibly the only difference was that each of these cars had a small blue sticker in the lower left part of the windshield bearing the letters, "C.P.H.A."

I stood at the back of the small auditorium, having arrived too late to find a seat. I pressed in among the other late arrivals just as the meeting was officially called to order. There was little notice taken of me; all ears were tuned to the monotonous recitation of the board's activities and recommendations. I took that opportunity to look over the board of directors and make a snap evaluation. I did not like what I saw. I especially did not like the president, who was presenting the case for the board. He was one of those dead-faced guys with a zero personality but more arrogance than a gang of peacocks. I don't know what made me bring the pocket recorder, but since I had, I turned it on to record.

The first question came from the floor about twenty minutes of boring recitation later. It was only then that I truly realized that the bozo who was president of this board had been systematically lying through his teeth. It all had to do with some legal action the board claimed was unavoidable. It was an action taken against a homeowner in Coco Palms. The questioner contended that it was a personal matter between the homeowner and certain members of the board. A quick look at some of the board members, and especially the president, confirmed the questioner's contention for me. The president was a liar. His problem, as I saw it, was that he was not a good liar.

The man who spoke from the floor was obviously a gentleman, but he was angry. He had difficulty getting out the things he wished to say. He stammered, and in that moment the president got some help from another member of the audience. Somewhere in the auditorium an anonymous voice shouted, "Sit down, Bridges." A few other anonymously rendered hoots heckled in agreement. The man Bridges looked around, lost his nerve, and sat down.

It was hard to tell whether the shouters were simply friends of the board members or planted in an effort to prevent any momentum developing from the opposition. I kept my eye trained on the spot where the first anonymous shouter was seated.

Before the president could move on, a second man stood to be recognized. The president tried to ignore him, but the man spoke out. "I would like to be heard on the matter of this security patrol." The room quieted. This was getting to be interesting.

"We will come to that in the proper order," the president said with a look back at the rest of the board.

"No," the man said, "we can talk about it now. You are raising our assessments by more than a hundred percent because of this patrol and I think we should have some answers."

The president banged his gavel down. "Let's not waste any more time on this at this meeting. If you want specific information, write a letter to the board and we'll be happy to send you what you request."

"I've done that," the angry man shouted back from the crowd. Other voices mumbled their agreement. "I was ignored. I want answers now." The voices mumbled again.

"Order," the president demanded.

"We have some serious concerns here. Why are we hiring all these extra patrolmen? Why is it necessary to—"

The president banged hard with the gavel to cut him off.

"That's enough on that," he said. He made an obvious motion
with his head, and from the doorway behind me I saw Charlie
Jessup start forward.

"Enough? We haven't even begun," the man shouted back in
exasperation.

"Sit down," came the anonymous voice and my eye caught
him. "Move if you don't like it, Garvey!" From a couple of
other spots in the room came similar shouts: "Sit down."
"Let's get on with it." "Shut up, Garvey!" I focused only on
the leader. He shrank down after he yelled out so that he
blended in with those sitting next to him. It was hard to believe this was happening in a community of such wealth. I was
sure that the net worth in that room had to run in the hun-
dreds of millions. It was a further indication to me that we are
but a half step from the caves after all.

Jessup and two of his men came up the side aisle and positioned themselves behind the directors. It was the grossest
form of intimidation I had ever seen. It was so overt it made
me laugh. I laughed alone. The rest took it very seriously.

The president said in his arrogant, pompous voice: "We
have business to conclude here tonight. As I said before, any
personal questions should be handled by a letter to the board.
We have no intention of turning this meeting into a free-for-
all, so please hold your questions. Now, our chairman of the
finance committee will give his report. George."

It all transpired with the poor abandoned Garvey still on his
feet. He withered finally, and silently took his seat, unable to
compete with the loudspeaker system which the finance chairman now controlled. George was more boring than the president, if that was possible, and I suspected just as big a liar, if
my ability to read men was holding up. I noted the nameplates
before each board member. The president's name was Doug
Dreckman. I was sure he preferred Douglas, but "Doug" made
him seem more like one of the boys. One of the boys he would
never be. He smirked at one of his fellow board members as
the other man made some private comment to him. I had the

feeling it was about us cattle assembled before them.

I watched Dreckman. He had things going very much his way and it was clear he thought nothing could be done to change that. I wondered why.

As the evening's business reached a close, I was surprised to see an old man in the front row stand to be recognized.

Dreckman said with obvious impatience, "Yes, Colonel Sutter?" I had the feeling that some big bucks were about to speak.

The old man faced the assemblage with a kind of ragged dignity and said in a weak voice, "I think some comments should be made in regard to the death of one of our home-owners, Mr. Leeds. I think a great many of us have concerns about this, and we need information. What is being done to solve it, and what is being done to ensure our safety?"

Dreckman turned and beckoned Jessup to him. He spoke in his ear for a moment before feeding Jessup off to the mike. He said by way of introduction, "I'll let the man in charge of that investigation answer. You all know Captain Jessup of our patrol."

Charlie Jessup took the microphone with all the confidence of a seasoned performer. If anything, he looked even bigger standing in front of that group. I checked my recorder. It was almost out of tape.

"I know you are all concerned about the incident which occurred here in the Palms. I know some of you were probably friends of Mr. Leeds. We all mourn his passing. But I am mad. I am mad that someone would kill a man like Wendell Leeds, but I am also mad that anyone would invade the sanctity of Coco Palms." Charlie Jessup said it all on one breath. When he paused to get another, he used the moment dramatically to look around. "You can rest assured that I will not stop until the perpetrator of this horrible deed is caught and brought to justice. As to exactly what is being done in that regard, I cannot say, except to tell you the investigation is ongoing."

He turned abruptly away from the mike to resume his place

behind the president. Dreckman said, "I think one of the questions about increased assessments for the patrol has just been answered." There was a mild rumbling of dissatisfaction from the assemblage, but no one stood to voice it openly. I heard the tiny click from my recorder as it reached the end of the tape and shut itself off. It was perfect timing, for the president adjourned the meeting at that point. He must have known I was out of tape.

The grumbling of the homeowners carried out into the parking lot, with neighbors collecting in small groups to complain among themselves. I approached the group around Samuel Garvey and waited. When he looked at me I extended my hand and said, "I'm Jake Sands. I just wanted to introduce myself."

The man's eyes squinted and then sharpened. "Oh, yes," he said, "how nice of you. You've only just built here, I understand? How do you like the Palms?"

"I'm not too sure, frankly." I smiled at him to let him know it was nothing personal with him. "I'm impressed that you know about me. Do you know everyone who lives here?"

"Most of the longer-term residents," he said with a soft politeness to his voice. "You mustn't take this current upheaval as the standard here, Mr. Sands. We're much better people than we're showing just now."

The man I had marked as the leader of the anonymous shout-downs was walking toward a far line of cars. He was moving at a rapid pace with his head slightly hidden. I nodded toward him. "Do you know that man? The one there in the light-colored jacket?"

Samuel Garvey turned his sharp eyes in that direction and studied the man closely. "No, I don't believe I do," he answered.

"He's not a resident?"

"Not one whom I know."

I nodded. "Well, I'll be going now. It was a pleasure to meet you, Mr. Garvey."

"Likewise, Mr. Sands."

I walked quickly to my car, keeping my eye on the man in the light-colored jacket. He stopped at a blue van. I got into the Porsche and watched him from behind the wheel. From the side I caught sight of Jessup and his two men leaving the back of the auditorium. They piled into Jessup's Wagoneer, which was parked beside the building, and made a fast exit. They didn't see me.

I followed the blue van toward Goleta, staying a good half block behind, as we went farther away from Coco Palms. He drove a straight line to Foothill Road, where he turned into a small development of very moderate homes. There were a lot of pickups on the street and in the drives. It was a blue-collar development where the lots were small and the houses close.

I stayed well back and killed my lights as he pulled into a driveway at the end of a cul-de-sac. He carefully checked the van to be sure it was locked before he went inside the house. I took a penlight from my glove compartment and walked to the van. My light picked around the litter inside on the passenger seat and floor. I could see papers, and envelopes, and junk mail discards. The name and address was the same on all envelopes: Mr. Claude Hayes, 1127 Vista Street. With a quick look at the house I verified I was at 1127.

I mulled it over on the way back to Coco Palms. It might be nice to know who had invited Mr. Claude Hayes to the meeting. I wondered if he had been paid by the hour.

10 🌿

The next day I made myself think about Greg Burley.

It was funny how I had begun to consider this hunt for Greg Burley as a job. I took it on to do some gentle poking around and either find the guy or not. It didn't matter much to me, either way, in the beginning. I had figured this as little more than an adult runaway. Now I didn't think so. Now I considered more and more the possibility of Greg Burley being dead. Although it presented itself, I never really thought of him as Toni Spence's killer. But then I couldn't rule it out. Not yet. Lovers? No way. She was old enough to be his mother. And what man would walk away from Kate? That still bothered me.

So what did I have? I asked myself. I had some numbers and some photos, and some impressions of his personality, character, and habits. Not much to find someone who might not want to be found. Well, I had done it before on less. I took a deep mental breath and waded into it all, trying to find loose ends that might lead to something.

After a couple of hours all I had come up with were the photos. There were other people in those photos who might prove useful. It was a shot in the dark, but what else did I have? I chose a few to blow up for detail and wasted the better part of a day trying to find a shop that would do the job from color prints. It was tricky because I wanted thirty-two by forty enlargements. I needed a poster shop, but I finally settled for half that size from a standard film processor.

I left the photos, with my instructions, with an able young chap named Kenny, who promised them to me by evening. He was true to his word, so at six I picked up the sixteen by twenty enlargements and took them with me to dinner. Dinner was at Tony's Beachside, which had long been a favorite of mine in Santa Barbara. The food was good, the service excellent, and the view not bad either. I was relieved to find that Tony was not there, because I didn't feel like talking to anyone.

Of the six blowups, I had pinned my hopes on only one. It was the one taken in front of the car owned by Toni Spence. I wanted a better look at the friend who stood with his arm around Greg Burley's shoulders. It was not much improved. The shadow from the hat was too deep to see any detail of the face.

Although I continued to study the pictures through dinner, I could glean nothing of interest from them. Finally, I put them away and, in fact, pushed the whole thing from my mind. I did not go directly home from Tony's. Instead, after leaving the enlargements in my car, I chose to take a walk on the beach. It was a nice night, warm and still, which made me want to walk close to the water.

Other nights and other beaches swam into my mind. I walked and thought about my life as I had seldom done of late. I let the thoughts of Trinia and Josh come. It was hard to remember the restlessness and lack of fear I had known before them. It was easier to remember the deep, soft happiness of them. I had not known then there was a price for that.

I sat down in the sand and let the soothing lap of the waves lull me into deeper reflection. I had never known pain until I lost Trinia and Josh. I had never cried before, from so deep a place. I had never sought oblivion the way I did when they died, or known I was that soft, or that I could ever be subject to something called clinical depression. I had learned about melancholy and how it always lurked around the edges of life once the wounds were opened. I had learned the only safe way to live was to live alone, and that real love put a person at risk. I leaned back and looked at the stars. After a while I closed my eyes. I went to sleep.

I awoke to the presence of two bums who were trying to decide if they could rob me. I was stiff and sore as I rose to my feet. It was enough, however, to discourage Mr. Flotsam and Mr. Jetsam from any move on me. I was tempted to run them both into the ocean. It made me angry that we could not be safe from these dropouts, but in the end I was satisfied to see them scurry away to their own havens.

I stretched and looked at the time. It was almost midnight. So what, I thought, no one was waiting for me. I had no pressing appointments in the morning. Why worry? Why hurry? Why anything?

That was more or less my mood when I returned home. I was self-absorbed in that babyish, self-pitying way that makes a person careless. Some things were automatic with me though, even when I was in a careless mode. I automatically checked out the garage before pulling all the way in. I automatically put the door down behind me as soon as I was in. I automatically noted the green light on the security system before I punched in the code. I automatically checked my little perimeter traps to see if one had been tripped.

I almost ignored it, even though I saw it. I almost turned the key in the lock and entered in spite of what my eyes told me. I stood frozen in a kind of inertia with the key in the lock, staring down at the piece of toothpick lying beneath the door.

I bent down and took a serious look. The toothpick was halfway under the door, which most likely would happen only if the door had been opened. The wind might topple it, but it would fall to the side. It was pretty clear someone had used the door.

I examined the lock to see if there were any marks that might indicate the use of something other than a key. There were none. I quickly assessed what else I knew. The alarm system had not been tripped, which meant it had been either turned off or bypassed. I moved to the door that led out to the back of the house. The thread I had attached between the door and the frame was broken. Now there was no question at all about an entry.

I reset the alarm, put my key in the door, and opened it. The blare of the alarm was even louder when I opened the garage door. I backed my car out and drove outside my gates to watch. When the system was tripped, it turned on high-intensity perimeter lights which gave a daylight atmosphere to my property.

I could imagine the procedure taking place at the moment. My phone would ring. That would be the patrol office seeking a code word and an explanation. If they received no answer a car would be sent. I checked my watch. I was interested to see how long it would take for them to arrive.

I was surprised. It was only a matter of minutes before a Coco Palms patrol car pulled up next to me. He shone his spotlight on me.

"What's happening here?" he asked.

"Don't know," I answered with a shrug. "I've been waiting for you to check it out."

There was a long hesitation before he parked his car. He got out with an apparent reluctance to go any farther until I joined him.

"You think there's been an intruder?" he asked as we approached the house.

"Don't know," I said in as noncommital a fashion as possible. "Could be the entry from the garage. I sometimes don't get it closed all the way."

He did not break stride as he altered course for the garage. I pushed the control for the door to the interior of the house.

"It's open all right," he said without a turn back to me. "Probably like you said, huh? Just didn't get it all the way closed?"

"Could be." I punched in the code on the alarm pad, shutting it down. "But maybe we better go inside and see. You okay with that?"

That brought his eyes to me. They were not nice eyes. He was on the verge of saying something that would go with the eyes, but held it in. Instead he said, "That's what I'm here for."

I went in behind him. He looked about in a perfunctory way before announcing, "It's clear. I can't see any sign of an intruder here. You ought to be more careful about closing that door, Mr. Sands."

"Right, thanks," I said. "Sorry to be a bother."

He grunted some incomprehensible reply on his way to the front door. This guy was wasting no time with me. It was almost comical how fast he was moving to get away. I stopped him at the door.

"What's your name?" I asked.

He turned as if to show me his name pinned above the pocket of his shirt, then said as if I could not read, "Fred."

"Fred?"

"Fred Stanner. I'm in charge when Captain Jessup isn't on duty."

"Well, Fred, thanks again. You an ex-cop?"

"Yes, sort of," he answered, putting some physical distance between us.

"Sort of? What does that mean?" I went with him as he backed away.

"I was military police."

"Oh, what branch?"

"Army."

I let him drift away without further comment. His big back stretched his uniform much as Charlie Jessup's did. I wondered if they worked out together.

In the aftermath I examined the house more intently. There was nothing missing, and as far as I could see, nothing disturbed. I heated some of the leftover morning coffee in the microwave and sat with it in the living room. It seemed that Fred Stanner had not said more than a couple of words to me the entire time he was here. It made me curious.

I mentally shook my head at what was beginning to look like a predicament. I liked things simple. I liked to be liked. I liked privacy. I liked to stay out of things that were not my problem. Nothing seemed to be going the way I liked it.

Without really thinking about it, I picked up the small file on Greg Burley and began to go through it. I seemed to do that a lot these day, whenever idle time was upon me. I sought out the scrap of paper that bore Toni Spence's number. The sight of it saddened me a little. Not so long ago that number represented a person who was very much alive, and now she was nothing more than the focus of an investigation in Monterey County.

I glanced through the other scraps, focusing momentarily on the block letter initials I had come to think of as Willie something or other Nelson. I supposed I would never get beyond that. On a whim I picked up the phone and dialed the number beneath the initials. It was well past midnight, but if anyone was going to be home anytime, chances were good it would be then. There was no answer. I tossed the scrap aside and picked up the blowups for one last look before declaring them useless.

It was still only the parking lot picture that held my interest. I tried to work without any preconceived notions as I looked at it. I wanted to let my eye lead my mind instead of vice versa. At first I seemed to focus on the car with the license plate "TONI." It was not an accident that Greg and his friend were posed in front of it. It was my guess that they had arrived in that car, or at least one of them had. It was also my guess that the person who had taken the snap was Toni Spence.

Though the face of the friend was too dark to read, there was something about him that put me into deep memory search. I took a magnifying glass to it, hoping to see a cleft chin, a scar on the cheek, anything that might be an aid in identification. There was nothing I could see. I ran the glass over the rest of the picture. I could not help but think how odd it was that a wife knew so little about her husband's friends.

I moved the glass to the friend's left hand, which hung lazily over Greg Burley's shoulder. No ring did not necessarily mean no wife, but it was worth noting. The nails were neatly trimmed in that way professional manicurists do. The slight gleam hinted at a good buff or clear polish.

I struggled to leave my mind open as I moved the glass around. The one thing I had always relied on was that little trigger inside that turned on all the lights. It had always worked for me, sometimes coming in the middle of the night out of a deep sleep, but it had always worked. I began to wonder if I had lost it, or if there was simply nothing there to see. Yet the picture drew me, held me, as if the answer was there.

I yawned physically and mentally and put the enlarged photo aside. I was satisfied that the marina in the background of the picture was Santa Barbara. I felt if I ever got a look at the photo friend in person, I could identify him by his hands. A few questions, perhaps, locating some of Greg's diving buddies, but it was a place to start, a place to look. Even so, what would that do for me? I began to wonder.

One step at a time, I reasoned with a tired brain. I didn't want to think anymore. I put out the lights and plodded back to my bedroom. I wanted a shower and needed one, but my mental torpor demanded sleep.

• • •

Sleep was a restless event, filled with dreams of unidentifiable deeds performed by unidentifiable persons. After an initial deep sleep, I wrestled with a state of semi-wakefulness which had me tossing from side to side, making a shambles of the bed. Tiny oversights have a way of becoming mammoth offenses in the early-morning hours. In the midst of flash dreams there filtered in the phone messages I had not bothered to play back, which became calls I had not returned, which led to one unpleasant conclusion after another. These intermixed with fast-action replays of moments, both stupid and ridiculous, in which I was a participant. Real actions mingled unsettlingly with my dreams. I imagined myself driving endlessly on the freeway with a Toyota dancing around me and the driver shouting obscenities and holding his hand out for all the world to see, giving me the finger. The driver was either Greg Burley or Charlie Jessup. The car became a police car. It pulled me over, and Charlie Jessup dressed in an M.P. uniform dragged me out and handcuffed me. He pointed a finger at me as we stood before the homeowners' meeting and shouted, "He killed Wendell Leeds."

I opened my eyes and stared at the ceiling. My tee shirt was wet with perspiration. It had happened, but I had lost it: the little inner switch was tripped, but I fumbled it. I fought off the need to change my damp shirt, trying to make myself sleep again, hoping to reactivate the trigger, but the discomfort got to me. I rolled out of bed and took off the shirt, while the lost images of my dreams floated away.

I was no longer in a mood to sleep. I lay in the dark with eyes wide open, knowing my day had begun, whether I wanted it to or not. It was there, I knew it. I had to find the trigger again.

I showered, made coffee, and wandered outside to a pale dawn light. I was about to sit and enjoy what poets would call a waking sky when I remembered what had awakened me. I had a mental image of Charlie Jessup standing before the assembly in the elementary school auditorium. I was sure I could remember his words, but it became important that I hear them again.

I went to my closet and found the jacket I had worn to the meeting that night. The tape recorder was still in the inside pocket. I rewound it a short way back while I walked to the living room. I pushed play and listened.

The voice of Charlie Jessup said: "I know you are all concerned about the incident which occurred here in the Palms. I know some of you were probably friends of Mr. Leeds. We all mourn his passing. But I am mad. I am mad that someone would kill a man like Wendell Leeds, but I am also mad that anyone would invade the sanctity of Coco Palms." I pushed the stop button. His words sounded in my brain like an echo.

I had not really needed to replay it. I remembered it. What I needed, I suppose, was a dramatic reinforcement. It is amazing how the mind grasps things without your noticing them, then dumps them on you at the most unexpected moments. You hear things you don't know you hear. You see things you don't know you see. That was what I had always trusted to happen for me. That was the trigger.

In the living room I rummaged through the scraps of paper I had studied the night before. I found the block letters I had mistakenly taken to be initials. I looked at them and heard them then as Charlie Jessup had said them, when he said the name Wendell Leeds. He had put a heavy emphasis on the first portion of the name. "WENdell Leeds."

That, however, wasn't all that pulled at me. I took the magnifier once again to the enlargement of Greg Burley and his diving buddy. I moved the glass slightly up from the left hand to the watch. Why it had escaped my notice before, I do not know, but the watch was a telling piece of information. It was like my own, a Promaster Diver, made by Citizen. The casing was unique and identifiable from a distance, with its alarm housing and four function buttons of polished brass.

The watch, the hands—I had seen them before, of course, and had not realized it. I had seen them when Wendell Leeds lay dying in the middle of Faring Lane. "Wen" Leeds, as Greg Burley most probably called him.

The sky awoke without me. I sat with cold coffee, idly holding an enlarged photo of two friends who had been diving buddies. I sat that way for a long time. A long time.

11 ❧

I checked my answering machine for messages from the day before. Only two people left their names, Jason and Katherine Burley. A couple of others left me a few seconds of dial tone. I took a moment trying to decide who to call first, and Katherine won.

Her voice came at me like a warm wind, sudden and overpowering. It was odd, the effect she had upon me. I was reduced to adolescent musings. My tongue got too thick for me to speak around. All at once the things I formed to say seemed too trite and silly for her ears. I tended to make noises rather than words.

"I'm sorry," she said, "I didn't understand what you said."

"I said, I'm sorry I didn't get back to you yesterday, but I got home pretty late." I seemed to run out of breath before I finished my sentences. Perhaps I was forgetting to breathe.

"Oh, that's fine. I was just wondering about some things," she said. "Big night on the town?"

"Pardon?"

"I was just asking if you were out doing the town last night. Forget I asked, it's none of my business." There was a lot of girlish flirtation in her voice. I seemed to constantly have the feeling with her that I had missed some transition between plateaus in our relationship.

I was less than glib. "I took a walk on the beach and went to sleep on the sand."

"How romantic," she breathed.

"Alone," I said too quickly. "I was almost mugged by a couple of examples of our nation's most current and most ardent concern."

"Did you know that you sometimes talk in riddles? I assume you are referring to the homeless. You are telling me that you were accosted on the beach by two bums, is that right?"

"Are you using the word 'bums' because you think that's my word for them, or is it yours?" I was sincerely interested in her answer.

"You've got me, Mr. Holmes. I had the feeling you were being polite and wished to identify them for what they were. And I share the sentiment. Was I wrong?"

"Nope," I answered, "you were not wrong. You just didn't go far enough."

A tiny silence marked an end to the banter. I cleared my throat to keep something happening on my end of the line. I felt it was up to me to pick it up again.

"Say, Katherine, I'd like to run a name by you and see if it rings a bell," I said. "Wendell Leeds? Probably you would've heard Wen Leeds or just plain Wen. You recall ever hearing that name?"

There was an extended moment that was easy to read as memory searching, but could have been something else.

"No," she finally answered. "Is that someone Greg was supposed to know?"

"I think he was a diving buddy. Would that be a possibility?"

"Oh, yes, it could be. I didn't know all his diving friends. That was something he really did apart from me. What is the significance of this man?"

"Significance?"

"How did you come to know about this man?" she asked.

"I think he's the man in one of the photos you gave me," I answered. "Actually he might be in several of the pictures, but I haven't nailed it down yet."

"What if he is? What does it mean?" There was no fun and games left in her voice.

"That remains to be seen. It's just something I'm checking out." I decided to get off it. "You said you were wondering about some things?"

She paused briefly. "Nothing specific. I was just thinking about it all and feeling sort of helpless, you know? It was nothing. It was silly of me to call."

"No, no, call anytime," I hurriedly countered. "I just haven't got anything solid to tell you right now."

She let that hang out in midair for a moment. I was about to smother it with more blathering when she finally spoke, in a voice I liked a lot.

"Next time you take a walk along the beach, invite me. I like to walk on the beach, and I could watch over you while you sleep." It was so intimate, the way she said it, it made me wonder again if I had missed something.

"Sure," I responded. "Sure thing, Kate."

"Bye, Jake."

"Bye, Kate."

It was easy for me to forget that I was looking for her missing husband. I put the phone down and thought about a walk on the beach with Kate Burley. Maybe someday, I thought.

Jason was barely civil when he answered. He made no pretense of being awake. I knew people who always sounded as if they had just been waiting for your call, no matter what time of the day or night you called. Four o'clock in the morning and they would say, "No, you didn't wake me. I was just sitting here playing solitaire. I'm so glad you called." Not Jason. If you woke him, he told you about it.

"What do you think I am, a farmer?" he grumbled.

"Not in this lifetime," I answered. "I've got some interesting stuff to chat with you about."

"Chat? Where'd you get that word?" He was not about to
be in a good humor.

"What do you prefer, rap?"

He paused. "Yeah," he said. "I think I do."

"I'll come down tomorrow night. How's that for you?"

"Fine. I thought maybe after your defeat last time, you were
afraid of me," he said, lifting slightly.

"Yeah, but you're such fun to rap with it keeps me coming
back." I hung up before he did. It was nice not to worry about
the amenities sometimes.

I held the phone in my lap because I still had something I
had to do. The enlarged picture of Greg Burley and his diving
buddy stared at me from the coffee table. I was stalling, sure,
because my next moves scared me a little. It was like walking
into a dark room I'd never seen before. I did not like to think
what it meant if I connected Wendell Leeds with Greg Burley.
I did not like the feeling of groping. I did not like the feeling
in my bones.

I knew I should call Tex Flanagan on this. I knew it in a
logical way. I even started twice to dial his number. Both
times I stopped myself. I had more thinking to do. I needed
more information. I needed to satisfy some of my own questions first, or maybe just raise some new ones. I gave myself
more time to think.

When I did make another call it was not to Tex Flanagan. It
was to Bob Claiborne.

*   *   *

"Hey, Jake," Bob called from the far end of the terrace at
the Tennis Club of Santa Barbara. I walked in his direction
while keeping one eye on the fine tennis being played on the
court just below.

"Not bad, huh?" He indicated the two players on court one.

"Not bad," I agreed.

"You know, just now watching those guys, I realized something I've been doing wrong on my volley. See how the lefty keeps his elbow forward? There, see that? That's what I haven't been doing. I've been letting my elbow down. It's the little things, Jake. Always the little things that make the difference."

I nodded as if he were making sense. As if keeping his elbow forward would make a bit of difference. As if the game Bob Claiborne played and the game the two Young Turks below us were playing had anything in common. I nodded again, and I tried not to smile.

"So, big guy, what's this about? Don't tell me you're thinking of selling? Don't do that now without giving it a chance over there." He was hard-pressed to keep his eyes off the action below.

I pointed to a table around the corner where we could talk, and where he could not see the tennis. "Over there, Bob. This'll only take a minute."

He followed obediently and good-naturedly. He was a good man, I tried to tell myself, though a little foolish and vain.

"You look serious," he said. "Nothing's wrong, I hope."

"Nothing's wrong," I assured him, "at least not with me. I want to ask you about Wendell Leeds. You said, if I remember correctly, that you were handling his house for him when he got killed. Is that right?"

"Wendell Leeds? Yeah, sure, that's right."

"Are you still handling it?"

"Well, no, it's not on the market anymore. It will be again probably when the estate is probated, but it's frozen now. Why, you know someone who's interested?"

"Me," I answered simply.

"You? I don't get it. You think you want to buy another house?"

"No, but I'm interested in Wendell Leeds's house. Do you think I could see it?" I tried to keep it casual.

"No, I don't think so, Jake. We're not empowered to show the house anymore."

"You still have the keys, don't you?"

He gave me a look of bewilderment. I countered with wide eyes.

"We are entrusted with the keys, yes, but we can't show the place. I'm sorry, Jake, but as soon as the court stuff is finished I'll put you at the top of the list. You'll be the first to see it when it goes back on the market, I promise."

"That's not good enough, Bob," I said more firmly than I intended. "I want to see it now."

"I just can't, Jake."

"It's a favor, Bob," I said with all the implications the word could carry.

He stared at me as if I had broken his heart. At first he shook his head slightly, but after a moment he grew still. His mind worked then as I knew it eventually would. I read the man too well. Self had a way of entering all Bob's considerations.

"This would make us square," he said.

I nodded, liking him less for it.

"When?" he asked, now conspiratorially.

"Tonight."

"Jeez, you can't see a house at night, Jake. Let's do it when you can see the place."

"Wouldn't you rather no one knew I was looking at it?" The question was unnecessary.

"Yeah, right."

"I'd prefer it that way too, if you don't mind. Let's keep this between the two of us, shall we?"

He nodded. "I'll drop the keys in your mailbox, okay? Get them back to me tomorrow if you can."

"You'll have them back tomorrow. By the way, you might also leave me one of those information sheets on the house, if you have one, and an alarm key or code if it's set," I said, and got to my feet. I put out my hand. "Thanks, Bob."

He took it and said, "This makes us even, Jake. Don't forget that."

"How could I ever?" I said, knowing the irony would miss him by a mile.

• • •

I worked out. I swam. I ran. I went through the motions of a normal day. I tried to suppress the bubble of excitement that was rising within me. I knew this stage of the game well. It was where the truth began.

After a small evening meal of pasta with a pesto sauce flavored with crushed walnuts, a lettuce salad, and fruit, I settled down with the Claiborne Realty sales presentation on the Wendell Leeds property. The information sheet I had asked for turned out to be a slick two-page brochure with good-quality photography, plus a separate sheet with the floor plan. It was more than I could have wished for, in that it gave me good preparatory information. I would not be going into the house cold.

I studied the layout of the house, the room sizes, the access points front and back. It was an estate, set well back off Faring Lane. I could see that I would need a few hours to do it right. On the floor plan I marked the key areas for my attention. I especially wanted thorough looks at the study, master suite, garage, and kitchen. There was much I had to learn about Wendell Leeds, and I felt I could learn most of it in those areas.

I made a small belt pack for myself. Along with the keys Bob had left, I put in a strong flashlight, a roll of Scotch tape, a pocketknife, a Canon half-frame camera loaded with high-speed Ektachrome, and my pocket recorder with fresh batteries and fresh tape. Then I waited with a cup of coffee for my mind to clear. Controlled breathing and the visualization of cloud formations did the trick, as it always had since my early training days in a South Carolina swamp.

At full dark, I donned navy blue sweats and headed for the Leeds property. I ran along the side of the street as a late-night jogger might. I did not intend to be seen, but if I was, I wanted something fairly plausible.

It was a couple of miles to Leeds's place, uphill and down, and the slow trot felt good. It loosened cobwebs and freed tensions by the time I got there. I stopped in front of the property for a quick look-see at the control box outside the gate, which housed a phone, alarm keypad, and key slot for the gate. Thanks to Claiborne's meticulous labeling I had no trouble finding the right keys. The gate swung open majestically. "Open Sesame," I said to myself as I walked in.

I entered by the front door and used all the thirty seconds of delay time finding the alarm shutoff. I got the alarm key in and turned just in time; the red light blinked to green as sweat began to trickle down my back. I hurried to the kitchen, following my memory of the floor plan and the beam of my flashlight. I found the master unit of the intercom and turned it on. Each switch was identified with a tiny label, obviously written by a person with a small hand and perfect eyesight. I squinted at the labels until I was finally able to focus enough to make them out. I found a button marked "Gate" and pushed it. I held down the listen switch and heard the gate closing. I turned off the intercom and relaxed.

I looked around the kitchen. It was some kitchen. The brochure said "gourmet," and I suppose that's what it was, but to my eye it was a bit too much for a house. It had two Sub-Zeros side by side. They were vintage models, but those two babies could hold enough cold and frozen food for a year. Nobody needed that much refrigerator. There was a six-burner commercial gas range with an additional electric two-burner and grill. The counter tiles and sinks were slightly old-fashioned, as were the cabinets. I was a little surprised to see that the kitchen had not been remodeled. I was sure it had been state-of-the-art when the house was built, but I read Leeds as having been a high-tech, modern fellow. Old-fashioned or not, the kitchen looked as clean and new as a showroom.

I found the pantry. This guy must have thought war was imminent he was so well-stocked. My respect for him sagged a bit when I spotted several jars of instant coffee.

The kitchen did not tell me much. It was too obviously the domain of a hired cook, and maid, and what have you. This was not a place where a guy slopped together a B.L.T. for lunch. Maybe the instant coffee was the cook's idea. I looked it over though, from top to bottom. I looked in every drawer and cupboard. The china, crystal, silver, and even the cookware were all top-notch. I was reminded of one of Trinia's observations: "It's in the kitchen where you can tell if someone really has money or not." Well, Trinia would have agreed with me. This guy had had it, loads of it.

I referred to the floor plan. I worked my way from room to room through the west wing. The master suite was upstairs at the far end of the house. The master bedroom was not all that impressive. It did, however, have the same orderly, unlived-in look as the kitchen. "Immaculate," I suppose, was the word that most fit it. The closets, bureau drawers, bathroom cabinets—all were so carefully organized they did not look real. I was beginning to feel it would have taken a very precise man to live in this house. My first assessments of him as he lay dying that night had been fairly true to the mark, it seemed.

I found a "hide-a-stair" in the ceiling of a closet. I pulled the cord, which produced a nicely crafted set of retractable steps. I didn't expect to find much in the attic, and I didn't. It was a tight fit up there, with a crosswork of pipes and electrical wires, but nothing struck me as being out of the ordinary. I felt a slight tug of pessimism as I came down from the attic and replaced the stair.

I gave the master suite a good once-over. Nothing turned up that even hinted I was on the right track. I slowed myself down and tried to think more of the fellow I had seen with the life running out of him on Faring Lane. Most of what I knew of Wendell Leeds I knew from those moments. I replayed the episode on that little movie screen behind the eyelids.

Finally, something began to seep into my memory about him. It sent me back into his closets for another look. I began a search in earnest through all his dressers and cabinets. The more I looked without success, the stronger my need for discovery grew. I went back to the main closet, a large walk-in affair with three walls of hanging clothes, a large center dressing area, and the "hide-a-stair" tucked neatly into the ceiling.

I stood in that center area and moved my light carefully around the walls. It would have been easy to miss had I not been so convinced that it had to be there. I pushed aside the clothes on the rack to give me access to the wall. I felt around; I pushed and prodded, to no avail. I moved my light about some more. I found it along the baseboard. It was a small plastic loop of the same color as the baseboard, almost undetectable. I bent down and pulled it. The upper section of the wall released. Two piano-hinged doors opened out, exposing a compartment of about four feet by four feet hidden in the wall.

I shone the light in on the shelves of Styrofoam heads. Each wore a slightly different toupee. There was a progression in them which ran from a fresh haircut to a rather shaggy need of one. This was no ordinary wig collection. This was a man's deep secret, calculated to an extraordinary degree.

Once I overcame my amazement, I checked the secret chamber more closely. There was nothing there but the wigs. I closed it again, carefully and almost respectfully. I couldn't help but be touched by the discipline such deception must have demanded.

I looked at my watch and was startled to see it was one A.M. I had been inside for two hours already without any real success. I would have to make some choices and move more quickly. I still wanted to check the garage, and I definitely wanted some time in the study. As I left the master suite, I did as I had done with the other phones I found in the house. I pushed the redial button. As with the others, there was no answer.

It was not your run-of-the-mill study. It was a large room with a library section at one end and a high-tech area at the other. A large partner's desk was more or less centered in the room. I did not know where to start.

I worked my way around the room, studying the framed pictures, hung in perfect symmetry along the wall, for a familiar face. I ignored the books, and the computer and attendant technology, because I did not have the time or the expertise. I wound up where I should have started, at the desk.

Neat beyond belief, as I expected. Also the most impersonal desk I had ever seen. This was not a working desk, merely furniture where someone sat. To do what? I wondered. I sat in the chair and tried to get a feeling for what Wendell Leeds might have done here. I found carefully filed correspondence which meant nothing to me, address books which were dated, meaning that he updated them on a regular basis, and various papers of the odds-and-ends variety. I checked over the address books, hoping a name here or there would ring a bell. After a few pages it was clear we moved in different circles.

I beamed my flashlight on the dial pad of the phone on the left corner of the desk. It was one of those speaker phones with a built-in memory storage for the numbers most often called. I noted that no names had been entered in the slots next to the speed-dial buttons. He either had not taken the time to enter the numbers or, for one reason or another, had not wanted to. I checked out the other functions and found the redial button. As I had done with all the other phones, I pushed it.

While the last number on this phone had called was being redialed, I took out my little tape recorder and stuck the suction mike to the receiver. I had it set to record by the time the strange bouncing tones of the numbers being dialed concluded.

It was all perfunctory, since I was not expecting the phone to be answered. I barely held the instrument up to my ear as I cast my light about the room, ready to transfer my attentions. I had already figured that odds were the last call on this phone had been made by someone other than Wendell Leeds: a police officer investigating the murder, a maid, a real estate person. I could imagine the phone ringing in some office somewhere with no one around but the cleaning lady.

What I did not expect was what I got. The sleep-heavy voice at the other end said, "Hello?" and for half a second my brain ceased to function.

"Hello?" came the voice from the phone. "Is anyone there? Hello? Hello?" Silence for a moment, and then the click followed by the dial tone.

I did not breathe. I don't think my blood flowed. I was as still as I knew how to be. Time, too, seemed to have slowed to a stop.

I did the mechanical things then. I replaced the receiver. I disconnected the suction mike. I pushed rewind, and I sat back to listen to the voice again. I did not need to. I knew it only too well.

For some reason I played it back again and again, as if I were supposed to. Finally, I sat with it and let it become part of the truth. My senses were dulled, but my imagination brought the scents of honeysuckle and jasmine to me. They went with the voice.

I had what I came for. I concluded that I had all I needed from Wendell Leeds's house for the time being. I was preparing to leave, when lights hit the windows. With a quick look through the shutters I could see a car pulling into the driveway. I moved into the hallway.

I crouched and listened to the sounds. I could hear the door being opened with a key. There was no stealth here; someone was entering quite normally. A light came on, and I heard the footsteps, one, two, three, to the control panel. There was a moment then when I could hear nothing. I imagined that someone was trying to figure out why the alarm was not on. Then the footsteps again, heavy on the marble entry floor, moving away from me. There was another sound which took a moment to identify. It was the jingle of keys hanging from a belt. I followed the sounds to the kitchen, where another light was turned on.

I was curious. I walked as furtively as I knew how, to a place where I could see a portion of the kitchen at an angle through the breakfast room door. I heard the rummaging in the refrigerator before I could get a look at the rummager. Then I saw a uniformed patrolman carry his loot to the counter to create his own version of a meal.

There was something ghoulish about it, to my way of thinking. Here was this security guard using the stores of a dead man as his own private restaurant. I was not forming a very high opinion of the Coco Palms patrol of late. It was the same patrolman who had answered the alarm at my house. I tried to recall his name. Stanner, it was. Fred Stanner.

He was a quick and sloppy eater. I could see him wipe at his mess in a halfhearted way before he left my field of vision. I heard the pantry door open, and what I imagined to be more rummaging. The heavy footsteps sounded again, accompanied by the jingling keys. The light in the kitchen went out, and Fred Stanner once more came into view heading down the hall toward the front door. He carried a large sack, which was no doubt filled with items he had taken from the pantry. It was his grocery store as well, it seemed. I heard him hesitate at the control panel. He was probably trying to decide if he should set the alarm or not. I hoped he would not, because I was not familiar with the locations of the interior traps and movement sensors.

As soon as the foyer light went out I edged toward it. Even as Patrolman Piggy was exiting the door, I was moving in to the control panel. No red light. He had opted to leave it as he found it. It spoke to me of a cunning and devious nature. No surprise there, not after watching him steal the food. I waited while he put his groceries into his car, started it, and slowly drove through the gates.

I let a few minutes pass before I too took my leave from the estate of the late Wendell Leeds. My impressions would take some sorting out. Upon first speculation it seemed that Wendell Leeds had put little of himself into his property. He had not altered it at all to meet what I had assumed to be a very modern, ahead-of-the-trend inclination. I threw that into the already overfilled basket of things to consider in the future.

I took extra precautions as I slipped out of the gate. I made sure no eyes were on me as I moved into an easy lope away. I fell into an easy rhythm, letting my feet carry me on an uneventful run home. My only difficulty came with what was working in my brain. The throaty voice still breathed against my ear. Around me the air was alive with the fragrances I had so long enjoyed. The fragrances of citrus blossoms, and night-blooming jasmine, and honeysuckle and Katherine Burley.

12 🔥

I awoke about nine, which was late for me, from that lousy kind of sleep that drains out all vitality. It left me with a sort of deep ache in my back somewhere I could not identify exactly. I was listless and indecisive, not wanting to get up but definitely not wanting to stay in bed. The pool proved to be the right place for me to be.

I swam longer and harder than usual. There was something angry in the deep strokes I took, yet oddly cathartic. When I finished, I sat dripping on the chaise, letting my wind and my heartbeat return to normal. By the clock it took a short time, but locked within my mind as I was, idle moments ran to eternity.

My phone rang.

"Jake?" Those who knew me were onto the fact that often I did not answer in conventional fashion. I was usually of the mind that the caller was the one who had something to say, so it was the caller who should speak. A silly premise, but one I leaned on when I was in a sour mental state. The caller spoke again. "Jake, how are you? It's Vera."

My spirits lifted instantly. I said, "Your timing's perfect, old pal, absolutely perfect."

"Hey, watch that 'old' crap. I get enough of that from my mirror." Years of bourbon whiskey and unfiltered cigarettes had made the voice. Life had made the woman. "You ever gonna have anybody see that place of yours, or is it so fagged up you're embarrassed by it?"

"Yep, Lonnie struck again," I said.

"Now don't tell me he did it in silks and laces. He knows what a macho type you are."

"To tell you the truth, I don't know what was Lonnie's doing and what was Albert's. All I know is this house just barely puts up with me."

"You know, according to Lonnie, there is no better architect in the world than Albert. He just did that singer's house. You know, the slut that struts? The blonde that looks like a hooker on a bad night?" She gave me a moment to reflect. "Anyway, friend, you should be proud and willing to show it off. Now when is the big bash?"

"I don't do that anymore, Vera. My party days are all behind me, I'm afraid."

"You simp, you have to have a housewarming," she barked. "It's unnatural to do what I've heard you're doing."

"Jason, right?"

"He for one. Word is you've stopped living. Why, Jake? You were always one of the guys Henry, God rest his soul, relied on to always be you. You were the center of our gatherings, didn't you know that?"

"No," I laughed, "and I'm not buying your line of bull either."

Her voice took on a more serious tone. "You never knew how much Henry valued your friendship, did you? He used to sit and talk about you after everyone else had gone. He used to quote you from the evening. Can you imagine that? Here I'd be getting ready for bed and Henry is repeating your bon mots as if they were worth hearing again. It was your character he loved. He used to say you were the last man of honor he knew."

"That hardly makes a party animal, Vera," I said.

"Well, I admit you were seldom the life of the party, but there was always something in the way you listened and watched, and always laughed at the subtle, good stuff that went over everyone else's head. The stuff that Henry was so good at." She threw in the last part with a kind of soft chuckle. "You and Henry seemed always to have a secret going. And Jason, of course. The three of you always seemed to be on a different wavelength from the rest of us."

"You flatter me, Vera. There was no one with a mind like Henry's. I sat at his feet, intellectually," I stated honestly.

"Enough of this crap," she said. She loved the word "crap." It was just common enough for her to feel earthy. "I want an answer. When do I get to see that place of yours?"

I wanted to see her. I wanted to hear more of her laugh and remember with her some of the wonderful evenings I had spent in her home with her and her husband and friends.

"You name it," I said.

"How about tonight?" she responded. "You can't say no, because I've got it all arranged. I took a certain liberty and lined up a few people. You see how well I know you, my dear? I know that it is very rare for you to make plans more than a few hours in advance. Also, with your new bent for isolationism I just knew you'd be home. Now, Jason's is closed tonight, so I'll pick him up and bring him with me along with all the food and drink. Lonnie and Albert are dying to see how you're living with their work, and there'll be Sebastian and Lorna, Lorna's new man, Fabio or Fabian or whatever, and a friend of mine you don't know, an actress, but not a ditz. You'll like her, she's a knockout. And letmeseeisthereanyoneelse? No. That's it, unless you have someone you want. So let's do it on the early side. Say sevenish, so we can see the outside and not stumble off into the ocean or whatever you have there. Okay, sweet?"

"Okay, Vera," I said, as usual overwhelmed by her. "I'm looking forward to it. Just one thing, if you will? When you pick up Jason, tell him I said for him to bring his kit."

"His what? His kit?"

"He'll know what I mean. See you at seven," I said.

" 'Bye," she croaked, and was gone.

The perfect tonic for a depleted psyche.

I did some dusting and straightening, knowing that it didn't make any difference but doing it all the same. I took a quick trip to the market for some odds and ends. I wanted to be sure to have Taittinger blanc de blanc and Jack Daniel's for Vera. She loved and drank both but seemed always to want the one that was not on hand. I got Glenlivet for Jason, Campari for Lonnie, Dubonnet for Albert, a nice Montrachet for Sebastian, and ginger beer for Lorna. Fabio and Vera's actress friend would have to take potluck. I picked up some of those cheeses that no one ever buys for themselves, some fresh nonexotic fruits, and a new blend of espresso beans.

The checker, who popped her gum, gave me the eye. I guess I hit a homer with something I was buying. She double-popped as she rang it up and handed me back the change. I hurried out before she went for a triple.

My afternoon workout started out as real labor. I warmed up with calisthenics. I still did the old-fashioned kind that started with jumping jacks and ended with double-clap push-ups. I stretched, but according to the new breed of sinew-and-bone-conditioning experts, my form of stretching was heresy. I even did the full-range sit-ups, in this age of quarter lifts where the lift is finished when the shoulders rise off the floor.

I thought of those things as the sweat began to bead and pour. I thought of the way some people constantly fiddled with stuff, fixing what wasn't broken until it was all in ruins. The fools who would forever go for the latest thing, shedding what fit for what was in. I had heard of some of the poor saps of yesterday who had spent fortunes on Nehru jackets storing them in cedar closets, waiting for the style to be revived. And there were those of today who let themselves buy the lumpy, ultrawide-shouldered coats that made them look like un-masked circus clowns. The more I thought about all this, the less I watched the workout clock.

I hit the heavy bag hard, feeling the impact in my shoulder. There was still a hint of pain, enough to remind me not to overdo. The ribs were fine, and my wind was improving. I still turned red and wanted to die after a hard drill, but each day there were tiny signs of improvement.

I ended with a little ropework. I was still wheezing and gasping for air when I collapsed onto the tiled bench in the steam room, ready to feel the spirit leave me any moment. Why did I do it? I asked myself. I was too tired to answer.

My recovery time wasn't bad. The half hour in the steam, another ten minutes to cool off, and five under the shower made me feel almost human. I lay back on the bed long enough to dry off completely before dressing. I closed my eyes to take a few moments of relaxation . . . only a couple of minutes . . .

I reached out at the noise. It was shrill and persistent. My hand came back with the phone, but my mind was still struggling with important things like, where was I? and who was I? I growled, thinking I was saying something in a clear wide-awake manner.

"Jake? Are you okay? Jake?"

The voice penetrated. It struck a nerve deep inside. I sat up. "Sure," I lied, not knowing yet if I was alive or dead. "Hi, Kate."

Her laugh convinced me I was alive. "What was that god-awful sound? It was hardly human."

"That was my pet," I said with a wild look at my watch. What time was it? What day? "I let him answer the phone from time to time."

She laughed again, even better than before. "Jake, you're either drunk or I caught you sleeping. Which is it?"

"Drunk," I replied. "I never sleep."

"Not at night anyway, is that it? You poor thing, don't you

know what comes from burning the candle at both ends?"

I recited " 'I burn my candle at both ends; it burns both day and night; but, oh, my foes, and, oh, my friends; it makes a lovely light.' Or something like that."

"Yes, something like that," she said. "Jake? Are you doing anything tonight? I thought we might meet someplace for dinner. I've sort of got the blues."

"You, the blues?" I tried to imagine if that was possible. "Women like you don't get the blues, Kate, you give them."

I braced myself for that back-of-the-throat chuckle, but it didn't come. The voice lowered though, and caught me with an uppercut. "Am I out of line, Jake? Did I presume too much?"

I was awake at last—not that I was any better off. That sensation she caused in me settled somewhere around the middle of my chest. It reminded me of the feeling I used to get on the downgrade of a roller coaster. What was it she had presumed? I wondered.

"No," I managed, "you're not out of line. I have some people coming over tonight, sort of a housewarming. Would you like to come?"

"Oh, no, I don't want to impose. I thought if you weren't busy we could have dinner. Another time," she said quickly.

"I want you to come," I said almost as quickly.

"Really?" A tiny pause. "Jake, are you sure about this?"

Her voice from the night before replayed inside my brain. *Hello? Is anyone there? Hello? Hello?* "I'm sure. About seven."

"I don't know if I should," she breathed. "Would anyone be there that I might know?"

"Jason."

"Oh, yes, Jason Meddler." She hesitated. "Can I think about it?"

"Sure. You come if you feel like it. You're welcome, and we'll be here."

I put the phone down and lay back with eyes open. The roller coaster plunged downward. I was on a wild ride.

• • •

The cars arrived together, with Vera's in the lead. She had a new limo and a new driver since the last time I had seen her, but then it had been a few years.

It felt good. We were all older, and different in so many ways, but there was a lot of it that played on familiar chords. There was that commotion which is part of arriving, when car doors are being slammed, and hellos are being said, and packages of things are being carried inside, and the oohs and aahs are being uttered. The hugs and handshakes brought back the old days when there were regular get-togethers. It made me think of family reunions, and Sunday dinners, and the kinds of occasions that normal people experienced. It gave me a feeling of warmth and well-being, but in a way it also made me feel like a fraud. I was a loner stealing a few fleeting moments of fellowship from this strange and diverse group.

Vera, of course, took charge. "Jake, this is Fabio, Lorna's squeeze—isn't that what they say these days? Isn't he a doll? And here, Jake, you must say hello to Melissa. Melissa, this is the infamous Jake Sands you've heard so much about." Vera whirled and turned, stirring us all with her great energy. She directed what was to be carried in, and where it was to be put. She had my kitchen under complete control in a matter of minutes, and in a few minutes more had command of my entire house. "Put on your Glenn Miller or your Nat King Cole, darling. Keep it soft though, I hate to be drowned with music."

I tried my hand at being a host by offering drinks, but Vera shooed me out. "Let Sebastian. He knows what everyone drinks in this group, don't you, Sebby?"

I couldn't imagine anyone calling that huge, dignified man Sebby. Anyone but Vera, that is. He smiled and responded, "I do indeed, my dear Vera, and I would be delighted to serve. Jake, I see you've put an ample supply here at our disposal."

I drifted into that closed-focus zone where things continue to happen but in a detailed sort of way. I settled in the living room next to Jason, who had been delivered his Glenlivet on ice first. Together we watched and listened with a shared sense of amusement at the general ado. We had the same eye, Jason and I, for human eccentricity. It made us smile in tandem at the acerbic wit of Lonnie and the reproving glances he received from Albert. We both noted the obvious interest Fabio was beginning to display in Melissa, and the arched brows of Lorna. It was fun. We both felt it, and we both needed it.

"I see what you mean about this house. You look about as much at home here as I would in a nunnery," he said.

"Wait'll you see the rest of it."

"I brought the kit," he said. "Now?"

"Later," I said. "There's no hurry."

Vera announced it was tour time, so everyone, with glass in hand, followed behind Lonnie, who took over as guide. He led us through the house, pointing out features of which he was very proud. Here and there Albert mentioned an architectural detail he thought we might have missed. Jason was practically bursting with supremacist glee. Lonnie led us into my workout room and disclaimed it immediately.

"Oh my, you must let me do this room properly. This is all so primitive," he minced. "What is that awful thing hanging there?"

"That's a heavy bag," I said. "It suits my needs, Lonnie."

"You've absolutely nothing here," he whined. "You've no Stairmaster, no treadmill, no Lifecycle. Really, dear boy you must let me do it right."

"I'm old-fashioned," I explained. I turned and left them to it. I could bear no more.

Jason hooted as he wheeled along behind me on my way back to the living room. I gave him a resentful look which only increased his amusement.

"Dear boy," he mimicked, "you are so déclassé." He loved to get a needle into me.

I settled onto the sectional with a shake of my head. "That workout room is the only room in this house I feel at home in. He calls it primitive. I guess that makes me a caveman."

"That's pretty close to it," Jason responded. "Let me tell you something. I kinda like your digs here. It may not be exactly you, but it's damned nice. I don't know what this style would be called—maybe Hawaiian modern or something, with all the lava rock—but I gotta tell you, old boy, I like it."

He meant it. It made me feel better about the place.

After the others had made their tour of the grounds and taken in the view of the ocean and the islands, they joined Jason and me in the living room. The praise for the place went, appropriately enough, to the proud parents of it, Lonnie and Albert. I was still the stranger there.

The evening moved on with me sitting around the edges of it as usual. The others drank their drinks, I my coffee, and topics were thrown into the center of the room and attacked from all angles until shredded and dismissed. For the most part I listened and let my guests express their outrages and delights. I became drowsy with the peacefulness of the evening. It was a comfortable place to be.

It wasn't until Vera mentioned dinner, and she and Sebastian began to put it out buffet style, that I thought about Katherine. I looked at my watch and saw it was nine o'clock. I had not really expected her. I wasn't even sure I had really wanted her to come. I still had not been able to put my thoughts in order from the night before.

I watched Fabio's casual flirtation with Melissa. Lorna watched it too. How many evenings in the past, I thought, had I watched similar scenes play themselves out. I wondered idly how many murders had resulted from just such evenings.

It seemed Fabio had been in movies in Italy. "It is a wonderful business, no?" he asked Melissa in his heavily accented English.

She trilled her laugh as only a woman much flattered could do. "I wouldn't say the business is wonderful all the time.

When you're working, then yes, it's the greatest, but when you're not it's the pits."

There were certain phrases I disliked, especially from women. "It's the pits," was one of them.

Fabio laughed a practiced laugh. "The pits? That is true, but you, I am sure, with your beauty cannot know the pits."

Inwardly, I gagged. Outwardly, Jason raised his eyebrows and tossed back the rest of the Glenlivet in his glass. The doorbell rang.

From the moment I brought Katherine Burley into the living room, the evening was different. There was a sudden and obvious center to everyone's attention, even Vera's. Katherine's grace managed to infect us all in some strange way.

Vera said, "I'm so glad you came, you beautiful thing you, because he's been moping around here all evening. I didn't know what was wrong with him, but now I can understand. I thought those sneaky looks at his watch were hints for us to leave."

Katherine's eyes sought mine as if to say, oh? "I'm sorry I'm late. Am I too late for food?" She managed to include everyone in her question.

In unison everyone answered, "No, of course not."

It seemed that they all rushed to the table to fetch a plate for her. Actually, it was Vera who did so.

It was also Vera who did the inquisition. "So, my dear, just how long have you know my boy Jake? You must understand, I am like his mother and I must know everything." Vera's own brand of charm was so practiced and polished it was endurable. She posed her question as she handed over a plate of food.

Katherine smiled without being coquettish. "Not long," she answered. "You must tell me about him."

Vera laughed her loud, whiskey-voice laugh. "Oh, my dear, if I did, you wouldn't believe me."

Fabio broke in, "You must be actress in films, no?" His perfect teeth gleamed out of his perfectly tanned face.

All she said was, "No," but with that one word and with

one quick look in his direction she dismissed him totally. It was the kind of thing that made a giggle rise in the throat.

Vera moved in closer to Katherine and said, "So, Kate—is it Kate or do you hate that?" She waited for Katherine to accept the name before she continued. "So, Kate, let me tell you about this group of strangers you've fallen in with here."

I relaxed inside. Vera had the reins. She gave an amusing and comprehensive bio on everyone there, telling it all in a way that both flattered and teased. I had forgotten how bright and bold Vera was, and what a knack she had for making a room come to life.

I drifted to the edge again, while the others kicked around the state of the world today. Kate joined in. She had opinions and voiced them as strongly as the others did. There was much debate and much agreement. It became an evening reminiscent of the many such nights spent with Vera and Henry.

The evening began to break up slowly, with Lonnie and Albert making their departure first. It was a long trip back to Hollywood at that hour and the day began early for them, they said. I saw them to the door and thanked them. Next Lorna dragged Fabio out. He had reversed his field again and made a move on Melissa who, having seen the example set by Kate, was having none of it. Lorna would most likely be alone the next time I saw her. Sebastian agreed to see Melissa home. She claimed to have an early interview for a commercial. It was my feeling that she simply wanted to get out of the reflective glare of Kate's beauty. At last it was just the four of us: Vera, Jason, Kate, and me.

"Let's move it outside," Vera said. "It's time I switched to champagne. How about you, my dear? Do you like champagne?" I could hear the slight slur in her voice. The Jack Daniel's had had its effect.

"I love champagne," Kate answered.

"Under the stars," Vera announced. "It's warm and beautiful outside. You can have one of your awful cigars, Jason. Turn up your music, Jake. It goes with this night."

We did as we were ordered. She was right, it was a flawless night. I took the champagne bucket, the Glenlivet, ice, and my coffee outside with us. We settled back to enjoy it.

Jason said, "Jake, we better do the check before I get too buzzed to pick it up." He sounded a bit buzzed as it was, so I could see the wisdom in his suggestion.

"Excuse us," I said. "We have a little chore. We'll be right back."

Inside, Jason opened his case and began to prepare the machine. "What's got you spooked?"

I kept it vague. "A visitor," I said. "A few nights ago. Nothing missing."

"Ah," he said as he adjusted a dial and put on a headset. "Well, let's see what we can find."

He moved himself around the house with the intuition that only a master of the art developed. This sort of thing had been his area of expertise. He had always loved the gadgets, and he had always been good with them.

As he worked his way around, I stood by the open French doors and listened to the muted conversation between Vera and Kate. "He was married?" Kate asked.

"Oh yes," Vera answered, taking a deep breath before beginning the story. "She was lovely, like you, my dear. Young and already a widow with a child when Jake met her. Her husband had been a flyer, I believe, killed on some sort of training mission. A real tragedy. Jake met her at a ceremony at that marine base down the coast. El Toro, is it? Her name was Trinia. Lovely, isn't it?"

I heard Kate say, "Yes, lovely. Tell me about it." I knew Vera was sipping her champagne and was probably studying Kate over the rim of her glass.

"They had a wonderful marriage, Trinia and Jake. He loved that little Josh like nothing you've ever seen. You'd never have known the boy wasn't his own. They even looked a little alike." She made one of her chortling sounds, followed by a pause for another sip at her champagne. "I can see the three of them still, walking along holding hands. They always held hands."

"How long were they married?"

"Four or five years. Trinia was expecting a child too. Eight months pregnant and a thing like that happens. God, it makes you wonder." Vera let it hang there. I imagined she was refilling her glass, possibly Kate's as well.

"They died?" Katherine asked.

"They were killed. Murdered in a fire. A man named Clyde Walls did it out of revenge. The guilt of it almost killed Jake."

"Revenge?" Kate asked. "Revenge for what?"

"You don't know much about Jake, do you? Well, I'm not surprised. Most people call him the Sphinx." Vera took a short moment. "He recovered things. Most of the time it was for people who had won court awards or settlements or some such thing. The Clyde Walls thing was of that ilk. He chased him up to Alaska and brought back all the things the man had stolen."

"When did they die?" Kate's voice sounded deep and hoarse.

"Four years ago, more or less." Vera's voice too took on the deep tones of somberness. "Jake was away when it happened. I thought he wouldn't survive it. I wasn't sure until tonight that he had."

"You mean you haven't seen him since it happened?"

"Not since the funeral, no," Vera said. "He broke all ties except with Jason. Then he went after Clyde Walls. That was probably the only thing that saved him."

"He chased a man for four years?"

"Oh no, my dear," Vera said with the gentleness of a nanny. "For most of that time, he was eliminating other possibilities. It was only in the last year that he was able to verify who did it. I understand he found him someplace in South America."

It took a moment for me to realize that Jason had moved up beside me. He sat silently listening with me to Vera.

"Well?" I asked.

Jason nodded and held out his hand. He had found three

bugs. One had been attached to the phone line. The others were room mikes. I examined them but could not immediately identify the make. I walked with Jason back to the living room and put them close to the music, before we rejoined Vera and Kate outside. Both women seemed affected by the champagne.

"So what was it, Jason?" Vera asked. "Did you find anything?"

She was so direct and open it sometimes startled me. Jason simply laughed and avoided answering directly. "It's a grand house, Vera. Sound as can be." He reached in his pocket for his cigar, held it up, and asked, "Anybody mind?" No one did so he teased the tip of the cigar with the lighter flame. After a puff or two he sat back in contentment with his glass of Glenlivet and a glowing cigar.

I stayed somewhat in the background, both physically and psychologically. I was wrestling with the concept of someone bugging my house. I was already working on the possibles.

"Is something wrong?" Kate asked, noting my withdrawal.

Jason explained. "Some poor fool has chosen to annoy our Jake. I pity the poor bastard, I can tell you that."

"Pity? Why pity?" Kate asked, still asea.

Jason laughed. "Oh, Kate my girl, they don't know who they're messing with. They just don't know."

Kate turned toward me. She stared into the shadow, where I remained, as if she could see me. Finally she said with a teasing lilt, "Who are they messing with, Jake? Who are you?"

I shrugged. I was not feeling sociable at the moment. I was feeling a surge of anger that someone would bug my house. I turned and walked inside. I looked down at the tiny transmitter microphones for a moment before I smashed my heel down on them, smashed them until they were flat and useless.

I carried out a fresh carafe of coffee to cover my absence, and held it up in offering. All three waved a rejection at me. I settled down to join the silence. There was still Nat King Cole, and the waves breaking down below, but in our little group there was silence.

Silence was not one of Vera's favorite things. She held up the bottle and offered, "Champagne?"

Kate said, "No, I really must go. I had no idea it had gotten so late."

They made their goodbyes, and I saw her to her car.

"You must tell me about you sometime," she said. "I want to know you."

"And you must tell me about you, Kate," I responded with more intensity than it required. "I want to know you too."

"There's no mystery to me, Jake."

"No?"

"Is something wrong tonight?" she asked suddenly. "I'm getting very strange vibes from you."

"What could be wrong?"

She slid her hands up behind my neck. She stared at me in that completely focused way she had. I tried to stare back but my knees were on the weak side. I was a teenager again and at the mercy of Mary Kaye McGee, who knew about boys, and French kissing, and petting in the backseats of cars. The sweat broke along my spine. She pulled me to her and kissed me sweetly on the lips.

She was well out of the driveway before I realized what a gentle kiss it had been. It took that long for the jumble to settle inside my brain.

Jason took one look and said, "Look out, old boy, you've got that zombie stare."

Vera was politer. "She's a lovely girl, Jake."

The use of the term, "girl" was not lost on me. I replied, "And married, Vera. She's a lovely, married girl."

Vera said, "You were a mere boy when Henry and Jason recruited you into that special unit of theirs. I still feel responsible for you. You understand that, don't you?"

Jason and I nodded in the same way. We were both remembering Henry and our ill-fated group.

"Henry chose a good name for it," she said. "Orion. The hunter. I always thought that was so fitting." She sipped at her drink. There was a trace of bitterness in her voice as she continued. "It was a good idea . . . if they had let you go ahead and finish the job."

"You forget, Vera," Jason said in a sober voice, "everyone in the Orion unit was killed except Jake and me and Henry, of course."

"Dear Jason. You *almost* died. You'll never know how Henry suffered over that." Vera shook her head at the memory of it. "He took that guilt to the grave with him. Henry was academia. He should never have been involved directly with it."

"It was his idea, and the President asked him. How could he not be part of it?" Jason asked, a little cruelly, I thought.

"Oh, you're right, of course." She sipped her champagne. "But he was not hard enough to be head of something like that. He couldn't take the losses."

"No, Vera, Henry was, as you say, a man of philosophy and dreams," Jason said. "But he was also the man who saw how to combat terrorism in its early stages. He believed in hunting terrorists down and killing them, so that there would be no safe havens on the face of the earth. I agreed with him then, and I still think that's the way to do it."

Vera had a smile in her voice as she said, "If I remember correctly, they had a hard time pulling the plug on you, Jake."

Jason answered for me, as he used to do a lot in the old days. "Jake thought he had to finish what we started. So he says. I think he was doing a revenge thing for me on the Jackal." He grinned in my direction. "Did I put that delicately enough?"

"And the Jackal?" Vera asked, knowing the answer already.

Jason answered as if I were not present, "Six feet under, whether Jake admits it or not. Jake went after him, and Jake always got what he went after."

Vera said, "Henry was very proud of you, Jake. He felt the training and experience you got with the Orion unit was part of what made you so successful with your recovery business. He considered himself your mentor and teacher to some degree."

"He was," I said. "In many things."

"In the end he felt you had surpassed him, as all good students must," she said.

"I'm sorry I wasn't here when Henry died." I found the words hard to say.

"You were in Paraguay doing what you had to do." Vera was repeating words I knew must have come from Jason. "We couldn't find you to tell you, but Jason spoke eloquently for you both. He was buried at Arlington, you know?"

I nodded, this time unable to find words.

They were both quiet for a moment. Jason's cigar was stronger than the perfume of the heavy, scented air.

Jason asked, "So who do you think planted them, amigo? Three bugs, Vera. Have any ideas?"

"Not yet," I answered.

Jason's grin gleamed in the night. "I like it. See, Vera? See the look? That's the look I love to see on old Jake's face. It means that he's down in there deep someplace figuring and sorting, and when he comes up again, by God, all hell can break loose." He laughed.

I felt myself smiling even though I didn't want to. Jason had that way with me. I could never take myself too seriously around him.

Vera shook her head. "What a pair. Henry always said you two were twin souls in different bodies, or something like that. Oh, God, I can't even think anymore. Here you've let me go and drink too much, Jake. Well, I think maybe it's time we got out of here anyway, Jason, and let this poor boy rest from our assault upon his castle. You held up very well, my dear, with all the fussing Lonnie was doing. I do think he did a fine job for you though. It's not nearly as fey as his usual work."

I laughed. "That's reassuring."

"Well, you know what I mean. Anyway, it's good for us to live against our type from time to time. You're doing well, and looking well, and we're going now so this evening doesn't run on too long. We must do this again soon, Jake. You must stay a part of this world, my dear." Vera rose with a liveliness that belied her age.

I saw them out with a promise to call Jason with whatever I learned about the bugs, and a promise to visit Vera soon. Jason said as he pulled the door closed, "I've left you the debugger kit. Use it every few days to keep things clean."

The chauffeur whisked them away quickly, probably thinking of a late date he could still keep. For my part I felt lonely when they left. I probably should have talked a bit more with Jason and Vera, but too much had already been said on this night, I thought. Too much of the past had been dredged up. I needed to pull myself up out of it and concentrate on the now.

Reentering the house, I remembered Jason's words to Vera. "Jake always got what he went after," he had said. I wondered if that was still true. But more than that, I wondered what I was really after.

13 ❧

Long after my guests had gone, I sat at my kitchen table viewing the fragments of the "bugs" through a magnifier. It was a convenient device with a strong light around the perimeter and a glass that could increase magnification tenfold with each of four switch positions. The first position gave me all I needed.

The small listening devices before me were very similar in type to the East German Hapler model that had made a name for itself in the American embassy in Moscow. These, however, looked like the Japanese copies. I was having trouble identifying the manufacturer. On such devices it was a common practice to stamp a symbol rather than a manufacturer's name. Sometimes even the symbol was vague.

My phone rang. I checked my watch and noted it was almost ten minutes past three in the morning. The phone rang again. I picked it up and listened.

"Jake, I do hope I didn't wake you," Kate said with some urgency to her voice. "But I had to call you now, because I didn't know how important this might be. Jake?"

"Yes, I'm here," I said.

"Well, do you remember you asked me if I knew someone named Leeds? Wen Leeds? Do you remember?"

"Yes, I remember," I said.

"It meant nothing to me at the time. It rang no bell whatsoever, but Jake, tonight when I got home I went into my bedside table for a book. I couldn't sleep, because of the evening and all, and I thought maybe reading would help. I started one a few weeks ago and I was looking for that book. Jake, I haven't looked in that drawer for weeks, or anyway, since Greg has been missing. I found the book and started to read. I fell asleep and dropped the book on the floor. I woke up and started to turn off the light, when I saw the book on the floor and picked it up. I picked it up by the back page. As I flipped it over, I could see that something was written on that page. You know, the blank part of the cover? The inside part?"

"Yes, I know," I coaxed.

"The name, Wen Leeds, was written there and a number. I remember now, Jake. He called me here on my line looking for Greg. I had just come out of the shower. It was in the afternoon on the day Greg disappeared. I remember it very well now. He said he had been trying to reach Greg on his own line and on his car phone but hadn't gotten any answer. He said it was very important. I used the book because I had no paper handy, and then I forgot it, with Greg missing and all. I guess Greg had given him my number for emergencies. Does this mean anything to you?"

"I think so."

"What?"

"It explains why and how Wendell Leeds called you."

"You knew he had called me?"

"Yes."

There was some silence.

"Did you find my number in Wendell Leeds's book or something?"

"On his phone."

"Oh, I see." I could hear her breathe. "You were in his house?"

"Yes."
"Will you tell me about it later?"
"Yes."
"Goodnight, Jake."
"Goodnight, Kate."
Still perfect.

. . .

The next day started better than most. I began to put things in order, looking for connections. I had a disappearance and two murders. Now I looked for the common bonds. With Leeds and Burley I had diving. I had nothing between Leeds and Spence except death. They had both died, and possibly on the same day. That connected with Greg Burley because that day he also disappeared. It was almost a circle. There were still some pieces missing.

A panicked Wendell Leeds had called Greg Burley. Toni Spence had been called at the coffee shop. The phone lines were busy that day. It could have been a simple business deal gone sour, or something more sinister.

I had to learn where Toni Spence was going when she was killed, or had gone. I needed a clearer picture of Wendell Leeds, and I had to determine, somehow, if Greg Burley was on the run as either a victim or a killer.

I took another crack at those snapshots Kate had turned up. The ones I didn't have blown up I put under the magnifier to grab a bit more detail. I concentrated on the photos with Wendell Leeds in them. I found something.

It's hard to keep the mind open enough to receive data in an unexpected form. It's hard to recognize when you find something you don't even know you're looking for. I had a history of being lucky at that. My luck held. I saw the case on my second or third look at one of the pictures. There was a large case, possibly a suitcase, at the feet of Wendell Leeds, who stood over it dripping wet. Behind him Greg Burley was just coming aboard, stepping over the railing of the boat. It was clear they had come up from a dive. I felt I had seen that suitcase before.

I riffled through the other snaps, then the blowups. It was there, sure enough. Greg Burley sat at a table with the case before him, looking up at the camera. There was something about the picture that suggested it had been taken for documentation. I could imagine he was on the verge of opening it. I tried to gauge the size of the case in relation to Burley. It appeared to be approximately four feet by three—a hard-shell case of the kind that became popular for air travel many years ago. I knew them mostly as the cases photographers used to transport their cameras and lenses. The rusty-looking, encrusted one in front of Greg Burley was hard to recognize as having once been a shiny, silver-skinned case, but I had no doubt about it. I could see the two parallel ribs that gave the case its distinctive design. Those ribs must have measured about two feet in length, and must have been about two feet apart. I was willing to bet they would match perfectly with the rust marks left in both Burley's Range Rover and Toni Spence's car.

Like that I had the core. I suspected that whatever had happened to them had happened because of that case, or rather what had been in that case. I had no doubt where the case had been for several years. Where was it now? I wondered. That was the thought I took with me for most of the rest of the day.

Late in the afternoon I called Jason. "I finally was able to read the markings on two of them. The house mikes were Diawachi Alfa series jobs. The phone mike was something else. I couldn't make it out."

Jason was all business. "What did its marking look like?"

"If I had to guess, I'd say something like a trident."

"That's a Diawachi too," he said instantly. "It's an antique."

"What do you call an antique?" I had a feeling that with technical stuff the term "antique" could encompass a wide range of time. I was right.

"It's third generation. I'd say five, six years old. Same as the Alfa series. It's low-grade stuff, Jake. It's a copy of good stuff but it's not too sophisticated." He puffed a couple of times and I could envision him lighting his cigar.

"Give me a bottom line. What does it mean that it's not high-quality?" I was pretty dense when it came to this kind of thing. I had used it in the past and knew it in a superficial way, but it seemed like cheating.

"Range," he said, and puffed. "These things have no range at all. You gotta be right on top of them to pick it up."

"What's right on top of them? A thousand yards, or what?"

He laughed. "How you survived all those years is a mystery to me. Try a couple hundred feet. I told you these are not very sophisticated. They're for the do-it-yourselfer. What you need to look for is a relay. These probably feed to some collector within two hundred feet that pumps it out big-time another several hundred yards. Shouldn't be difficult to find, amigo. It will be about the size of a paperback book, and most likely attached to the outside of your house someplace."

I promised chess in a couple of nights and rang off. I had to locate the relay, and leave it in place. Someone would come to check it out soon. I needed to be there when they did.

It took me two hours. It was at the end of the garage at the far end of the house, neatly concealed beneath the branches of an azalea bush. It was just as Jason had described. It looked so innocent but for the small antenna extending from its top side.

My next move was one I should have made earlier. I reset the code configuration in my garage and gate openers. I had to do it for each garage door and for each gate. It was time-consuming, and when I finished resetting the remote controls as well, I had used up another hour.

It was time for a run. I jogged down to the beach entrance. There were a few stragglers left from the day of volleyball and sunbathing, but for the most part the beach was as deserted as usual. I ran away from the sun for a mile or so before I turned back. I made sure no one was around as I left the tide line and moved in tight to the cliff. I got my bearings easily by the stand of tall eucalypti that marked the edge of the property next to mine. I studied the cliff face carefully. It would be night the next time I saw it and I wanted to know it well by then. After my close inspection, I resumed my run back down the beach. The lingerers were still there when I left. That was the way with a good day. It was hard to let it go.

• • •

Tony's Beachside was packed that night. I sat at a window table over a cup of after-dinner coffee with Tony across from me. He waved often to departing customers, or smiled, or nodded. The amazing thing about it was that none of it was phony.

"Yeah, I like this town, Jake. It's not like the old days in Santa Monica and Malibu though. Those days were the best. You agree?"

"I don't know," I mused. "Malibu was great in its time, but it wasn't a town."

"Yeah, I hear you. Look at that over there. Now don't you know that in the old days we would've been all over that?" He nodded to a girl a few tables away. The girl was tall and busty, and burned nut brown by the sun. She was typical of what I had always seen at beach communities.

I grinned at Tony and said, "The old days? What's wrong with these days?"

He made the exaggerated chin thrust gesture that was part of his communicative skills and said, "Yeah, maybe. But with AIDS and all the other junk around, I'm more careful. How about you? You drop in out of the sky. What's with your life these days, huh, baby?"

"I'm new here, Tony. I'm just feeling my way."

"Yeah, well, like I told you last time you were in, you could've dropped me with a feather when you said you'd moved up here. You in Santa Barbara? Come on. And baby, when you said Coco Palms. *Come onnn.* We're talking oil and water here."

"Just about the reaction I had when you moved up here," I reminded him.

"Yeah, but that was twelve years ago, and I'm Montecito, not Coco Palms," he countered. "Lotta difference, baby. Lotta difference. That Coco Palms crowd is snob city. I can always tell a customer from the Palms by the way he sniffs the room."

Tony had an infectious smile. I smiled with him.

"Ever hear of a guy named Dreckman?" I slid it in as casually as possible.

"Hey, Jake, what do you think here, I'm some sort of hick jerk? Come on. Do I know Dreckman? Dougie boy? Of course I know Dreckman. Now you tell me what you want to know, okay? Let's just assume that I know everybody worth knowing in this burg, okay? That'll make it a lot easier. Anybody I don't know isn't worth knowing, okay? Now tell me, what is it?" He was a Big Apple kid and it came out in his inflections and gesticulating hands and, of course, his chin thrust.

"Is he a square guy?"

Tony tilted his head to the side with eyebrows arched high and his hands turned palms up and out like petals of a flower opening. It spoke volumes. His lower lip jutted out and he said, "Ehh."

"How about Captain Jessup, head of the Coco Palms security patrol? Anything there?" I could see his interest rising.

"I hear things," he said in a lower tone. "He know who you are?"

"Just that I live there," I answered.

"Oh, baby, I want to be around." His big grin left me for only a moment as he nodded farewell to a group passing by our table. "I hear some heavyweight bad stuff on him." He waved across the room to some people just entering.

I looked out the window at the tourists wandering in a sunburned daze toward the pier and the ocean. They were experiencing paradise for the first time. They were innocent and believed in what they saw; they had not yet learned that their eyes would lie to them.

"Such as?" I asked when Tony's attention returned to me.

"Just rumor, but there's been talk about some shakedown

stuff. You remember a fellow named Beloit? Big-shot inventor or something? A year or two back, maybe more? Suicide? And the Giardellas? You ever hear of them? Murder-suicide? Also a couple of years back? All Coco Palms people. Now, Beloit killed himself in a motel in Las Vegas and the Giardellas did it in the desert, but, baby, something stinks in Coco Palms. And the accidents. Two deaths there of people getting a little careless. One went over the cliff and one drowned off the beach there. All in the last four years. The drowning just happened to be a girl who had claimed to Mom and Dad she was beat up and raped by Jessup and his pal Stanner. You met that musclehead yet? Mom and Dad couldn't get anyone to listen after Baby goes for the deep six. She was crazy, the powers said, and Mom and Pop moved on out of Coco Palms to pick up what was left of their lives. And how about that Leeds Nancy getting zapped right on Main Street Coco Palms. It adds up to funnyville to a lot of heads around here, baby. And a lot of fingers point at Jessup. But not so you would notice. Oh, no."

"You mentioned Fred Stanner? You know him?" I was trying to absorb what I was hearing.

"I've seen him," he said with squinted eyes. "He's a barhopper. Always on the make. He picks girls off at their cars when the bars close. Word has it he likes to hurt them."

"Anybody ever try to take him?"

"I don't know, but I hear he's tough. A black belt in two or three of those killer kung fu things. Dirty too. He killed a stranger in a cowboy bar out in the valley a couple of years ago. Got off scot-free, after a lot of witnesses showed up to say the stranger picked the fight. The stranger was a banker from San Francisco visiting relatives in Santa Ynez. He played bridge and golf. Chances are good that he'd never had a fight in his life, according to the relatives. That tell you anything?" He talked to me, but his eyes stayed alive with the room.

"A lot," I answered. "Thanks, Tony. I better be off now and let you roam. I'll be in again soon."

He got up with me. I dropped bills on the table. I knew if I asked for the tab, I'd never get it. It was like with Bernice and

Todd Parsley at the White Gull. I had to guess at it. He walked
me to the door and stepped outside with me.

"Look at all the schnooks. Are they the jerks or are we?"
He made a wide gesture with his hand.

I knew what he meant. After all, we weren't in Topeka
tracking around their city and taking up space in their parks
and restaurants. We weren't there making them add to their
police force and city maintenance services. We weren't using
their water and crowding their streets. They were here.

"I've never figured that one out," I answered.

"So, Jake, Jessup doesn't know about you, huh? Is he messing with you?" Tony was grinning.

"Not so you would notice," I answered, borrowing an earlier phrase of his.

Tony's grin widened. "To anybody else I'd say don't under-
estimate him, but with you I figure it doesn't matter." He
dropped his grin and leaned in to me. "Jake, if I can do anything on the info front, you call. I hear things, you know?"

I was about to take my leave, when something he had said
rushed back at me. "Tony," I said quickly, "one thing you said
I'd like more on. You referred to Wendell Leeds as a Nancy?"

"Yeah, I guess I shouldn't use that these days. I'll probably
have gays and lesbians marching in front of the joint calling
for my nuts," he said. "I've always called them Nancys or
Marys. What do you call them?"

I thought of my decorator and architect. "Lonnie and Albert," I said.

His laugh was loud and raucous.

"But Wendell Leeds was gay? You're sure?" I asked.

"Well, I'm not sure. I mean, I was never there, baby, but if it
walks like a duck, and quacks like a duck . . ."

"I get you," I said. "Thanks, Tony. See you soon."

"My best to Lonnie and Albert," he said as I headed to the
parking lot. I could still hear him laughing as I rounded the
corner. I felt a twinge of guilt at using Lonnie and Albert for a
cheap laugh. They were, after all, friends of mine. I liked myself a little less for it.

It was just after ten o'clock when I turned off Ocean Avenue before it became Coral Ridge Road and entered Coco Palms. I parked my car on a side lane, where I changed into a pair of dark-colored pants and a dark shirt. I locked the car and took a well-stuffed backpack with me to the steep and ill-defined trail down to the beach. It was a path used, for the most part, by the younger residents of the adjacent properties.

I rested at the bottom of the cliff for a few minutes, and let myself wonder again why I did such things. No answer came to me, so I picked myself up and continued my mission for the night. It was a good mile before I came to the section of beach that ran beneath the Coco Palms cliffs. It was another three-quarters of a mile before I found the markings I had made that afternoon.

I put on a cap with a light mount on it for the flashlight. I put on climbing gloves and wrapped a nylon rope around my shoulders. I did not let myself stop to think about it. I climbed. Loose rock crumbled away from my hands and feet. Fingerholds quickly became empty air and ledges disappeared. I resorted to the use of pitons after struggling for half an hour: it wasn't worth it. I drove in the pitons and used the other end of the climbing hammer to dig fingerholds. I felt the same as when I cheated on a diet, but I was getting too old to always do it the hard way. It was time I stopped perpetual training and used the tricks I already knew.

I did not bother with stealth. It was my own property. I reached the top, stumbled through the shrubbery that stood sentry between me and the cliff. I checked out the house and the perimeter of the property, then I recovered the sleeping bag I had stashed earlier and slipped inside it. Beside me was the shell cluster attached to nylon filament surrounding the relay box. The natural sounds of the shells would be enough to wake me, but not enough to sound the alarm to the intruder. Confident that I was ready, I smelled the air, thought of Kate, and drifted off to sleep.

14

After an uneventful night, I awoke with a need for all the amenities. I had not realized how accustomed I had become to that big, too soft bed of mine. The hot shower eased out all the kinks. A close shave and a pot of coffee made me near human again. I hoped I would not have to spend too many nights out there before someone came to tend to business.

I waited for a decent hour to call Kate. She did not answer and there was no machine. I was partially relieved, in that I still did not know how I was to broach the subject of her husband's relationship with Wendell Leeds in the light of what I had learned from Tony. It had some bearing, and I would have to know, but it could wait. I was on the late side for an appointment with the skipper of the *Reef Queen,* the dive boat I had seen in the background of some of the pictures.

After a jog out the Coco Palms gate to my car, and a fast Ocean Avenue drive, I pulled into the marina only a few minutes past my ten o'clock appointment. I hated to be late, and I hated to wait. Talk about a Catch-22.

Walt Haber owned and captained the *Reef Queen,* and to my relief, talked freely.

"You might say they were regulars, Greg and Wen," he said. "They hung together and dived together. For the longest time I had the feeling they were looking for something."

"Did they ever find it?" I asked.

"Not off of this boat, they didn't," he answered. "But I think the answer is yes, they did. I got word from a pal of mine that they rented his boat for four days running. It's a small dive boat, not equipped like mine to carry large groups."

"Were they looking in any particular place that you can remember?"

"I think so," he answered with a pull at the loose skin under his chin. "I have a regular schedule where I anchor different locations. Some folks have favorite areas they like to dive. Then I have days where it's mostly new divers and such. Well, Greg and Wen always went out on the Tuesday, Thursday, and weekend runs, even when it was with the beginners. Those were the days I cruised the channel between Santa Rosa Island and Santa Cruz Island. They never once wanted to dive San Miguel Island. That struck me as odd, because being such good divers I would have thought San Miguel would be right up their alley. I told them so, but they said no."

I unrolled the poster-sized blowup that showed Wendell Leeds standing over the suitcase, and Greg Burley climbing over the aft railing. In the background was a coved formation of land.

"Do you think you could recognize that place by what you can make out of the background? The rocks there seem to be unusual in the way they stair-step down to the water. See that?" I pointed to the formation. "Do you recognize it?"

"That's Hack's boat allright," he said in a mutter just loud enough for me to hear. "Yep, I'd say I got the spot. That's the leeward side of Santa Rosa, just outside the channel between the two islands. I'd say that's pretty sure it."

"Could you take me out there?"

"Sure thing. You check with me next week when we're up and running again and I'll let you know which day we'll be anchoring closest to it."

"Today." I took out my certification card and showed it along with a couple of hundred dollar bills. "I need to get out there today."

He shook his head. "This is a week for cleaning and refitting. I can't do it."

"What if you took your friend Hack's boat? Name your price."

He pondered it a moment before he went to the phone. It was several minutes before he came back.

"You got gear?" he asked.

"Nope, I'm going to need everything."

He looked me over. "I won't have a wet suit that'll fit you. You'll have to make do, I guess."

He led the way back to an equipment storage area. He pulled out a decent-looking regulator and handed it to me, then with a sweep of his hand indicated the rest.

"Pick out what you need. I'll get Hack's boat up here. And friend, it's gonna cost you five hundred—can you handle it?"

I put the money in his hand. He nodded and was off. I found the largest wet suit and took it without trying it on. I tried the fins and face masks until I found what I wanted. I put together a weight belt with more weights than I would need, just in case, and found a decent buoyancy control vest. I couldn't help but remember that when I started diving, there was no such thing as a buoyancy control device or a regulator like the one Walt Haber had tossed to me, with an attached module giving up-to-the-minute readouts on all the critical data needed below the surface. Back then it was a double hose, with no purge, and a J valve to give you a five-minute reserve. The only problem with that was half the time the valve got tripped and there was nothing there when you needed it. There were some modern advances I got along with, especially when my life was on the line.

I grabbed a backpack and sorted through the tanks. I was looking only at steel tanks of the eighty-cubic-foot size. I looked specifically at the markings on the necks, and found a couple that had fairly recent manufacture dates and had been hydrostatically tested within the last year. The tape over their valves indicated that they had been filled, so I lugged them outside along with the rest of the gear.

Walt Haber could sure handle a boat. I had barely stepped aboard with my gear before we were in a wide U heading for the islands. He didn't talk much, which was fine with me.

While he anchored us in a spot that was a close approximation to the one in the picture, I suited up. He loaned me a wrist compass, which I strapped to my right wrist, and a dive knife, which I strapped to the inside of my left calf. I felt ready.

He said, "You showed me a master card there, Sands, so I have to assume that you know what you're doing."

I nodded and moved to the stern. He followed behind me, giving me a buddy check for my equipment.

"I can lower a sounder for time underwater if you want." He stood with me at the port side while I looked out at the current playing by the anchor line. I shook my head and raised my watch, assuming he would recognize the sounder housing on it. I set the watch and nodded to him that I was off. "I've never lost a diver yet. Don't you go spoil my record." It was a funny line said in a serious way. I nodded again and stepped up and over the railing. I surfaced long enough to give him the okay sign, and to adjust my weight belt. Then I dove into the current.

I went to depth in stages. It had been some time since I had last been down, and equalizing the pressure in my ears was a slow process. I finally settled to the bottom at about sixty feet, where I set my compass and determined my course. It was a good sensation to be back underwater, even at so shallow a depth. I could feel the relaxation like warm oil on my body.

The world was one of filtered light and graceful, weightless motion. It was a world reduced to what was visible from the face mask. As the mask turned and took in different sectors, so did the world change and become isolated to that sector. I put my left arm straight out ahead of me with my right hand grasping the left biceps. In that way I could keep my eye on the compass and my course straight. It all came back to me with the ease I had anticipated.

I followed a search pattern using a grid method, moving quickly because I needed to cover a lot of territory. I swam into the current on the search out; I always wanted the current with me on the way back to the boat. There was nothing worse than being out of air and far downcurrent from your boat. It went smoothly and before I knew it the clear tone of my sounder let me know that it was time. I reversed my course and searched the other side of the field in a zigzag back to the anchor line. The current was strong enough to push me back in easily half the time it had taken me to swim out.

Aboard, I checked my stopwatch against my bezel setting and marked the time and depth registered by my regulator gauge onto my dive-table chart. Walt watched and waited for instructions, which I gave him as soon as I had calculated my next dive.

"Walt, move us around that jut there. I have a surface interval of about twenty-five minutes, so try to get us planted someplace in that time if you can. I don't want to build up any credit. I need the time below."

He knew what I meant. He could probably figure a dive table faster than I could. He knew all about having to spend a certain amount of time on the surface for the amount of time spent below at a certain depth. He knew about extending your total time by stretching your surface intervals and building up credits. He would know if I began to press it. He would know about such things as decompression and nitrogen narcosis. He would not want them and neither did I.

At the next location I searched the same grid pattern, and at the one after that. I was working my way toward the open mouth of the sizable channel that ran between the two islands. My total time down and my depths were reaching a point of higher mathematics. I spent my time on the surface figuring how to stretch my No-Decompression Limits, adding in the residual nitrogen time to the actual bottom time, and moving from one dive table to another.

"How you feeling?" Walt asked.

"I feel good," I replied as I put the mask on and prepared to go in again.

"What kind of depths you getting down there?" he asked. I knew he was trying to keep a kind of mental table going on me himself.

"Forty to sixty," I said. "See you."

I went straight down. I no longer had a problem equalizing, and I was familiar now with all the borrowed equipment. At bottom I checked my position on the compass and started to move out on my usual grid search. I had hardly begun when I saw the underwater cave. It would have been easy to miss, and it was probably just luck that let me catch it, but as soon as I saw it I knew that was it. That was what Greg and Wendell had been searching for. It had to be.

The entrance was small. I pulled my light out and made sure it was functioning, and attached a nylon cord to a rock spike at the entrance before I swam in. It opened up considerably when I was inside. It was like going to another level. Underwater caves held a special magic. Especially those with tunnels, as this one had.

I worked my way through the tunnels, tracing some to the end and finding others intersecting. It was then that I let myself think about what specifically I was seeking. It was probably a mechanism I used to prepare myself for finding it. I was looking for the body of Greg Burley; that was what my eye was programmed to look for. When I saw the case, I took a moment to recognize it.

I settled to the bottom six feet from the metal-shelled suitcase and stared at it. My God, I thought, they tried to put it back. One of them or all of them had come back down here with that case trying to undo what they had done, trying to save their lives, probably.

I swam to the case and lifted it. It was heavy, as I had expected it to be. I turned and pulled lightly on the nylon cord. It came to me easily, floating in serpentine freedom toward me. I swam back along its route until I saw the end waving like a reed along the bottom of the mazelike tunnel. I didn't stop to speculate on how it had come loose.

I took the most obvious courses, which only led me to dead ends. Then I backtracked and searched again for some sign of the way I had entered. I was lost without my home line, the cord to lead me back. So I guessed. I guessed wrong, and guessed again, and again guessed wrong. I swam this way and that, pulling the heavy suitcase with me.

You do not run out of air all at once. It doesn't happen that one minute you're breathing air and the next there is none. It's a gradual thing where at first you only think you detect the draw on the air is a little harder. Then you are sure it's not pulling as easily as before. And then it becomes a chore to get the next breath. Then it's definite that the air supply is getting short. If you're the panicky type, that's the time for it.

I felt rather sure that I would find my way out. I had a sense that there were not that many wrong turns left. Not after all the ones I had taken. I kept my eye on the current when I could detect it and tried to imagine it as part of the sea surge. It proved to be a fairly effective imagery: it enabled me to read the movement as ebb and flow. I followed it and grew more confident that I was on my way out. My problem was, I was on my last pull of air. I had sucked the coating off the insides of that bottle, I was sure.

I was tempted to drop the case, but I didn't want to have to come back down for it. I struggled to the entrance fighting that little gag switch that makes you want to spit out your mouthpiece and breathe water. As I got to it, I realized the hole I was going out of was not the same one I entered. It didn't make a lot of difference at that moment. I wiggled through the small opening into the most glorious sight I had ever seen: open sea. I was still sixty feet underwater though, and caution was the order of the day. I began to exhale as I let myself up slowly. I tried to ascend just behind the bubbles escaping from my mouth. One of the wonders of diving, which is very hard to trust until you have to, is that when breathing bottled air underwater, your lungs expand with it as you rise. So, as you go up you have more air to exhale, without ever having to inhale. You only get into trouble when you go up faster than those little dime-sized bubbles.

I hit the top a hundred yards from the boat. Even from there I could see that Walt was suited up and sitting on the dive platform, ready to go in. I liked him for that, and I knew he would not like me for making him worry. I swam with the current, pumping with the fins to support the extra weight of the case. Walt jumped in and grimly helped me take the case aboard.

"Out of air?" he asked matter-of-factly.

"And in a cave," I answered, giving him more than he had bargained for. "Looks like you were coming to get me."

He stared at me, then shook his head and said, "Glad you made it back."

"I didn't want to spoil your record, Walt," I said.

He smiled, which eased our tension, and together we hauled in the anchor and got under way. He even brought me a cup of coffee from the galley, after he had put the boat on autopilot. We sat with towels over our wet heads, looking like two monks, and sipped our coffee in silence while the boat plowed a straight course for the marina.

"You know," I said after both our eyes had gone to the case, "that might be something there you don't want to know anything about."

"It's a little late for that now, isn't it?" He had a way of delivering irony seriously.

"Maybe," I said. "Pull her back to idle. Maybe this should be left at sea."

"You don't know what's in there?" he asked.

"I haven't got a clue. It's caused some problems though, I can tell you that."

He gave me a crowbar. The brass lock was not of the same vintage as the rusty, crusted-over suitcase. It held together, but the once shiny, innovative, trend-setting piece of luggage tore loose from it. I pulled the top of the suitcase, which still held the unyielding padlock, open on its rusty hinges. It fell back, losing much of the old rubber stripping which had kept it watertight. Inside, there was apparently nothing more than the empty shell formed by the molded lead that lined the case and gave it its weight.

"That's a good bit of lead, but it don't strike me as much of a prize," Walt said.

"Me neither," I answered. I bent down to examine the lining more closely. It had been melted and poured to fit the form of the case. It was clear that the case had held something of great value or great concern to someone.

In my past I had seen so many different ways people could hide things that I automatically looked beyond the obvious. I had learned that linings could be great hiding places. I ran my hands over the lead on both parts of the case. It was almost undetectable but it seemed to me there was a thicker part to one side of the case. It was enough to be curious about. I shrugged to Walt. "Nothing here. May as well go on in."

The boat's engine revved up with a throaty rumble and once again we were slashing through the wave troughs toward the marina. With Walt busy at the wheel I studied the thick part of the case. I pried the lead away from the shell with my knife and found a second set of rubber seals. While Walt was still looking forward I pulled an oilskin-wrapped object from inside the lead lining. I managed to slip it away inside my wet suit just before Walt turned back to me. I shrugged and opened the case upside down to signal that nothing had been found. Having established that it was only a lead-lined metal shell, I threw the case in a wide arc out away from the boat.

"Seems a shame to see you throw that case away. You paid a pretty penny to get it," Walt said at my elbow. As if to remind me, he added, "Five hundred bucks."

I thought about it a minute or so. "Others paid more," I said.

. . .

It was nearly midnight when I finally climbed the cliff face to my house. I checked it all out to make sure that my visitor had not come in my absence. No visitor. This could get old real fast, I thought, when I was able to grab a bite and take some rest in my own kitchen. I checked for messages. Two from Tex Flanagan, one from Vera thanking me for the evening, and one from Bob Claiborne demanding his keys back. None from Kate.

I dialed Kate's number again. I had tried to reach her as soon as Walt Haber docked but had gotten no answer then. I got no answer now either. Although I knew the time, it made me look at my watch to verify the hour. Where was she at midnight? There weren't that many possibilities, and those I considered, I did not like. Was that a little touch of jealousy I felt bite at me?

Before I went outside for my night watch, I took out the envelope that held the keys to Wendell Leeds's house. After careful consideration, I made wax impressions of them before returning them to the envelope and sealing it. It was very possible that I would have to visit that house again.

I also took another look at the oilskin-wrapped object I had retrieved from the lead lining of the metal case. It was a thin, leatherbound book which at first appeared to be some sort of diary. It was of high quality, with the initial "G" on the front cover. It did not take much time to determine that the notations inside were in some code.

With the book safely put away, I went outside to resume my vigil. I slipped into the sleeping bag and checked my makeshift alarm system to be sure it was free of snags. Secure in my preparations, I put my head back and thought about how close it had been out there in that cave. Something had cut my nylon homing line. Or someone. One thing was fairly certain.

Walt Haber had not done it. He had been dressed and ready to come in, but his suit had been bone dry. I would give him some time and then ask him about it when he was off guard. There was always the chance he knew who, if anyone, had been in the water with me. I wondered about that as I drifted into the heavy mist of sleep.

15 🌿

He was clumsy. The shell alarm gave a slight tinkle at my ear, but I had already heard him. He never did hear me. I moved around until I had the breeze in my face. I let him get in a position where he was bending down to the relay box, before I hit him with the light. It was a high-beam spot that must have seemed like a noonday sun to him. He froze in his down position, which is just where I wanted him.

His face began to work in tiny tic movements. He was mentally assessing his predicament. I stood between him and the driveway, which meant freedom. Not only that, he had no idea who was behind the high beam. I let that play a little longer. There was something familiar about the guy, but I was having trouble placing him.

"You're in trouble, sport," I said.

He took on the facial expressions of a caged chimpanzee. I had just given him information he did not need.

"Come on out here," I said, and backed off with the light a few yards. He followed obediently. I stopped him on the driveway and ordered, "Hit the ground, facedown, arms and legs spread."

He lay perfectly still while I checked him out. He had on a

standard electrician's belt, loaded with tools and components, but no weapon. I nudged him over, with my foot, onto his back. He blinked into the light but made no other movement.

"So, sport, let's start with a name. Yours."

"Claude," he said in a choked-off voice.

"Claude?" It rang a bell. "Claude what?"

"Claude Hayes."

Then I remembered. This was the guy that had made all the noise at the homeowners' meeting. The guy I had followed home to the foothills in Goleta.

"How's that blue van running, Claude?" It had the desired effect: it got his attention. "And that nice little house you live in, Claude? You must feel pretty safe on that cul-de-sac. Do you still feel safe, Claude?"

His eyes were wide. "No sir."

"On your feet." I stepped back and let him rise. "Who sent you here tonight?"

He stared blankly at me.

"I've got a pretty good idea, Claude, but why don't you tell me anyway so I know you're the cooperative type?"

"I don't know. Really, I don't." He sounded scared but sincere. This was no pro. This was just some dumb clod who was being squeezed.

"What were you told to do here?"

"Put new batteries in the receiver, transmitter, and check it to see if it was working okay. That's all." His face was quieting down.

"Do you know what it's for? What it picks up and transmits?"

He hesitated. "I guess it's from RF mikes."

"What do you know about them?"

He spoke more freely. "Not much, just that they don't have a very big range. Look, I'm an electrician. That's my trade. I'm just doing a job I was told to do, honest. If I'm doing something that I shouldn't, then I'll go, okay?"

"No, not okay. Did you set the mikes?"

"No. Look, mister, I thought this was an up-and-up job."
His voice was moving into a panic zone. I knew he was close
to trying something. I hoped, for his sake, he wouldn't. "Now
I don't want no trouble, so I'll just leave."

I let off the light so he could see some of me. He tried to
move by me, and I moved his way. He could see no weapon, so
he grew braver. I said, "We have more to talk about, Claude."

"I got nothing to say to you," he said, sensing that I was
running a bluff.

"How about to the police?" Then, because I wanted to get
his reaction, I said, "Or the Coco Palms patrol. I'll call them
and let them take you in."

He was feeling much more confident suddenly. I was not
surprised that he was not afraid of the patrol. He visibly relaxed. I was expecting to have to deck him, because I could
see in his eyes the decision already made. He was ready to try
to make his move.

"The police?" he asked, buying another few seconds of
time.

"Unless you want to tell me who sent you here," I said,
watching his eyes closely.

He was a pure amateur. He went at the part of me he could
see, which was the fool's play I had offered him. As he reached
for me I dropped the flashlight. I chopped his wrist and locked
it in an overgrip that turned his side to me. I lifted my knee
and drove the heel of my foot into the bottom of his rib cage.
The floating rib gave and he whooshed in pain and disbelief.

He stumbled back against the garage, trying to hold both
his damaged wrist and side. It had happened too fast for him
to comprehend. He only knew that he had made a mistake. I
bent to pick up the flashlight, and in that moment he took another reckless chance. He ran.

I put the light on him, not bothering to chase because he
was going in the direction of the cliff. There was nowhere for
him to go there, so I let him find that out for himself. I
watched him run headlong into the line of shrubs at the cliff-

side. He stumbled around and seemed ready to come back toward my light, when he fell. It was one of those awkward, comic falls with the arms flailing in small circles as if one were trying to fly. His scream was swallowed by the sound of the surf even as I ran to him.

I shone my light over the edge of the cliff and saw his crumpled form below. It was not a position a living body could assume. I began my descent to check him out and worked my way down as quickly as I could without getting reckless. All the way down I thought of what I could have done differently to prevent his fall. I could have taken out his knees instead of his lower ribs, but at the time, the ribs seemed to be kinder. I could have chased him and caught him perhaps, but he had gotten a pretty good jump in that direction. I could have kept him on his face, or kept a hold on him, but I had been playing him for information.

He was dead. I sat with him for a few minutes and hoped there was no family expecting him home. I considered what I had learned from him. He was no simple working stiff, that was sure, but he was no pro either. It was possible that he had not known who gave him the orders, but that was a very remote possibility. He had known all right, and if I had had him a few minutes longer, I would have known too. I thought I knew anyway.

I climbed back up and took out the pitons. I moved the body well down the beach and erased all signs of my presence. Then I ran along the tide line the mile and a half to where my car was parked.

I saw dawn come up from the window of a Denny's along 101. I sat over coffee, mulling the tangled mess of things I was involved with. It seemed the more I thought about it, the more complicated it became. I dialed Kate's number at about seven. No answer. I didn't like it. I didn't like it all the way back to Coco Palms. I found the blue van parked a few hundred yards from my property. I hot-wired it and moved it another half mile or so.

I was in need of sleep. My bed looked tempting, but there were things I needed to do. A swim and a shower did wonders. That and another pot of coffee saw me through to a decent enough hour in the morning when I felt I could call Samuel Garvey without waking his household.

"Mr. Garvey, this is Jake Sands. We met at the homeowners' meeting," I said. "I hope I'm not waking you."

"Oh, yes, Mr. Sands, I remember you. No, you're not waking me at all. I'm up and in my garden by six-thirty every day."

"Do you have some time for me today?" I asked, leaving much unsaid.

He was a very smart old man. He left it unasked. He responded simply, "Would eleven do? At my house? I'm on Lemon Hill Road, 1120."

"Perfect," I replied. "I'll see you then."

I was there at eleven on the dot. The gate was open to a long, winding drive which led up to a grand old George Washington Smith mansion. Smith had been the most sought-after architect of the thirties for Spanish-style houses in Southern California. His were distinctive in their use of pillars and arches. Samuel Garvey's house was one of the better examples. He was standing in an open front door waiting for me.

"Thank you for seeing me, Mr. Garvey," I said as we shook hands.

"Sam," he corrected. "I'm honored that you would visit, Jack."

"It's Jake," I said with a smile.

"Ah, yes, Jake," he said without embarrassment, stepping aside to let me enter. He closed the door behind us and then led me into a huge living room. There were paintings, which looked to be of museum quality, on all the walls. The furnishings appeared to be the heavy mahogany of the Chippendale era.

"Would you mind if we sat outside?" I asked.

"Not at all." He led me out through French doors to a lovely open patio overlooking a view of the mountains to one side and the sea to the other.

As we settled across from each other over a glass-topped table, a maid appeared with a heavy silver coffee and tea service. After I indicated coffee, I waited while she poured. I gave a closer inspection of the sculpted ironwork of the furniture. The verdigrised finish on the cast iron made it look as if it had been lifted directly from the Tivoli Gardens. The Garveys knew good things, and what's more, they could afford them.

"Now, Jake, I think we can talk," Sam Garvey said when the maid had left. "I must confess to a curiosity about your caution."

"I always think it's better to discuss things of a certain nature with as much privacy as possible. I want to know about some people whom you may have known or known something about."

"Known?"

"Beloit? Giardella? Did you know them?"

His face became a stiff mask. "Very well. Why?"

"Do you think Charlie Jessup had anything to do with their deaths?"

He took a deep breath and leaned back to rub his eyes. He kept his head slightly tilted back. He could have been talking to the tops of the Monterey pines. "There is a growing sense of distrust in Coco Palms, Jake. Neighbors don't trust each other anymore. People have been scared by anonymous phone calls and letters. When Jim Beloit was alive, and the Giardellas, we often talked about the problems around here. We were all quite determined and brave. Then Jim makes that strange out-of-character trip to Las Vegas, a place where he had never been in his life, where he commits suicide. A short time later the Giardellas die in a murder-suicide in Palm Springs. A more unlikely pair for that sort of thing, you could not find."

He paused and shook his head at the memory. He brought his head forward and looked at me again. "Yes, I think Charlie Jessup had something to do with their deaths. I can't prove it, but I think it. And that poor young thing, Karen Bayless, and the whole Bayless family who suffered so, I think he, and

that Stanner fellow, definitely had something to do with that.
And more. A lot more."

"Sam, why have you stayed here? Why haven't you moved?"

"Many have, Jake, but not me. Never me. I came here to live
out the rest of my life, and by God, I'll do it." He paused for a
moment of reflection. "I've tried to tell the others, this will
pass. This was a good place to live and will be again as soon
as we can get rid of that board. They are self-serving, dishon-
est individuals who have created something even they can't
control. But it will pass. Once we get rid of Doug Dreckman
we'll be able to get back on the right track."

"You said anonymous calls and letters?" I prompted.

"It worked—and for all I know, still does work—like this.
Let's say two of us sit and discuss some problem or complaint
about the way things are being run here in Coco Palms.
Within the next few days what we've said to each other comes
back to us in the form of a letter, unsigned, or a late-night
phone call from some threatening, unidentified voice." Again
he shook his head. The discouragement was there, but so too
was the determination.

I picked it up from there. "Each person then thinks the
other has talked, and everybody clams up, is that it?"

He nodded wearily.

"Why not you? You still speak up pretty strongly." I had to
ask it.

"There's nothing they can do to me. I don't scare and there's
not a damned thing in this world they can threaten me with.
I've never cheated on my wife or my income taxes, so where's
their leverage?"

"You think that's it?" I asked. "Someone's putting the
squeeze on, using information like that?"

"Extorting, yes," he answered sadly. "How they gain their
information, I do not know."

"Maybe I can answer that one for you," I said, "but my one
question about all this is, why?"

"I don't have that answer either. From me they've only

sought my silence. Perhaps from others they've asked for more."

I nodded and sipped my coffee. It tasted of chicory. He watched me but said nothing.

"Sam, do you know what a bug is? Like when someone taps into your telephone?" I asked.

"Yes," he said cautiously, "I've heard of such things."

"I think some of the houses around here have been bugged. Yours for one." I smiled at his intense face. "Mine for another."

His comprehension grew into a kind of childish glee. I was surprised by his reaction. I was even more surprised when he got to his feet and slammed his right fist into his left palm and said, "Yes. By God, yes. I knew it had to be something like that." Then he turned to me. "How can we find out, absolutely?"

"I already know about mine. That's a definite. I would wager big on yours. There are professionals who for a fee will do a sweep of your home and phone lines. I can call them for you if you wish."

"You had yours done by them?"

"Mine was done by a friend." I moved to change the subject. "Have you kept any kind of file on what's been happening around here? Any letters you've exchanged, or notes of conversations, or even any of those anonymous mailings?"

"Sit tight," he said, and bounded inside with such apparent vigor I had to smile. He was back in a moment with what looked like a scrapbook.

"This is something I started after things were already in a bad state around here, but I think you can get a feeling from it. I got so that I'd just keep anything about the Palms."

I opened the pages to find more than I had hoped for. It was a collection of newspaper clippings, letters, and handwritten notes going back two or more years. There were the big stories of the Beloits and Giardellas, and Karen Bayless, but there were also tiny items of no apparent significance that dealt in some way with Coco Palms or Coco Palms residents. In its own way it was a remarkable collection of data. It was not, however, a neat and careful work.

Sam seemed to be complimented by my careful study of his file. I pored over each page up to the current ones. The last clippings dealt with the murder of Wendell Leeds. I found the glaring headline page that read, "COCO PALMS MURDER." It had been torn raggedly from the paper, leaving portions of other stories around it. I noted part of a picture from the lower left corner of the page. Something about it rang a bell, but I could only remember that it had captured my attention the first time I saw it. Evidently it had given me pause even then.

I looked up at Sam Garvey, who was watching me with hawklike attentiveness. "There was another big story on this page, with this picture here. Do you remember it?" I asked.

He looked at the torn picture I showed him. He shook his head. "No, I don't."

I couldn't say why exactly, but something was telling me I had to see that story again. "You wouldn't have a copy of this whole front page, would you?"

He smiled tolerantly. "Lord no, Jake. I think I kept quite enough as it is."

I closed the book and stood. "Sam, I have to go now. Thank you for your hospitality and all the information. It's been very enlightening."

"About those people you were going to call . . ." he said, as he followed me toward the French doors.

"I'll have them come tomorrow, if you'll be here."

"I'll be here," he answered excitedly. "All day."

He saw me to my car. He was smiling as if it were something he'd just learned to do. "By God," he said, "I feel like I've just turned back ten years."

He looked it, too, in the last glimpse I had of him in my rearview mirror. I drove directly downtown to Anapamu Street and the central library. I went to the periodicals desk and gave the woman there the date of the *News-Press* issue I wanted.

"One moment, please," she said. She started away then and stopped to inform me, "That will still be in hard copy. It will not go to micro for more than two months from now."

"Hard copy will be fine," I said, not knowing what else to say.

She went away happy and returned with the paper in hand. I took it to a table and looked at the front page. In the lower left-hand corner was the picture of a sign crudely printed and left as a statement among the high weeds of what had been an abandoned house. The sign read, "Care for the Homeless," and supposedly it had been left by the homeless man who had burned himself to death, along with the abandoned house, in protest. Then I knew why I'd had to see the story again.

After I read the story a second time, I had a copy made and returned the paper. I stopped at a pay phone on my way to my car.

Tex Flanagan was in a good mood.

"Podner, you been among the missin'. Where you been keeping yourself?" He was munching on something.

"I've been around, Tex, just a little busy is all." I tried to keep my voice calm, although I did not feel that way inside.

"You're as tough to find as a quick-footed quarterback on an icy field. I was thinking we oughta get together and maybe compare notes. I ain't got much, but I was sorta hoping you'd found a thing or two." He chewed his food loudly.

"I think I have. I have to pick up something from my house and then I'll come to your office. Half an hour okay?"

"I'll save you a cookie," he said with a laugh.

I wouldn't hold my breath for that, I thought as I put another quarter in the phone and dialed Kate. No answer. I was worried but partially relieved.

I walked out to the car with the copy of the newspaper story in my hand. I sat behind the wheel looking at it for a moment before starting the engine. I studied the picture of the crudely drawn sign. I didn't believe in coincidences, but I did believe in hunches. If my hunch was right, there was not going to be an easy way to tell Kate I had found her husband.

• • •

Tex stared at me as if I had gone mad. He shook his head and rocked forward in his swivel chair to slam both forearms onto his desk. The arms were like two sides of beef coming down. I had forgotten how huge the man was.

"You're runnin' at the wrong goal line, podner," he said. "There just ain't no way this fella in this paper here was Greg Burley. This fella was a vagrant that burned himself up. Probably crazy as a bedbug. Anyhow, we got a positive ID the next day."

"From whom?"

"One of his hobo buddies. He only knew him by his hobo name, Cardboard Charlie or something. That's why we still got him listed as John Doe, but for our purposes we got the ID."

"If he was killed, that ID could have been bought. Where's the fellow who identified him now?"

"Skedaddled, I'd guess. We don't spend a lot of time around here keeping tabs on these no-accounts." Tex made it clear he was finished with the idea.

I persisted. "You're not going to let this close on the word of some bum off the street?"

"So what've you got that says we shouldn't?" he challenged.

I read from the notes I had brought from home. They were the ones Kate had written out for me when I'd first started looking for Greg. I read from the physical description first.

"Greg Burley is five feet eleven inches tall. He weighs one hundred seventy pounds. His hair is brownish blond. His eyes hazel brown. He has several distinguishing marks—"

"This tramp was burned to a crisp. You think distinguishing marks would be left? Come on down to earth here, Jake," Tex said. "This is not very smart. I know you want to find the man, but don't try to force this, 'cause, podner, it just won't fit."

"So prove me wrong," I argued. "Pick up the phone there and get the physical detail report on the John Doe. If they match, you got something to go forward on. If they don't, we drop it and I keep looking."

He sat looking at me as if I had done something socially unsavory. His mouth had a nasty twist to it. He would not be a pleasant man to cross.

I said, "I'm going to push this thing until I get an answer, Tex, so why not humor me? What've you got to lose?"

He pulled at the lobe of his ear, then turned to the phone and punched in some numbers. He put it on speaker so I could hear.

"Mitchell here," after three rings.

"What say there, Al? I'm a-sittin' here with a good old boy who coulda been a Texan if he'd been born proper." He laughed and winked at me. "I'll make a little introduction on the phone here. I'm on the speaker, Al. Al Mitchell, say howdy to Jake Sands."

"Hello, Jake," came the voice from the speaker. I responded with, "Hello, Al."

"Now that you boys know each other, let's get down to business. Al, someplace in your files there you got a physical on that hobo that burned himself up. You know the one I mean?"

Al answered immediately. "I know the one. It's here under a John Doe. What do you need?"

"General description," Tex said. "I suppose it'd be your best guess, since he was barbecued."

"Hold on," Al said. He was away from the phone for a short time, which Tex and I used to avoid eye contact. Al's voice signaled his return. "All right, I got it here."

Tex said, "I'm lookin' for a male, five foot eleven, one seventy, brown hair, brown eyes . . ."

"Yes, you've got a match," Al said.

"But that's just a guess, right?"

"No, not really. We can reconstruct a very accurate image of the deceased."

Tex was disturbed by the news. He did not like to lose at anything, that was clear.

Al continued; "Twelve fillings, four caps on the upper fronts, crowns on both lower rear molars. Old breaks to left leg and left big toe. Fresh breaks to fingers left hand—"

I jumped in. "What does that mean, fresh breaks?"

Al said, "Two of his fingers were broken, I'd say within hours of his death."

Tex and I stared at each other. Tex said, "Okay, Al, thanks. What would you need to make a positive ID?"

"Dentals," Al said without equivocation.

After Tex had concluded the conversation with Al Mitchell, he regained some of his calm. A fresh sack of corn chips seemed to help. He offered, but I declined.

"So, we got a coincidence here, maybe," he said while munching loudly.

"Maybe," I replied.

"Probably," he amended.

"You don't seem too enthusiastic about this."

He leaned back and laughed, spewing small bits of chips onto his desk. He said, "You get a wild hair, and I'm supposed to go full bore chasin' it? Podner, I call the plays in this huddle, and I just don't read the same defense as you."

"A hundred says I'm right," I offered on my way to the door.

"Make it five," he countered.

As soon as I left him I called Kate again. I let the phone ring ten times before I hung up.

On the way home, I stopped by Bob Claiborne's office. I gave him the envelope with the keys and thanked him.

"I was getting a little worried there," he confessed. "I left several messages."

"Yes, I know."

"So, how're things with you?" he asked, as if I thought he cared.

"Fine," I said, putting a solid period to it. "By the way, Bob, a friend of mine has some dealings with a real estate lady named Chandler. Do you happen to know her?"

"Chandler? I can check her out. I have the book right here."

He reached into his drawer and consulted a small book I took to be a listing of all the local real estate companies and agents. He held the book at arm's length to read the small print. I wondered if he knew how silly he looked contorting his head back and squinting like Mr. Magoo. His vanity had overcome his good sense.

"Oh, yes," he said, "Yes, I know her. She's listed here with Parks Realty. It's a Summerland office. Does your friend want property in Summerland?"

I looked away from him, at the collection of things on the wall behind him. He was a very civic-minded fellow according to the plaques. I could not resist pulling his chain a little, but I couldn't watch him while I did it. "Yes," I said. "I think he might be. Big bucks. Big."

"I deal with Summerland property, you know? I can find him anything he wants. Why don't you send him to see me? Hell, Parks Realty is small-time. I'll treat him right, Jake. What's his name? He looking for land, a ranch, what?"

"You don't think this Chandler lady can do the job for him?" I asked innocently.

"Parks does rentals mostly," he said in a rising voice. "This Chandler woman wouldn't know how to handle a big deal if it fell on her."

"You mean the Parks office doesn't handle the large properties?"

"Only for rentals," he said. "And anything they can do I can do better."

"Isn't that a line from a song?" I said as I got to my feet. "Well, I don't pretend to know my friend's business. Perhaps it's a rental he's interested in."

"You should have called me, Jake. Any friend of yours is a friend of mine. You tell him about me, and let me have a shot at finding him something, okay? If it's a rental, that's okay too. I can do it all. You know that."

"Well, maybe it's just a whim," I said, passing it off. "I'll let you know if he gets serious, Bob."

He saw me to the door, reaching up to pat me on the back.

"You ever think of moving out of Coco Palms?" he asked. His realtor's glands were oversecreting.

"Could be," I said, seeing his dangling chain still within reach. "It's not what I expected."

He nodded his head as if in agreement. "I could sell your place easy. Say, I've got something that you might find interesting. It's a building right down by Tony's Beachside. It's commercial except for the top floor. Got a great penthouse apartment. Want to see it?"

"Maybe later," I said, and left him with visions of a double sale.

I drove to Summerland. It was a great day, and I hardly noticed the oil-drilling platforms polluting the channel. I thought briefly of the local furor raised by Chevron or somebody, who wanted to transport their oil through that delicate channel. It was not enough that they had cluttered the view and exposed the entire Santa Barbara coastline to a possible environmental disaster; now they wanted to force that community to live with even greater odds of potential catastrophe. I didn't think I liked them very much for that.

The gates were open, so I pulled up the long driveway and parked in the same place I had parked when I'd been here before. The difference was that Kate was not waiting at her door to greet me. The place was closed and empty-looking. I took a pick kit from my glove compartment and a multipurpose knife with magnetized tweezers. That knife was the most useful tool I had ever owned. I looked for tape but there was none. Oh well.

I went around the house peeking in each window and door. I could not detect anything out of order. I chose a door at the side that was not visible from any other property and worked the lock with a double-tine pick from the kit. The bolt slipped back after a couple of minutes. That part was simple. Then I went to work on the alarm. I guessed it was a standard closed circuit job which used magnets to complete the loop. I used the tiny foldout scissors on the knife to cut small pieces from the mesh of a window screen. I put the pieces on the blade of the knife and extended it to the upper edge of the door, concentrating on the side away from the hinges. I thrust the knife blade in as far as I could with a tilt so the fragments of screen could move. When I saw them pulled off the blade, I marked that point of the door. I thrust the magnetic tweezers into the space above the mark, held my breath, and opened the door. It worked. The tweezers kept the circuit closed. I forced the knife blade into the wood to hold them in place while I roamed.

My first search was for some sign of Kate. I was relieved when I did not find her. It was what I had feared most about coming here. I then took a less frantic look at things. Everything was in perfect order. I worked my way through to Kate's room, where I found the book Kate had mentioned with Wen Leeds's name and number written on the inside of the back cover. It brought her voice back to me, which I didn't need.

In the kitchen, I went directly to the list of numbers next to the phone which I remembered from my first visit there. I copied off the name and number of the dentist. I was happier to get it that way than from Katherine. I wasn't ready to make the explanations that would demand.

I moved on about the house checking drawers and closets, finding nothing unusual or consequential. I worked my way to the garage, where in one bay the Range Rover was parked. I looked around briefly before taking on the car. I had, from the beginning, held some undefined questions about it. Instinct told me Greg Burley had put the car in that auto repair shop to safe-house it. The question that remained for me was, why?

I opened its doors, again marveling at its pristine condition. I sat in each seat, enjoying the feel of the car. I checked out the overhead lining, the seats, and the panels on the doors. It was like new. It was also high-tech. It even had a fax machine attached to the car phone. The thing I envied was the sound system. I could see at least four speakers in the doors. Besides the stereo radio, there was a tape deck and a CD player. I noticed a cassette in the tape player but no CDs. That seemed odd to me, considering the superior sound of the CD. I pulled the tape out. The label identified it as an old Mamas and the Papas tape. I saw "Monday, Monday," and "California Dreamin' " listed and felt a small nostalgic tug. I replaced the tape in the deck with a feeling that my general picture of Greg Burley had just been derailed. A high-tech yuppie didn't connect to an early Sixties music buff.

I ran my hands over everything, feeling for unusual lumps. There were none. The only imperfection was a very slight separation of the rear carpeting from the channel sheath at the right rear door. It was hardly enough to notice, but it was the only thing to notice, so I did. I bent down and felt it. There was nothing to feel. Reluctantly I pulled at the carpet. It came away from the casing more freely than I expected. I lifted it up enough to insert my hand beneath it. I could feel only a folded sheet of paper, which I withdrew.

I put the paper aside and pulled back the rest of the carpet for a more thorough search. There was nothing more. Finally I replaced the carpet and closed up the car. I took the paper into the house. It was a yellowed diagram of shapes and lines with notations all over. It was too much to absorb without some careful study. It was, however, vaguely familiar in form.

I left the house without tripping the alarm and relocked the door. I drove home numbed by the day. Breaking and entering was not a relaxing way to spend time.

At home I delayed my study of the paper until I had made myself something to eat. I cooked up a simple omelet, which I ate while looking for local news on television. I found the NBC affiliate in the introductory phase of its evening broadcast and left it there. Jason came to mind when I saw the newsreader with the frozen hair begin to do his thing. He was a robot to be sure. The voice was perfect, but the soul was dead. A Dan Rather clone.

The lead story was the one I had tuned in for. The robot told us about the body of Claude Hayes having been discovered on a beach in Isla Vista. Isla Vista? In an apparent accident the man had fallen to his death from the Vista Mesa cliffs. The robot looked appropriately solemn, concluding his report with the information that there was an ex-wife and a surviving son, both living in Arizona.

I switched off the television and pondered the details I had just heard. Isla Vista was quite a distance form Coco Palms. Somebody had taken the body of Claude Hayes on a long ride, probably right up the beach in a four-wheel-drive vehicle, if I had my guess. I had not expected that, and it left me with more than I could deal with. I was much too tired.

Even a shower did nothing to revive me. I lay down, still slightly damp, and with the lights on and much left to consider, I fell asleep. I heard the phone ring. It rang two different times that night, but I was confident that my machine could handle it.

16 🌿

Dawn came up without me. I rode a dream into a more decent hour before I let go. Once up, I stumbled around for a while before I showered, shaved, and dressed myself in denims and a soft Sea Island cotton shirt.

As my first order of business, I called Burley's dentist, Dr. Dunn. I kept my fingers crossed that Burley had been in for more than a teeth cleaning. He had, and Dunn had his complete dental file on hand. He agreed to messenger Greg Burley's dental records, including X rays, to Al Mitchell at the county building. Then I called Al Mitchell and told him to expect the messenger. I said it was urgent and asked for a callback with the results. He sounded a little vague in his reply, but it was in the vicinity of a yes, so I went with it.

I had a cup of coffee and downed a bowl of Grape Nuts, before I remembered I had to make a call for Sam Garvey. I checked my book for the number of a very special service company called the Paladin Group. They could do a lot of things, but all I asked for was a sweep of Sam Garvey's house. I gave them the address and they promised a man would be out by noon.

I noticed the message light and pushed playback. I mentally crossed my fingers as I sipped at my coffee and listened to the first message. It wasn't a hang-up. Someone was there, but whoever it was said nothing. There was a sound, however, which at first I mistook for heavy breathing. It took a minute to recognize the sound of the surf. It was the same sound I had listened to several times while looking at the stars out by my pool. There was a subtle message there which someone had gone to the trouble to deliver with a cellular phone.

The beep for the second message caught me in midspeculation. I felt the sudden jolt of her voice like a shot to the gut. "Jake? I know it's late but if you get in and get this message tonight, call me. It doesn't matter what time, okay? I miss you. Oh, this is Kate." There was that little throaty laugh and she was gone.

Without thinking, I reached for the phone and dialed.

"Hello?" she said on the second ring.

"It's Jake."

"As if I wouldn't know," she said with an instant tease. "Get my message?"

"Yeah, this morning."

"Sleeping on the beach again?"

It took a minute. I responded, "No, in my own soft bed. Fact is, I was already asleep when you called."

"I believe you," she said with the laugh in her voice. "Have you been very busy?"

"Yeah," I said. "Kate, can you meet me for lunch today?"

"I thought you'd never ask. I would love to."

"Do you know Tony's Beachside?"

"Near the pier?"

"Right. Meet me there at one. I may have some news," I said. "And Kate, it may not be good news."

After a pause she said, "I'm a big girl, Jake. See you at one."

I worked out and waited. It was noon before I got the call. I would have preferred Al Mitchell. What I got was Tex Flanagan.

"You keep up your stunts, podner, and you an' me are gonna walk the streets of fist city." His voice was mean. "You get my drift, cowboy?"

"Is that in California?" I decided on flip because I didn't

trust myself with any other kind of answer.

He surprised me. He laughed. It was the deep, obnoxious kind that makes you cringe. "You must be tough," he said. "You got the gall of a real tough nut. You just be glad I like you. Okay, you kept the ball on an end around and your luck held, podner. You scored."

"The John Doe is Greg Burley?"

"Right as rain. I reckon I owe you a hundred," he mumbled.

"Five," I corrected.

"My aunt's fanny, five! You didn't take me up on five," he protested.

"Whatever you think's right," I said. "So, what do you do with it now? Any suspects?"

He guffawed. I could imagine spittle flying in all directions. "Suspects? We're not even chalking up murder yet. So far the only difference is we got a name for the John Doe. It still reads the same."

"I see," I said. "Okay, Tex, you call your own game." Damn, I thought, he had me doing football metaphor.

"I don't play if I don't," he responded in kind. "Jake, what say we get together for a little powwow meal here pretty soon. You're a real smart fella, and you might have an idea or two that I'd like. Anyhow, I want to hear how you're coming with Charlie."

"Charlie? Oh, Jessup. Sure, why not? I'll call you," I said.

"I'll pay. That'll make us square," he said, as if he were making a great gesture. I wondered if he knew Bob Claiborne.

"Sounds good," I said. When I put the phone down I thought for a mad moment of destroying it, as if that would eliminate the fools who were slowly taking over the world.

• • •

Tony wasn't due in until later so I waited for Kate outside in the parking lot. It was a nice lot as far as lots go. It was surrounded by shade trees with a few interspersed down the middle. It was set back on Cabrillo, which ran along the beach, and which made it pretty expensive real estate. On the back side of the parking lot was a three-story building with a nice facade. The lower floor of the building had a dive shop fronting on an access road, and a bookstore facing the side street. The middle floor appeared to be warehousing. The top looked very interesting. It showed awninged terraces with lots of potted plants. The penthouse, I thought, and the building that Bob Claiborne had mentioned. I studied it until I heard the little beep of Kate's horn announcing her arrival.

She floated on my arm to our table, and we must have talked because her lips moved, and she reacted to things, and she reached across to touch me in emphasis, but I don't remember what was said. It was just stuff. Polite stuff. Simple, impersonal stuff. I let us eat, and I let myself tour her face and eyes for as long as I dared. I let her enjoy her wine and whatever she wished while I waited for a time when I could tell her.

She made it happen. She folded her napkin neatly and put it aside and said, "So, tell me."

I fiddled with the things in front of me, arranging them just right. I nodded and took careful aim and said, "Greg is dead."

There was a flicker. It was like watching a film that has a glitch. Everything slides a notch, and then it's back to normal as if nothing's happened. I tried to wait her out because I wanted her words, but the moment stretched too long for comfort. I added, "I'm sorry."

She nodded. She blinked. She stared, not really at me or at anything. She just stared.

"Are you okay?" I asked. It was a fool's question.

She was gracious enough not to make a vocal reply. It was a blink, and a pinch of the mouth, and a smile to me from the eyes.

When at last she spoke, it was a question. "Are you sure?"

"Yes," I said. "They made the positive identification this morning." I needed to get it all out. I told everything I knew about it: the fire, the deserted house, the story in the paper, and the day he disappeared.

It landed like blows, or I imagined it did. Nothing showed on the outside. I had to guess at what was happening inside. I reached across and held her hand. She dropped her head for a while, so I could not see her eyes.

I looked out the window at normal people doing normal things. It made it all surreal. The setting was wrong for this sort of thing. We should have been in a quiet, dark room.

"And now?" she said.

"The coroner will tell you," I replied.

"Can we walk?" she asked.

I nodded and quickly paid the bill. We walked among the normal people who prattled on around us about normal, silly, meaningless things. I wished we were doing that. I wished I could help her.

"I need to go now," she said finally. I walked her to her car, where she turned and looked hard at me. "Can I call you?" she said. "Can I still see you?"

"Anytime."

After she had gone I looked again at the building behind the parking lot. It was too close to the normal people, I thought.

• • •

Jason beat me easily. I was in another world and he knew it. He reaped no great joy from his victory.

"Well, we got that out of the way," he said as he wheeled himself over to his bar. "I once went to see a singer at a club down on Wilshire. The Horn, I think it was. Anyway, I was down in front where I was as lit up as the stage—by the lights, old pal, not booze. This comic comes on. His stuff is all political, not very good, and on the wrong side from me, but I thought I was reacting fine. He stopped cold and stared down at me and said, 'I'm sorry I'm ruining your evening. I know you came in here to see the singer. I'll hurry and get out of your way.' It embarrassed the hell out of me."

He swirled his freshly poured drink into the light. It was a beautiful amber. He wheeled himself back to face me. "Since then I always think of the insignificant things that fall before the important moments as the 'comic.' Now that we've gotten rid of the comic, let's get to it. What's going on with you?"

"When did you meet Katherine Burley for the first time?" I asked.

He did a little take, like someone on the receiving end of a short straight jab. "You mean the date?"

"Was it before or after Greg Burley disappeared?"

He did not have to think about it. "After."

"You never saw her with him? Ever, even at a distance?" I leaned into the question.

His eyes probed back at mine. "No," he answered. "She called me and said that she knew Greg was a regular customer. She asked if she could come talk to me about him. She came, we talked, and that's when I learned he had gone missing. Then I called you."

I nodded, taking it in. He waited. I said, "Greg Burley was killed. He was burned to death. Made to look like a vagrant who committed suicide. Greg Burley was linked, and to what degree I'm not sure, to the guy who got shot in Coco Palms. You remember him? Wendell Leeds?"

He nodded and moved his glass in a constant rhythm, but he was not drinking. He was making a silent little whistle.

"There was another person linked to them who was killed in an automobile, made to look like an accident but had murder written all over it. I don't know her connection to them."

"Her name?"

"Toni Spence."

"Oh, yeah, you mentioned her before. Toni with an 'i.' " He pulled at his lower lip. "Any relation to Anthony Carl Spence, I wonder?"

"The lawyer? I never thought of it. Maybe."

"Spence and something? Big-time San Francisco firm. I seem to remember reading where he died a while back, and I believe his partner, too, a year or so earlier. Want me to check it?"

"Why not?" I said. "How well did you get to know Greg Burley?"

"We talked a few times. He was here quite a lot. Fit in well with the poker crowd. Started coming about a year ago, I'd say."

"Do you remember who brought him in?"

He thought about it a moment. "Yes. Bob Claiborne."

I was surprised. "You sure?"

"I'm sure," he said emphatically. "Claiborne was his real estate agent, found him his place in Summerland, I think."

"Did Greg talk much about Katherine?"

"No, not at all."

"He ever mention that he was separated?"

"Yes, I think so, maybe . . . or divorced, or not getting along. I don't remember exactly." He put his hands up in a halting motion. "Wait a minute here, Jake. If I hear you right, Greg Burley has been located. Why do I get the feeling that you're not dropping it there?"

"I have to know some things. When I know what I need to, then I'll drop it."

"Wouldn't have anything to do with Kate, would it?"

"Everything," I confirmed.

"So, what have you got in your leather envelope there? I swore to myself I wouldn't ask. I was gonna wait you out, but to hell with it. Tell me."

"I'll show you," I said. "But first let me tell you this. Greg and Wen were divers. They were intentionally looking for a spot near the Channel Islands. They found it, and they found something there that I think got them killed. Now this is just my guess, but I think they tried to make it look like it hadn't been taken, maybe just long enough for them to clear out, but it didn't work. I found what they left, an empty case, but what I don't think they knew was that there was something hidden in the lead lining." I passed the small, diarylike book to him. "I don't think they ever saw this."

" 'G,' huh?" he said, more to himself than to me, as he ran his finger over the gold initial on the front. "Cipher?" he asked after a casual glance into the book.

"Either that or G is a lousy speller," I said. "I thought I might leave it with you, because it's going to take some work. Right up your alley."

"It's nice to be needed," he said with his wry smile. "So it was something worth great risk? Something other than money?"

"I'm thinking that," I agreed. "And this may have been part of it in some way. I don't know."

I took from my portfolio the paper I had removed from the floor mat of the Range Rover. I spread it out before handing it across.

"Has a few years on it," he said with a look at the yellowing of all the exposed portions.

"How old, do you think?"

"I'd say about fifteen years. Maybe more. Hard to tell." He was quickly becoming absorbed by the diagrams on the paper. "Have you made out any of these notations? Do you know what this is?"

"The diagram in the corner seems to be a house or building of some sort, and the major drawing could be streets, rivers, canals. There are a lot of numbers that could be times or dates, and a lot of shorthand and abbreviation."

"You know what this reminds me of, Jake?"

He turned the diagram around to gain a different perspective on it. Suddenly he looked up at me and said, "It's a control map."

I leaned in. I turned my head so that I might also see it from different perspectives. "Possible," I said.

"No. It is," he stated. "It's just like the control maps we used to draw up for missions in the old days. You remember the very first missions that were planned but never carried out? Before we had access to satellites, and zoom booms and minicom systems, we made these kinds of plans. Ours were better. This baby is crude, but it's a control map. A blueprint for some kind of action."

I was involuntarily nodding my head. He was right. I could feel Jason's interest heighten. He was never happier than when he had a puzzle.

"So what country is this in? Is it a killing, a robbery, what? And when?" I asked aloud the most basic questions I had about it.

Jason wheeled himself to his cigars and went through his lighting ritual. "Let me ask you," he said. "Is this just curiosity pushing you, or are you serious here?"

"I'm serious," I answered.

"Okay, then let me make a copy of this thing and see what I can do in the daylight. If it's what we think it is, then it should have all the answers right there on it." He took the map and wheeled into the office. In a moment he had returned.

"It conjures up a lot of memories to see a control map again," he said. He handed back the original.

"Any of them good?"

I had to guess from the look on his face that some of them were. He was still wearing that expression when we shook hands and said goodnight. I wondered if at times like that he was thinking about how life had been with two good legs.

• • •

It was always my instincts that had given me the edge. They had even, in some instances, kept me alive. I relied on them and, to a great degree, took them for granted. But then, there were always those times when I would become a little too loose or too preoccupied. As I drove into my garage that night I was very preoccupied. I was thinking about the control map and how it figured in with everything else.

I had never been hit with a Taser gun before, but I knew instantly what it was that slammed into me. It was a jolt that hit me high in the back and took my legs out from under me. I dropped to the side, trying to fall away from the assault and buy time. It didn't work. There were two of them.

I took a wild kick to the back of the neck as I tried to roll. A second Taser barb struck me, taking what little strength I had left. The double jolts brought convulsions. I felt like a fish floundering on dry sand. The assailants were quiet and efficient. I was hoping their intent was just to send a message.

One sound penetrated the fuzz that was building in my brain. It was the dull tinkle of keys, bunched and fastened to a belt. I remembered hearing that sound somewhere else. I listened hard to the jingle of the bunched keys, trying to force the memory of where I had heard it before. A foot connected with my temple before a bright light, which rose from the back of my skull, brought a flash of pain and then inky darkness.

I came to a semiconscious state with my head beneath the car. It must have been an instinctive move I had made, right at the end. I had pains all over. My head, my neck, the spots on my back where the high-voltage barbs had hit me, all let me know that I had been worked over pretty good. Maybe not as much as they had thought, but still pretty good.

By the time I got myself under the cold water of the shower, I was thinking fairly straight. I replayed it through the ache in my brain. Most of it was sounds. The scuffling feet, the muted voices, and the keys. I had it. I could not only hear those keys in my memory, I could see them as I had last seen them, clumped on a ring and attached to the belt by a leather strap.

I called the patrol office. "No, Patrolman Stanner is not working tonight." And "Captain Jessup is not available this evening either."

I opted not to leave a message. I'd be seeing them soon, I said.

• • •

The Coco Palms Homeowners' Association office was dark and locked up tight. It was an easy matter to enter and bypass the alarm, an old-fashioned model which had never been updated. It made me wonder where the money we were being assessed was being spent.

I found the personnel files I needed and xeroxed the pages on Jessup and Stanner. I really only needed the home addresses, but then you never knew when it might all come in handy.

While I was there I thought I might as well take a little look around. I spent another hour nosing through other files and desk drawers. I found a small file cabinet, locked and labeled

"Private." That, of course, got my attention. I opened it and pulled out the contents. It was, for the most part, a record of actions taken by the board of directors during executive sessions. I understood quickly that executive sessions meant board only. No outsiders. No minutes taken. No record, other than what I had found, which in itself was a raging testament to the arrogance of Dreckman and the rest. Dreckman seemed to feel impervious to reprisal. It was time he got some reality. I xeroxed everything that looked interesting. Garvey would know just how to use it.

I drove first to Charlie Jessup's house. He lived well. Too well for a security man. I was about to check out his garage when he saved me the trouble. He pulled up in his Wagoneer. I watched from a short distance as he drove into his garage and closed the door behind him. He was in for the night. At least he thought he was. That was all I cared about.

I made the quick drive to Fred Stanner's. It was time I began to find out some things and to reduce the odds. Fred Stanner was the logical place for me to begin. Besides, I owed him. I didn't like to let such debts linger.

He still wasn't home when I got there. I checked my watch and noted that the bars were still open. He seemed like the type that might stay until last call, so I went inside his place to make myself comfortable. He did not live well. That is, he did not live neatly, or cleanly. He was a pig in more ways than one.

I took the opportunity to find out what I could about Fred Stanner. I did not bother to hide the fact that I ransacked his closets and drawers. In fact, I took great pleasure in adding to the mess. What I found did not surprise me. One drawer was filled with Polaroids of females of various ages in varying stages of undress. Some of them seemed to be enjoying it while others showed a definite level of distress. I pulled the drawer out. Taped to the bottom was an envelope containing more pictures, somewhat more graphic in detail. Stanner costarred in some of them, and in some I recognized my old

friend Charlie Jessup. They were quite a pair. They obviously
partied together. In picture after picture it was either Stanner
or Jessup clutching onto a naked girl who seemed terrified by
her dilemma. There were some where the girls were either
bound or handcuffed. I wondered if one of those girls was
Karen Bayless.

I also wondered why the pictures were in Stanner's hands. A
tiny alarm sounded in my brain, but passed as I scanned the
rest of the pictures. It was clear the females they were using
were victims, but some of the pictures could be made to look
like something else. Was the purpose of this collection
pornography or blackmail?

I moved on in my search. He had several guns. I found two
handguns and four rifles of various types. Nothing with a
scope though. I also found his bankbooks. He was getting
some very healthy money from some source. It was regular,
too. That built a case for blackmail.

I heard the garage door opener start its pull, so I cut the
lights and went to the door leading to the garage. The car
pulled in, and then when the engine died I thought I could
make out voices. That was not what I expected. I listened
more closely and did not like what I heard.

A girl's voice on the edge of panic said, "Please, you
promised to take me back to my car. Please, don't."

"You can get out nice or I can break this arm here, but
you're gettin' out, and you're not going to make any noise."
Fred Stanner's tone was nasty and maybe a little drunk.

He must have done something to hurt her, because she
screamed. It was the wrong thing to do. I slipped as quietly as
I could through the door and eased down in front of the car.
He pulled her out and she made a noise of protest. He hit her
again. She bounced off the car and fell to the floor. He bent
and picked her up. His strength was impressive. Probably
practiced three-hundred-pound dead lifts with Jessup every
day just for this purpose.

He carried her inside the way a normal person might carry a

bag of groceries, in one arm. With the other hand he closed
the door behind him. The bunch of keys jingled in his wake. I
waited for perhaps thirty seconds before following. Evidently
the additional mess I had created did not make an impression
on him, because he took his prey directly to the bedroom. He
did not bother turning on lights either. He was content to use
the faint illumination from exterior lights which peeked in
around the edges of dirty shades. I could hear her crying. I
could hear him slapping. I moved quickly.

He had already torn her blouse away and had both hands in
the band of her jeans ready to rip them down. I put the high-
beam flashlight straight on him and said, "By the count of
three you be on your feet and against the wall. One, two . . ."

He moved then, having figured the odds were that whoever
had him also had a gun. He tried hard to peer through the
beam to read me, but I kept his eyes with the light. The girl
was a mess. Her face was red, her nose bloody, and her jaw
hung slack and swollen, signifying a break. She grabbed at her
blouse, not knowing what to do. She made pathetic little animal noises.

I said, "Go on out of here now. Take his car wherever you
need to go and leave it. You can wreck it if you want to, or
blow it up or whatever. I can guarantee this guy won't ever
give you trouble again."

She was frozen for a moment. When she did move, it was
slowly. She was in real pain, and I feared she might pass out.

"Are you going to be able to drive?" I asked.

She nodded dumbly. The tears finally began to subside. I
imagined they would really pour later. She held her left arm
with her right hand. "He hurt my arm," she said.

I looked at it. It was badly bruised, but otherwise appeared to
be okay. It was her jaw that would bring her the pain tomorrow. "Your arm is going to be all right," I said. "Now go."

She left without ever getting a look at me, which was the
way I wanted it. I waited until I heard the car leave the driveway.

"Hello, again, hotshot," I said.

"This some kinda joke or something?" he said hopefully.

"Nope," I answered, "no joke. Matter of fact, this is one of the more serious nights you'll have in your life."

His head was clearing. He was beginning to make some calculations. He was getting smart to the light and keeping his head turned slightly away from it. I switched it off. The dark was worse for him than for me. It took him longer to adjust, and in that time I moved across the room and kicked him very hard in the stomach. I moved back to the doorway and hit the overhead light switch in time to watch him drop to his knees.

His look of surprise was comical. It was then I realized he thought they had killed me in my garage. He and his pal had left me for dead under my car after the Taser gun attack. Too bad for him I caught that look. It made me angrier.

"You're in for a hard night, Freddy boy. One that will change you forevermore," I said. "On your feet, we're going to the other room."

He shook off the effects of the kick and rose. I could see the cunning little pig eyes assess the situation. I could almost see the very moment he realized there was no gun. He pretended to do as he was told. He was not a good actor. He was almost bad enough to make the grade in today's films. His move was low-grade kung fu, slow and clumsy. He was strong though, and when he came in at me he came with power.

I backed him off with a double jab to his forehead. It hurt my hand more than it did him, but it was enough to take the steam out of his rush. He groped at me as I moved backward into the other room. His fighting style changed to basic street-animal stuff. I popped him twice more on the cheek and nose before he got to me. His hands grabbed at my shirt like steel claws. He pulled me in for a head smash, which I suppose he had seen in some movie or maybe learned from some sensei at a local martial arts dojo. The only problem with the head smash is, you have to be perfect. You have to hit the other guy in the face with the hardest part of your head, which is the curve just above the forehead. If the other guy should, for instance, drop his head as you are swinging yours forward, then it turns into a very bad move. I let him hurt himself on my head; then I pulled myself free of him and drove a right hand into his face. His nose came apart, and he dropped like a sack of potatoes.

I was having fun. I was remembering the sounds the girl had made, and I had made her a promise. "Can you hear me," I asked close to his ear. He held both hands to his nose as he looked up at me.

"You've . . . made . . . big mistake," he said.

"Nope, you made the mistake." I grabbed him by the hair and pulled him up. "Now let's talk."

"Nothing . . . say." He glared at me over his hands. He backed away, and I knew exactly what he was thinking and where he was going.

"Don't do it," I said. "I know what you're thinking, but let me tell you some truth here. If you get to a gun, I'll use it on you. Don't do it."

He did not listen. He figured his chances were better than I had painted them. He rolled away from me over the table and grabbed a handgun from the lower bookcase cabinet. He had it coming up nicely when I jumped, feet forward, to kick it away. I felt my back go on me a little bit, and had a funny, fleeting thought of how ridiculous this whole thing was. I'm sure my move hurt me more than it did him, but it kept him from firing. He tried to aim the gun at me again, so I kicked him in the groin. I decided that maybe he should be the one hurt the most. I let him double over before I pulled him up by the hair once more and pushed the heel of my hand into his face. He yelled and fell back against a table. The gun dropped at his feet. I picked it up.

"You're about as smart as I thought you were," I said with an ample amount of disgust. "Who was with you tonight at my place? Jessup?"

"I wasn't at your place," he blustered.

"No, but your keys were, and I'm still going to punish you

for that," I said. "And then there's the promise I made that girl, and of course, the warning I gave you when you went for the gun. I hate to do this, but I have to, you understand. You have to know that when I say I'm going to do something, I do it."

I aimed the gun at him, held it, lowered it to his knee, and then pulled the trigger. He went down in a crumpled heap of mewling agony. I let him roll and twist with it before I nudged him over with my foot.

"That's just a knee," I said. "There's more. You want to answer a few questions now?"

He looked up at me, still in shock, but with a new horror in his eyes. He was probably genuinely afraid for the first time in his life. Slowly he nodded.

"Good," I said. "Now who was with you tonight? Jessup?"

He nodded again.

"What's your game? What's going on with Jessup?"

He closed his eyes against the pain. "No game. He learns things about people and uses it . . ."

"Where did Claude Hayes figure?"

"A guy Charlie used to do odd jobs. He was an electrician by trade and—" He stopped suddenly and looked at me with new understanding. "You did him, didn't you?"

I thought it might be to my advantage to let him think so. I said, "He was uncooperative." I let that sink in before I asked, "Why me?"

"You were a positive ID leaving the Palms the night Leeds was shot. Charlie figured you saw something . . . thought he could put pressure on you."

"Who ID'd me? Who shot Leeds?"

"I don't know. It wasn't me."

"Jessup?"

He shook his head. "No. I don't think so."

"That little car dealer MacGribb didn't identify me, so who did?"

"I don't know. Jessup just said it was positive," he answered. "Please, my leg."

I remembered how the girl had pleaded. I kicked his thigh,

which moved his knee, which made him scream in pain.

"How many houses are bugged in the Palms?" I asked.

" 'Bout twenty," he moaned. "Please, I can't stand this. I can't breathe."

"Which ones?"

"I don't know exactly. It moves around. We keep one on Dreckman and the rest of the board, and on Garvey and the other mouths, and on a few special cases like you." He was beginning to hyperventilate.

"How long have you been doing it?"

"Don't know. Charlie had it set up before I came. Three years maybe."

"How many people have you killed, Stanner?"

"Nobody," he said with a violent shake of his head. "I've put the scare, but I ain't been part of any killin'. On my mother's eyes, I swear."

"And Jessup?"

He did not want to answer. He put it off by moaning. I gave him something to really moan about. I kicked his knee.

"Jesus," he yelled. "I don't know. Not for sure. He was away at the same time Beloit got it and the Giardellas, too, but I ain't sure he did it." The pain was getting to him. "I don't know nothing else about it. I need some help, please." He began to shake in a convulsive way.

"What about Greg Burley and Toni Spence?"

His eyes began to roll up. He was about to go into shock. I brought the phone to him and pulled his head up, using his hair again. I said, "Call nine one one. You tell them you shot yourself in the knee."

He took the phone and began to dial. I said, "You don't have to mention that I was here."

He got an answer and told the voice on the other end what I had told him to say and gave his name and address. They evidently told him to hold on, but I gave him the sign to hang up. He obeyed me.

"You've got a week to get out of here," I said. I took one of the Xerox copies from my pocket and looked at it. "And I mean clear out of California. It says here that you're from Ohio. I think you should go back there. You will never see that girl again, and you will not go inside Coco Palms again. Ever. Because if you do . . ."

I pointed his gun between his eyes and held it there for a moment. He tried to turn his head away. I prodded him.

"I'll always find you, sport, no matter where you try to hide, so don't be dumb. You do what I say and you might hobble into old age."

His eyes had dulled with the pain, but I could see that my words took deep root.

" 'Night," I said, and laid the back of my fist into his jaw. He toppled to the side. I dropped the gun beside him and hastily departed his premises. I had just gotten to my car when the ambulance arrived. I waited until they had taken him out on a stretcher. He was conscious again and screaming openly with the pain. It was a pathetic sight, I had to admit. But then it was hard to feel sorry for a guy like that.

17 🌿

I slept in a bit and awoke with a jumbled brain and a few sore spots. I went through a short routine of very careful calisthenics to ease out some of the muscle distensions. There wasn't much I could do about my brain except coffee. I called Bob Claiborne as soon as I was up to speed on the day, and made a date with him for later in the morning. Then I called Sam Garvey.

"You were quite right, Jake, about there being listening devices in my home, by the way, and your Paladin people were most efficient in finding and removing them," he said.

"You should have them sweep your friends' homes as well," I suggested.

"My thought exactly," he readily agreed. "So I called several people here in the Palms and in fact, set it up for them with the Paladin Group people. But I did it stupidly. I forgot that their phones might be listened to as mine had been. Evidently at least one of them was. I'm afraid I blundered."

"Why so?"

"Last night I received a call . . . very menacing. Anonymous, of course, but I know who it was."

"Tell me."

"It had to be Jessup. Or his henchman, Stanner. They've become so brazen in their tactics of late that they feel they can get away with anything. I'm genuinely afraid now."

He sounded it. "I don't think you have anything to worry about, Sam," I said. "They won't be stupid enough to try anything with you."

"I wish I could be as sure about that, Jake. I keep remembering Beloit and the Giardellas. This caller last night mentioned my daughter and her family and even knew where they live."

"Do you trust me?" I asked. "If I say I'll handle this for you, will you believe me?

"Yes," he answered without hesitation.

"Stanner won't be with us any longer," I said. "Don't ask me why or how, and don't mention to anyone I said so. I'm going to drop some papers in your mailbox this morning. I think they'll give you what you need on Dreckman. The whole board actually."

"Jake, you give me anything on Dreckman and his bunch, I'll blow them right out of the water. I'm set up with all the firepower I need. Only the ammunition is missing."

"The ammunition will be in your mailbox. Okay?"

He sounded better when I hung up, which gave me a slight lift. I did as promised, then headed into town and Cabrillo Boulevard.

I parked in Tony's lot and walked around to the side-street entrance to the building. Bob was there waiting for me when I arrived . . . and I was early. He was a very anxious real estate man.

"Jake, I want you to see what you've got here," he said after the amenities were observed. "On the lower floor facing one street you've got that dive shop, on the other is the rare-book store, and facing the lot here is a ladies' boutique and the best art gallery in town for my money. All steady, long-term rentals. The middle floor is set up for warehousing. I mean, what could be simpler? And you live on top of it all in the penthouse. This is one in a million, Jake."

He rattled on as he led me to the elevator. "This elevator is yours alone. It only goes to the penthouse. Phenomenal, isn't it? There's a stairway too that only serves the penthouse. See, the guy who built this building made all this for himself, but he never moved in, and then he died, and the building got tied up in a probate thing, and well, you know how that goes."

I hadn't come here out of any interest in the building or the penthouse. I wanted to talk to Bob about Greg Burley, but I also wanted to keep it subtle. I figured it was easier to do that with him showing me something he had for sale. Now I was wondering if that had been such a good idea. I liked what I saw.

We stepped out of the elevator into an entry foyer. He led me into the apartment, still talking about the guy who had built it and the problems of the probate, and on and on. I stopped listening and started looking. It faced the beach, the pier, the islands, and Cabrillo Boulevard on one side, and the city and the mountains behind on the other. This was some place. There was a terrace all the way around with a lap pool along one side. I was impressed.

Bob never stopped talking. "All the ceilings are ten or twelve feet high. You need that, Jake, for your size. And look at the room you got here. Phenomenal square footage, and wait'll you see this. Just look, Jake, look at this kitchen. Is that a kitchen or what? The latest thing. Real gourmet. Phenomenal."

I ached to see a kitchen some real estate shark didn't declare to be "gourmet." I followed him through the apartment. The rooms were large and plentiful. As much as I wanted to resist it, I had never seen anything quite like it.

"It's one of a kind, Jake." He droned on without letup. "It really is you. You know what I mean? I look at a place like this, and I say this fits you to a T. I bet I could sell your place and make a deal for you on this one where the rentals would cover the mortgage on the difference. Or plenty close anyway. Jake, this really is a phenomenal place."

I wondered if he had just picked up the word "phenomenal" and was trying it on me. I also wondered if he was hanging out with a new and younger crowd.

"You're right, Bob, this is impressive," I said. We walked through the rooms twice more, and I tried to ease into it slowly. "This place got all hung up in probate, huh? Like the Leeds property?"

"No, a different thing entirely. You know, it comes out now that Leeds wasn't the deeded owner of that property. It was some law firm in San Francisco holding it in the estate of a client. Big mess. But this place is clear. You give me the right offer and you could sail right in."

"That reminds me," I said, hanging on. "You knew Greg Burley, didn't you?"

He looked stricken. "Yes," he answered. "I read about it in the paper this morning, him being identified after all this time." He shook his head sadly. "It's really awful, isn't it?"

I hadn't seen the paper. "What?" I asked.

"Why, him burning himself up that way. It's hard to believe he'd do a thing like that. Like a Buddhist or something. I didn't know he was such a fanatic. And over the homeless? My God, he never struck me as that type at all."

"How'd you get to know him?" I asked innocently while looking out at the view.

"Oh, I spent a lot of time with him showing him properties," he told me. "We saw every big house from Goleta to Carpenteria. He looked like a sure thing. It was Wendell Leeds, in fact, who introduced us. Greg was down from San Francisco looking for a place and Wendell put us together. They were business associates, I think. God, I think of all the time I wasted on him."

"Yeah," I said, as if I had a glimmering of empathy for his complaint. "What do you think of the wife?"

"Whose wife?"

"Greg's. Mrs. Burley."

"I never met her," he said regretfully.

That got my attention. "Never?"

"He did all the looking alone." He leaned forward and took a more confidential pose. "Well, sometimes Wendell would go with us, but most of the time he was alone. If he was married it comes as a bit of a surprise."

"How so?"

He gave a knowing little smile. "Well, Wendell was a bit on the light side, if you get my meaning, and so I just figured that Greg was, like, his boyfriend. I never figured him to be married."

"So you didn't get to know him socially at all?"

"Not beyond a certain point, no. I took him around to some of the clubs. I even took him to dinner at Meddler's. I introduced him to Jason Meddler, because he'd mentioned that he was addicted to cards, and asked me if I knew a place."

"What clubs?"

He raised his eyebrows at the question. "Well, Valley, of course, Birnham Woods, Montecito, and the new Summerland C.C."

"Not Coco Palms?"

"No," he answered. "I didn't think he'd want to go all the way over there with good clubs right at his doorstep."

"And you never met *her*, huh? She never went to the clubs with you?"

"No. I've never met her."

"Phenomenal."

He looked at me with new respect.

"Then after you sold him the house on Palmetto Lane you didn't keep in touch?"

"I didn't sell him that house. He just leased it." Bob was perturbed. "I didn't get a penny out of it. He went through another agent out in Summerland. I think of all the hours I spent showing him houses, and the miles I drove . . . There's no telling what I spent on lunches and dinners and all. Hell, I should have gotten something for it."

"Would you know who that agent was?"

"It was that Chandler woman you mentioned that your friend was dealing with. The Parks agency? By the way, how's that going for him? Did you tell him about me?"

"Oh, that," I said. "That's a dead issue, Bob."

I promised to get back to him about the penthouse. I wasn't sure if I had gotten answers or simply opened up new questions.

I left my car in Tony's lot and took a walk across Cabrillo to the beach. I drifted down toward the pier, and used the pay phone that was farthest out beyond the last concession stand. The pier creaked and moaned beneath me as I waited through ten rings. She didn't answer. I hadn't expected her to. I picked up the phone book and found the Parks real estate agency. In less than a minute I was talking to a lady named Chandler. I mentioned Greg Burley to her and we each expressed bewilderment at his demise.

"Would you happen to remember your last conversation with Greg Burley?" I asked. "Approximately when it was and the content? Things of that sort?"

She answered immediately, with an animated voice. "I certainly do, Mr. Sands. He returned a call to me from his car phone. The exact date I'm not clear on, but say around mid-month sometime. It's my feeling that it was on the very day he died, according to the paper."

"And the content?" I asked, hoping she would not balk at the question.

She hesitated briefly. "I suppose it would do no harm to tell you. We discussed his vacating the house."

That caught me off guard. "For what reason?"

"His lease was up," she explained. "Actually, it's not up for another week, but he was vacating early. He held a year's lease on the house, and did not wish to extend. The rent was terribly high."

"So, he informed you he was leaving? How soon did he say?"

"In a day or two I believe. Then we received the call that the house would be occupied until the last day of the lease, so we are not even allowed to show it for another few days. It seems a bit odd with him found dead, but it's not unusual for people to allow friends to take vacated accommodations for the remainder of a paid-up lease. That happens most frequently."

"Who called you?"

"That I don't know. I didn't take the call myself. It doesn't really matter to us as long as the house is vacated promptly when the lease expires."

I changed course slightly. "Has anyone from the sheriff's department talked to you about any of this? About that conversation?"

"No. Someone did call, a short time back, checking out this number to see who Mr. Burley had called that day from his car. I said it was I. That was all." She waited for more.

"Did you ever meet Mr. Burley's wife?" I held my breath.

She took a prolonged breath. "Well, I did happen by one day, the only time I ever went by actually, and did meet a woman there I took to be his mother. I suppose it could have been a wife, but she was much older than he. There was never any mention of a wife, however. None at all."

"Was that older woman staying there? Living there?"

"It appeared so. She was certainly sleeping there. It was in the morning, and she was still in robe and slippers."

After I hung up I went to the very end of the pier and leaned against the railing to look out at the islands across the channel. I thought through the jumble of deaths and deceptions I had stepped into. I couldn't make the pieces fit. I didn't like the questions I had. The only thing left for me was to stir things up a bit.

I left the pier and walked in the opposite direction from my car. It was just far enough to be good exercise without being work. It was a nice day, and I had a lot to think about.

Walt Haber didn't see me until I was almost next to him. He was working on his boat with the kind of dedicated masochism that afflicts most boat owners. I stopped and let him discover me. It unnerved him.

"Jeez," he said, spilling some soapy water on himself.

"You're a little jumpy, aren't you, Walt?" I had wanted to catch him off guard, and it seemed I succeeded.

"I just don't like people sneaking up on me," he responded. "If you're thinking of going out again, forget it. I'm way too busy."

"Got any coffee?" I asked.

His shoulders slumped forward as he thought about it. He put aside his work and got to his feet. "Yeah," he said. "I could use a break."

We sat at his worktable for a few moments over the coffee. I finally said, "Walt, I went into a cave to get that case out there. I set a home line, and it sure looked to me like it was cut. Got any ideas on it?"

His eyes remained steady though they widened a bit. "Cut? Damn, I thought maybe something was foul there."

"What do you mean?"

"Sit tight, I'll be right back."

He was gone for five or ten minutes. I watched the slow movement of a sloop under sail making the age-old maneuvers as it prepared to berth. He returned with a lean, brown man with crisscross lines on his face and nicotine-stained fingers. The man nodded and took a seat at the table.

"Jake, this is Hack. Hack, Jake Sands. We used one of Hack's boats when we went out the other day," he said by way of introduction and explanation. "You tell him, Hack."

Hack nodded solemnly. His voice had the croak of bad lungs and phlegmy vocal cords. He offered a cigarette from a slightly crumpled pack of unfiltered Camels. I refused. He shrugged as if to say, to each his own. He flicked back the lid of a vintage Zippo and in the same motion had a flame at the tip of the Camel, then with a tiny wrist motion flipped the lid closed. I expected to hear the small scrape and click that was distinctive to the Zippo. It was silent—the waterproof seal around the wick made it so. He moved the lighter around on the table with one hand and smoked with the other.

"I cut your line," he said. "I wasn't meaning you harm. I was just trying to keep you from looking too deep into the cave. I figured as soon as you felt it loose you'd come out. I waited on the other side of the cove, just out of Walt's sight, to see if you got out okay."

"You have a reason?"

"It's kind of a long story."

"Take your time."

He sucked in on the cigarette. He smoked the way I remembered Bogart smoked. His eyes had the same wet look that Bogart's had had. Maybe it was the smoke.

"I was in the navy. I was a U.D.T. man, a frogman. That was way before the SEALs, or I guess it was the forerunner of them, but anyhow, when I mustered out I come here and worked for a diving company. Lotta work for divers then with them oil platforms starting up and all. I borrowed a few bucks and began a charter boat operation when the diving work slowed down." He looked into his own smoke as if the vision of his past lay there. He flicked away the ash and took a long hard draw on the cigarette, all the while turning the lighter with his other hand. The Bogart eyes burned when the acrid smoke hit them.

"One day a fella comes to me and asks to rent my boat. I remember when he first seen me he was looking me over real careful like. Studying me, you know? Anyhow, I took him out to the islands for some diving. Two, three days in a row he come back and I took him out all over the channel. Then this one day we're on our way back in when he comes up and cuts the engine. Scared hell out of me, I can tell you. Then he said, 'Hack, do you know me?' Now here we was out in the middle of the channel there and I'm looking at this guy that for my money I'd never seen before in my life. But still there was something familiar about him. I'd felt it from the first, and then when he asked me if I knew him, I was sure I did, but I couldn't place it. I don't mind saying, I was a little spooked."

I waited through another long drag on the cigarette, which

seemed to prepare him to continue. "Thing is, I didn't know him when he first showed up because he looked so different. His nose was all changed and his eyes. He didn't look anything like I remembered. And he'd changed his name. I'd known him as Phil Logan. He was going by the name of Lomax here. It was spooky, real spooky. He had to tell me, and when he did, well, then I could see it. I mean, after he told me who he was I remembered him real well from the navy. But man, his life had really changed. He was rolling in dough. He asked me how I was doing and I told him the truth. I was up against it and stood to lose the boat. That's when he offered to back me. He wanted to be what he called a silent partner. That was fine with me, so that day, right out there in that channel, we made a deal. He bought the boats, and I ran the company."

"Where did he get the money?" I asked. "Did you find out?"

He shook his head. "Nope," he answered. "I never asked. I figured it had to be from some bank robbery or something, and I didn't want to know. He made me swear to keep it all secret, and kinda sealed it by telling me that if anybody found out about him, and me knowing him, my life wouldn't be worth a plugged nickel."

"You mean he threatened you?" I asked.

"Nope, it wasn't like that. It wasn't him threatening me much as it was him warning me. Like there was some others out there that better never find out about me knowing him. Scared me kind of. But then I can tell you this, he was always a strange one. Loved guns and could shoot the eye out of a bird in flight. Always on the tough side. Anyhow, I figured even if he had stolen the money, I was clean on it. All I really had to do was keep my mouth shut. It was a good opportunity for me. Turned out to be, too."

He seemed startled by his own memory. "You know, I remember when we was in the navy we put in here for some training dives on the islands out there. I can remember him saying that if he ever got the big bucks, he was going to come live in Santa Barbara. He sure as hell called that shot."

"Where is this Lomax now?" I asked.

"He's dead. Died a couple of years ago."

"What does that have to do with you cutting my line?"

He nodded quickly as if agreeing to get back to the point. "See, when we first started up the boat business him and me would go out diving almost every day. I didn't know it then, but he was looking for a place to hide something. He found it one day, and the next he showed up with these two suitcases. Both of them was heavy. I know because I had to help him aboard with them. Then we went out where we'd been the day before and he took those cases down with him. It was into that cave you were diving in."

"I only found one case," I said.

He nodded and stubbed out the small butt. He lit another automatically. His hand unconsciously employed the same slick action with the lighter. It was flick-flick and the cigarette was lit. "After those first weeks, he didn't come around very often. He'd come about once a year and go down and bring up a case. He'd come back with it a day or two later and take it back down. The last time, he never took the case he brought up back down. And he never came back neither."

Hack looked out at the marina. "I was supposed to see that the place where he'd stashed the cases wasn't messed with. I was supposed to keep an eye on it and let him know if anybody started diving out there. That was easy at first because there wasn't that many folks into diving. It got tougher later on, but by that time I pretty much had the diving under my thumb around here."

He looked at Walt, who nodded his agreement.

Hack coughed a few times and then continued. "Logan got stranger all the time. Got so I'd only see him maybe once or twice a year when he'd call me to come to his house. It was weird, real weird. He was scared of sounds and everything. He had this big estate all covered with a security system. I had one instruction if anything ever happened to him. I mean if he was killed or died. I was supposed to call a lawyer in San Francisco and say, 'Lomax is dead.' Then I was to send this envelope to him."

"What kind of envelope?" I asked.

"It was one of them padded ones."

"How large?"

He indicated with his hands the size of an eight-by-ten picture. He said, "Not too. It was something small and kinda flat. Sorta square. I could tell that by feeling it. It made a little noise when I shook it, but I ain't even got a good guess at what it was. All I know is what I'm telling you."

"Do you remember when he gave it to you?"

"It wasn't too awful long before he died. I remember he got it off a shelf and gave it to me. He made it seem real important at the time."

"What do you mean he got it off a shelf? Was it with other envelopes?"

"No, wasn't in an envelope. I remember now it was something that he picked up and put in an envelope. I didn't see what it was, but he wasn't trying to hide it from me. I just didn't see it."

"But he put it in an envelope and then handed it to you?"

"Yeah, but first he wrote on it."

"The lawyer's name?"

"And address and all. He told me to mail it like it was if anything happened. That's just what I did, too."

"Do you remember what else might have been on that shelf?" I was groping. I could not get a fix on any of what I was hearing.

He shook his head. "I dunno, it was a while back. I'd guess it was books and magazines and records and things. I just don't know. It was kinda cluttered, I do remember that."

I asked, "How did he die?"

He squinted through his smoke. "I dunno. A stroke or something." He paused, taking his time. "Went on vacation and them two fellows you know about found the cave. I checked and saw the case was still there, so I figured it was all back to square one. Then you came along. Guess I wasn't thinking straight. I don't mind telling you, I was gettin' a mite scared about what might be in that case. And it was nothing, huh?"

I looked at Walt. "Just some lead," I said. "Who was the lawyer you were supposed to contact?" I asked.

"Name of Maher," he said without having to reach too deeply for it.

I was disappointed. I was expecting him to say Spence. "Maher?" I repeated.

He spelled it for me. It didn't help. Then he said, "I called when Lomax died. Never talked direct with him, but I left word anyhow. They thanked me, and that was it. Then I sent the envelope. Never heard another word. Not another word. Course I didn't leave my name or nothing. Lomax made it clear I shouldn't, if I knew what was good for me. Didn't really matter, because Lomax had already signed over the business to me."

"Looks like you made out okay," I said. I stood up and extended my hand. "Thanks."

He got to his feet with his hand out. As we shook I nodded toward the lighter in his other hand. "Mind if I look at that lighter? Haven't seen one like it in a while."

The Bogart eyes wavered. He tossed it up to me. It was smooth and cool to the touch. I tried the lid action and spun the flint wheel and admired the flame. I nodded approvingly while I turned it in my hand, studying the inscription. The medallion on the side was much too worn to read, but beneath it I could make out the words "Subic Bay, Philippines." I tossed it back.

"Nice," I said. "Makes me think of my own days at Subic."

"Navy?" he asked automatically.

"The Corps."

"Oh," as if I had said something distasteful. His face held that kind of stark innocence some men get when they grow

older. It was hard to imagine him in any other light. He
dipped his head in a quick nod of conclusion and made his departure.

Walt walked me out to the entrance. He voiced my thoughts
exactly. "Sounds like that fella Lomax was down to just Hack
and his lawyer for people he could trust. He picked a good one
in Hack though. Long as I've known him, I've never seen him
play it any way but square. Except for what he did with you,
of course, and that's all kinda tied in with his loyalty to that
Lomax."

"Well, he sure seemed to come clean with me," I offered.

"Hack's a good guy," he said. "He never meant to do anything that'd hurt you, I'm sure."

I agreed with him, and we flipped each other a little wave
goodbye. Maybe I walked faster, but the walk down Cabrillo
seemed shorter on the way back to my car.

18 🌿

With Trinia it was always goose bumps. With me it was a sort of buzz in the head . . . almost audible. It was a signal that the brain had latched onto something abstract and begun to fashion it into a reality. I was hearing the buzz as I drove to Goleta to meet Tex Flanagan for a late lunch. Or perhaps it was an early supper. No matter, it was in a restaurant and it was food and it was getting on in the afternoon.

Tex had been most insistent when I called him that we not discuss anything on the phone. He had named the restaurant and the time. I was happy to oblige.

He waved me over to where he sat already half through a plate of ravioli.

"Am I late?" I asked.

"No, no, podner, I'm just getting a little head start," he answered. "What's your pleasure?"

"Nothing to eat. I'll have coffee."

He shrugged it away with one shoulder and loaded his fork with ravioli. He stuffed it in his mouth and washed it down with beer. Somehow he managed to wave to the waiter at the same time and get my coffee poured.

"Never had good Eye-talian food till I left Duval. Now I cain't get enough of it," he said without missing a beat in his munching rhythm. It was a little like watching a lion feed.

"Duval?" I asked. "A small town?"

"Town?" He looked at me in a studied way, as if he suspected me of mockery. "County. Duval's a county."

"In Texas?"

He was clearly uncomfortable at being the one on the receiving end of questions. He shrugged it off and said, "That's right. Down near Corpus."

"Corpus Christi?"

"Yeah, around there. A couple of counties over. Down there we go by counties. Towns don't mean much." He took a short peek up at me. "Duval ain't that obscure, let me tell you," he said, as if imparting wisdom. "So now you got my roots, let's get to this trouble-in-paradise thing you were trying to tell me on the phone."

"A nest of snakes, Tex. That's about the way I'd describe Coco Palms. There's everything there from extortion to, and probably including, murder."

"What is it with you, pard? You see murder everywhere you look? You still think Burley was burnt by witches or something?" He let himself enjoy his little joke.

"Let me turn that question back to you. Do you still think Greg Burley, who had everything in the world going for him, doused himself with gasoline and burned himself to death? Do you really believe that? And as a protest for the homeless?"

"I've seen stranger," he answered calmly. "You still nosing around that thing?"

I ignored his question. "What have you got on the Leeds shooting?"

"Not much. Why? You got something I oughta know?"

"I was wondering if you had taken a good look at your old friend Charlie Jessup's part in it? He seems to be at the core of all the trouble in Coco Palms since he's been there. Incidentally, how long *has* he been there?"

"Four years more or less. Yep, we looked in his direction. He's clean."

"Tex, tell me the truth. Do you not see a connection between Leeds and Burley?" I put it as straight as I knew how.

He pushed his empty plate aside with his huge forearm. His eyes made contact with me for the first time. He said, "Yep, podner, I surely do, but you're not gonna like it one little bit. I can't prove it so I'm not pushing it, but I think Burley shot his boyfriend and then in a deranged state did himself in."

"And Toni Spence?"

"I don't see that it matters. She doesn't figure into it. Anyhow, she was full of drugs and booze. That one's closed and gone, pard."

I sipped my coffee and watched him rake bread crumbs with one beefy hand into the other.

"How long have you been in Santa Barbara, Tex?" I asked.

"Three or four years." His look to me lost some of its casualness.

"Why here?"

"There was a chief deputy opening," he said. "I was overqualified, but I was tired of big-city crime, and changing seasons, and people that all talked like me. Fact is, I just tired of Dallas."

He did have a certain flair about him that made me smile. I knew it was a little like trying to pet a shark. "So, it just happens that about the time a man you don't like comes here, you too make a career change and happen to wind up in the same place. Quite a coincidence, Tex."

"Well, podner, I'd think that might give you a hint that I would've been all over his hide on the Leeds thing. I won't deny I been looking," he said. "And I don't deny that I might've come all this way to nail him either, but he's as clean as can be. Course, if you come up with something I'd be grateful."

"You haven't found anything in four years?"

"Nope." He shrugged. "*Nada.*"

"Well, maybe I can bring you something."

"Fine. Fine." He eased back to let the waiter place what appeared to be a double order of apple pie before him. He accepted it with a nod, somewhat as a king might accept a liege's gift. With a huge bite in his mouth he said, "Don't know if you heard or not, but Fred Stanner is in the hospital. Shot himself in the knee. Bad. Gonna be crippled up in that leg, it looks like."

"Too bad," I said noncommittally.

"Says he's going back home to Ohio soon's he gets out of the hospital. Seems odd. I thought he liked it here."

"He a friend of yours?" I asked.

"Nope. He's a friend of Charlie's. That's what seems so odd about it." He chewed, and swallowed, and shoveled in more pie. "Claude Hayes was a friend of Charlie's too. He went off a cliff. It's got me thinking."

"There are species of animals who eat their young," I offered.

"You think Charlie's eatin' his young?" He laughed. "I like that. You got a funny way of looking at things, podner, but I like it."

I was glad he liked it. The more I saw of him, the more I did not want to be on his wrong side. I didn't know, though, how many more meals I could sit through with him. It tended to kill my appetite.

• • •

On a whim I hit 101 going south. Tex's attitude about his "roots," as he had called them, stuck with me. Part of my drive across Santa Barbara was motivated by curiosity, and part of it was because I had some spare time.

I got off on the Olive Mill Road exit in Montecito. The Coffee Mill was quieter than I had ever seen it. Of course, I was used to the breakfast crowd, a much racier group.

My timing couldn't have been better. Peggy Cooley was just finishing her day. She gave me a lively smile. "You're a little off your routine today, aren't you?" She automatically picked up the coffeepot as she approached.

"I was passing and thought I'd stop for a quick cup," I said as offhandedly as possible.

"A spontaneous fellow," she teased. "I like that. So, that's all you want? Coffee?"

I nodded. "And maybe a little Texas lore. You did tell me you were an authority."

"So, not so spontaneous after all. More questions, cowboy?"

"Jake." I grinned, hoping enough little boy would come out to soften her up.

She leaned back against the chair behind her. "So?"

"It's a little hard to put into a question, Peggy, but I was wondering if it's a common thing in Texas to identify your home by its county?"

She thought about it before she said, "I'd say yes if a person was from a really small town. What county?"

"Ever hear of Duval County?"

"Haven't you?"

"Not until today, no. Should I have?"

It was possibly not a conscious move, her edging closer to me. Or the lowering of her voice. She looked hard for something in my face before she continued. "Duval is a very famous little county in my part of the world. The rumor mill links it to a lot of ugly things."

"Like what ugly things?"

"Like politics, like big-time corruption." She paused to gather her thoughts. "Duval is one of the counties that put Lyndon Johnson in the Senate. Jim Wells County, Duval County, there were two or three of them that were sort of run by one man down there. I think he was called the Duke of Duval County. He's why it became famous in some quarters."

"How did Duval County put Johnson in the Senate?"

"The way I remember my daddy telling it was that the votes got recounted in Jim Wells and Duval and some other county, giving Johnson the primary against a man named Coke Stevenson. It was by only a few hundred votes, and folks started calling him Landslide Lyndon because of it. As my daddy told it, later when they checked it out, most of those

names on the voter registrations were either long dead or
didn't exist."

"This Duke of Duval, as you call him, is he still running
things down there?" I asked.

"Oh no." She gave it one of her raucous chuckles. "Everything is run from Dallas now by a local from my neck of the
woods, a slick by the name of Garrison. David Lee Garrison
to be exact. Country club type, very civilized, Texas style.
That means he's a hunter, a golfer, and a poker player, holds
the doors open for the ladies but still has people killed who
cross him."

"Is this widely known about Garrison?"

She considered that. "I wouldn't say so. He's more known on
the society pages. He married the most beautiful gal in the
state, a Miss Texas, and had a girl child, which gave a lot of
folks a smile, him being such a macho and all. Raised the girl
like a boy until her mama sent her off to one of those finishing
schools back east. Her name is Jenny Lee. Those that know her
now say she's a harder case then her old man. That's about it."

"You seem to know a lot about the Garrisons."

"I went to school with Jenny Lee until the eighth grade,
when she was shipped off east." There was a wry twist to her
smile. "That was when my daddy still had money and we lived
in Turtle Creek, not too far from the Garrisons. I even played
on their tennis court once or twice when I was a kid."

"I've heard of Turtle Creek. That's high-rent."

"It used to be," she said. "And I used to be a princess."

There was a sadness in her voice, but her face did not lose
its characteristic self-confidence. "Anything else?" she asked.

"No, thanks, Peggy."

"*De nada*," she said in her flippant style. "I'm outta here."

She left me with a full cup of coffee and quite a lot to think
about. What got most of my attention was the fact that at one
time Peggy Cooley had been in the money.

• • •

I charred a steak outside and ate by the pool. It was a breezeless evening, still and quiet. It was almost fully dark when that idiotic chirping sound had me reaching for the telephone.

Jason's voice started in as soon as I raised the phone. "Got something for you. Anthony Carl Spence did leave a daughter as the only surviving member of his family. Her name was Toni. Married three times—Toni, that is—no children. How about that?"

"When did he die and how?" I asked.

"Little over a year ago. He was up there in years. Eighty-something. Had a heart attack at his club in San Francisco. Still practicing law though. Kept the practice open on his own the last year."

"What does that mean?"

"His partner died. Most people thought he'd hang it up then, but he didn't. Kept the firm name and everything. Spence and Maher. World famous."

That caught me in a soft spot. Maher. I struggled to adjust all my thinking to include the forgotten information.

"That's it—Maher was Spence's partner. Damn, I didn't connect it. Everybody's heard of Spence and Maher."

"Yeah. Maher was younger, but he went first. Big reputation, that firm. They did things all over the country." Jason was enthusiastic about his information. I could hear a new lilt to his voice.

I took deep mental breaths to slow myself down. Then I told him about Hack, and his instructions to call Maher, and about Logan. He muttered small exclamations as I talked.

"And how do you figure Logan fits into all this?" he said after taking it all in.

"I'd say it's pretty simple at this point. Logan did something that brought him a big payday. Robbed a bank, held up a train, or did an extraordinary favor. At any rate, he brought it here with him, whatever it was, and stayed in hiding the rest of his life."

"And Maher?" he pressed.

"My guess is that Logan went for Spence and Maher because they were famous and he'd heard of them. He probably took them something from one of the suitcases to keep for him as a form of insurance."

"Do you think it was some form of blackmail? Maybe the stuff he left with Maher was the proof. Pictures?" He was getting on track.

"Could be, which then went to Spence," I said.

"And you think the daughter came down here to get the loot?" he supplied for me. "Which they knew was sunk in that cave?"

"Something like that."

He made a humming sound for a moment. "Let me think about all this. I'll get back to you."

"How you coming on the cipher?"

"Nothing yet, but I'll have it."

I did not doubt that for a minute. While I still had the phone in my hand I dialed Kate. No answer. My steak was cold, but then I wasn't hungry anyway. I let some time pass. I nodded off. Like an old man, I thought, I'm beginning to nod, and most probably snore.

I felt trapped in my own skull with thoughts of the control map, the book, and all the players in the game. There was too much to think about. My brain was mush.

I needed a break. I took a shoreline drive. It was relaxing and nice, but it made me miss the convertible days. It was not quite the same to drive along the ocean in a closed car. You really couldn't feel it the way you could in a convertible. Even cool nights were fun with the top down and the heater on and all the windows up. I drove home in a much easier frame of mind, thinking about little more than the days and nights of my old convertibles.

A car blocked my drive. Her car. She sat calmly waiting for me as if we had a date and I was only a few minutes late. I pushed the remote. The gates swung open and she drove inside. I pulled on back to the garage, fumbled with the alarm pad, stumbled in the dark, and finally made it to the front door in what would have passed for record time. Women like Kate should not be kept waiting on front door steps.

"You said anytime," she said when I opened the door.

I nodded and tried a grin. It must have worked, because she smiled back. "I've been trying to call you," I said.

She nodded as if she knew it. "Can we sit out under the stars awhile?" she asked, and led me without my answer to the back.

I offered a drink. She declined. I followed along in her wake, not quite sure of her mood or intentions.

We settled onto chaises set at a V angle. Our feet were the closest part of us to each other. That allowed me to see her better. To my eye, she had never looked more beautiful. I had never wanted to look at her more.

"I seem to think of you when I need to be with someone," she said in a voice rimmed with whimsy. "What do you suppose that means?"

"That I'm precious and adorable?" I was out of my league and knew it.

The throaty laugh floated to me. "You are," she said. "Precious and adorable. Is that what your mother used to say to you?"

"No, my dentist." I tried to keep out of the whirlpool that was just a few feet away. "You go out of town?"

Again she nodded. "Would you put on that nice music you were playing the other night. That singer with the satin voice?"

"Nat King Cole," I supplied. "Sure."

I put on the music and in her honor switched on the exterior speakers. By the time I returned she was in the pool. I sat and looked at the stars while she swam. She did not summon me or gain my attention in any way. She was swimming, and I was sailing among the tiny fuzzy lights millions of miles away.

"Could you get me a towel?"

When I returned with it she stood at the edge of the pool with her head tilted far back, smoothing the water out of it. "Thank you," she said, as if she were not gleaming wet and naked in a soft moonlight. I said, "Of course," as if my throat were not constricted to the point of suffocation.

There was no hurry. We both knew we could have the night. We talked of childhoods and other places we had been. We took our time in our silences to feel the night around us. She sat with me on my chaise and went to sleep more than once against my chest. While she slept I traced the line of her cheek and jaw with my eye. I looked for flaws, but there were none. None anywhere. Still perfect.

After a while we went inside. I pulled back the curtains in the bedroom and opened the French door wide so whatever magic there was in the night would stay with us. The sound of the surf was carried in on perfumed air. It was her perfume. The scent of night flowers.

It wasn't hard to forget the circumstances of our meeting. I was glad I had never known Greg Burley, because it could have put a pall over the night for me. As it was, there was nothing and no one grabbing at my conscience. I couldn't speak for her. She seemed to have a passion that ran free and on its own. When she let it go, that whirlpool I'd been dancing around finally got me. I dove in. She filled up every thought and sense I had in those moments. It lasted a long time.

Then we slept. I didn't dream. I didn't need to. She was there against my skin and in my brain, chasing away the demons that lived in the night shadows.

19 🌿

I moved my arm around in search of her and stretched my legs into the cool emptiness of the other side of the bed. I sat up and forced my eyes open. Had she gone in the night? I wondered.

I threw cold water on my face and brushed my teeth. I could see that she had done the same. A new toothbrush had been taken from the cabinet. I must have been in a deep sleep.

I saw her when I stepped outside the French doors. She was swimming the same kind of concentrated laps she had swum the night before. She saw me and waved. I went back in to make breakfast.

She sat across from me in one of my terry-cloth robes, looking small inside it. Her hair was bound up in a towel, somehow appearing stylish. The day was starting with bright sunshine, lending an unrealistic hue to the blues and greens around us. I suddenly felt we were a couple out of a movie I had seen somewhere. Even the distant sound of an early-morning gardener's mower seemed placed there for effect.

She stole my thoughts. She said, "Nick and Nora Charles," and laughed.

"You're too young for those movies," I said.

"You are too, probably," she replied. "Bet you know them from television just like I do."

She was right, of course, but still I felt those films were of my generation, not hers. "You win," I said.

She continued to press her point. "Even that music you like so much," she said with a teasing squint, "is slightly before your time."

I let the phone chirp. I wasn't interested. She was across from me and there wasn't anyone else I cared about at that moment. It kept chirping. She gave me a look that said, please, so I picked it up.

"I'm coming up there, Jake," Jason said without preamble. "I don't want to talk about this on the phone. I know something. I've figured something out. Jake? You there?"

"Yes," I said. "Okay, when?"

"You tell me, but right away. This is something I want to talk about."

"I understand," I said. "This morning then. Whenever you can make it. I'll wait for you."

"You're not alone, are you?"

"No, but I will be."

"Good," he said. "This is definitely not for other ears."

"Why don't I come to you?" I suggested.

"No. It's better I come there," he said emphatically. "This is big, Jake, real big."

"I believe you." I added, "You're overselling."

"You'll see," he said, and hung up.

She was up and collecting her clothes from the night before. There was a bounce in the way she moved that reminded me of a little girl. She had no doubt been the apple of her parents' eyes. I remembered she had told me her father had taught her to ride, swim, and shoot. As I moved toward her I said, "You were probably always Daddy's little girl, weren't you?"

She stared at me without answering.

"Did I say something wrong?"

Her face softened into a smile. "No, you never say anything wrong."

"So, were you?" I pressed.

"A daddy's girl?" She looked away to think about it. "Yes, I was. I was also a mommy's girl. You aren't the only one who is precious and adorable." She moved close to me. "Oh, that's right, it was only your dentist who called you that."

"I should have never confessed that," I said, going with the gag.

Her eyes grew more serious. "I wish you would talk more about yourself. I mean the real things, Jake," she said before she let some of the lightness return. "Want to have lunch with me at the club later?"

"I can't," I said. "I've got a meeting this morning."

"Yes, I gathered." She continued to smile at me as she went inside. "Just don't make any plans for tonight. Okay?"

I put my hands up as if I were making a great sacrifice. "That's really tough with my busy social calender, but okay."

When she was in her car and ready to go I leaned into her window and said, "It really happened, didn't it?"

She touched my cheek with her fingertips. "Yes," she said. "Are you surprised?"

"Very," I answered.

"Not me," she said. "I always knew."

• • •

I spent a tough morning waiting for Jason. It got tougher, the longer I waited. I made myself work out. There was still some soreness from the kicks I had taken from Stanner and Jessup, and those Taser guns had left their marks, but it all began to ease out as I worked up a good sweat.

I took a short steam, shaved, showered, and dressed. I must have looked at my watch a dozen times while I waited. I got tired of pacing inside. I went to the front and walked back and forth in the driveway. It was the first time I had spent much time looking at the front. I had to admit I admired the house and the landscaping, yet I still had the feeling that the house belonged here but I did not.

My impatience made me snap around at the sound of a car. I saw him well before he saw me. Charlie Jessup slowed at my driveway and looked down toward the house. I moved into his line of sight as he stopped. He stared at me for a moment in surprise at being caught peeking in. I walked toward his Wagoneer. He was not in uniform, and appeared to be unshaven as well.

"You on patrol, Captain?" I called out to him.

His upper lip involuntarily drew up into a sneer. His eyes became mean. "Always," was his answer.

As I got closer I saw he was somewhat disheveled overall.

"Late night?" I poked at him with it. Sort of like you would do with a long stick and a rattler.

His big arms flexed and his eyes closed down to slits. He didn't seem to like me at all. He looked somewhere down the road and let me see how much effort he was putting into self-control. "I spent the night at the hospital with a friend. Someone made a very bad mistake in hurting a friend of mine."

"Gee, it must be comforting to have a friend like you, Jessup." I made my face as empty as a disco dancer's.

"I'll find out who did it," he said. "And when I do he'll pay."

"Golly," my Mayberry voice croaked, "maybe it was somebody we know."

"You're going to wish you'd stayed out of it," he said from the two tight lines that formed his mouth. "You're going to wish you'd showed some respect."

"No, sport, let me tell you what I'm going to wish. When the time comes I'm going to wish you had lasted longer. And leave the respect line to the wiseguys in the east coast mobs who know how to use it," I added from some angry depth.

"You're a pissant, Sands. Something that can be stepped on anytime I want to," he said in a rising voice. "You'll get in my face once too often, mister."

I smiled sweetly. "Tell me something, Captain Jessup. How

can you afford that fine house over on Travis Circle? You must put in a lot of overtime." I got to him with that. He didn't like my knowing where he lived. He tried to even things up a bit.

"That lady going to be spending every night here now?"

"Cute," I said. "You don't want to get too cute, though, Charlie. Cute guys don't last."

"We'll see who's cute when I get finished with you," he said angrily.

I leaned into his Wagoneer. "You seem upset." I turned on my most knowing smirk. "Maybe you and Stanner were closer than I thought."

I couldn't read his face then, except for the veins popping on his forehead and the flush of red around his eyes. He left some rubber behind as he gunned the Wagoneer away. I had stirred enough, I thought. He was due to explode. Now my problem was avoiding the fallout.

I checked my watch again. That little exchange hadn't taken much time. It was well past noon though, and my impatience was getting the better of me. It might have been the way the sky to the south was filling with rich dark clouds, but whatever, I did not like it. I went inside to the phone. No answer at Jason's. I tried his cellular. Nothing.

I spent some time trying not to think about anything. As a result, I thought about almost everything. Nothing fit. All I had were questions, and there didn't seem to be any answers. My mind began to lock up on me when I began to factor in Kate.

Without an abundance of thought behind it, I dialed the Coco Palms Country Club. I got the administrative office and a Miss Downing.

"Yes, Miss Downing, I'm Mr. Good with Brewster, Mullen, and Good, the accounting firm?" I took a very brief pause to allow it to settle. "Our client Mrs. Burley, Mrs. Greg Burley, is getting incomplete statements from the club there, we think. Could you pull up her account please?"

"I have it before me now, Mr. Good, on the computer. What seems to be the trouble?"

"A minor problem with the statements. Where are you instructed to send them?"

"Nowhere, sir," Miss Downing stated. "Since she is not a member of the Coco Palms Country Club, the account was settled on a weekly basis. She closed it out entirely, however, today."

"Closed it?" My act slipped.

"Why, yes, sir. She said they were off on the next leg of the honeymoon. Hawaii, I believe she said."

"Honeymoon? I'm a bit confused, Miss Downing. You mean, she isn't a member at Coco Palms?"

"No, sir. We granted her a twenty-one day courtesy guest membership, while she and her husband were here on their honeymoon." She took my silence to be the confusion it was. She explained: "In accordance with the reciprocal policy we have with certain other clubs."

"That means a member from a club in another city can have temporary membership here?"

"Very select clubs, you understand?"

"I understand," I responded obediently.

"Perhaps your problem is there, with her home club in Pebble Beach?" she offered. The subtle tone of suspicion began to rise in her voice. "Who did you say you were again, sir?"

I knew the game was up. "I think you've put your finger on our problem here," I said, trying to focus. "Thank you, Miss Downing, you've been most helpful."

The sound of a car in my drive caught my ear as I hung up the phone. I sat where I was for an extra moment, allowing the confusion to subside. It only got worse. Jason was already out of his car by the time I opened the front door. He saw my face and laughed.

"Worried, Mother?"

"No, but a little ticked off. It's afternoon already, and you were going to be here midmorning." I tried to cover my real concern with a gruffness I didn't sell well. It only made him laugh again.

"*Mea culpa*. I need those cases from the back. I'll see you inside. Looks like rain, doesn't it?" He wheeled in, leaving me speechless.

I opened the rear door of the specially equipped Rolls and lifted out the two cases. I put them on the floor of the living room where Jason had already positioned himself at the coffee table. He opened one of the oversized briefcases and spread out a replica of the map I had found in Greg Burley's Range Rover. He placed a plastic overlay on top of it, without inviting me to look yet. Jason loved his games.

I sat down and let him do his thing. When he finished with his fussing, he turned to me and pushed out his big hand. "Hi," he said.

I shook his hand. "You're a piece of work, my friend. Now, what's this all about?"

"Get your original and look at it."

I did as I was told. When I had the original map spread before me, he said, "You are definitely looking at a control map. I know when, where, and what, but more important, I know who."

"You mean who did it?" I asked.

"I mean who it was done to. I assume your man Logan did it, or at least was part of it," he answered, and adjusted the overlay for his report. "This was a hit, amigo. A major, major hit."

I studied what he had done. All the abbreviations were spelled out. He had highlighted the most pertinent data and had placed a circle around the corner of two intersecting double lines marked on the overlay as Wenonah and Fillmore Streets.

"So, tell me," I finally had to say. My mind was still grappling with the knuckleball I had just taken from Miss Downing.

"Does anything you see there mean anything to you?" he asked.

"No," I said. "I see you've filled in street names, and some dates, names, and times, but none of it rings a bell. Should it?"

I was surprised to see how serious he had suddenly become. He said, "Looking at it as a control map, and taking your guess that the diagram showed us a street corner, I took it as a definite action against that building diagramed at that corner. I wasn't getting anywhere with the shorthand until I got to the notations at the top where it says, 'Wed 18 or Th 19.' I read that as Wednesday the eighteenth or Thursday the nineteenth. I put the computer on it and did a calender run, where I turned up several different months in a lot of different years that had Wednesdays and Thursdays falling on the eighteenth and nineteenth. I took that to the library downtown and pulled the micros on the *New York Times* where I concentrated on things that might have happened on one of those combinations. It looked a little daunting at first, but I'm sure I finally came up with it. There was a front-page article in the *Times* dated June 21, 1975. You want to guess who got bumped?"

"Seventy-five? Wait a minute." I gave it some thought. "Hoffa?"

"Good guess. Hoffa did go missing in '75, but the date was July 30. In fact, word had it that this guy put out the contract on Hoffa."

"Whoa," I said. "Mob stuff?" He nodded. I cleared my mental decks and searched for it. The "G" on the leather diary swam into the picture. "Genovese. Vito Genovese."

"You went from hot to cold. Genovese bit the dust in 1969. Want to try again?"

Then I had it. "Giancana," I said.

"I've always told people you weren't as dumb as you look," he said. "Sam 'Mooney' Giancana was knocked off in his home in Oak Park, Illinois, the night of June 19th, 1975. And his address was?"

"The corner of Wenonah and Fillmore Streets," I supplied automatically. "The 'G' on that little book sort of nails it, doesn't it?"

"That did it for me," he replied. "Incidentally, I'm having no luck decoding it. I'll need more time, but I didn't feel this could wait."

"You've made a pretty good read here, Jason. It all figures."

His grin filled out. "I really am a genius, Jake. One day you'll admit it."

"I admit it," I said, and studied the map. "And these other notations?

"Lookouts, a dump site for the gun, things like that." He pointed to various notations which he had translated from the shorthand of the original map. "You can see airport departures are even listed here. It's pretty complete."

"I wonder if this is the real thing?" I asked, aloud but rhetorically. Jason didn't bother framing an answer.

We contemplated the map for a few moments in silence, as if gleaning the last scraps of information from it. Actually there was nothing more the control map could tell us now that Jason had translated it. Finally, he placed both hands palms down on the table and exhaled.

"Which brings us to the present," he said. His eyebrows had that lift which meant I was supposed to read his mind or be forever branded an idiot.

"You're thinking that perhaps I've bitten into this long furry thing which turns out to be a tiger's tail."

He nodded. "I took the liberty to open your little repository in the basement of my place and pick up a few of your old tools." He thrust his chin in the direction of the second of the cases I had carried in for him. "I didn't know if you had anything here or not."

I looked at the case at my feet. "I don't think so, Jason."

"You don't think so?" There was a slight flush to his face. "Jake, this is not like turning down green tea for dinner. I know you've undergone some changes that have to do with this sort of thing, but listen, amigo, this is not the time to make a bad move. There were a lot of folks peppered around that killing field, and you can be sure a bunch more were hiding in the shadows."

"It's got nothing to do with me."

"Like hell it hasn't. Let me ask you something. Now that
you've come to understand the map for what it is, who do you
think killed Greg Burley?" Jason's eyes snapped at me and
dared me to argue.

"I don't know," I responded. "And you don't know. It's farfetched, what you're suggesting, and I'm not buying into it."

"And how about the Spence babe and Leeds? Three people
who were messing around in something that brought them
this map at the very least, and God only knows what else, all
find themselves very dead. What is that? Farfetched? Coincidence? You still believe that, I've got a bridge to sell you."

"I believe it was something they had in common all right,
but not necessarily this map. Who knows when Burley found
it or if he found it. It might not be related." My argument
sounded lame even to my own ears.

"Of course he found it. I don't believe he knew what the hell
it was. He probably took it, along with other things, out of
that case and held on to it thinking it had to do with more
goodies, but he was a proven fool," he said, letting his vehe-
mence show. "So, okay, amigo, what do you do? Jake, this
could be the real thing, or it could be a fake, but why take a
chance? Your worry right now is not who was behind the Giancana hit, but who's doing the current crop. You got three
dead. You are definitely in the line of fire here as soon as they
catch on to you."

"I've been a little careless," I said with what passed for a
smile.

"Why don't I take the names we got here to Paladin? Let
them run a check on everybody. There may be some wild cards
here we haven't spotted. Okay with you?" At my nod he asked
another question. "You are using the debugger I left with you,
aren't you?" Again I nodded.

"Good," he said on the way to the door. "I'd hate to think
that all my gems of wisdom were shared with the bad guys,
whoever they may be."

"There's a San Francisco connection here, Jason. Run that
by the Paladin Group with the names of the three deceased,

the law firm of Spence and Maher, and Katherine Burley." I took a pen and scribbled on a piece of paper before handing it to him. "May as well have those names checked too. This afternoon if you can."

"I'll be back," he said.

"No, I'll come to you," I answered. Things no longer felt safe in paradise. We shook hands and he left. I wandered back into the living room in a kind of stupor. I sat and looked at the case he had left behind. It took me a while before I pulled it to me and opened it. It was as if I was taking an irrevocable step into uncharted territory.

I placed my two weapons of choice on the table before me. Both were 9mm automatics. Each was small enough to carry in the belt at the small of the back or under the arm without making an obvious bulge. The Sig Sauer P228 was the better of the two for my money. But the Glock could go places the Sig Sauer could not. The Glock was made of ceramics and could pass through metal detectors. When in doubt I carried both.

There was an oversupply of ammunition in the case, from which I loaded the double-stack, fourteen-round magazines, mixing hollow-point rounds with teflon-coated ones. The laser sighting attachment was there, but I opted to leave it off. I felt modern enough with a ceramic gun.

After hefting them for sight and feel, I put both guns on the table and leaned back against the cool leather of the sofa. I closed my eyes, wondering if I had stumbled into this thing or been pulled? And if so, why?

I felt old and tired. My mind wavered between soft oblivion and a renewed assault upon the problems at hand. I staggered into an odd contemplation: Did old men nap in the afternoon to escape their pasts or their futures? Drowsiness sealed my eyes and emptied my mind. I had chosen soft oblivion. A vision of Kate drifted in upon me. I took her hand and let her pull me slowly with her. I kept asking, "Where? Where?" She only smiled.

20 🔥

I awoke from my little nap, slightly disoriented, to a late afternoon darkened prematurely by rain. The clouds of morning had finally produced a gentle but steady downpour which had turned the world outside quite lush.

Rain or no rain, I needed exercise. I substituted a nylon windbreaker for my usual cotton sweatshirt and added a baseball cap in deference to the weather. I ran without any conscious decision in the direction of Faring Lane. Random thoughts flared and died like tiny charges of light. I pushed them all aside and concentrated on the run.

Five miles, more or less, and I was back at my own house. I hit the control that opened the gate as I slowed to a jagged walk. I had sprinted the last hundred and had lost my ability to breathe about fifty yards back. I put my hands on my hips and my head back and took in as much soggy air as my fragile lungs could handle. Why, I wondered, did I do it? Did it really make life better?

I decided it was best to walk a bit before going inside and aimed myself a couple of hundred yards down Coral Ridge Road. As I made my turn back toward my house, I noticed a package attached to the outside of the rural-type mailbox of a neighbor. Something about the package alerted my senses. It was a padded envelope, encasing a squared shape in the center, with the return address to a video club.

I remembered Hack had said that Logan had given him a padded envelope to send to his lawyer, Maher. It got me thinking about Hack.

I showered and shaved and combed back my hair, which seemed to have more gray in it than I had noticed before. That distracted me for a few mintues while I thought about all those old actors who still played guys my age and even younger. They didn't have gray hair. Were they genetically blessed or did they dye it? And the news guys? They had to be dyeing theirs. All those old faces peering out at us from beneath that young hair.

By the time I was dressed I remembered what I had failed to do when I returned home after my talk with Hack. I went to the kitchen and rummaged through my odds-and-ends drawer until I found the Zippo. It was, as I remembered, a close relative to the one Hack had used so expertly, waterproofing and all. I flipped the lid. It did not move as smoothly nor did it light when I thumbed the flint wheel, but on its side was the imprint, "Subic Bay."

I looked up Channel Charters in the Yellow Pages.

Hack's phlegmy voice did not sound happy to hear from me. He said, "Sure, Mr. Sands, I remember you."

"I got to thinking, Hack, about that lighter of yours. I've run across another one almost like it and started wondering about that outfit you were in at Subic. Do you remember most of the guys in your unit there?" Another shot in the dark.

"Not really. Been a lot of years since I've seen any of 'em."

"Except for Lomax," I corrected.

"Logan," he countered. "Yep, he was in the Subic outfit, but I don't suppose I'd remember him either if I hadn't run into him later like I did. Lot of lighters like that, you know?"

"I know. You've never run into any of the other guys from your outfit in later years?"

"Nope. Only Logan."

"Was there anyone, other than you, in your unit that Logan was close to?" It was another long shot, but I was figuring that Logan had to go back at least that far to find anyone he could trust.

"I don't remember anybody," he said. "And we wasn't all that close. No more than anybody else in the outfit."

"I don't suppose you'd have an old roster list or anything like that from those days, would you?"

"Nope. Just some snaps is all." I could almost hear him try to draw the words back as soon as he said them.

"Do you mind if I come by and look at them?" I could hardly get the question out fast enough. "I can be there within the hour."

He hesitated half a beat before agreeing. I hung up fast before he could change his mind.

I poured a cup of coffee to take the edge off the dryness left in my throat from the run, and watched the rain. It had turned heavy as the light began to seep out of the west behind it. I was drawn to the sound and look of hard rain. There was a potential for disaster in it even as it soothed and mesmerized.

· · ·

Hack sat hunched over the cigarette butt he was grinding into the ashtray, peering at me as I studied the pictures he had laid out for me. I looked up, and he dropped his eyes.

"Did Logan know you had these old pictures?"

He shook his head. I went back to the photos. Hack had identified Logan for me in as many pictures as he could be sure about. I studied the other men around Logan in the snapshots.

"Drink?" Hack asked. "I got whiskey and beer."

"No, thanks." Hack mumbled something about sailors and the rain. I could hear the sound of a bottle touching a glass. When I looked up again he held a glass of whiskey neat.

"Were these all taken when you were in the Philippines, at Subic Bay?" I asked.

He nodded. He was withdrawing. I sought to bring him

back. I reached into my pocket and produced the lighter. I held
it up so he could see it before I tossed it to him. "That lighter's
the one I mentioned to you. What do you think?"

He turned it in his hand and compared it to his own. He
nodded slightly as if recognizing a species. "That's the way we
proofed 'em all right."

Again I returned my attention to the pictures. If there was
one thing to be said for Logan or Lomax, it was that he was
unremarkable. He would have made a perfect spy, so ordinary
it almost gave new meaning to the word. Average size. Average, unmemorable features. Average postures and expressions.
It was hard to recognize him from one picture to the next.

I had almost gone through the batch before I could detect a
face that recurred in most of the photos, usually close to Logan. It was a handsome face, and mean.

"You said you couldn't remember many of the men in the
unit. How about this guy here? Do you remember his name?"
I went to Hack with the picture and squatted next to his chair.
Hack squinted at the picture.

"Yeah, that's Buddy."

"Buddy?"

He suddenly looked a little sheepish. "What's this all about,
huh? Why're you asking all these questions?"

I sensed he needed just a little push to tip over whatever he
was balanced upon. I decided on the truth.

"Your friend Logan was mixed up in something very big
and very bad. What you know can get you killed if the wrong
people get on to you. The more I know, the better my chances
are of keeping that from happening. That's it, Hack, in a nutshell."

He had already decided to trust me. It was simply a matter
of making a transition. But first, because he was at heart a
good man, he had to clear his soul. He gulped the whiskey and
clunked the glass down on the table beside his chair.

"I lied," he said. "When you asked me if I knew of anybody
else in the outfit that was close to Logan, well, I got scared of

the whole thing and said no. I reckon I thought it would all go away, but it ain't gonna, is it?" He lifted a Camel to his lips. We both squinted through its acrid smoke. "Yeah, there was. That's him, Buddy Mapes."

I looked at the fading snapshot. The more I studied the face, the less I liked it. "Tell me about him."

Hack's Bogart eyes dipped into the recesses of the past. "He was a running mate of Logan's. They were always going into town together to raise hell. Into Olongapo. Buddy Mapes was a real bad number. I heard rumors that him and Logan use to rob the queers that worked the street just over the bridge from the base. Benny boys, they called them over there. Got so that a lot of the Benny boys started winding up in the Olongapo River with their throats cut. That ended when they transferred Buddy Mapes out of Subic. They never got him for it, but he was that type. Mean to the core. I don't mind telling you, I was scared of him."

"Do you know where he is now?" I asked.

"Dead," he answered simply. "Logan and me got to talking about the old unit one night, not long before Logan himself died. He'd been drinking when I got to his house, and I could see he was in one of his down moods. Only it was worse that night, a lot worse. He wanted to talk, mostly about the old days. That's when he told me Buddy Mapes was dead."

"Did he say where Buddy died or when?"

"Someplace up in the middle part of the state. Logan had backed Buddy in a ranch, sorta like he'd backed me in the charter boat business. I figured out that he used Buddy to peddle whatever it was he was taking from the cases."

"Buddy came here?" I said, surprised at the prospect.

"No. Logan never let on to Mapes where he lived, or let him see his new face. He had some system of drops in different towns that let them pass things. But I think Buddy might've figured out that Logan lived in Santa Barbara."

"You think that, or know it?"

"It's what Logan said. He was real strange that night.

Talked more than he'd ever done before. Said he thought Mapes had figured it out somehow. He wasn't sure until Buddy was killed, but that capped it. Kept saying, 'Just a matter of time.' Said that over and over."

"Do you know when Buddy died?"

"Three, four months before Logan did. But from then on, Logan became a real hermit. Scared of his own shadow. You reckon Buddy Mapes *was* killed?" Hack was a true innocent.

"Yes," I answered. "That would be my guess. What happened to Buddy's ranch? Do you know?"

He said with a shrug, "Buddy didn't manage things very well. He was hitting on Logan for more money all the time. Sorta blackmailing him it sounded like. I'd guess the ranch got taken by creditors."

"Would you say this Buddy Mapes was a tough guy? A stand-up guy?"

He mulled it over before answering. "You mean do I think he'd sell out a friend, don't you? The answer is yes. In a New York minute he'd do it if there was something in it for him."

"Like maybe his life?" I asked. That brought it home real fast.

We sat in silence for a moment while I tried to garner my thoughts. He lodged his cigarette in the corner of his mouth while he poured himself another shot of whiskey. He smoked and sipped his drink and looked outside at the rain.

"The lighter I brought tonight belonged to Logan, didn't it?" I asked. He nodded.

"Buddy Mapes is dead, Hack, and so are a couple of fellows named Leeds and Burley and a woman named Toni Spence. And it's all about this same thing." I too looked at the rain. "Hack, I don't remember if you've ever said where Logan's house was?"

His expression didn't change. His eyes didn't come in from the rain. He said. "Fancy town. 411 Faring Lane, Coco Palms."

Leeds's house, I thought. Those poor dumb fools. Leeds, Burley, Spence. They hadn't known what they were playing with. I began to fill in parts of the puzzle. It gave me some concern for Hack.

"I found you, and that means they could too. Be careful, Hack."

"Would it do any good to be careful?" he asked with the innocence of a child, in his old man's voice.

"Probably not," I answered. Outside the small office the rain fell straight through the beams of the spotlights. Water poured from the eaves, drowning out the other sounds of the marina.

"If they come, they come," he said.

"Maybe they won't," I said without much conviction. "Like I said, I'll do what I can." I went to the door.

From his chair, Hack raised his glass in toast.

"That's probably more than I deserve," he said.

• • •

I turned my car toward Summerland. Kate was either not at home or not answering her phone. It didn't make much difference. I had to go there. It was a little like trying to yawn and not being able to. I was feeling that same level of discomfort with my mind. There was a yawn in there that wouldn't come. For some reason I kept thinking about Kate's house. I had to see it again.

The rain had settled into a less aggressive dribble by the time I turned onto Palmetto Lane. I put the wipers on intermittent and cracked the window a smidgen. Decorative lamps gracing the pillared walls of Palmetto Lane lent a festive air to the night. Each estate glowed in the abundance of perimeter lighting. The electric bills must have been enormous on Fame Lane.

Kate's gates were open as usual. I wondered if they were ever closed. There were a couple of spots on, which were probably photocell jobs that automatically turned on at night. I parked and walked around the house to the ocean side. I could see through the windows to the main security panel, which showed no red light. I was relieved to see the alarm was not set. It saved me some trouble.

I tried the doors and found the rear sliders open. It was almost too easy; I wasn't sure I liked the feel of it. I slipped inside and listened to the stillness around me. I knew I was alone in the house, just as at times in the past and in other houses I had known I was not. I turned on the lights. The furniture was still there, but the house read empty. The deserted kind of empty.

I went from room to room, turning on lights, looking for the switch to my own memory. I went to Kate's bedroom. What I had noted the first time I was there but failed to properly register was the way the whole house looked like one of those model homes in real estate developments. Perhaps now knowing the house was being rented furnished gave me a different perspective, but I could get no feeling of real people inhabiting the place. I had accepted the furniture as evidence the last time. Now I could see that the furniture was all there was.

There were still clothes in the wardrobe and the other basic accoutrements that spoke of her, as did that scent of jasmine barely adrift in the air. It did not say more, however, than that she had spent time here. I was splitting hairs, I knew, by allowing that feeling deep in the pit of my stomach to take over. The feeling intensified when I made a closer examination of the clothes. They weren't the kind Kate wore. They were more befitting a woman of fifty. More befitting a woman like Toni Spence. I tried the redial trick on her phone. It rang my number. I hung up when I heard my own voice from my answering machine.

The kitchen was the same as the last time I had seen it. I don't know what I expected to find that would be different. I looked anyway. Beside the wall phone was that efficient list from which I had taken the dentist's number. The list was legible enough, done in carefully printed letters and numbers. It was a work of penmanship, more or less, the quality of my own: a step below average. Kate's, on the other hand, was of excellent calligraphic standards. I could still visualize it from the first time I'd seen it at the table in the White Gull. Odd also was the content of the list. There was nothing there especially hers. I was grasping at some strange straws. Without much thought behind it I lifted the receiver and pushed the redial button on the wall phone. I heard my own voice again.

I looked over the rest of the house quickly. It was the same as before. Tidy and clean. It allowed some evidence that the dead had resided here, but of the living all I'd found out so far was that Kate had called me from both her room and the kitchen. I wondered when.

The garage was empty except for the Range Rover. I opened the storage cabinets and found nothing. There were no boxes, suitcases, broken toasters. There was not even one of those useless wicker flower baskets that everyone seems to have but no one knows what to do with. I stood in the center of the garage and looked around. Nothing but the car. I opened and looked in.

That little mental switch I'd come here hoping to trip finally clicked. I'd found it odd before when I saw the Range Rover's exceptional sound system, complete with CD player, and noted an old-fashioned cassette in the tape player. I still found it odd. I reached in and pulled out the Mamas and the Papas tape. It was what had been bothering me all along. It just didn't figure. A high-tech guy like Greg Burley wouldn't settle for the inferior sound of tape when he had the CD player available. I couldn't see him going for the Mamas and the Papas either. He wasn't the "California Dreamin' " type in my book.

I left things more or less the way I found them. Somehow I had the feeling that it didn't matter anymore. By the time I hit the on-ramp to 101 the rain was back to a three setting on the wipers. I felt a kind of giddy comfort in the cockpit of the Porsche with the rain rolling and misting off the sleek surface. The click-clicking of the wipers was the only sound I heard. There was warmth and isolation as the windshield reflected the dashlights back to me.

When I was ready I pushed the cassette into the player and turned it on. All the years of being conditioned to believe the labels on things must have had some staying power. I almost still expected to hear the Mamas and the Papas.

"If you're listening to this, then I'm dead," the voice said. It was slightly high-pitched but hoarse, with an accent I would have placed as from New Jersey or New York. "So you can open that big envelope you been keeping for me and read what's in there. It's a confession, I guess you'd say. Everything said in there is fact. My fingerprints on it you can check against my navy record. My real name is Philip A. Logan, just like I signed on the confession. Nobody made me write nothing. I just did it. Okay?"

The static from the tape made the short pause dramatic. I had unconsciously slowed, drawing an angry double horn blast from the car behind me. I pulled off the freeway onto Olive Mill Road and headed toward the beach.

"Say, I don't know if I'm talking here to you lawyers or to the feds. Same difference, I guess. So, okay, here it is. Now you got it all in the confession there about the hit on Mr. G., so I ain't giving you all that crap again. But there's some things that prove what I wrote there, and some stuff I got no use for no more. It's all yours. Maybe you'll make me famous now. That'd be a laugh."

I came to a stop just beyond the Coral Casino Club in front of the Biltmore Hotel. The ocean side of the street was ink black. The sound of the waves pounding into the sand below was barely audible in the rain. I shut off the engine and the wipers, leaving myself cocooned inside the car with the voice of Phil Logan.

His ragged laugh sounded a bit on the drunk side. "So, first thing is the gun used in the hit. I heard they found it in a park. I don't know, I didn't toss it. But if it matches up with a Duro .22 ten-shot target job with a four-inch barrel with a gag can on it, then that's the gun."

He coughed then, nervously, and mumbled something that

was indistinct. "I took it all. Every damned bit of it. I ran with the plans, the money, the dope, and the book. Oh yeah, baby, I got the book. That's what all this is about. They might have let it alone after a while if I hadn't run with the book."

He was starting to ramble. His tongue was loosening as he got more used to the recorder.

"We used Johnny R. to get in because he was an old friend of Mr. G.'s. You know what they did to Johnny, don't you? They chopped him up and put him in a barrel down there in Florida. That's what they'd have done to me, too, you can put money on it."

He coughed and laughed. "I'm not some dumb punk off the streets, baby, I know the score. That's why I had my run all set up before we did Giancana. Johnny should've done the same. And anybody that thought Mr. G. was gonna blab to that committee don't know the man. He wasn't gonna talk. Why should he? But he'd kept a book. That was what everyone was afraid of. They were afraid there'd be a warrant thing that would grab the book. Then all the connections would be made and all the politicos blown."

A car pulled up slowly behind me. The lights startled me, and before I was aware of moving I had the Glock in my hands with the saftey off. At some point I had also turned off the tape player. I was low in my seat watching the lights move leisurely from behind to beside my car. It did not stop on its way by me. It was a Lexus with a man and a woman in it. They looked in my direction before proceeding to the entrance of the hotel. I relaxed and put the gun aside. I hit the play button again.

"I ran with the money that was supposed to pay the hit team. That was about a hundred and fifty grand. I coulda done all right on that, but before I left Chicago I looked at the book. Most of it was mumbo jumbo. It didn't mean nothin' to me, but the back page was plain English. It was a list of public lockers with combo numbers. I knew what that had to be, so I hit a few of them before I went under. I was like a kid grabbin' candy. There was all kinds of stashes, cash, jewels, dope, everything. I took out what I could carry. I ran with about ten million bucks' worth of pure uncut heroin, unlaundered cash, and jewels. I forgot about the book. I mean I knew I had it, I took it off his body, and that's how I found the stashes, but what I forgot was what was in the rest of that book. If I had just thought about it, I would've hand-carried it to Dallas and then run. But what the hell, I did my change act, came to Santa Barbara, and sunk the book with the rest of the stuff." He laughed a hard, bitter laugh.

"It's all in a cave out in the Channel Islands. No more cash, but the dope and diamonds are there along with my own little list of stash sites. Worth millions, but I got no use for it anymore, so go get it. I went through most of the cash, so I ran some of the heroin out through Mapes. Too risky to do too much of it. Could be that's what got Mapes killed. The bastard. He was trying to snake me, so I don't much care that they got him. I never let him know where I was or how I looked with my new face, but somehow I think he figured out there at the end that I was here in Santa Barbara. It's odds on that he said that, so it's just a matter of time. With all the wiseguys and such on my tail I can bet you it won't be long till you'll be getting this tape. I can feel 'em closing in on me, you know. I can feel 'em."

He paused briefly. "Hell, I don't care. I got no life anyway. So, I've got two lockers loaded with stuff. The directions to the lockers and the keys are with half the dope down in that sea cave. Here's what you do. You go out to the islands straight off the pier. Straight out. Aim right of Santa Cruz and cross the channel to Santa Rosa. Stay on the leeward side of Rosa and look for a cove that has like steps around it. You'll know it. Nothing else like it out there."

He made it sound a lot easier to find than it was. Another car passed, but I was under control. I watched it go by in the rain while I listened.

"You'll find a cave down there with lots of twists and turns.

Stay right. Go to the end, and there it is, boys, the golden goose. You'll be heroes. And there's more. There's the names of the planners and the one name that'll make it all. The man behind the game, and the proof. Everything is there in the little book with all the dates and backup stuff. Oh man, I'd love to see the fireworks this is gonna cause. Just knowing it's gonna happen is gonna give me the last laugh when they do me."

I thought that was it. I was reaching to turn it off after half a minute of static, when the thin voice cackled its joyless laugh.

"I just thought of something. One of you shyster lawyers might try to shortstop this thing and fill you own pockets. Okay with me, pal. It's your funeral. You think you can make the run with it, more power to you. Just get the book to the white hats, okay?"

Those were his last spoken words. He started to sing "The Eyes of Texas," but after the first line continued the tune with, "da, da, da, da, da," until he grew tired of it and stopped. I listened to the static, waiting for more, until I was sure he was finally finished. The hollow, mocking voice haunted me like nothing I had ever heard. Rain streamed against the car, punctuating the sudden silence within.

Without conscious thought I started the car and headed for home. I was feeling the need for a safe haven. It was possible I was heading in the wrong direction.

21 🌿

I found messages waiting: Flanagan, Jason, Vera, Bob Claiborne, no doubt wanting to sell me something, and Kate. I played Kate's message back several times. I had a strange need to hear her voice. Maybe it was the rain.

"Jake, forgive me, but I can't see you tonight. I've had to make a quick trip out of town. I'm not sure how long I'll be gone, but I'll call you soon . . . very soon. I already miss you, darling. Please believe that. You're a very special kind of man."

There was something at the end, in her voice, that made me think she was about to add something but stopped. It was a tiny sound, but I listened to it again and again. It said more to me than all the words.

I called Flanagan and was patched through to his car.

"Podner," he said in a cheerful mood, "how're they hanging?"

"Loose and tender," I answered. "What's up?"

"Nothing much. I just thought if you're not busy, we might have a little powwow."

"Now?"

"We could meet at the Rainbow and we could settle that little bet I owe you," he offered.

"The five hundred?"

"Always the joker, aren't you," he said. "The hundred, or dinner, remember?"

At least he remembered the debt. I was hungry and curious, so I said yes.

The Rainbow was a small café on State Street, which had been there for years. It reminded me of places I had known as a kid. Places that had Wurlitzer jukeboxes with individual selector units at the tables. Where chrome-topped sugar, salt, and pepper shakers flanked the ersatz silver napkin holders along with bottles of ketchup and hot pepper sauce. I remembered the coffee mugs had been heavy, tan ceramic, and the coffee had steamed into the faces of the men who sipped at it between drags on cigarettes and loud, hearty laughs. The smoke and the laughs had given sight and sound to rooms already alive with the scents of bacon and other grill-fried foods.

I found Flanagan sitting in a windowed corner joking with a waitress. There was no jukebox, and the mugs were dark brown and glazed, but the similarities were there. They lived in the nature of the place.

"Blanche, say howdy to Jake here," Flanagan boomed. "He's a little citified, but he's still a good old boy underneath."

Blanche and I nodded at each other. I shook Flanagan's powerful hand and sat across from him.

"I know the field here, pard, so let me quarterback," he said, preempting my right to choose. "You bring us both a Philly Dip sandwich, and don't go stingy on the fries. You like spuds, don't you, Jake? And coffee for my pardner, honey. Lots of it. Right?"

I nodded, as if it made a difference. Blanche cheerfully went with our order. I liked the Rainbow and wished I were there alone. I doubted I would enjoy dining across from Tex, the human food disposal.

"Now you can't say I don't pay my debts." He beamed. Perhaps he thought I didn't see the blackboard at the entry listing the Philly Dip as the special for the day at $5.95. The whole menu at the Rainbow, I estimated, wouldn't make a hundred. "You're looking a mite peaked, pard. You off your feed a little?"

"No, tired is all," I answered.

"That's a dangerous condition. A man makes mistakes when he's tired."

I couldn't tell if there was a cryptic message there or not. Tex didn't let it linger. He stepped right into a story that pertained to some "old boy" he used to know who slept one hour a night. It was a long story, the kind we used to call a shaggy dog. I missed the point, but then I wasn't really listening. I was watching him. I was trying to read through the words and the image of the man to see who lived inside.

Blanche brought our Philly Dips. The sandwich didn't slow Flanagan. He talked right through it. His continuously open mouth chomped the food into an unsightly mulch as he babbled on.

"Don't hear the name Blanche much anymore," he noted. "Too old-fashioned. What you get now are names like Tiffany, Brittany, and Crystal."

"But then a lot of today's men wear earrings," I offered.

He acknowledged my comment with a laugh, and continued his diatribe about old-fashioned names like Sylvia and Melba. Certain words caused a spray of his pulverized mixture to come my way. I moved back from the table with my coffee, abandoning the rest of my sandwich.

In time the meal was over. Blanche, a pro waitress, had the dishes cleared in a flash. Tex and I sat facing each other over our coffees as his string of commentaries slowed. All the while, I was studying him, learning more about him.

"You look like a linebacker trying to read a quarterback's mind," he said suddenly.

"I am," I answered. "I'm curious about you, Tex."

"For instance?"

"For instance, why did you want to see me? I don't figure you for a man who does anything without a purpose."

He allowed me a grin. "You and me would've made a good combo if we'd met up a few years ago, pard. I like your style. Okay, so you cut right through it, and so do I. I want to know what's going on with you. Did you work over Stanner?"

"Have you asked Charlie Jessup?"

"Whether he did it or whether he thinks you did it?"

It was my turn to allow him a grin. "Either way."

"Okay, I didn't expect to get a straight yes or no. I think I'd have been disappointed if I had." He sloshed down the remainder of his coffee. Part of it dribbled down his chin. As he wiped at it he said, "I get the feeling that what I know about you is only part of the story."

"I get the same feeling about you, Tex."

"That supposed to mean something?"

I gave it a little shrug. "It's just a feeling." I wanted to deflect him. "So, you got anything to tell me?"

"Let's just turn that question around there, podner. You got something to tell me?"

"Can't think of a thing. Nothing new, that is," I said blandly.

He squinted. "We got a deal, you and me, about sharing information. Don't you forget it, Jake. Don't you get the idea that I'd take kindly to you calling your own plays around here."

"That's not an idea I'd entertain for a minute," I said. "I do have a question, Tex. You care to tell me the bore of the rifle that took out Leeds?"

He hesitated long enough to give me a scowl. "Big bore," he said. "Deer rifle or maybe even bigger. I don't remember the exact size. Is that something you need to know?"

"Oh, no," I said with eyes wide. "I was just curious. You'd never mentioned it before."

"That's why I still think maybe it was an accident. Coulda been somebody shooting off a round accidentally, and they haven't got the guts to own up to it. Can't say as I blame 'em," he added with an empathetic lift of his brow.

"Are you a hunter, Tex? Deer, birds?"

"I done my share. Used to go to Tulsa once a year for a big quail hunt. Sorta miss them days," he said, as if he meant it.

"You ever hunt with a fellow named Garrison out of Dallas there?"

"Garrison?" he repeated with no change of expression. "I know a Bill Garrison from Abilene, but he don't hunt."

"David Lee Garrison," I said. "And he hunts."

"Nope, don't know the man," he said as he reached for the shaker of toothpicks. "Lotta folks in Dallas, podner, and I didn't know 'em all."

"That's odd," I said. "I thought he was a big man down there."

He laughed. "There's lots of five-hundred-dollar millionaires in them parts. All of 'em think they're big men."

"I've enjoyed our talk," I said, and stood. He put his hand out over the table so I had to lean in to shake. He pulled me slightly forward as if to say he still had power over me. "Thanks for dinner," I managed to say without sarcasm.

"Don't mention it," he said. "That squares our bet."

He and Bob Claiborne had gone to the same school of accounting. I hoped he was a big tipper. I hated to see a good waitress like Blanche get stiffed.

The rain had slowed to a soundless mist. I was grateful for that small blessing as I turned away from home and headed for the 101 freeway. I had a long drive ahead of me that night. And much to consider on the way.

• • •

I used up most of the night driving up the coast, and pulled into Carmel with dawn not far away. I took a room at a good motel, where I hoped the excessive rate ensured that the maids would honor the Do Not Disturb sign I affixed to the door.

It did not. I was awakened an hour earlier than I wanted to be by the tap-tap of a key against my door. I let the door be opened against the security chain and slammed shut again without responding. I was afraid of what I would shout at the maid. I could hear her speaking to her co-worker. She was complaining in Spanish about the sleep-ins.

"*Silencio,* dammit," I yelled at the door. I stood in the center of the room feeling somewhat childish as I accepted the silence I had demanded. I knew it was too late for me. I would not go back to sleep, but it let off some of the steam I felt rising.

I showered and shaved, then wrote down the number of a local print, copy, and fax shop I got out of the phone book. I placed a call to the Santa Barbara County medical examiner's office and got Al Mitchell on the phone. I was confident he would not remember my voice, but I still disguised it slightly. I identified myself as John Good, an investigator for Monterey County. I asked him for the complete autopsy data on Wendell Leeds, along with a cause-of-death report on Phil Lomax, and gave him the fax number of the copy shop. He agreed without hesitation. I then notified the copy shop that I, John Good, was expecting something. They were happy to have my business.

After a breakfast of shirred eggs with sausage, and casaba melon in a local restaurant called the Daffodil, I tackled my day's chore. I drove to the renowned seventeen-mile scenic road that winds picturesquely through Pebble Beach. Pebble Beach and Carmel are, in a sense, to San Francisco what Santa Barbara is to Los Angeles. They are bedroom communities to those cities, but at the same time they are elegant resort areas.

There was no other way to do it, that I could see. I had to visit the clubs in Pebble Beach. I needed some answers that I could only get in person and on site. It was not tough work to journey along that magnificient road. It made me forget I was troubled by what I was seeking.

I struck gold on my third stop. The Cypress Hill Country Club was as exclusive as they get. It was empty, too, as most very expensive clubs seem to be. It's an anomaly, to my way of thinking, that the more people pay for a membership, the less they seem to use it. I entered the luxurious clubhouse as one might enter a fabled museum. It was old and grand. A family of twenty could have lived quite comfortably in the entry hall.

I located the golf shop, which was staffed by a man who avoided eye contact as a matter of courtesy. From there it was easy. The membership and handicap listings were posted in the hallways leading to the locker rooms. On the men's side I noted the name Anthony Spence. I seemed to remember he had died on a golf course. I wondered if it had been Cypress Hill. There was no Greg Burley. Nor was there a Katherine Burley on the women's side. There was a Toni Spence.

"Excuse me," I said to the averted eyes. "I have a question regarding the membership listings."

The eyes turned to me. The man behind them said, "Yes, sir?"

"I've noticed that a name is still on the list even though the man is deceased. Mr. Spence?"

"Ah, yes. That is usual at Cypress Hill, sir. The deceased are carried on our membership lists until the estate has resigned it. Mr. Spence is still a member, sir, although he has been deceased for some time now. He was a fine golfer."

His eyes fell away from me, ready to be recalled if it was my wish. It was not. I left the way I had entered and walked down the cobblestoned pathway to the tennis courts. The tennis shop had a female clone of the fellow I had just left. I wandered past the shop to the lounge next to it. Inside against the back wall was a tastefully done rankings chart. My hopes rose. I was sure that as good a player as Katherine Burley would surely be ranked in any club where she was a member.

The rankings were dated as of the first of the current month. I looked carefully over the names, starting at the top with number one. I grew more pessimistic with each name down the list. Since she was not listed, I had to conclude she was not a member.

On the way out I noticed the trophy case next to the door. There were trophies dating back to the thirties. Most of them had names engraved on them with dates and events. I began to read them, working my way into the modern era. I almost missed it. It wasn't what I was looking for at all.

I was into the latter years when my eye caught the name Maher. It read, "Mixed doubles champions, K. Maher and J. Smythe." I had not thought to look for Spence's late law partner among the memberships at Cypress Hill, but it was possible that I had come across him by accident. I quickly scanned the other trophies. It took a moment to register, although the name was spelled out on several of the cups and platters. She was as good a player as I had thought. Maybe better, considering the number of trophies that bore her name. Katherine Maher had won in every category of competition. She had won singles, mixed doubles, and women's doubles. A bit much for the woman I had watched play, the woman I knew as Katherine Burley, but it seemed obvious that she and Katherine Maher were one and the same.

I had a big part of what I had come for. The rest of it I pondered as I drove. I proceeded along the extraordinary scenic route back toward Carmel without seeing it. I was going to have to find Toni Spence's address the hard way. It was not available through the usual means because she was too well insulated through corporations and trusts. The only addresses that were publicly available on her were business addresses. I wanted to find her home address, and it seemed that was something I would have to do on a local level, and most probably through trial and error. I did not relish the chore. I lingered over a lunch of pasta shells in a creamed almond and anise sauce. It sounded good on the menu but just missed. The coffee was fresh-ground and good, so the Pasta Garden wasn't a total loss.

My thoughts were in a jumble. It took me an hour to decide on my next move, which took me back to the phone book. I looked up Spence and Maher both. There was a number but no address for Spence; however, K. Maher was listed at 45 Carter Lane. It wasn't hard to find.

I half expected to see her BMW in the drive. It was neither there nor in the three-bay garage, where by peeking through the windows at the side I could see a Mercedes sedan and two empty spaces. The house itself looked very empty. I took a short tour around, looking in where it was possible. I tried to check out the mailbox, which was a slot drop type that took a

key to open, but I was able to squint and verify the name
Katherine Maher on a letter inside. I decided to come back
and do a more thorough job later.

At that moment I needed to locate Toni Spence's house. Her
phone number and Katherine Maher's were the same through
the first four digits. That raised the possibility they were living
in the same general area. Just how small that area was I could
only speculate. In rich rural areas of estate-sized properties I
had noticed that the names are usually prominently displayed
on the mailboxes. I needed to be lucky, but it was all I had.

I spent an hour or more reading names on mailboxes and
stealing peeks at the mail inside those without names. It was
discouraging work. The negatives mounted up as my search
took me farther from Kate's house. I was beginning to lose
some of my optimism when I finally read the name Toni
Spence on the crush of mail inside an unmarked box in front
of a house set well back from the road. I checked the mail a
second time to be sure I had the right place, before I turned
my attention to the house. I dreaded what I had to do next.

The house was nestled in a forest setting. It was of moderate size, but obviously very expensive. I had no trouble getting
inside. The rear doors were standing open. It was the sort of
thing burglars did, opening all the doors while they were inside: it made escape easier. This, however, had been no bur-
glary. The major items of value remained. This had been a
search, thorough and destructive.

It struck me as odd the police had not been here, until I
thought about it. She had been declared a suicide, and all her
assets were held in trusts and corporations. There was probably a desk someplace with a file on it and an overworked bu-
reaucrat behind it that represented the delay in the process.
The authorities were in for a big surprise when they finally did
get around to checking out Toni Spence's property.

The interior of the house was tastefully done. I imagined a
decorator had been given a free hand along with an unlimited
budget. Lonnie would have been in heaven. But now, the evidence of frenzied ransacking was unmistakable throughout the

house. I followed the trail of it to the master bedroom, where I could see some affirmation of my hunch that Toni Spence had been tortured before she died. I did not like to think what might have happened to her on her own bedroom chaise. It was fouled in ways that spoke of sweat-drenching horror. Whiskey stains surrounded it, supporting my belief that it had been forced down her. It was clear to me that what had happened to her had happened here. She had, most likely, died here in her own bedroom in a miserable, terrifying way. They had probably cleaned and dressed her body for the short trip to that Monterey cliff.

I spent some time looking in the few places I thought they might have missed. Whatever she had was not with her when she died, I surmised. It was my guess she had talked. She had given at least two names: Greg Burley and Wendell Leeds. I wondered if there were others. My search was neither long nor intensive. I was convinced that she had given up everything she knew or possessed before she died.

I wiped my fingerprints off the things I had inadvertently touched and closed the house up. I made my way carefully back to my car as a slight rain began to fall. I tried to walk on leaves and hard areas to avoid leaving footprints. If ever I wanted to stay clean on something, it was this.

I parked down the road from Katherine's house and crept in to check out the garage again. Still empty except for the Mercedes sedan. The house too had that vacant feeling to it. I returned to my car, where I could watch the road from both directions. I tried to keep thoughts of Toni Spence and the way she had died out of my mind. It was hard. I was inclined to personal rage over such things. I could not afford that.

The day was moving out from under me too quickly. I checked my watch constantly against the impending darkness. I had the idea early on that Katherine was not coming back to this house. The longer I sat there, the more sure of it I became. Night settled in around me, isolating me with my thoughts. It was a lonely place to be.

When I left at nine, I took one long, last look at Katherine's house. Perhaps I was trying to glean some piece of her, the Kate I knew, from it. It did not look like her to me. I could not feel her there.

I made it to the copy shop just before it closed at nine-thirty. The fax from Al Mitchell was there and waiting. As John Good I paid the bill and took the three-page report with me to dinner at the Captain's Table restaurant. I ordered grilled shark with potatoes and salad, while the busboy poured my coffee. I liked busboys. They were much easier than waiters to summon for refills. I opened the report.

Wendell Leeds had been forty-four years old. His body showed multiple contusions to the torso. One rib was broken. He had died from a gunshot wound to the back of the head. I read down the page to the section on detail of injuries. The marks on the torso had most likely been caused by blunt objects approximately four inches in diameter. Fists, I thought. The wound to the head had been caused by a small-millimeter, fragmenting shell of high velocity, .22 to .25 caliber. He had died from severe trauma to the lower rear quadrant of the cranium.

I didn't need any more. I knew he'd been worked over, and I knew he had not been killed with a deer rifle. It was my guess that he had gotten away from his interrogator before he'd told all of his story. He hadn't gotten far enough away, was all.

The information on Phil Lomax was short and simple. He had died of cancer of the colon.

The shark was good. So was the cobbler I had afterwards. It helped me quell the bad taste of death that was rising in my throat.

I had enough from Carmel and Pebble Beach for the moment. I would come back another time to visit and enjoy, to stand on the cliffs and look out at the sea. I wondered if that was the sort of thing Kate did, and if it was something I would ever do with her. I thought not.

22 🌿

I drove through the night. I made it as far as Paso Robles before the lead weights on my eyelids became too heavy to lift any longer. I found a small, clean motel and pulled in for a nap. I dropped off right away and must have slept for an hour or so before my mind turned my dreams on me.

A long time ago they were only names, but somewhere along the line they had become people to me: Wendell Leeds, Greg Burley, Toni Spence. It was hard to say which of them had died the hardest. Possibly it had been Greg Burley. He had burned. Leeds probably got off the lightest. I saw him die. But it was Toni Spence I kept thinking about. Women and children weren't supposed to suffer like that.

I lay on the undersized bed with my eyes open, thinking. I couldn't stop the anger. It came like waves of a rising tide. I couldn't remember what my intentions had been, other than to follow the trail of information wherever it led. Perhaps it had never been more than that. Yet at some time the indignation had begun, and the anger had started to simmer. It had become a need to speak the names of the dead to their murderer, and to answer for them as they could not.

As I pulled onto 101 South I felt more at peace with my

anger. I let it come. I would need rage to do what I had decided to do. I wanted one or two more pieces to the puzzle so I could be sure, but deep inside I felt I knew. Just as I had known from that same spot in the gut a long time ago that it was going to be my fight. It had been inevitable. The only thing left was to fill in the blanks so I would know who all the players were. My first talk would be with Peggy Cooley.

The sun was well up by the time I got to Santa Barbara. I passed on through to the first Montecito exit. The Coffee Mill was buzzing with its usual morning group. I took a table by a back window that was being vacated by a man who looked vaguely familiar. His eyes were level with mine as he passed, which gave us both slight pause. He grinned at that while my tired mind groped with a name to put with the face. I was sure I knew him and started to speak, but he was already gone. He made a graceful exit as a few heads turned in his wake.

I watched from the window as he stopped in the parking lot to talk with a comedian I recognized. Both names escaped me.

"Stargazing?" came the honey-smooth voice at my ear.

I tried to shrug it away. "Just watching humans in their natural habitat."

She lifted the five from under the half-empty bowl of oatmeal and gave it a little wave. "Cute and generous is my favorite combination," she said as she uprighted a clean cup in its saucer and poured my coffee. "You hungry, honey, or did you just come in to leer at my leanings?" She leaned big bosoms toward me as she said it. I tried not to notice.

"Poached eggs on English muffins," I said. "No potatoes."

She nodded it in and cleared away the empty bowl. "All he ever eats, oatmeal. Coffee and oatmeal."

She knew I wanted to ask his name, but I wasn't asking, and she wasn't saying. It was the kind of standoff I could see she enjoyed. Peggy Cooley was a tease through and through. She left me watching the two men outside. The comedian was "on" and the big man was a good audience. He laughed while the two of them drew more than a little attention from the

passing motorists. He's an actor, I thought stupidly, but still
could not find his name. So many actors and famous people
from every walk of life settled in Santa Barbara that it was a
common occurrence to see them.

Peggy was back in a moment with a paper folded to the
crossword, which she plopped in front of me with a pencil
while she topped off my coffee. It was all done so quickly and
silently I didn't have time to say thank you, much less start a
conversation. I obediently transferred my attention to the
"down" column of clues. I was into the "across" group when
my breakfast arrived.

I finished the puzzle, and my eggs, and the potatoes she had
mischievously put on the side. I had more coffee and waited.
The place cleared out somewhat before Peggy found her way
to me with a grin at my empty plate. "You want another side
of potatoes?" she said.

"You're an imp, you know that?" I said. "You got a minute?"

"I read you pretty good, Jake," she answered, settling her
lush form against the back of a chair. "I said to myself, 'Peggy
girl, the man has come to have words with you.' Now the
question is, cowboy, is it my bod or my mind you're after?"

"You remembered my name," I said with an appreciative
nod. "That's flattering."

"Oh, I think you'd be very flattered if you could read my
mind, chum. So, if it's my number you want, I'll write it down
for you. On your chest if you so desire."

"On paper will do fine." I shared the smile in her eyes.
"Peggy, I'd like to talk a bit more about some of the things we
discussed last time I was in, about Texas, and about Garrison."

"Jenny Lee? My old school chum?" she asked.

"No, her father, David," I corrected.

"I never knew him personally," she said. "I've already told
you all I know about him."

"Well, how about his reputation? Would most people in the
state know his name?"

She pondered it a moment before answering. "No, I wouldn't think so."

"Tell me again who he is. Tell me more about him and this Duval place, the fellow you said ran things down there and all that."

"Oh, Lordy," she said with a huge sigh. "He was called the Duke of Duval County, and some folks I knew, who knew about such things, said it all tied to the boys way off in Chicago. I never could figure out quite how, but I do know there were a lot of scandals. You remember Billy Sol Estes? Bobby Baker?" I nodded at the picture of Texas in the Johnson era.

"And there was a federal agent of some sort who was supposed to have committed suicide by shooting himself in the back seven times with a rifle. Lots of that sort of thing in the rumor mill." She let it hang there for me to gather in.

"This Duke of Duval County figured in all that?" I asked.

"That and a lot more. I'm not going to draw the lines for you, but you put one dot on him, and one on the Chicago mob, and one on Kennedy, and then a great big one on Lyndon Baines Johnson, and what kind of picture do you come up with?" Her raised eyebrows marked an end to our conversation.

I could hear Logan's rendition of "The Eyes of Texas" playing in the back of my brain.

"And this Duke of Duval is retired or what?" I asked.

"Old news is what he is," she said. "He was small-time compared to Garrison. Jake, what I know about all of this is just rumor, understand? The rumor makes Garrison the big cheese, dating back to the Duke's big days. They say Garrison is one of the most powerful men in the country. Who knows? But no matter which end of the rumor you hear, the connection to the mob boys in Chicago always comes up. At least that's the story I hear. Okay?"

"Would a cop, a former cop from Dallas, know who Garrison was?"

"Sure," she answered simply. "Like Hoover knew Dillinger, and Ness knew Capone, he'd know David Lee Garrison."

"It's just the civilians who wouldn't know him?"

"You got it," she said, eyebrows asking if I was finished.

I nodded my thanks as she pushed herself away from the chair in answer to a customer's raised hand. Her perfume rushed to me. It was reminiscent of good soaps and sandalwood.

As I passed her on my way out, she held a piece of paper toward me. I took it with a nod.

"I can swim, ride horses, ice skate, play tennis and golf," she said. "I don't like boats, museums, or dirty movies. I can cook. Don't be bashful, chum."

I already was, which, of course, she already knew.

• • •

It was a twenty minute drive to Goleta and Travis Circle. I waited while the neighborhood spit out its white-collar workers in a staggered procession of fancy cars. The Wagoneer was among the later of the daily morning commuters to take the street. I let it get around the corner and well away before I approached the house. I went in at the back, where I found a door unlocked.

It initially struck me as odd that a security man should leave his own door unlocked, and even odder that there was no alarm system hooked to the house. Then I got a look at the interior. It was neat and orderly to what I would describe as an obsessional degree, with few personal items. There were no pictures, no mementos, no letters or books. There was little of the man who occupied the house other than his clothes and daily-care items. One room, however, was all Jessup. It was walled in mirrors and filled with racks of weights and weigh-lifting benches. I checked the weights left on one of the Olympic-standard bars and stopped counting at 350 pounds. A very strong fellow, Jessup.

I had the feeling that Jessup had been in that house longer than he'd intended to be. He had probably kept extending his lease. It became obvious, the more I studied the place, that the house was a temporary stop for him. He was ready to move at a moment's notice.

The garage was the last place I looked. The cabinets along the rear wall were padlocked. I was not too careful in breaking them open. It was beyond the point where such things mattered. I exercised the same disregard for the locked trunk I found inside: I hammered it open, careful only not to damage the contents. I needn't have worried. Guns are hard to damage.

I found what I was looking for. It was a specially scoped .22 rifle designed for long-range shooting. The shells were long loads, and the lead slugs were hollow-points. On closer inspection I could see the circle on the tip of the slugs which indicated a plug had been taken out and replaced. I was sure that inside each of those lead tips was the tiny drop of mercury that on impact turned the bullet into deadly shrapnel. Dumdums.

I took the weapon. Inside me, the rage was growing.

At home I went through a tough regimen fed by the anger. I forced my body to limits I had not reached in recent months. I swam afterwards as if in a sea of my own thoughts. Each stroke brought new speculation. I was still struggling with some confusion.

I called Jason and gave him a few additional items to pass on to the Paladin Group.

"How you coming on the book?" I asked.

"Something's haywire," he replied. "It looks like a straight transposition cipher, but when I break it down to letter frequency tables and do my digraph and trigraph work sheets—that's two-letter and three-letter formations to you less informed—all I get is gobbledygook for a decipher."

"So maybe you're making words in another language," I offered.

"What are you saying?"

"Try to translate what you've got into Italian, with a strong Sicilian influence," I said. "Giancana was Sicilian."

A moment of silence preceded his comment. "It galls the hell out of me to be outthought by you on a cipher. I hope you're wrong."

"I'll see you this evening," I said. "I've got something for you to hear."

"I can come there."

"No, definitely not. Things are in motion here, Jason. I'll give you some of it when I see you."

He understood what I was not saying and let it go. As I put the phone down I checked my watch. I needed to get some sleep. I had time to make up for what I had lost the night before and possibly what I was due to lose in the night to come. I secured my bedroom, closed out the light, and lay down. A distant rumble signaled the return of the dark clouds from the day before. It was a welcome sound to my numb and muddled brain.

• • •

It was too early for the usual crush at Meddler's. I sat at the long bar with the drinkers who didn't go by the clock, and had some of the Count's good coffee. Lorna and Eddie weren't working yet, and Sebastian was scurrying—if you could call the movement of a three-hundred-pound man scurrying—to and fro preparing for the dinner crowd.

Sebastian, his immediate work done, settled on a stool next to me. "Jason should be back soon," he said. "You sure you don't want to wait upstairs?"

I shook my head. He read my face and gave the Count a look. They left me alone as I sipped from the delicate Rosenthal cup, which the Count kept filled. I wasn't there long before the parking attendant was at my side. "Mr. Sands, Mr. Meddler is here. I told him you wanted him to wait in the car, like you said."

Jason's car was idling beneath the portico like a huge black animal awaiting its prey. I tipped the attendant as he held the door for me, and slipped into the front passenger seat.

"Where to?" Jason asked, as if this were an ordinary oc-
curence. I shrugged and he put the car in motion. I fiddled
with the seat, getting it as far down and as far back as it
would go. My knees were still against the dash and my head
against the top. I was amazed at how a car as big and cumber-
some as the Rolls Royce could have so little interior room.

I took the tape from my pocket and pushed it into the tape
player. Jason turned onto the Pacific Coast Highway toward
Malibu as the voice of Phil Logan replaced a New Age clar-
inetist. The dark-tinted windows of the Rolls, the rain, and the
words of Phil Logan made a powerful combination. Jason
finally pulled off the highway at Malibu Canyon Road into the
parking lot of a trendy shopping center. We idled there listening together to that most remarkable tape.

"Incredible," he said when the last haunting notes of "The
Eyes of Texas" had vanished into the static of the tape.
"Where did you get that?" The trappings of adulthood had
dropped, leaving an awestruck kid who could have been asking his friend about a "totally fantastic" bicycle or baseball
mitt.

I told him. I told him the rest as well, which I had not had
the time or the inclination to tell before. When I was finished
he knew what I knew, and he began to know what I was
thinking. Then it was his turn.

"Okay, now let me fill you in on what I've learned from Paladin. Some of it overlaps what you've already figured out. I
just came from there, incidentally," he said, an adult once
more. To prove it he snipped the end of one of his Cubanos
and lit it while I waited as impatiently as he intended. "Leeds
was a lawyer, and guess what firm he worked for?"

"Spence and Maher," I answered obediently.

"Can't fool you," he said, and puffed. "Spence and Maher is
still in business, by the way. I guess it doesn't matter that
they're both dead. It's like any other corporation. Toni Spence
had inherited operating interest." He took a large envelope
from the console between us and passed it to me. "It's all in

there, along with some of the other stuff you asked for. They did what they could in an afternoon."

He studied the symmetry of his burn in the dim light of the dash, then patted the cigar against the ashtray. "My bet is that like the old baseball double play that went Tinker to Evers to Chance, this went Maher to Spence to Leeds. When Spence died, Leeds and his boyfriend decided to go for the goodies."

"Old man Spence might not have been so clean on this either," I speculated. I turned on the overhead light to better read the reports from the envelope. "Otherwise, why didn't it all go public? They've got a confession from Logan spelling out the whole thing."

"You can lay money that that confession is no longer in that law office," he snorted.

"Leeds worked it so he'd come down to Santa Barbara to handle Logan's property, and moved in so he could search it thoroughly." I thought aloud from one part of my brain while I absorbed the report with another. "Burley rented the Summerland house so they'd have a base to work from. They could take their time, dive at their leisure, and dispose of what they found in slow, careful steps. A sweet plan, except they forgot that people might be looking for Logan and his stash."

"Why do you suppose they hung on to that control map? It wasn't any good to them."

"They didn't know that. It was like the lighter. Logan had saved them more as mementos, probably, than anything else. Leeds and Burley thought they meant something, maybe clues to finding the book."

"That makes sense. Leeds knew the thing was blown, so he ran with the only evidence of Logan he had, the lighter. He probably was trying to pass it off to you there in the street."

I nodded agreement without taking my eyes from the papers I was reading. A gust of wind pushed the rain against the car. It made noise, but the heavy car did not rock at all. Neither would a tank, I thought. A car should move a little.

"You'll notice that Charles Jessup was an outstanding line-

backer at Texas A. and M.," Jason said. "Made all the all-
American picks. Makes you wonder why he didn't go on to the
pros, doesn't it?"

"A better offer," I answered, flat.

"I don't like it, Jake," he said. "You're out in the open on
this thing. You don't know all the players, but you can bet the
farm they know you."

"I think I know all the ones who know me." I placed the report back into the envelope and tapped it for emphasis. "This
has told me a lot."

"So, Katherine Burley is Maher's daughter or something?"
he asked from behind his smoke. "Must've found out things
from the Spence woman and came down to follow up herself.
She's played a smart hand, wouldn't you say? Pro stuff if you
ask me."

I thought about what I had just read in the Paladin report on
Katherine Maher. "Did you read this report on her?"

"Not any of the detail work, just the summary sheet on all
the reports," he replied. "Something there I should know?"

"I'll fill you in later," I said.

"She could be in deep trouble, couldn't she?" he said. "They
must be onto her by now."

I answered with a nod and changed the subject. "Anything
more on the book?"

"It's like you said, written in Italian, and then put into cipher. I've only done a few pages so far, but I can tell you,
amigo, it is dynamite. And I'm talking about the kind that can
blow up in our faces if we're not careful."

"I need to get back."

The traffic was light heading in the direction of Meddler's.
Jason stared ahead at the mist and glisten from the rain. We
rode in silence.

"What now?" he asked me at my car.

"I'll know more tomorrow. I'll call or come down." I paused
with my hand on the door handle. "I think I have it," I said.
"All but one last piece. It's odd how I felt I was being pulled

in different directions by different problems, when all along they were connected."

"Can't I help?" he offered.

"You have," I answered. I held up the envelope. "You've helped a lot. I wouldn't have figured it out without you. Talk to you tomorrow."

We shook hands. It could have been my imagination, but it seemed to me he held on a little longer than usual.

23 🌿

There was no need to stop at my house. I had brought everything I needed with me. I parked my car well out of sight on Vista Laguna. The rain was light enough, so I didn't consider parking any closer. I buckled on a hip pack, stuck the Sig Sauer 9mm in the belt behind my back, and jogged to 411 Faring Lane.

I used the keys I had made from the wax molds. One opened the gate, one the door, and one turned off the alarm. Once inside, I turned the intercom to the on position and put the switch to FM radio with the volume low. Next I went upstairs directly to the large closet in the master suite, where I pulled down the "hide-a-stair" steps to the attic. As I ascended, my eye caught the break in the wall where the hidden door to Leeds's private wig collection hinged. I felt the same sudden tug of sympathy for him I had experienced before. Maybe this night would make it better, I thought.

In the attic I crawled along the crossbeams until I found the loosely strung wires of both the intercom and the security system. With the aid of my flashlight I isolated the wires I wanted. I took the operator's headset from my hip pack and pressed the button to recheck the battery strength; I got a green light. I scraped away the plastic sheathing of the intercom wires and attached the alligator clips of the headset wires to the exposed copper line. The sound of KRUZ-FM came through loud and clear. I depressed the talk switch and could hear my voice transmit. Only one thing left to do.

Using the phone in the kitchen, I dialed the patrol office and asked for Jessup.

"He's not in at the moment, sir," came the militarily formal voice. "May I take a message?"

"Tell him to meet me at Logan's house. He'll know where that is and he'll know who this is. And tell him it's urgent," I said.

I hung up on his question, whatever it was going to be. I moved the selector switch from FM radio to intercom before I returned to the attic for the hard part. The waiting.

It had been difficult for me to learn to wait. The good ones could remain silent and motionless for twelve hours without losing the alertness of senses it required. I was never a good one. I could last two or maybe three hours before my mind began to wander. Fighting the drowsiness was another chore. I hoped I was not to be put to the test in that attic.

The rain picked up, reverberating against the roof just over me. I lay in the dark on the crossbeams listening to it. It was like the sound of the ocean. No matter how loud it got, it was always soothing and soporific. I felt its tug. Without my earlier nap I would have been halfway to dreamland. It was hard enough as it was.

I had been fighting the inner battle to remain still for some time before my finger holding down the listen button began to get stiff in the joint. I changed fingers, and when I did I realized that, for I didn't know how long, I had not had the button fully depressed. With the rain, I had not noticed the absence of the slight static. I could have entirely missed the sound of a car arriving, or a door opening, or the entry I was awaiting. Again the rain could have masked those sounds. I had been depending on the headset. When I pushed the listen button down

fully, I heard the static and something more. I heard the sound
of footsteps on a hard-surfaced floor. Where? I wondered.

Feeling a little behind in the game, I pushed the talk button
and said into the headset, "Hi, Charlie. I guess tonight's the
night, huh?"

I listened closely, but all there was to hear was the static.
What else had I missed? It was always the little mistakes that
got you killed.

"Why don't we talk a little before we get to it, okay? You
up for some talk, Charlie?" I prodded the silence with my
voice as much as I could. I waited through the static for some
reply. I was beginning to doubt that it was Charlie Jessup who
was in the house with me. And for how long?

Finally, I did hear something. It was hard to make out at
first. I strained against the earphones with my volume control
at high trying to get it. Whispering, I thought. I was hearing
someone whispering. That meant Charlie Jessup had not come
alone. Or he had an imaginary friend left over from his childhood. Then came a sound like the clearing of a throat. My
guess was that they had decided to talk to me so they could
find me. Sure enough, Charlie did the honors.

"So, smart guy, you must think you're something, huh?"
Jessup said. I could imagine him looking around into the darkness. Him and his partner. "Now what is it we're going to get
to, Mr. Sands, sir?" The sarcasm was thick and angry.

"You and me, Charlie," I said with an equal dose of mockery. I had a lift in confidence as he fell into my game plan.
"It's been coming a long time. But maybe you'd tell me a few
things first."

"Things?"

"What brought you here to Coco Palms? How'd you get
onto Logan?" I knew he was moving, because I could hear
him as he went from one intercom station to the next. He
would soon get frustrated, or his partner would, and then
they would make their mistakes.

"I don't know what you're talking about," he stalled.

"It was Buddy Mapes, wasn't it? You had some kind of

track on the dope he tried to market, didn't you? What did
you boys do, follow every heroin trade that wasn't from your
store? Is that how you found Buddy Mapes? Just nod, I can see
you." I thought I'd play with his head a little.

I could hear his sudden quick head movements. His uniform
fabric was too stiff for this kind of work. He would never
have made it in my old unit.

"So, you know it all? Okay, what else do you know?" He
was stalling to get his head clear, or to confer with his partner.

"What do I know? Well, I know that you've been here too
long. You didn't find what you were sent here for, did you?
Your little extortion sideline has kept you busy, but the boys
aren't too happy with you, are they? They keep asking for Logan's stash." I threw out the big net. I wasn't sure what I'd
catch.

I could imagine his ear cocked to the room around him. His
voice came back at me with a sharp difference in it. "Sands,
where are you coming from on this thing? Maybe we can
work together."

"To do what?"

I must have sounded interested. He hopped on it. "Recover
a few things. That's what you do, isn't it? You may already
have found some things we might be interested in. The people
I work for can be very generous."

"Haven't they already told you to take me out like you did
Leeds, Burley, and Spence?"

He laughed. "They don't know about you yet. There wasn't
any reason to mention you until now. What you were was a
personal nuisance, but I can forget about that if you want to
play ball."

"You mean you're calling the shots?" I asked.

The pause was longer. "Sure, why not?"

"Because nobody's dumb enough to put you in charge of
anything, Charlie. You're a big, stupid boob who can't get out
of your own way." I listened into the silence that was his
anger.

"Where are you, Sands?" he said with that now familiar

tightness. "I'm tired of this game. I thought you said we were going to get it on. Lose your nerve?"

I could hear him then, below me, in the master suite. I pulled one of the earpieces aside to get a better feeling for his movement. I let my imagination make visual images to go with the sounds I heard. He was making a quick check: the bathroom, the sitting room, the bedroom, and finally the closet. He paused before the intercom.

"So, you're out of things to say, huh, smart guy?" He made his comment into the intercom and hastily took off for the next room. I let his footsteps fade away before I unclipped the headphone and worked my way to the drop ladder. I lowered it and moved down as quickly as my stiffened body would allow. I took my position in the bedroom behind the open bedroom door.

It was more waiting. A different kind though, with the game on. It was adrenaline-charged stuff. I had always thought it was probably like what an actor felt waiting for his first entrance on opening night. The toughest part was keeping the head straight. The tendency was always there to over-imagine the things that could go wrong. I had learned a while ago that was the one sure way to make things go wrong. It was better to use the time doing what would make the odds swing home. I used isometrics. It was like charging the battery in every muscle group.

As I had figured, Charlie was making a second check of the rooms. It was a much more slipshod survey than his first search. His feet moved heavily toward the master suite, giving me ample time to calculate his entry. I needed to time my movements very carefully.

He was ten feet into the room before I moved. I slammed the door shut and locked it with one hand, and with the other I hit the light switch. He was completely thrown. His eye was glued to the night scope, and the sudden light made him blink. It was a little mistake, but enough to give me an edge. I disarmed him easily. Too easily.

He dropped the scope and gave up the gun with almost no
resistance. A distant part of my brain was recognizing the
danger even as it occurred. The rest of the brain was trying to
keep me upright. I held the barrel of Jessup's Smith and Wes-
son .357 and leaned back onto my heels. Jessup was moving
forward as I pulled at the gun. It was not an easy discipline to
learn, jujitsu, but its application was simple. All you really had
to do was go with everything the other guy did, then use his
momentum against him. It worked in theory, it worked in
practice, and it worked with Jessup.

I felt his hands push against my balance. It was like judo in
that regard, so I fully understood what was happening to me:
he was controlling my center of balance to gain an advantage
of leverage. I did as he had done. I went with it. I took the
fall, with a complete tuck and roll back to my feet. He stayed
with me, however, and struck me hard with a two-thousand
pound wrecking ball, which looked a lot like his right fist.

I went with it again, but came up out of a side roll looking
for him. He was there. So was the wrecking ball. He laid my
nose flat against my face and slightly to the side. Stabbing icicles of light and sound invaded my head. Blood leaked into my
mouth. If there was one thing I disliked above all others in
this world, it was the taste of my own blood. I dipped to avoid
the follow-up in the combination and felt the icicles pierce the
tender parts of my skull.

I slipped another big swing and turned to my left away from
him. It was my luck he was trying to take me out with the one
big shot. It gave me a chance to duck and move and clear my
head. My vision cleared too, and I didn't like what I saw. Jessup was six and a half feet of mean and muscle. He was also
fast, which complicated my life no end. Adding to that was
the fact that he knew his way around a fight, I came up with
some short odds.

I found myself thinking about a fellow I once knew who
used to say that experience, age, and treachery would overcome muscle, youth, and skill every time. All I was lacking at

the moment was the treachery, which was evidently the key ingredient in the equation. It was strange the way my mind flipped to things like that at such moments. Or things like suddenly noticing that Jessup had a small patch of blue in his otherwise brown left eye. I did not want that to be my final thought in this life, so I moved quickly toward the chaise, getting it between us and giving me a few more needed seconds of recovery.

Jessup didn't slow. He came right over the chaise after me. Not that I thought he would show any regard for the furniture, but I did think the chaise would offer a better barrier than it proved to do. He took me in a wrestler's hold around the neck. His strength was awesome. I flashed on the three hundred pounds of weight on his barbells and opted against a muscle contest. As he started to twist me to the floor, I slipped beneath him changing the angle of his hold. As he started to adjust, I braced my hands against his arm and pulled free. I side-kicked from the floor at his knee, which gave me another second and let me get back to my feet.

He set himself into a slight crouch with his left side facing me in his next approach. I needed to collect myself. I had to put aside the ache in the center of my face that used to be my nose, and the bright fuzz that filled my head, and the tinny taste of my blood. I needed to think about Toni Spence.

I stepped in with a sure thing. I hooked a left into the meat of his forward biceps. He started a counter with his other hand, and I turned a right over into the inside of that bicep. He looked at me with some surprise. I did it again, both ways, and then followed it with hooks to the outsides of his upper arms. I took a punch to the high part of the head in the process, but I came out way ahead on the exchange.

Jessup moved back from me shaking his meaty arms at his sides. The big muscles that had absorbed the blows would start to feel very heavy very soon if I could keep pounding them. I edged forward and feinted to the face. His arms came up, and I pounded into them. He moved back, and I went with him. I hit his shoulders and arms almost at will. His return punches had already lost some of their steam.

To add to his confusion I changed my stance abruptly to a zenkutsu-dachi ready position. I kicked out against the inside of his forward thigh. Something at his hip seemed to give, causing him to sag away from me. He held his balance though and caught me in the ear with a roundhouse kick. It was the reminder I needed that he was a dangerous quarry.

We continued to spar with no apparent advantage going either way. I knew though that each blow I landed on his arms was taking a toll. He seemed to take some confidence from the look of my face. It had to be puffed and red with the broken nose beginning to swell. The blood must have made it look much worse than it was. His eyes went to the door, as did mine, when the knob turned. There was a gentle pressure against the door before the knob was released. Jessup smiled as if he were playing with a marked deck.

"So, smart guy, you give us what you know and you may walk. You ain't gonna make it if you don't."

I moved in on flat feet, sort of a shuffle, and flicked two quick jabs at his face. One landed, the other didn't, but his arms rose, and I came up on the inside of one with all the power I had. I knew I had ruptured something in there by the way the arm moved out at the shoulder. He stumbled and went down.

"Tell me, Charlie, why do you call me smart guy?" I asked as if the answer were important to me.

"What's going on, Sands? What are you after? Who the hell are you anyhow?" He couldn't seem to make up his mind which question he wanted me to answer. I decided to answer them all but in reverse order.

"I'm your mistake, Charlie, that's who I am. It's you I'm after, and what's going on here is some payback. Okay?"

"Payback?" He looked genuinely confused.

"Yeah, you owe some skin and some pain, Charlie. I'm the collector." I watched him closely. He was like a bad swimmer in deep water.

"I don't get it. Who sent you? Who is this about?"

"Leeds. Let's start with Leeds. That was a good shot you made in that light. What was it, about three hundred yards?"

At some point he had decided to play it straight. He said, "Yeah, about that. It was you that took the gun, huh? So, what are you to Leeds?"

"And Greg Burley. Did you do the torch job on him?" I pressed.

He shook his head. "That wasn't me." He had worked his way up to a standing position and edged closer to me.

"But Toni Spence was you, wasn't it?" His face told me I was right. "It was on a chaise a lot like the one in here, wasn't it? You worked her over pretty good, Charlie. She must have spilled it all. Told you about Leeds and Burley, didn't she? That how you got onto them?" All I had to do was watch his face. "And the boys got onto her the same way they got onto Buddy Mapes. She tried to put something on the market, didn't she? The boys back in Chicago picked up on it and sent you after her? Is that about the way it happened?"

"I don't know about those things," he said with some of his bravado returning. His eyes were taking quick looks at the door. It was possible he had heard something I missed. I let him think, with a short look at the door, that he had turned my attention. He moved cat quick with a lead kick. I moved the leg aside with a chop block and kicked into it as I had earlier. He sagged again before I kicked him in the chest, sending him back against the wall.

He tried to being his arms up, but they didn't work quite right. I moved inside and landed hard shots to his face. I took my time, and I picked my shots. I did the same kind of methodical work on him I imagined he had done on Toni Spence. His face was pulp when I stepped back to do what damage I could to the ribs. I don't think he was conscious for that. He was sliding away from me down the wall. Finally, I let him fall.

I experienced an odd sense of disappointment. I had expected him to be a tougher fight. Maybe that was what kept my rage from abating. I still felt it, and I still thought of Toni Spence.

"I think it's time I met your partner," I said to Charlie Jessup's unconscious form. I made a quick survey of the room and spotted the night scope, which I put into my pocket, but I could not find the gun. I checked his pulse before turning off the lights and opening the door. There was not a sound to be heard. I stood beside the door for several minutes, then slipped to the floor and wriggled my way down the hall.

It was slow and tedious, moving on knees and elbows an inch at a time. It was also silent and invisible to the watching eye. All it required was a good bit of patience and, or course, arms and legs that were willing to perform in ways unpracticed for many years.

I found it easier going on the stairs, and in what seemed like a little less than a week managed to get down them. At the bottom there was a barely appreciable shaft of light from the outdoor floods which made me change my course to the living room. I took the longer way down the hall, but I stayed invisible. It was not a time to take chances. I entered the living room from the dining room side, which was opposite the stairs. I crawled in toward the protection of a large chair, really only a shadow against the faint hint of light from the other side. The living room was the center of the house and seemed a logical place to position myself. If Jessup's partner was still in the house, then sooner or later we would meet in here.

I could hear movement on the stairs. It had to be Jessup, because of the uncertain rhythm of the steps. The sound of the stumbles and bumps against the wall made it pretty clear that someone was having trouble negotiating the stairs. He made it to the bottom and stopped to catch some breath through his splintered nose. My only consolation was that his was worse than mine. He sputtered and coughed, probably on the blood he had inhaled, and stumbled toward the living room. He was partially caught by the dim shaft of light when he stopped. I could just make out his hand with the .357 in it. I did not know where he was headed, but that was as far as he got. From a deep corner of the room came the puff from a muffled gun. Charlie Jessup fell hard into the living room. From the source of the shot to the point where Jessup took the hit it figured to be sixty feet. That was one hell of a shot in the dark.

24 🌱

I focused Jessup's night scope on the part of the room where the shot came from, but I didn't need it. I knew who his partner was and where. Once I confirmed it, I put the scope down and settled back behind my chair for a moment to collect my thoughts. I eased the Sig from its place in the small of my back. The gun felt alive and ready, which was more than I could say for myself. The initial numbness from my nose and cheek had been replaced by an ache with its very own pulse. It made it hard to focus on what I had to do.

"Nice shot," I said. "Wrong man though."

The darkness was thickened by the sudden tension. It was no time for me to have random thoughts, but there I was, noting how the rain had stopped, and how the heat had come back into the night. It reminded me of tropical rains and other nights and other places.

The laugh brought me back from my side trip. "It was a fifty-fifty," the partner said. "He was dead tonight either way."

"A shame he didn't know that. He might have put up a better fight."

Again the laugh. "My money was always on you."

"Any reason we need to sit here in the dark?"

"I suppose not." There was a moment when I heard some slight movement before a floor lamp across the room was illuminated.

"Howdy, podner."

"Hello, Tex."

He sat behind a grand piano in the far corner of the room. It was a perfect fortification with the corner of the two walls guarding his back and the piano offering him a forward shield. He was leaned over the keyboard onto the piano top, holding the silenced pistol in front of him.

"You're a mighty clever fella, Jake." He gave a single shake of his head without moving his eyes. "I must say I didn't hear you or see you come down them stairs. How'd you do that, pard?"

"Maybe I was never upstairs," I replied.

"Oh, you was there all right." He laughed. "Your face tells that story. You and Charlie must've had a dandy. I'd like to have seen that one."

"Yeah, I'll bet you would. You're a real fan of Charlie's work, aren't you, Tex? Did you like watching what he did to Toni Spence?"

He grinned. "I didn't mind. It's always kinda fun to watch a fella enjoy his trade."

"You did Burley?"

"Now, you should appreciate that one, Jake. I thought that was real clever. I even made a statement for the homeless."

"Was he dead when you burned him?" I had to ask.

"Not quite," he answered with some amusement. "He was a bit of a whiner, if you know what I mean. Passed out a lot. Begged, too. Not our kinda fella, Jake."

"Oh, I don't know. You didn't get everything you wanted, did you?"

He paused over that. "Not everything, but you never get everything."

"Sure you do. You got everything Mapes had, didn't you?"

"Buddy? You know about Buddy? Say now, you're pretty deep into this thing, aren't you, Jake? How do you know about Buddy Mapes?" His interest was intense.

"Mapes gave up Logan to you, but he didn't know too much, did he? He was able to pinpoint Santa Barbara and maybe even Coco Palms, but he didn't know Logan's new name, and he hadn't seen him since he'd had his face changed, so it didn't do you much good, did it? Jessup never could find him. Incidentally, was it the heroin that tripped up Mapes?"

Tex Flanagan had an ugly grin. I was getting tired of it. "We're pretty good, ain't we, podner? Loose drugs is a mighty hard thing to catch onto."

"Not if it's pure, uncut heroin. Not a lot of that around. You put a watch on Mapes, didn't you, after his first sale?"

Tex waved his gun as one might waggle a finger. "Oh, no, podner, both cows gotta be milked here. You tell me some things, I tell you some things. Only one of us is coming outta here. Might as well be with a full pail. Won't matter to the other one, now will it?"

"Not all that much I can tell you, Tex. I don't really know anything."

"You know about Logan and Mapes. I'd kinda like to know how."

I looked across the room at the hulk of man leaning incongruously over the piano. I tried to ignore the silenced pistol he leveled in my direction. I wondered if he was trying to ignore mine. I decided to lie.

"I've had a bug on Jessup."

"Son of a bitch!" he exclaimed. "That useless piece of horse dung didn't do one damn thing right since he came here. I should've killed him a long time ago. Well, well, you ran our own plays back on us, looks like."

"Did Jessup know what he was after and why?"

He took a moment. "Nope."

"Did you?"

He nodded his head with his pig eyes asquint.

"I would imagine it really hit the fan when somebody woke up to the fact that Logan had run with Giancana's book. The

poor bastard probably didn't even realize what he had at first."
I was feeling my way along with it. "It's funny when you think
about it. He changed faces and names, came here to Santa
Barbara, where he sank his loot out there in the channel, and
lived like a prisoner in a gilded cage. You couldn't find him
though. Cancer took him before you could get to him, and
you never even knew where he lived until you tumbled onto
Burley and Leeds. That makes your outfit look a little stupid,
Tex."

"You know something, pard, we can still play in the same
backfield," Tex said with his best, good-old-boy charm oozing
from the words. "I think we can do some business here and
both of us come out fat and happy. You ready to talk a deal?"

I laughed as unkindly as I knew how. "You can't deal, Tex.
All you can do is what your old hunting buddy in Dallas tells
you to do."

His face went hard. I had crossed some line he had drawn
internally.

"So you have made that connection? I was afraid of that,"
he said with the slightest movement of his lips.

"You made a bad play there when you pretended not to
know David Lee Garrison. You might say that's where you
fumbled the ball." I pressed him hard, sensing a crack in his
composure. I trusted the Sig Sauer to give me the edge in any
exchange of fire.

There was a sudden movement well to my right at the other
entrance to the living room. Out of my peripheral vision I
could see Jessup coming up slowly from his facedown position. Tex Flanagan was too intent upon me to see it. I had a
problem in that I was totally exposed to Jessup's view. He
moved again, raising his gun in my direction, and I gave a
quick flick of my eyes toward him.

The *pfftt* of Flanagan's silenced gun seemed to reach me
long after I was hurled backward by a heavy punch thrown by
an invisible fighter. It had landed up somewhere around my
shoulder, and I lay on my back looking at the ceiling, wonder-

ing if that attack of stupidity was to be my last.

I was vaguely aware of Flanagan rising from behind the piano. It was all slow motion. My own gun suddenly felt as if it weighed six hundred pounds and the invisible giant who had hit me was holding it down. I struggled with the giant to get the Sig up to fire. Flanagan moved so fast for a man his size I couldn't help but admire it. My Sig was miles away from its target when something exploded. Flanagan looked surprised. His huge face turned away from me as another explosion shook the room. Flanagan's face spurted red, and he moved backward with his arms flailing cartoonishly. He crumpled against the piano, then slowly slid to the floor.

I turned the Sig toward the sound of the explosions, but I needn't have bothered. Those two shots were the final burst of life for Charlie Jessup. He had probably died as he pulled off the kill shot to Flanagan's head. Even as I sank toward oblivion I was impressed with the way those two men could shoot.

I went into a short blackout which might have been a few seconds or a few minutes. My system had simply said, "enough," and shut down. It took great effort to swim back up out of it, because it was thick and heavy and very comfortable. My ears opened first, as they always did, to the definite silence of death. My nose picked up the smell of cordite and night flowers, and finally my eyes opened to a view of the ceiling, which was very far away.

I raised myself slightly into the stillness around me to view the bleary confusion of shadows thrown across the huge room by the single lamp. Flanagan and Jessup were merely inert objects tossed on the floor. With the giant trying to hold me in my place I finally made it to my knees. I paused that way, holding my wound and gasping deeply for breath. The dizziness passed and after a time, beyond my ability to measure, I got to my feet. In my surprise to be alive I stumbled blindly from one dead body to the other, assuring myself that each was dead. I bid them a grateful farewell and staggered to the door and the fresh air outside.

I heard the car start from someplace not so close, but some-place not so far. My ears sought it in an eager attempt at hu-man contact. In a slow, even acceleration it abandoned me to the exile I felt as the sole survivor of the night. I did not let my-self think about that car—I had other, more important issues to deal with, like breathing, and walking, and staying alive. I was about to embark on the longest journey of my life. I had to make it to my car, and in my car I had to make it home. The rain-freshened air helped me believe I could make it. I drank it in with a deep thirst for anything that tasted of life.

As I moved, I improved. The night air was good to me. It slowly brought me around to a reasonable state of conscious-ness where I was able to manage my passage home almost nor-mally. Once there, I parked at my front door and entered the house, leaving the door open behind me just as I had left the front gate open.

I took great gulps of water from the tap while I washed the dried blood from my nose and then pressed a towel to my wound. It still bled too much, but there were things left for me to do. I noticed my message light blinking, but that too would have to wait. I put on my music and opened the French doors wide. With a glass of chilled coffee from the refrigerator I went poolside to collapse onto one of the designer lounge chairs. For the first time the chair, welcoming me with its abundant com-fort, no longer seemed to be too soft. I settled into it gingerly, afraid to jar the tear in my upper chest. The towel had stanched the flow of blood, which gave me time. I had no idea how much of it I would need. All I could do was wait.

· · ·

I don't think it was long. I either fell asleep or blacked out again, but when I awoke it was because the sudden scent of night flowers had penetrated my torpor. I lifted my head and pulled in the mixture of jasmine, citrus blossom, and honey-suckle. When I opened my eyes, she was standing near me, but not too near.

"Is it bad?"

I shook my head. "I don't know," I answered honestly, "It feels bad, but then everything started hurting after I turned forty."

"Your face is a mess." She started to say more but stopped herself.

I did a mental lean toward her sympathy, but lost it in midair somewhere and took the fall. I put a hand to my shattered nose as if I could shield the unsightliness of it. It didn't matter—she wasn't looking at me anyway. She was looking around at the house and pool and had one ear cocked to the music.

"That's nice," she said "Who is it?"

"The Four Freshman," I answered. "Music from my youth. It helped me form some of my romantic dreams."

"Did your dreams come true?" It was in her to tease. It was possible she couldn't help it.

"Some of them. And sometimes. But not all of them, and not all the time." The light from the pool made a moving glimmer upon her. It caught her eyes well.

"Life makes that happen," she said. "I wish it didn't sometimes."

"Yeah," I said to the night shadows behind her.

"You left your door open, you know, and your gate?" She posed it in a questioning way by turning it up at the end.

"For you."

"How did you know I'd be coming?"

"It was the logical place after you left Logan's house."

"I was at Logan's house?"

"Your perfume was," I said. "And I heard your car start. I knew if you weren't here before me, you wouldn't be long. It's my guess that you went to make a call. I don't suppose you'll tell me about that, though." She was so good to look at.

"It could have been nice here with you, Jake, in this house, in this place." Then, in a soft voice: "If it weren't for other things."

"Yeah, those other things," I said. "So what do we do now,
Kate? Okay if I still call you Kate? It would be a little hard for
me to get used to another name this late in the game."

"Another name?"

She was very smooth. I made a sound like a chuckle so she
would know I admired her technique.

"That Katherine Maher curve was a good one. I almost
bought into it except for a couple of things that didn't fit.
One, the dates on the trophies I saw at the Cypress Hill
Club. Two, the girl I saw hitting balls at the Coco Palms
Club—you—was not the kind of player who could have
racked up wins like that. The girl I saw was well schooled in
the game, and hit all the shots with a classic style, but there
was no fire in them. The woman who won those trophies was
a hard-core competitor on the tennis court; the girl I saw ral-
lying wasn't. And the other thing I picked up from a minor
little detail in a routine report on Katherine Maher. She, like
Toni Spence, was a woman in her fifties. That sort of iced it
for me, Kate."

She took it well. I expected her to.

"Are you going to make this hard for me, Jake?" There was
a wistfulness in her voice that chilled me.

I ignored her question and said, "Is she dead too, Kate? Was
Katherine Maher killed after they found out Toni Spence had
confided everything to her?"

She nodded casually, as if I had just commented on the stars.
Her eyes opened wide, and I remembered how they had looked
to me that first night in the White Gull. I remembered, too,
how perfect she had seemed to be. That should have been my
first clue.

"They were probably friends all their lives, those two," I
said, thinking aloud.

"Do you have any of the things, Jake?" she asked straight-
forwardly.

"Do you?" I asked back.

She smiled a perfect smile. "Do you have it, Jake?"

"Why don't you be more specific."

Without hesitation she answered, "The book, Jake. Do you have it?" She stared hard, willing me to respond. "No, I didn't really think you'd give it up. I'll still get it, Jake. You can't stop that."

"Is that you speaking, or your daddy?" It was a serious question which sounded like a taunt. Her eyes left me before I finished my thought.

I might as well not have spoken. She stared briefly at the pool, as if swimming were something she wanted to do. I let myself remember how she swam and how she looked and felt afterwards. When she turned back to me, I was sure that she too was remembering. There was a look of agony on her face.

"I wish there were other possibilities, Jake. I wish I could stay with you and take care of you, or leave you as you are and keep you as a memory, but I can't. You understand that I can't, don't you?"

"I guess that brings us back to my earlier question. So, what do we do now?"

"I do a hard thing, and you an easy one," she said simply, and raised her arm from her side. I couldn't make out the make and model, but at that point a gun was a gun.

"I'm a little tired of having guns pointed at me tonight, Kate." As if that would make a difference.

"This will be the last, I promise." The gun sagged slightly back from me. "I wish you'd look away from me, Jake. I don't want to shoot you facing me, but I will if I must."

"Tell me about your daddy, Kate." I was trying to rock her attention. "You've never said much."

"You would have liked him. As he was, before the stroke. He was strong like you, Jake. Could you imagine living in a wheelchair? I must do for him what he can't."

"So you're trying to prove to him that you're as good as a son would have been," I said. "It wasn't enough to be Daddy's little girl?"

My right arm dangled beside the chaise. In my hand under

the chair I grasped the Sig Sauer P228. Her gun tracked a bit away as she listened to me. It was all I needed. With one quick move I had my arm up and the gun sighted perfectly to fire. She was a vulnerable target. She was frozen. Her breath caught and held as I controlled that small portion of eternity. I too stopped breathing while I studied the face I was about to shatter. Her eyes frozen in fear were no less beautiful. The mouth no less inviting. The skin no less radiant. The face no less perfect.

She would have been an easy kill. My finger was squeezing, but the rest of me was begging not to pull the trigger. The rest of me won. The moment passed. I lowered my gun.

She knew the threat had passed before the Sig was fully down. Her action was immediate. Her own gun centered back on me, unsteady at first, but stilled by her own return to calm. Then came the anger. I had seen it happen before. Release from paralyzing fear could sometimes breed irrational anger. It did with Kate.

"You're dead," she said, her voice becoming a shriek. "You should have given me the book, because now I'll have to get it from your friend Jason. And Jason I will feed to the sharks."

Not Jason, I thought. I said, "I can't let you do that." But it was too late.

The red beam of the laser attachment touched my chest. I rolled to the side as the pop of the gun filled the space between us. I felt the bullet punch at the area between my neck and shoulder as I capsized. I fell face forward to the deck and rolled onto my side in my best imitation of death. I had no time to assess my injury. Bad was bad, and it looked as if it was about to get worse.

Kate moved in quickly for the insurance shot. She braced herself for a slug to my head. I rolled and fired, hitting her high and spinning her away from me. I put the second shot right at the heart. She dropped like a puppet suddenly released from its strings.

I lay in the blood from my new wound with my arm and

gun outstretched toward Kate. I forced myself up and went to her, confirming that she was dead. A bundle of emotions swarmed, but I had to put them on hold for later. Now was not the time to lament my actions.

I managed, with great pain and difficulty, to get her body into her car. I drove her to 411 Faring Lane, where I put her into the room with Flanagan and Jessup. I pressed my Sig Sauer into the stiffening hand of Tex Flanagan and put Flanagan's gun in hers. After using Flanagan's handkerchief to wipe my prints from key areas, I studied the scene for flaws. It read pretty well.

I let myself have a moment with her. She could have been asleep, the way she looked. The calm and beauty were back in her face. I touched her cheek with the backs of my fingers, trying to understand who she had been. The skin was cool already. It was time for me to go. I said goodbye to the woman I had known as Kate, who was still, even in death, beautiful. But no longer perfect.

I left the car some distance from my house and barely made it home. I staggered the last yards in an awkward progression of steps and stumbles. Somehow I made it inside, and somehow I got to the phone. I must have dialed because Jason answered before it finished its first ring.

"Jake?" he said in the voice of the worried father.

"I need help," I said in the voice of the child.

25 🌿

There was a warm breeze coming from the wrong direction, which the natives called a Sundowner. It was a Sundowner that had been responsible for the Painted Cave fire as well as most of the other bad ones in Santa Barbara's history. It blew in from the mountain side and out toward the ocean. The heat of it felt good to me.

After a little time spent in a private hospital tucked away in the deep recesses of Malibu Canyon, and another stretch of time spent in idle recuperation in Hawaii, I was home. While I waited for the good Kona I had brought back with me to brew, I though about the last few months. It was something like sorting out data for filing. Naturally, it was Jason who had kept me informed on the events affecting my life. It was the memory of Jason's words that chronicled the recent past for me.

"Sam Garvey said to tell you that they've thrown the bums out," he had said. "Whatever that means. He also said to tell you that Doug Dreckman faces criminal charges including extortion, and something about corporate something or other. Anyway, he said that Coco Palms is cleaned up for the moment, and you should consider keeping your place there.

Seems the whole world knows you've put it on the market."

I had heard the things Jason said to me, but they had meant very little. I had slipped into a deep hole. There had been no thought down there. There had been no past, and there had been no future. Even the doctors, with their poking and probing and serious faces, had failed to rouse my interest. I had heard them in the hall once saying, "He doesn't seem to care if he gets well." I had not been sure if that was so or not.

"Bob Claiborne says he's got one offer for the list price from some TV actor from L.A., and one on the burner from a local wanting to move up. He wants to know if you want him to get the two of them in a bidding thing. And something about a building you were interested in with a penthouse and all? This building I gotta see."

Nights had been the worst. Nights had brought home the waste that cluttered the past. In Maui it had been better. Vera's house on the beach had been a good place to sit and do nothing and think nothing. That's where Jason had delivered the Giancana book, deciphered and translated, to me.

"This thing is too hot to mess with. If all the judges and politicos documented in this thing are for real, then we better be careful what we do with it. Some of them are in very high places now. What do you say we hold it until we find somebody clean at the top and then send it in anonymously? And before I forget, Claiborne says the TV actor wants the house as is, with all the furniture. He's willing to pay well for it. What do you say? And the building's yours. Gonna be a pretty hefty mortgage, though."

The parts they had operated on had healed up okay. The nose had never been a thing of beauty. When they reset it they had, if anything, improved it.

"Lonnie has promised to do the new place like you say. In his words, in all that wood and leather traditional crap. You've got a lot of guts to trust old Lonnie a second time, Jake."

I hadn't bothered to explain to Jason about that little twinge of guilt that had made me feel I owed Lonnie. Maybe I couldn't have explained it, who knows?

"It looks like the investigation is all finished now. They released an official statement that Special Deputy Flanagan
killed Jessup and was killed by him." Jason had paused, unsure about mentioning the rest of it. "They still have no
identification on Kate, or as the police refer to her, the Jane
Doe they found dead on the scene, also killed by Flanagan.
Oh, did I tell you, they found Katherine Maher's body? In the
trunk of her own car, a Mercedes, in her own garage. She'd
been worked over pretty badly and died from blows to the
head. Not a pretty sight, I'm told." He paused again. His voice
had taken on a different tone. "She and Toni Spence had been
best friends since childhood. What a terrible thing."

My routine had resembled a sleepwalk. I had meandered
from the beach house to the Wailea Club for meals and to
watch an occasional good tennis match. In the evenings I'd often wandered to the Wailea Beach Hotel to have dinner at
Raffles. I had developed a fondness for their mahi mahi in
cream tarragon sauce. When I began to consider that the high
point of my day, I had realized it was time to leave.

"You're all moved into your new place now, Jake. Anytime
you want to come home it's ready. Claiborne wanted to stretch
the escrow out, thinking you'd at least want to visit the house
before the actor moves in, but I told him you said no. Oh, Sam
Garvey said to tell you, when you get back from your vacation
he and the new board want to give you an expression of their
gratitude. It's a lithograph, and I don't think the rest of the
new board had a damn thing to do with it. My guess is that it
came right off his own wall. I'll take it if you pass. It's a Norman Rockwell. This vacation thing is getting to be a hard sell.
You better come back so folks can see that you still exist."

So, I was back. I leaned on the terrace railing and looked
out at Cabrillo Boulevard, alive with tourists. Tony's Beachside, below me, was busy. The beach across the boulevard had
a lot of couples walking at the tide line, some of them holding
hands. I felt my spirits sag. The hole closed up around me.

I went inside, opened the cabinet and took the bottle. I went back to the terrace with a glass and plopped down on the Brown and Jordan chaise to pour the Jack Daniel's. I looked hard at the bottle before I poured. The amber liquid had been calling to me for some time now. I held the glass at my lips, smelling the rich bourbon whiskey.

Once I had hidden for sixty-one days within its mindless haze. That was when the thoughts of Trinia and Josh were open wounds. That was when I was looking for a way to go with them. I had to ask myself if it was the same thing again. Was there an open wound? I wasn't sure of my answer, but I knew that when I compared it to the loss of Trinia and Josh, it paled. The mere comparison seemed a sacrilege.

I poured the bourbon back into the bottle and replaced it in the cabinet. I poured myself a cup of the Kona coffee and wandered onto the terrace again, where I leaned against the railing, looking inside. It was the unfinished aspect of this business that was bothering me.

They had still not officially identified the woman who had not been Kate Maher, nor Kate Burley, but who had died with Flanagan and Jessup. No one had come forward to claim her and put a name to the beautiful face. I couldn't let her go that way, as if she had not existed, as if she were a figment of someone's imagination and not a real person whose fingertips had burned a memory into my brain. She deserved her rightful identity, and I had to be sure.

I called Jason and told him to tell the police where to look. He leaked it through the Paladin Group.

The Sundowner phase lasted for three days. On the third day, in the late afternoon, I got a call from a friend at the Paladin Group. He had heard from a source that the police had finally identified the female victim in the Coco Palms triple shooting. He gave me the name and the details. It was finally over.

I felt suddenly freed from a heavy weight and able to see the world around me differently. I could settle down and enjoy my new home. All things considered, it was a perfect fit. Lonnie had filled the place with Kargas pieces. The heavy, carved wood tables, armoires, chairs, and such were very much to my liking. "Right up my alley," I could hear Vera say. And suddenly I needed to hear her say it. I needed friends. I called her.

"The hermit lives," she said.

"I'm ready to have you all meet the digs," I answered.

"Dear boy, I was beginning to wonder if Lonnie had done it to you again. Tell me it does not look like a queen's lair. I know he tried this time."

I laughed. "It's great, Vera. You'll love it. It's the sort of place Henry would've loved."

She snorted. "That's probably true. You and Henry saw eye to eye on all such things. But darling, I always thought Henry had the worst taste in furnishings of anyone I knew. Is tomorrow too soon?"

"Tomorrow's perfect," I said.

"One of my neighbors has a niece visiting. Perfectly gorgeous. A TV anchorperson in San Diego. Shall I bring her along?"

"No," I said before she had finished. She sputtered something and again I said, "No, Vera. No."

We hung up with Vera complaining about my tendency toward seclusion, and me saying something about her tendency to meddle. It had always been so with us, and I hoped it would never change.

My spirits were on the rise. However, a few deep breaths on the terrace and the view of a runner on the beach reminded me it had been a few months since I had exercised. I moved my arms about, testing my upper chest. I could feel the aftereffects of the wounds, but it was time to start the process. There was always that first day back. There was always that moment when it was all so painful and hard that it didn't seem worth the effort.

What the hell, I thought, why put it off? I put on my gray cotton sweats, and plain, no-frills sneakers and went to the beach. As I walked across Cabrillo a car passed with Texas plates. I thought briefly of Tex Flanagan, and of the tape made by Logan, which was still in Jason's safe along with the deciphered book, but most of all I thought of a man named David Lee Garrison. I wondered if he ached somewhere deep within his soul for the little girl he had taught to ride, and swim, and shoot. Or for the adolescent he had sent off to learn tennis and golf and the other trappings of respectability. Or finally for the young woman whom he had taught the angle of his trade, taken into his ugly business, and given the reins of power. I moved into a slow trot across the sidewalk and the green park area and toward the water.

I was sure Jenny Lee Garrison had been a beautiful child. She had been a beautiful woman. It would be a long time before I would smell the scent of night flowers and not think of her.

I moved it up a notch when I got to the firmer sand at the tide line. The legs stretched out, and the lungs filled and emptied, and before long the wheeze and sweat began.

No question about it, I was out of shape.